BEDLAM BURNING

BEDLAM BURNING

GEOFF NICHOLSON

THE OVERLOOK PRESS
WOODSTOCK & NEW YORK

First published in the United States in 2002 by
The Overlook Press, Peter Mayer Publishers, Inc.
Woodstock & New York

WOODSTOCK:
One Overlook Drive
Woodstock, NY 12498
www.overlookpress.com
[for individual orders, bulk and special sales, contact our Woodstock office]

NEW YORK:
141 Wooster Street
New York, NY 10012

Library of Congress Cataloging-in-Publication Data

Nicholson, Geoff.
Bedlam burning / Geoff Nicholson.
p. cm.
1. Mentally ill, Writings of the—Publishing—Fiction. 2. Universities and colleges—
Fiction. 3. Impostors and imposture—Fiction. 4. Psychiatric hospitals—Fiction.
5. Book burning—Fiction. 6. Novelists—Fiction. 7. England—Fiction. I. Title.
PR6064.I225 B43 2002   823'.914—dc21   2001051172

Manufactured in the United States of America
FIRST EDITION
3 5 7 9 8 6 4 2
ISBN 1-58567-239-4

BEDLAM BURNING

Then

I

I first met Gregory Collins at a book-burning party given by my Director of Studies in his college rooms in Cambridge in 1974. I was as surprised to be invited as I was appalled to learn that such things went on in what I took to be an enlightened and liberal institution. I was, I admit, extremely young and extremely naive.

My Director of Studies was Dr John Bentley. We called him Dr John the Night Tripper, which was the least appropriate name we could come up with. He had a reputation for intellectual audacity, not to say offensiveness. He embraced 'tradition', the Augustans, Milton, Hobbes, right-wing politics, beagling, Wagner, the *Salisbury Review*, although, in retrospect, I'm sure he did much of it to annoy. He could also on occasions be extremely surprising. Once, in a tutorial ostensibly about Dryden, he delivered an extraordinarily detailed and well-informed, if ultimately dismissive, critique of the early films of Andy Warhol. It came as no surprise that he dismissed them, but it was pretty amazing that he'd taken the trouble to become informed about them at all; and not only was he informed, he'd actually been there at a showing of the full-length version of *Empire* at the Arts Lab, in London in 1967.

'I wouldn't have taken you for a fan of experimental cinema, Dr B,' I'd said at the time.

'I'm not,' he'd replied. 'I'm a fan of good jokes.'

We students wanted to find him both hateful and ridiculous; but we could never convincingly write him off as either, especially not when he was known to be such a good host. His parties, even the ones that didn't feature book burnings, floated on limitless reservoirs of college claret.

At first I thought the invitation must have come to the wrong man.

3

I have a woefully common name – Mike Smith, a name shared with all sorts of people: the English cricketer, the keyboard player in the Dave Clark Five, to name but two. But I spoke to Bentley and he assured me there'd been no mistake.

The invitation wasn't at all explicit about how the party would proceed, but before long lots of information came my way. It was as though I'd joined some secret society. People I'd never spoken to before came up to me in Hall or in the bar, as though they were about to discuss, if not offer, drugs or sex, but all they wanted was to share gossip about this party. Some had actually attended previous ones, but mostly they'd just heard rumours, and they all wanted to know what book I was going to take along, and when I said I had no idea, they took the opportunity to school me in the various strategies.

The format, I was told, was quite simple. Each guest had to bring a book, just the one, and towards the end of the evening, when everyone was good and drunk, we would each in turn briefly state our reasons for wanting to burn our particular book, and then throw it into the fire in Bentley's study.

Of course, I was not the only one to be shocked by this flirtation with the imagery of Nazism. I was told there were those who got round the problem by bringing along a book that was itself fascistic, *Mein Kampf* or a volume of Nietzsche or Ayn Rand. Another option was to go for books which, if not evil, were at least transparently worthless: Agatha Christie or Barbara Cartland or Frederic Raphael. Other people apparently took what seemed to me a rather silly option and burned the Bible or Shakespeare or Chaucer, a reaction against being forced to read these texts as part of their education rather than because of anything the texts actually contained.

But in a way, it seemed to me that all these gestures somehow missed the point. From knowing the man a little, I felt Bentley's real interest was in castigating what he took to be the trendily, vapidly liberal, the emptily left-wing. Bentley didn't want us to burn the great works of English literature, he wanted us to burn Barthes and Marcuse, Chomsky and Foucault. I had actually read something by all these people and if I was cornered I'd probably have been forced to agree about their vapidity, but I tended to think they shouldn't be burned, if for no other reason than that they clearly annoyed and threatened people like Bentley.

I knew I should have turned down the invitation to the party, and yet there was some perverse honour in being invited. No doubt Dr Bentley chose his guests carefully, for their sense of irony or perhaps their moral ambivalence, and if some people went along with trepidation, or even with an urge to denounce the proceedings, that was all part of the show. Bentley didn't want to invite a bunch of Nazis to his book-burning parties; that would have been too easy. He wanted to invite a group of self-conscious, self-regarding students who had pretensions to civilisation and intellect, and he wanted to watch them squirm and implicate themselves.

His rooms were comfortable in a dusty, bookish, scholarly sort of way. There were a couple of leather wing chairs, a pair of frayed *chaises-longues*, a few upright chairs; but there was certainly not enough seating for the number of people at the party, so most of us stood awkwardly by the fireplace, or wedged in against glass-fronted bookcases filled with the dark, bare spines of English literary texts. These were serious, scholarly works in standard editions, nothing so frivolous as a paperback, nothing so gaudy as a book jacket. There were a few paintings on the walls, dark landscapes and still lifes thickened with the painters' disdain for brightness or colour. This seemed somehow deliberately joyless. The walls of my own room, naturally, were decked out with posters: Raquel Welch and Frank Zappa (not the one with him on the toilet – I thought that was a bit corny), and there was a reproduction of *Hylas and the Nymphs*, a painting I'd found indecently erotic when I first saw it, although the effect had started to wear off now that it had been up there for the best part of two years.

If Bentley's rooms were masculine, he was not. Like plenty of other Cambridge dons I'd met he managed to be effete without appearing at all homosexual, to be soft without being feminine. At the time he seemed ancient to me, a fading old scholar who had been immured with his books and his thoughts for decades. Now, I realise he could only have been in his mid-thirties, and his patrician, musty air had no doubt been developed precisely to disguise any vestiges of youthfulness or frivolity.

The invitation said 'lounge suits' were required, and I did happen to own a suit. My parents had bought it for me in my last year at school, saying it would come in handy for university entrance interviews, if nothing else. It still just about fitted me. The suit was sober, grey, smart, precise; everything I didn't want to be. Yes, I had worn it to interviews and it had apparently done no harm since I'd got in to Cambridge, a surprise to everyone except me, but I liked to think that my hair, long, thick, clean but out of control, did something to subvert the meaning of the suit. To make the point even more forcibly, I arrived at the book-burning party wearing a scruffy orange T-shirt under the suit, and if Dr Bentley wanted to bounce me for being improperly dressed, that was just fine by me. I intended to treat this party with at least some of the contempt it deserved. But Bentley didn't remark on the T-shirt at all, and welcomed me to his rooms with easy, effortless politeness, and then a college servant, a sullen, understandably resentful seventeen-year-old from the town, handed me a glass of wine.

The others at the party, a dozen or so undergraduates, plus a few research students, had made less effort to be subversive. They were all wearing collars and ties but most of them looked very ill-at-ease in this regulation dress. This was a time of shoulder-length hair and ornate facial fuzz, of faded, flared denim, of cheese-cloth shirts and grandad vests. Just about everyone wanted to look like a hippie, even some of the dons, but Gregory Collins was untouched by such influences.

He stood out from the crowd because he looked so at home in his suit. It was certainly not a smart suit and certainly not fashionable. It was a baggy three-piece, thick, hot, hairy, and looked as though it might have been handed down through the family, but Gregory inhabited it comfortably. He wore his hair in a short back and sides, and it shone slickly in a style reminiscent of Brylcreemed footballers from the nineteen-thirties. He was wearing what looked like an old school tie, perhaps one that he'd had since the second form.

He was big but not fat, not yet anyway, but he had difficulty manoeuvring his clumsy, uncoordinated bulk, and he moved as though constantly correcting himself, reining himself in, struggling to keep control of legs that threatened to walk into furniture, of arms that were constantly about to knock over glasses or elbow people in the stomach. He had one of those heads that appears to widen as it approaches the neck: the top of the skull a small dome, the cheeks slanting outwards, the jaw wider than the ears, disappearing into what one day soon would be heavy jowls.

There was something amusing about his clumsiness, and yet he was a person who demanded to be taken seriously. His size, his awkwardness, his uncompromising look of being out of place, gave him a presence, a gravity that had to be dealt with. I'd never met him before, in fact I only knew one or two people in the whole room, but he came across to me immediately and said, 'I saw you in some play or other, didn't I?'

I admitted this might be so. I'd had a brief, humiliating fling with the world of student theatre.

'Aye, I thought it was you.'

By now I'd taken in his voice, an unembarrassed, even ostentatious, Yorkshire accent. This was not an unfamiliar ploy at Cambridge. Although some people at university tried to disguise their origins, either because they were too fancy or too humble or, as in my own case, simply too dull, others wore them like a badge. Personally, I was trying hard to appear classless and deracinated, and I admit that I did feel a little superior to Gregory Collins, not because he was working class, whereas I was more solidly, boringly middle class, but because he felt the need to turn his origins into a performance and I did not.

'You looked the part all right,' he said, 'but every time you opened your mouth, I thought, What a twat.'

His criticism was undoubtedly justified but it still took me aback. It did so happen that I was a good-looking young man at that time. I took no particular credit for it. I knew it was completely accidental, that it carried no morality with it, but others seemed to see it far less clear-sightedly than I did. Some people liked me because of the way I looked. People were willing to trust me, they were willing to make allowances, willing to do me favours. Sometimes they wanted something in return, perhaps there was an occasional sexual motive, people who fancied me, although they were almost always the wrong people. But sex wasn't the whole story, not even very much of the story. People attributed qualities to me because of my attractiveness. They wanted me around. They wanted me at their parties. They wanted me for their friend. I had an advantage that I thought the likes of Gregory Collins would never have.

And so, thinking I might be able to do something with these accidental good looks, I had gone into student amateur dramatics. The majority of the other people involved didn't seem to think of themselves as either students or amateurs. They preferred to think of themselves as serious young thespians, artists who were on the springboard to great things in the professional theatre, and I might

7

have been willing to go along with the self-deception, but my few appearances on stage had convinced me I was absolutely, irredeemably amateur.

I tried to be good. I wanted to be charismatic and magnetic, the kind of performer audiences couldn't take their eyes off. But they could, and they did. Such charisma and magnetism as I genuinely seemed to have in my real life evaporated completely the moment I walked on stage. No doubt the whole audience thought, What a twat, but none of them had expressed it quite so directly as Gregory Collins.

At that point the sullen boy came round asking if we wanted our glasses refilled and Gregory Collins said, 'That'd be champion.' I thought he was trying to be funny, but no, 'champion' seemed to be a regular part of his vocabulary.

I discovered he'd seen me in a minor role in an experimental production of Huysmans' *Against Nature*, a project that would have been quite bad and ludicrous enough even without my own contribution. He said, 'I should think that's a book you wouldn't mind seeing burned.' I smiled thinly. The fact that he was almost right didn't make him any less annoying. I got away from him.

Our choice of book had to be kept secret, so we had arrived at the party with our volumes in sealed envelopes as though it were the Oscars or the Miss World Contest. But I did notice that Gregory Collins brought his offering in a locked metal case. This surely was taking things too far.

I spent the rest of the evening trying to keep my distance from him. He seemed like a bore. The party went on for a long time and nothing much happened. We all got slowly but not extravagantly drunk, and it was nearly midnight before the book burning started. I managed to get one of the few seats in the room from where I could see the proceedings clearly yet appear detached from them.

Bentley stood unsteadily on a footstool, called for order, and the burning began. He chose the sequence in which guests had to make their denunciations, but there seemed no particular pattern to it. I was hoping he'd choose me early so I could get it over with, but perhaps he sensed that and deliberately kept me waiting.

Envelopes were opened, books were produced, displayed, jejunely denounced and tossed into the fireplace. A couple of people played along with Bentley's prejudices. Someone burned Kate Millett's

Sexual Politics. Someone went for *Mythologies.* But naturally there were also more liberal, combative elements present, and someone burned Henry Miller's *Tropic of Cancer* for reasons Kate Millett would have agreed with.

A slight, red-haired Scot with a squint and asymmetrical, triangular sideburns had brought along a copy of Ray Bradbury's *Fahrenheit 451,* not because he thought it deserved burning for anything it contained, he explained, but simply because of the title.

'When you consider it,' Bentley said thoughtfully, 'I don't suppose four hundred and fifty-one degrees Fahrenheit can really be the temperature at which all paper burns, can it? Paper comes in different varieties, made from all sorts of materials, and it's treated with any number of different chemicals and acids and so forth, depending on the quality and the purpose. So different kinds of paper must have widely differing flash points. Still, it's a catchy enough title.'

The fire burned erratically in the hearth, swallowing up books, occasionally choking with paper and ash, and requiring Bentley to attend it with a poker and tongs. He did it cheerfully and fastidiously, and he muttered ironic phrases about the dignity of labour.

Then a big fleshy bruiser took the floor. He was called Franklin, a medical student, treasurer of the JCR committee, captain of the college rowing team, who made pin-money by selling cheap pocket calculators to science students, assuring buyers that these little plastic suckers were going to change the world. Most of us were not convinced.

'I'd certainly like to rid the world of this novelettish little volume,' he said.

He opened his envelope and displayed a copy of *The Diary of Anne Frank,* and in one movement he whipped it across the room like a frisbee, so that it thwacked into the fire back, creating a messy little eruption of ash and soot.

'Oh, come on,' I said loudly, 'that's not funny.'

'Wasn't trying to be funny.'

I started to get up from my chair. I don't know precisely what I had in mind, whether I was going to flounce out of the party or whether I was going to offer to horse-whip the anti-Semitic bounder; but inevitably I did neither and Bentley did his amused best to placate me.

'You shouldn't take this too seriously, you know,' he said. 'We

9

aren't actually trying to rid the world of these books. That would be as wearisome as it would be futile. We're simply engaging in a little active, symbolic literary criticism.'

I was usually quite good at thinking on my feet and coming back with a snappy answer, but I couldn't think of anything worth saying, so rather awkwardly I sat down again, had another drink, and I was still gently glowering when Bentley said, 'So, Michael, have you solved your own liberal dilemma in this area?'

'You mean, have I found a book I want to burn?'

He pursed his mouth to show that he thought I was being a little vulgar and needlessly explicit.

'As a matter of fact, I have,' I said.

I stood up and opened my own envelope, and I took out a small volume of literary criticism. It was called *Palpable Obscure* and it was written by Dr John Bentley.

'My reasons for wanting to burn this book are fairly straightforward,' I said. 'Because he's the kind of author who approves of book-burning parties.'

The hush around the room was gratifyingly brittle. The guests reacted as though I'd committed the most terrible social gaffe. It was all very well to toy with fascism, but it was something quite else to insult your host. Dr Bentley looked at me sadly, as though he was trying hard to suppress the condescension he felt towards me, but wasn't quite succeeding.

'Someone does this every year,' he said. 'Not very original, but it does ensure at least the occasional small royalty.'

He raised his glass to me and of course I had to raise my own in return. I don't suppose I'd really imagined that my simple little insult would reduce him to quivering shame, but equally I couldn't show my disappointment at how successfully and urbanely he'd dealt with it.

It might have made for a rather sour end to the proceedings, which I suppose had been my intention, but we'd reckoned without Gregory Collins. It was now his turn. Grandly he took his place at a side table and placed his metal box on it, roughly shoving bottles and glasses out of the way. With unnecessary and comical ceremony he opened up the box. What he took out was not a book at all, but a typed manuscript some three or four inches thick. The pages were loose and unbound, and as he gripped them they slid around in his fingers.

'This is my contribution to the proceedings,' he said. 'I've grafted away for the last two years trying to write the great bloody Cambridge novel, and here it is.'

I knew nothing at all about Gregory Collins, but it still came as a surprise to find that he'd written a novel. He didn't look the type, although my idea of what the type looked like was utterly uninformed.

'Anyway,' he said, 'the bugger's finished, and it's absolute tripe, and I can't think of anything better to do with it than chuck the bloody thing in the fire.'

The manuscript was too big and cumbersome to be thrown easily or accurately and so he walked across the room and carefully placed it in the grate. By now there was already a great deal of ash and burned paper in there and the sheer bulk of the manuscript threatened to extinguish the fire altogether, but after a while the pages started to curl and smoulder, then blacken and separate, never bursting into a grand, satisfying conflagration, but nevertheless being very effectively consumed and destroyed.

There was some muttering around the room that this was a brave, rash and foolish thing to do, although simultaneously a couple of people sneered that it was probably only a first draft or a Xerox, and there could easily be another copy safely stashed away somewhere. But I didn't think that. I could believe that Gregory Collins was a poseur, but I didn't think he was a fake. Dr Bentley was finding the whole thing delicious, and was giggling like a schoolboy. It had been a great finale.

And that was the end of the burning, though not quite the end of the party. A couple of people came up to me and said it had been pretty smart of me to burn Bentley's book, but there was no doubt that I'd been upstaged by Gregory Collins. He briefly became the centre of attention, although he had very little to say for himself. When somebody asked him what the novel had been about he refused to give details. 'I've burned the bastard,' he said. 'You don't expect me to turn it into a bloody oral tradition, do you?'

Then Bentley put on a record of *Siegfried*, clear signal that it was time for the majority of us to leave. A group of us were going back to someone's room to smoke dope and listen to a Captain Beefheart bootleg, and we invited Gregory Collins along, but he turned us down, saying it sounded a bit too rich for his blood. I think we were all relieved. But before we went our separate ways he shook me very formally by the hand and said, 'We made a great double act, eh, Michael?'

Far less formally, Dr Bentley saw us to the door, and as I made my way out he looked at me with a tenderness that made me very uncomfortable. 'So pretty,' he said, 'and so empty.' I felt less threatened by his words than I did by his look, and perhaps recognising that he added, 'But not quite pretty enough or quite empty enough to be truly appealing.'

2

It's tempting to think that all this happened a very long time ago, in a completely different age and time, yet I'm sure that the feelings we had about ourselves then were surprisingly similar to the ones we have now. We felt ourselves to be very modern, very complex, very in control. But I also remember we felt bombarded, overloaded, surfeited. We felt ourselves to be awash in a superfluity of goods and services, products and messages. The shops seemed full of crap. Our roads seemed too full of cars. The world seemed polluted. We felt we were besieged by advertising, media images, information. Even from the academic quietness of Cambridge the world seemed too noisy and busy and demanding. Our perceptions weren't inaccurate but, of course, we'd seen nothing yet. If anyone thought the future would be so drenched in the stuff of computers and electronic entertainment they were keeping rather quiet about it, although admittedly some people seemed to see the future more clearly than others, certainly more clearly than I did.

As our lives as students came to an end, there was a great settling out, a clarification of who we were, of who we had been all along. Those who had appeared subversive and anti-materialistic now expressed an interest in the law or accountancy. Those who'd enjoyed a dandyish, decadent reputation as students now thought they might become television researchers. Those who'd been involved with concrete poetry and avant-garde film thought they should get a job working for the *Daily Telegraph*. And in most cases they got what they wanted.

I had absolutely no idea what the future held for me, not even what I wanted it to hold. I would have been happy enough to stay on at the university, to spend a few more years in lecture theatres, libraries and seminar rooms, to be a continuing if not exactly an eternal student.

But I knew all along that my degree wouldn't be good enough to allow me to become a Ph.D. student. I'd even talked to Dr Bentley about my prospects. If he retained any resentment about my burning his book, he refused to show it, and he said he was prepared to put in a good word for me, but on balance he thought I shouldn't set my sights too firmly on a career as an academic.

I had a lot of ambivalence towards what I only half-jokingly referred to as the 'real world'. Certainly the world of the university appeared at times both inauthentic and stifling, but the world out there, the world of jobs and careers, of grown-up relationships and ambitions and money, seemed an infinitely tough and frightening place, and nothing in my education had prepared me to deal with it.

So, since I knew I couldn't be part of academe I did what seemed like the next best thing, or at least an extremely obvious thing. I got a job working in London for a firm of rare book dealers. They were called Somervilles, a good old name in a small and highly specialised field. They bought and sold English and American literary first editions, Joyce at the very top end, down through Greene and Waugh, all the way to Kingsley Amis and Ian Fleming. They also sold authors' manuscripts, everything from single postcards and letters to complete archives. It sounded like something I might enjoy, that I might be quite good at.

At the interview I had been told this was a job with a future, that it might involve bidding at auctions, negotiating with literary estates, perhaps eventually going to America to visit university libraries who were amassing literary materials. Both my potential employers and I could see that my charm might be very useful in this area, and I was keen to do well at the job, willing to put a lot of energy into this world of fine bindings and limited editions, but what I did day to day was a lot more humble.

I was supposedly learning how to catalogue books and manuscripts, so they might be accurately described for our mail-order customers, who were many and rich and sometimes quite famous. Tom Stoppard and George Steiner were on the mailing list, as were any number of Cambridge dons, including Dr Bentley, though I checked the records and saw it was years since he'd bought anything.

The job of cataloguing was a precise, formal and pretty dull business. I had to be able to discern the difference between a fine copy, a nice copy, a good copy, and a good reading copy. I learned pithy descriptive phrases – 'some wear on the spine', 'with the author's autograph inscription on the fly leaf', 'front edge somewhat faded', 'wrappers frayed'. I learned what foxing was.

A couple of months after leaving university I found myself sitting at my desk when my boss, Julian Somerville, placed two books in front of me. Although he shared the family name, he was a sufficiently distant relative that they didn't feel the need to share anything else with him, such as the family fortune. He managed the shop part of the business, not that they called it a shop, preferring the term 'showroom', since that sounded classier and snootier and more likely to keep out passing trade, but let's face it, a shop is what a shop does. As far as I was concerned, Julian was the shop manager and much of the time I was his shop assistant.

Julian Somerville was a long, thin breadstick of a man, with perfect manners, who dressed in multiple layers of brown: corduroy suits, khaki waistcoats, beige shirts, knitted tweed ties. The two books he placed in front of me were both copies of Scott Fitzgerald's *The Great Gatsby*, both English first editions, both in fine condition, but one had a dust jacket and one didn't.

'Lessons in book dealing, number one thousand and one,' said Julian brightly, and he indicated the book without the jacket. 'This copy is quite desirable, quite collectable, and would set you back about a hundred pounds.'

I nodded, doing my best to appear the keen student.

'This copy,' he said, indicating the other, 'with the jacket, is worth about five hundred. The moral of the lesson: in this trade if in no other, you can judge a book by its cover.'

'Far out,' I said. It was the kind of thing I liked to say. I was surrounded by literary tradition, by solidity, by locked glass-fronted bookcases, by leather-topped desks. I felt the need to inject the occasional bit of 'modern' terminology. Julian frowned at me indulgently.

His lesson filled me with a certain ambivalence. If a jacketed *Great Gatsby* was worth so much more than an unjacketed one, the jacket in effect became far more valuable than the book itself. I well understood how this might offend literary purists. They would say that being fixated on the materiality of the book, the edition, the binding, the jacket, was clearly missing the point of what books were about, that texts were somehow invisible, incorporeal, that they floated free of the solid matter of the printed object.

Yet I wasn't quite such a purist. I liked books. I liked their form as well as their content. I thought they were nice things to have around, to touch, to look at. A few of them furnished the small horrible room in Shepherd's Bush where I lived. They seemed like a reasonable thing to spend money on, not that I had any money to spend on books or on anything else. The rare-book world was not a place where an entry-level graduate could make his fortune. I had known this all along and I didn't feel particularly aggrieved. The fact that some books cost as much as I earned in a year was just a fact of life, and one I could by and large live with. Nevertheless, when some rich customer, usually American, usually too fat and too well-dressed, breezed into the showroom and casually spent a four-figure sum with rather less premeditation than I'd give to buying a Mars bar, I admit I could feel resentful.

However, this resentment was somewhat free-floating. Partly I resented the American for being so rich. Certainly I resented my employer for paying me so little, and as a corollary to that I resented the world for being so expensive. But I was also fed up with myself for not having any valuable skills that I could sell in the market place. Or maybe it wasn't about skills, anyway. I sensed there were plenty of young men out there who were successfully making their way in the world, and who weren't any more skilled than I was. So what was it they had that I didn't? What secrets did they have access to? I disliked myself for being so feeble, so ignorant of how to plug into the world of achievement, success and money.

And money was probably the least important of the three. I told myself I'd have been happy to work for little or no money if I was doing something I really liked, that really mattered, but in the event I seemed to be working for little or no money, doing a job that didn't matter in the least. I couldn't have said that I hated the job at Somervilles exactly, and I was well aware that there were millions of jobs I'd have liked far less, but I had a profound sense that I was wasting my time.

If, in that old existential sense, we are what we do, then I thought I was nothing because I'd done nothing, experienced nothing, at least nothing that seemed to matter either to me or to anyone else. I'm always amazed and irritated when I see people interviewed on the TV news or in documentaries, and there's the interviewee's name and a one-line, or even one-word, definition of who and what they are: Michael Smith 'Student', Mike Smith 'Friend', Mick Smith 'Disgruntled employee'. Of course, most people who appear on TV or in documentaries have rather more dramatic captions than these. To be newsworthy they need things like 'Orgiast', 'Father of Siamese Twins', 'Unrepentant Nazi'. I'm depressed by this too. It seems so limiting. Like anyone else, I had always wanted to be more than the labels attached to me, but at least I'd have liked the labels to be somewhat impressive: Michael Smith 'Wit', Mickey Smith 'Lover of Women' Mike Smith 'A Man to Watch'. What I didn't want, and what I suspected would have been the most appropriate was Mike Smith 'Pathetic Bastard'.

And I was confused too. I'd had this supposedly privileged English education; privileged enough that millions of my fellow Englishman would be quite prepared to hate me for it, to consider me a snob and an élitist. It was supposed to open all doors, to plug me into some pernicious old boys' network. So why was I no more than a not much glorified shop assistant? And why was I living in squalor, in a horrible room in Shepherd's Bush, instead of the Chelsea penthouse that I inhabited in my dreams?

The other extant myth about Cambridge that I was finding to be completely without foundation, was that it supposedly provided you with friends for life. Since leaving university I'd seen hardly anyone. In a few cases there were good reasons, my friends had got married, gone to work abroad and so on, but even the ones who lived and worked in London stayed out of contact. Oh sure, I got a few party invitations, was sometimes called upon to be the 'spare man', went out for the occasional beer or pizza with somebody, but it wasn't quite the gilded social life I'd been hoping for. Perhaps the truth was I didn't have any friends any more, and that made me think perhaps I'd never really had any in the first place.

But at least I had a girlfriend of sorts. She was called Nicola Campbell and I'd known her a little at university. I'd seen her at lectures and in the coffee bar, and had regarded her as a good acquaintance rather than a friend. Nicola had a clean, scrubbed, healthy quality that a lot of people found very attractive, very sexy. I could see, in a theoretical way, that this was true, but some sort of chemistry was lacking in my case. At university I'd never quite fancied her, never thought of pursuing her, but in London it was different. I ran into her going into a cinema on a Sunday afternoon. We were both alone, and maybe there is something especially depressing about going to the cinema alone on Sunday afternoons, and maybe we both thought the other one was more lonely and desperate than either of us really was. We sat together in the cinema, and then went out for a drink, and later we went out a few more times to see other films, then we had sex once, and then we had sex a couple more times, and somehow, before we knew it, it appeared we were going out with each other, albeit in an uncommitted, half-hearted sort of way.

Nicola was a good person. She was attractive, intelligent, charming, witty; just like me. We made a good, or at least a good-looking couple. We liked each other, but I think we both knew we didn't like each other quite enough. Nothing was wrong and yet we had a sense of how things might be better. We thought our relationship would do for now, but we keenly hoped that something more passionate and interesting and substantial was not too far around the corner.

The main thing I remember about Nicola from those days, is how little odour she had about her. Sometimes she smelled of soap, and occasionally of expensive, understated perfume, but she never smelled of herself. She never smelled of sweat or sex or garlic or anything robust like that. Her breath, her hair, her body, were all quite odourless.

We fell into a pattern. We saw each other twice a week at most, and went to the cinema or for a cheap meal. We always went Dutch. She too had moved to London straight from university and was doing a job that seemed to have certain parallels with my own, although hers sounded much better since she was 'working in publishing'. It seems absurd to me now but that phrase had a magic to it then, and not only to me. Publishing was spoken of as a glamour profession, something a graduate might aspire to and only be accepted into if you were one of the brightest and the best. It was a hundred times better than working in rare books.

Nicola was doing her best to rid me of this illusion. She said her colleagues were grey, tubby men and women who chain-smoked and wore cardigans. They regarded her as dangerously glamorous and well-groomed and therefore frivolous and insubstantial. Her work, much like my own, was a mixture of the clerical and the dogsbody, but there was one part of her job that sounded to me like a reasonable amount of fun. She was in charge of the 'slush pile'. She had to deal with the unsolicited manuscripts: the military memoirs, the spiritual confessions, the travel diaries, the experimental novels sent in by the talentless, the desperate and the disturbed. It sounded fine to me, but Nicola felt otherwise.

'It only confirms how pathetically low on the totem I am,' she complained. 'Everything in the slush pile is, by definition, crap, otherwise it wouldn't be in the slush pile. So basically I'm wasting my time. And if by some strange chance something good managed to creep in there, and if I spotted it and said we ought to publish it, my bosses would still reject it, because they wouldn't trust my opinion because they think I'm just the imbecile who's in charge of the slush pile.'

There was reason enough for both of us to be dissatisfied, but one of the best things to be said for living in London was that it was always easy to see people around you who were far worse off than you were. And that was how I thought of Gregory Collins when I next met him.

He came into Somervilles one drab, wet afternoon. I suspect that if it had been anyone other than Gregory Collins I might have been embarrassed to be seen going about my dreary shop-assistant duties, but I felt so sure that whatever he was up to had to be less interesting and fulfilling than what I was up to, I greeted him quite warmly. And he was even warmer in return. He greeted me like the oldest of old friends. Perhaps he thought our experience at the book-burning party had created insoluble bonds.

'This is a posh place you're working in,' he said. 'You must be doing all right for yourself.'

Poor old Gregory.

'It's OK,' I said. 'What about you? What are you up to?'

'Teaching,' he said dourly, and my sense of superiority remained quite intact.

'In London?'

'No, up in Harrogate. Grammar school. One of the last. Teaching history.'

Yes, that fitted perfectly.

'How is it?' I asked.

'It's champion,' he said. 'Teaching's my life. I'll always be a teacher.'

I felt better and better.

'So what brings you down to London?'

He snorted and looked unhappy.

'London,' he said, dismissively. 'I came all this bloody way for a meeting, and the bugger wasn't there. He'd called in sick. I'm going to be demanding an apology.'

He wandered about the book shop, opening cabinets, picking up very expensive items, a signed Wyndham Lewis, a Gertrude Stein letter. He seemed to find them interesting enough, but he handled them the way he might have handled the morning paper.

'I've got a few hours to kill before I get the train back up north. Do you want to have a bevvy after you finish work?'

I said sure. I had nothing better to do, although I wasn't certain I'd have anything to talk to him about. I didn't think I had much in common with Harrogate schoolteachers. The shop was open for another hour, so I expected Gregory to go away and then come back when I'd finished work, but he hung around till closing time, clumsily handling extremely rare and expensive items. Julian Somerville watched him with mild disapproval but was too feeble or polite to say anything. I was glad when I could finally get Gregory out of the shop and into the pub. He drank half his beer in one big gulp, then considered the taste carefully. 'Not bad for a southern ale.' His professional northerner act was even more irritating in London than it had been in Cambridge.

'So, have you done any more acting?' he asked.

'No, of course not,' I said. 'I think I've grown out of it.'

'Very good decision,' he said. 'I suppose we ought to be drinking champagne really. Not that I like champagne.'

'Something to celebrate?' I asked. I wondered if he'd found a good Yorkshire woman to marry him, although that seemed highly unlikely.

'Actually, I've not been quite straight with you, Michael. I'm trying not to be showy about it, but the fact is I'm down in London to see a publisher. *My* publisher.'

'You have a publisher?'

'Aye, I just said so.'

'Is this for history textbooks or something?'

'No, it's for a novel.'

The connection between Gregory Collins and novel writing was one that I still found hard to make.

'I thought you burned your novel,' I said.

'I burned one novel. You're allowed to write more than one. The first one was crap. This one's bloody good, if I say so myself.'

'That's great. Congratulations.'

I hoped I sounded convincing. Undoubtedly it was great for Gregory and there was no reason why his minor success should make me feel bad. I didn't think I was competing with the Gregory Collinses of this world, and yet I knew I probably didn't sound quite as pleased for him as I should have.

'What's it called?' I asked.

'*The Wax Man.*'

'Good title,' I said.

'I'm not dead keen on it actually,' he said. 'I wanted to change it to something with a number in the title, like *Slaughterhouse 5* or *Catch 22*, or *BUtterfield 8* or *The Crying of Lot 49.*'

'Why?' I asked.

'I don't know exactly. I just think titles with numbers in them are dead catchy. Anyway, the publishers reckoned it was a daft idea.'

'I suppose they know what they're doing,' I said.

'I wish I had your faith.'

'What's it about?'

'It's a very hard book to summarise,' he said, and I was rather glad of that.

'I'll just have to read it when it comes out.'

'Aye, you will. It's a serious book,' he said. 'A dark book. But funny, and very clever, very ironic, full of literary pranks and japes. I love a good literary prank, don't you, Michael?'

It seemed an innocent enough question at the time.

'Oh sure,' I said. 'So will you be giving up the teaching job?'

'Oh no. I wouldn't want to be some poncey full-time writer. Like I said, teaching's my life. Besides, I couldn't afford to give up the day job. They're paying me bugger all for my book. You won't believe this, but they aren't even doing a proper author photograph. I talked to this lass today and she said I'm supposed to send them a bloody holiday snap or something. I told her it's very short-sighted of them. You know, they always say Truman Capote was a success because of that sexy picture of him sitting under a palm tree or whatever. If they'd used a holiday snap it would all have been different.'

This thought made him very miserable, as if he was already anticipating the failure of his book, already seeing that having a novel published mightn't be the great joy he'd anticipated. I still knew very little about Gregory, and absolutely nothing about his writing, yet it seemed odd that he would have chosen Truman Capote as a role model.

'Why not have some photographs done professionally?' I asked, but he didn't think much of the suggestion.

'With my face, what would be the point?' he said. 'I know I'm an ugly git.'

He became even more miserable. Again I was surprised. He was undoubtedly right about his unattractiveness, but given how little effort he made to present himself attractively to the world, I'd assumed he somehow revelled in it.

'It's all right for you,' he said sulkily.

'Is it?'

'Yes, it is. You're a good-looking bloke. I bet you get lots of girls.'

'Oh yes, thousands.'

'Well, I bet you get a damn sight more than I do.'

No doubt this was true but admitting it would only have made him feel worse, so I said nothing. I suppose I might have tried to tell him where he was going wrong, suggested that he grow his hair, wear clothes that weren't a couple of decades out of fashion, but I had no desire to play Henry Higgins.

'Well, I'm no Truman Capote,' I said, and I bought another round of drinks and tried to change the subject.

'Are you in touch with anyone from college?' I asked.

'Nobody at all,' he said. 'Although I'm going to get in touch with old Bentley. I'm going to send him an advance proof of my book, ask him to give me a quote for the jacket.'

'Will that improve sales?'

'I don't know. If I was on first name terms with Anthony Burgess I'd ask him instead, but I'm not, am I?'

Gregory's depression was becoming infectious. An excess of beer seemed to be the only way to get through the evening and we went for it. Drunkenness didn't make Gregory Collins any less gloomy, but it made me a lot more tolerant of him. Our conversation didn't progress much. He was firmly stuck on the twin topics of his book and his lack of sexual appeal.

'I'll bet you're a photogenic bugger too, aren't you?' he said.

I had to admit this was true. Being photogenic was another one of those worthless qualities I happened to possess.

'And you *do* like literary jokes,' Gregory insisted.

I repeated that I did, but only because I thought in some vague, unconsidered way that saying so might make him less miserable.

'OK then, do me a favour. Give me a photograph of yourself and I'll send it to my publisher and tell them it's me.'

'What?' I said.

'They can't tell their arses from their elbows at that place, and I've never so much as seen my editor, and it's not as if authors ever really look like their publicity photographs, anyway.'

'What do you mean? You want me to pretend to be you?'

'No, you wouldn't be pretending to be me. I'd just be using your picture to make the reading public think I'm a decent-looking bloke.'

We were both well drunk by this time, and after some encouragement from Gregory I agreed that it sounded like a fairly amusing thing to do, but I had no real intention of doing it. I knew that by the next morning we'd both have sobered up and it wouldn't seem like such an amusing thing after all. But then Gregory looked at his watch, panicked, and said he'd missed his last train to Harrogate, and would I put him up for the night? I didn't feel I could say no, much as I wanted to, so I agreed to let him sleep on my floor.

We took the last tube back to my horrible room and while I made us some coffee Gregory rifled through a box of photographs I kept on the mantelpiece. I was anal enough to want to have my past documented but not anal enough to organise the photographs by, for instance, putting them in an album or any sort of order. He took out a moody head and shoulders portrait of me, not a bad one, actually, that the cast photographer had taken as a publicity shot when I was in a college production of *The Local Stigmatic*.

'But look,' I said, uneasy with all this but not quite capable of clear thought, 'how's this going to work with your friends and family? They'll see your name and my picture. They'll think that's a bit odd, won't they?'

'Don't be daft. I'm not telling my family. They already think I'm a right nancy boy for having gone to university. If they ever found out

I'd written a book, and especially if they found out what's in it, they'd bloody lynch me.'

I wondered what kind of shocking material it contained, but the thought only lasted a second.

'But it'll still have your name on it,' I said.

'So what? This might surprise you, Michael, but by and large the members of my family don't spend a lot of time combing the bookshops or reading the literary reviews. And if by some bizarre chance they ever saw a book with my name on it they'd just say, "That's a funny thing, a writer with the same name as our Gregory".'

'And, of course, it would have my picture on it.'

'Right.'

He said this triumphantly, as though he'd finally got a point across to one of his dimmer pupils. For my part, bleary as I was, I felt sure he hadn't dealt with all the possible objections and problems, but what the hell, it was late and I was pissed, and it was easier not to argue. I unrolled a sleeping bag for Gregory, and I got into my narrow single bed and fell asleep in a leaden, drunken haze.

When I woke up next morning Gregory Collins had gone. He'd taken the photograph and he'd left me a little thank-you note saying he'd invite me to the launch party for his book, if the bastards gave him a launch party, which he doubted. In the cold light of morning I had even bigger qualms about him using my picture, but I told myself he'd think better of it once he got home. In any case, I realised I had no way of getting in touch with him. I didn't know his address, didn't know which school he taught at, certainly didn't know the name of his publisher; and I really didn't feel inclined to start pursuing him. That would have been making far too much of it. So I forgot all about it. I decided that Gregory Collins was one of those people who would flit through my life every once in a while, never become a friend, and certainly never become important to me. Stupid or what?

3

I really didn't have much idea what Gregory Collins' novel *The Wax Man* was all about, and as far as I could see neither did most of the reviewers. Yes, I read it, and yes, it did get reviewed, respectfully if not widely, and although most of us couldn't make head or tail of it, we all somehow felt it was rather good.

If I'd been asked in advance what kind of book I'd have expected Gregory Collins to write I suppose it would have been something gritty and stolid, realist and urban, possibly set in a northern town and featuring a dedicated history teacher. But I should have known that Gregory Collins was always going to be a man who confounded easy expectations.

The book opens with our hero, a nameless, stateless, ageless man without qualities, finding himself embedded in a solid block of white wax, completely unable to move. There's wax in his ears so he can't hear, and in his eyes so he can't see, and no doubt he can't smell or taste much either, though the book doesn't go into details about that. And he certainly can't speak; although by some method or other he is able to breathe.

And so, being unable to do much of anything else, he does a lot of thinking and philosophising. He asks himself who he is and where he is and how he got there. He doesn't have any answers to these questions, so I suppose he's a sort of amnesiac, but he realises the mere fact that he has the ability to ask them must mean he once had a life outside the wax block, a life in which he was able to develop concepts of being and language.

This kind of philosophical, or I dare say ontological, stuff takes up a good half of the book, although mercifully it's divided into shortish chapters, and they're interspersed with some rather more upbeat material. In fact, the people who disliked the book worried that these non-philosophical chapters were nothing more than pornography, in which a man, who may or may not be the same one who's in the block of wax, performs just about every conceivable sexual act with men, women, animals and objects, in every imaginable permutation. This, I supposed, was what Gregory didn't want his family to read.

Although I didn't personally like the book all that much, and found a great deal of it hard going, the porno parts no less than the philosophical ones, it seemed to me to be a very clever and knowing book. It didn't exactly have something for everyone but I thought it had the right combination of high and low concerns, of philosophical and prurient elements, that would draw people to it. The philosophical passages seemed rigorous and serious enough, and the sexual passages had a trippy, druggy, hallucinatory feel to them that people still found appealing in those days.

The book didn't make the bestseller list or anything like that, and Gregory Collins didn't become a star of the literary heavens, but the book was talked of here and there as being an exciting and relevant new work by an interesting new writer. What more could anybody ask from a first novel?

I had received my own copy of the book direct from the author a few weeks ahead of publication. He had been right not to expect a party from his publisher, and an accompanying note apologised for that. I was a little surprised that he knew my address, although of course he had been to my bedsit. I was disappointed still to be in the same place and not to have moved on. Nothing in my life had changed at all: same job, same girlfriend, same discontent. The book was signed and inscribed, 'To Michael, thanks for helping me improve my image.' And there, sure enough, on the back flap, rather grainy and in high contrast was the photograph of me.

It was strange to see myself on the book jacket, and I was surprised Gregory had gone through with it, but basically I thought it was no big deal. As hoaxes went, literary or otherwise, it felt harmless enough. If the public was being deceived, it was not a very wicked or dangerous deception. And yes, there was something funny about plain old Gregory Collins transforming himself into the moody, high-cheekboned character in that author picture.

I didn't see what repercussions there could be. It was only a book, after all. How many copies could it possibly sell? Just how widely would my face be seen? I was not going to be mobbed in the street by rabid fans of Gregory Collins, now was I? And if, somewhere along the line, somebody did discover the hoax, we'd simply be able to come clean and admit we'd played this mildly amusing and slightly silly joke. I didn't think it was a hanging offence.

Nicola saw it differently. She had never met Gregory in her university days. Cambridge was, in some ways, a big place, and Gregory hadn't got around much. 'You're out of your mind,' she said, when I showed her my copy of *The Wax Man*. 'You've been exploited.'

'Yes?'

'Yes. Collins is using your image to make himself more presentable. That's not right.'

She seemed to think Gregory was some kind of satanic manipulator. If only she could meet him, I thought.

'It's a joke,' I said.

'Not a good one,' Nicola insisted. 'What if some plain middle-aged female writer had used a good-looking young model to pose as her in order to sell more books. What would you say then?'

'I'd say it was the same joke.'

'You wouldn't say it was pandering to rather fascistic notions of worth, based on physical beauty?'

'No, I don't think I'd say that,' I admitted.

'What if you ever want to write a book of your own?'

'I promise you, Nicola, I absolutely swear to you I'll never write a book.'

And then she started to thumb through the book. Her reaction was more extreme than I could ever have imagined.

'Shit,' she said. 'Shit and derision. I know this book. I've read this book. I read it in manuscript. It was in my slush pile. I tossed it straight back. I thought it was the most unutterable crap.'

'Well, maybe it is,' I said. I wasn't going to debate Gregory's literary genius.

'Yes, but at least it's publishable crap. And if I'm supposed to be a publisher I have to be able to tell publishable crap from unpublishable crap. And apparently I can't.'

This realisation made her despondent, and I could see why. It soured the evening. We agreed that neither of us would ever again refer to Gregory Collins and his works. That didn't strike me as much of a hardship.

Nicola and I were continuing with our rather frustrating lives and rather insipid relationship. It wasn't what either of us wanted, and although we could easily conceive of better things, we weren't quite prepared to take the uncertain and uncomfortable steps required to obtain them. We both knew we were settling for second- or third-best, but it was much, much better than nothing.

Then came the phone call from Gregory. He called me at work and when he said, 'Hello, Michael, how's it going?' I really had no idea who he was. He wasn't in my thoughts at all. I assumed it must be some customer being overly familiar. But we cleared that up and I asked him how his book was doing.

'They tell me sales are moderate,' he said grumpily.

'Well, if having my photograph on the back has in some small way contributed to that moderateness then I'm delighted.'

'There are plenty of precedents, you know,' he said, with what I thought was quite unnecessary defensiveness. 'Thomas Pynchon sent a stand-up comedian to collect a literary prize he'd won, and Andy Warhol sent an Andy Warhol impersonator out on a lecture tour pretending to be him.'

I sensed he was trying to justify or explain himself to me, but I thought no justification or explanation was required.

'It's all right,' I said, 'it's no problem,' but I could also sense that he was leading up to something he considered to be important and ominous.

'Yes, it is a problem, Michael, and I'd really appreciate your advice and help.'

That was even more ominous. Gregory Collins had managed perfectly well without my advice till now.

'I've been invited to do a reading,' he said. 'In Brighton. A reading and a signing. You can see my problem.'

'Sounds like it's time to come clean. Or you could just turn down the invitation.'

'I don't want to turn it down. You can't turn down publicity.'

'Then you'd better come clean.'

'I don't want to come clean.'

'What then?'

'You could do it for me.'

'Don't be silly.'

'Wait on. It's not as silly as it sounds,' he said gravely. 'All you'd have to do is read from the book for a bit, then maybe answer one or two daft questions and sign a few books. You could do that. It's money for old rope.'

'Money?' I said.

'Well no, there's no money, but they'll pay your train fare and the woman who runs the bookshop's offered a bed for the night if you need it. And let's face it, I know you fancy yourself as a performer.'

'Do I?' And the moment I voiced the question I saw the pointlessness of denying it. Perhaps Gregory knew me better than I knew myself. Although I had no urge to do any proper acting, in the form of plays or amateur dramatics, the desire to perform, to show off, to say, 'Look at me,' was still there, was perhaps there more than ever now that I was stuck in a job that required me to be so undemonstrative.

'I'd be right grateful,' Gregory said.

'Yes, I should think you would.'

I knew I ought to be saying no. For one thing, I knew Nicola would be furious with me, but I was finding the idea very appealing, and perhaps making Nicola furious was part of the appeal.

'So how exactly would this work?' I asked, but I knew it wouldn't really matter how it worked. Whatever the arrangement, paid or unpaid, with or without overnight accommodation, I wanted to do it. I knew that wasn't necessarily very healthy. I could perhaps have pretended I'd be doing it as an act of subversion, as a slap in the face to the literary establishment (whatever that was), but the truth was I'd be doing it because I was so bored with my life. Boredom seemed like the real enemy. It could drive you crazy, drive you to drink or drugs, to acts of self-destruction or crime, to simple insanity. But it was driving me to pretend to be a promising first novelist.

However, I saw that this matter of pretence wasn't absolutely straightforward. Yes, I would in one sense be pretending to be Gregory Collins, but I wouldn't be trying to impersonate him. I wouldn't be trying to act the part of a dour northern history teacher. I'd simply be myself but by another name, although a self who was pretending to have written a novel. Still, I thought I was up to it. I thought I could do as good a job of reading from the book as most authors ever do, certainly as well as Gregory would have done; and I'd read and heard more than enough literary twitterings to be able to bluff my way through the question and answer session. I would surely be able to come up with a few witty or amusing replies, far wittier and more amusing than Gregory. I was game. I was raring to go.

I sensed that Gregory was surprised by my immediate enthusiasm, that he'd imagined he'd have to do some arm-twisting, and I think he felt cheated, as though he'd wanted to revel in exerting his own powers of persuasion. We said we'd talk nearer the time in more detail, but, as far as I was concerned, by the time I put the phone down I'd made a firm and irrevocable commitment.

Sometimes it's surprising just how little it takes to make a person happy. The knowledge that I would be doing my little performance as Gregory Collins in a few weeks' time made my immediate life immeasurably more tolerable. My job seemed far less constricting, my bedsit less claustrophobic. Perhaps I should have taken that happiness as a warning sign. The fact that something so small could seem like such a highlight was no doubt an indicator of just how miserable I really was, but I was glad of any bright spot, and I didn't psychoanalyse it too much.

Even my relationship with Nicola seemed easier. Naturally, I knew it wouldn't remain that way once I'd told her I was going to do the reading. I knew she'd be furious, so I was saving it up, waiting for the right moment, the last possible moment, the day before I was due to do the reading, and then, when she reacted with anger or contempt or whatever, I thought that would be all right too. It wouldn't matter. It would be water off a duck's back. I had an exaggerated sense of my own well-being.

When I eventually told her, she said, 'This is terrible. This is the worst thing you've ever done to me.'

We were standing in a cinema queue in Leicester Square, in line to see A Star is Born, and I was baffled by her remark. I wasn't aware that I'd ever done anything terrible to her in the past, I didn't think I was doing anything very terrible now and, in any case, I didn't see in what sense I was doing it 'to her'.

'Don't think you can charm your way out of this one,' she said. 'I find it very hard to respect someone who's capable of deception.'

'But I'm not deceiving you. I'm being perfectly honest with you.'

'So you say. But if you're capable of deceiving the world about something like this, then who knows what you're deceiving me about?'

'What?'

'Who knows what you get up to on the nights when you don't see me?'

'I hang around my bedsit and read books.'

'That's what you tell me, but as we now know, you're quite capable of anything.'

I couldn't believe she was taking this so seriously, that it mattered so much to her. At best I thought she was being melodramatic, at worst I thought she was being crazy.

'This really isn't very important, you know,' I said. 'It's just a laugh.'

'Then don't do it. Tell Gregory Collins you won't do the reading.'

'I've no reason to tell him that.'

'The reason is because I'm asking you to. It's important to me, but not to you, so what does it matter?'

She'd got me. She could tell that this event was in fact all too important to me. I didn't want to cancel, and if she wanted to raise the stakes I was prepared to raise them too.

'Are we really going to fall out over this?' I asked.

'That's up to you.'

'No, it's not,' I said. 'It's up to both of us.'

'If you go to Brighton and do this absurd reading, then yes, we might very well fall out.'

'But we might not?'

Until that moment I hadn't wanted to fall out with Nicola, but now the prospect seemed surprisingly attractive. 'I'll let you know,' she said. 'Goodbye, Michael.' She walked away, and I wasn't sure whether or not she was walking out of my life for ever, and I wasn't sure whether that was going to make me miserable or actually quite happy. I was tempted to go chasing after her, but I knew it would only be prolonging a disagreement that couldn't be settled there and then. I stayed in the queue and went to see the film alone. It was rotten. I walked out halfway through.

4

I was nervous on the train down to Brighton but I wasn't afraid. I had the feeling I was going to be good. I'd selected some passages for the reading, rehearsed them quietly in the cramped privacy of my horrible room, and I felt I could do a good job with them. That first part of the evening, the actual reading, I saw as being really quite simple. The question and answer session, I thought, would be more difficult, and would require a certain amount of improvisation. I'd prepared a few answers about working methods, sources of inspiration, favourite authors and so on, and I felt I was in good shape. I hadn't made this stuff up out of nothing; I'd gone back to the source, talked to Gregory Collins and asked him to supply me with his views. Some of these, however, were a little stilted and dour so I'd been working on ways to make them pithier and more entertaining without falsifying them completely.

The hardest part of the performance, it seemed to me, would be the time spent, as it were, off stage, the time spent chatting with the owner of the shop, speaking informally to the fans, going out for a drink afterwards. This would require a much freer, more long-form improvisation. This mightn't be too easy, yet I had no great fears about it. I felt confident and in control, and I was certain I'd be able to cope. I would do my best to be a convincing Gregory Collins, but if the worst came to the worst I'd just be me.

The woman running the event, Ruth Harris, sole proprietor of Ruth Harris Books, was meeting me at the station. This was unnecessarily good of her. I'd have been happy to make my own way to her bookshop, but I was pleased to be treated so well. Obviously I didn't know what she looked like, but as soon as I got through the barrier at Brighton station I heard a perky woman's voice behind me say, 'I see the author photograph wasn't flattering at all. The flesh is even more engaging.' And then she slapped me on the bum.

I turned to see a woman of a certain age, say fifty; a woman who must once have been rather glamorous in a Bohemian sort of way. Her hair was still blonde, though obviously dyed, her lips and eyes were darkly painted, and she was showing a lot of crêpy cleavage. She smoked a thin, waxy cigar.

I was of an age when I couldn't imagine anyone over forty even having a sex life, much less being sexually attractive, yet in retrospect I know Ruth Harris was a sexy, good-looking woman, and I'm equally sure that many men would have been happy to have her slap them on the bum. I, however, found myself a little terrified.

'I'm Ruth Harris,' she said. 'Pleased you could make it.'

'Gregory Collins,' I said, and jutted out a hand to be shaken. I tried to appear firm, forthright, professional. I was aware this was the first time I'd ever lied about my name.

'I hope you won't mind me saying this, but I don't think you look much like a writer.'

I did mind. I felt as though my impersonation might be coming unstuck already, but in fact she was flattering me again.

'No, you're far too good-looking to be a writer,' she said. 'In my experience writers are a paunchy, bearded, dandruffy, halitosis-ridden bunch.'

'Are they?' I asked. 'I thought they were supposed to be romantic and wild-haired and wearing capes.'

'Only in my fantasies,' she said mistily.

She led me through the station car-park and we got into a crippled old Volvo estate car full of cardboard boxes and books. The windscreen was cracked, the tailgate was tied shut with washing line, and in order to sit in the passenger seat I had to rearrange carrierbags full of old magazines and papers, and I held a grubby bundle of *National Geographic*s on my knee for the length of the journey.

'I'm expecting a good turn-out,' Ruth Harris said. 'I've issued a three-line whip to all my friends and regular customers, and I'm sure you're the kind of writer who brings out the fans.'

'I wouldn't go that far,' I said.

'No? How far would you go?'

She was being flirtatious, even coquettish. I didn't know what to do with that at all. I smiled uncomfortably and she appeared to find my discomfort rather endearing. That was even worse.

The bookshop wasn't far from the station, and we soon stopped outside a narrow shop-front, a single window with a dark, chaotic interior. The door was locked and the shop was shut. Ruth Harris Books was evidently an entirely one-woman operation, and she'd had to close up in order to come and collect me.

She let me into the most overstocked bookshop I'd ever seen. We had to limbo and rumba our way in. The shelves were not just full, but so tightly crammed that books would need to be prised out. Wobbly stacks of paperbacks rose up from the floor and blocked the aisles. A couple of tables were piled high with miscellaneous, tatty old volumes. Most of the stock was second-hand, if not umpteenth-hand, though I did see a few new bestsellers, and there was a small mound of *The Wax Man*. My eye ran along the titles, observed the sort of books that were on sale, and I could see that most of them were worthless old rubbish: war stories, romances, condensed books, out-of-date travel guides and technical manuals, bound partworks. My assessment of their worthlessness wasn't just literary snobbery; they didn't appear to have any monetary value either. Someone could have come in and bought the whole lot at the asking price and it still wouldn't have made Ruth Harris a rich woman.

'I can't be doing with any of that high falutin', pretentious, first edition, literary nonsense,' she said. 'My customers want a good read and they want it cheap.'

Then why, I asked myself, though not her, had she invited Gregory Collins to do a reading? It seemed to me that whatever else might be said about *The Wax Man*, nobody in their right mind could possibly describe it as a good read. If Ruth Harris's stock said anything about her customers I had a feeling that Gregory's book, and my reading from it, might be a serious disappointment to them.

I looked around, wondering where exactly I was supposed to do the reading. There was scarcely enough room to stand up, much less accommodate an audience. However, seeing my confusion, Ruth Harris took me through the narrowest of book-lined corridors to a back room, in fact a rickety lean-to shed tacked on to the rear of the shop. The roof was corrugated iron, and the walls were constructed out of tongue and groove planks that didn't quite interlock. Cold air seeped in from all angles, and caused the single bare bulb to sway from the ceiling. Crowded together in the space were twenty or so splintery chairs, stools and packing cases that had been arranged in rows as seating, although they were pushed so tightly together that nobody would have any leg-room. Piled in the corners and on bookshelves were heaps of even less valuable stock, copies of *People's Friend* and *Titbits*, mauled football programmes, cookery books crusted with batter.

'I know it's not the London Palladium,' Ruth Harris said, 'but we've had some spectacularly successful literary evenings in here. A night when we presented some readings from John Fowles stands out particularly clearly.'

We returned to the main body of the shop to await arrivals. I was already sensing disaster, but I assumed it could only be a small one. The setting was too mean and parochial to threaten anything on the grand scale. And, as the scheduled time of the reading approached, I took some comfort from seeing that nobody had yet arrived. It occurred to me that perhaps nobody would turn up at all, in which case I could get the next train back to London. That would be a dull end to the adventure, but as Ruth Harris became ever more attentive, trying to foist herbal tea and fig rolls on to me and discussing where we might go after the reading for a little light supper and a tête-à-tête, it was starting to seem like a very desirable option.

Then suddenly the front door of the shop was thrown open and a young, intense-looking woman in a flapping red greatcoat came sweeping in, oblivious to the piles of books and magazines she was knocking over, a woman who was about to change my life in a rather dramatic way. If we'd been in a movie there'd have been a gush of appropriate music: a series of rising chords suggestive of transformation and infinite possibility. As it was I had absolutely no idea. I just thought she was strikingly beautiful.

I suspect it's always hardest to describe those people you like the most. You want others to feel the same way about them as you do, and that's undoubtedly asking too much. You find a woman very attractive and so you begin to describe her: the mass of red hair, the brown eyes, the long, lean body (all of these the new arrival possessed). But perhaps the reader isn't partial to red hair or brown eyes or long, lean bodies, so for him or her you're describing someone who by definition isn't that attractive at all.

So maybe you use more generalised words, like saying she had fine features, an elegant body, a warm presence, since surely nobody could dislike fineness, elegance and warmth; but the problem is it sounds as if you're describing an idea of a woman rather than the woman herself.

So maybe you get a bit poetic, say her eyes were like stars or limpid pools, or whatever. I'm not entirely sure how star-like eyes actually look, but they sound unobjectionable. Limpid I have no idea about at all, but I know it's an acceptable way for eyes to look. But some people don't like poetry, and star-like, limpid eyes sound like clichés anyway.

So maybe you can do it by giving the person's features moral qualities. You say she had proud breasts, a noble chin, wise eyes. Again, nobody can object to pride, nobility and wisdom, can they? And maybe the simple word beautiful comes into this category. Perhaps I should just say she was very beautiful and leave it at that, let the reader fill in the outline, colour in his or her own ideas of what constitutes beauty, of what a beautiful woman looks like. But that seems pretty feeble.

Possibly the telling detail is the way to go. The first thing I noticed, after the flapping red greatcoat and the red hair and so on, were the glasses. She wore a pair of formidably ugly hornrims, the kind that beg to be removed so that someone could say, 'Gosh, now that I see you without your glasses, why, you're quite, quite beautiful.' But the removal of the glasses would have been superfluous. She was obviously quite beautiful even with them, at least to me. The glasses emphasised her seriousness, made her appear substantial. I, who spent so much of my time feeling unserious and insubstantial, found this very appealing indeed. There was nothing bland about her, nothing half-hearted. She looked strong in every sense: a strong presence, a strong personality.

Ruth Harris and I stared at her, but she wasn't the kind of woman who was intimidated by being stared at. 'I haven't missed the start, have I?' she asked loudly of nobody in particular and then she saw me, obviously recognised me from the author photograph, and said, 'Oh my, this is really mingling with the stars, isn't it?'

I smiled at her as beguilingly as I knew how. She was someone I'd have been very pleased to beguile. I decided that even if nobody else arrived I would still be happy to go ahead with the reading. This woman's presence would make it all worthwhile. I looked at my watch. We were already well past the scheduled starting time, but Ruth Harris said we should wait a few more minutes. Then the rest of the audience arrived; two more people: Gregory Collins and Nicola.

'Sorry I'm late,' Nicola said briskly, as though her presence was the most natural thing in the world. 'I got lost. Then I met up with this nice man. I asked for directions. He was coming here too and he was lost as well but, anyway, we're here now.'

Gregory and I looked at each other and tried to think of something to say.

'I'm Gregory Collins,' I managed at last, as I shook his hand.

'I'm Bob,' said Gregory shamelessly. 'Bob Burns.'

What kind of name was that?

'Nice to meet you, Bob,' I said.

'Not *Robbie* Burns?' Ruth Harris said with a trilling little laugh.

'No. Robbie Burns was an eighteenth-century Scottish poet who died in seventeen ninety-six. So obviously not,' said Gregory, and nobody could tell whether they were supposed to laugh at that.

I could only guess at Gregory and Nicola's separate motives for coming to the event. Gregory, I thought, might have come hoping to share in some reflected, not to say refracted, glory. Perhaps he had wanted to see how popular he was and who his fans were. Tough luck, Gregory. But perhaps he was also there to keep an eye on me, to see that I didn't misrepresent him. That seemed a little untrusting.

Nicola's game was harder to understand. She knew that at the very least her presence was bound to make me feel uncomfortable, and no doubt that suited her; but she'd come a long way if that was all she wanted. It occurred to me she might be there to denounce me publicly and, if so, I wondered whether she'd do it during or after the reading. I didn't give her the chance to do it before. The moment she and Gregory arrived we all trooped into the back room and I began to read.

I'd decided it was best to start with some of the more salacious parts of the book. I had calculated that even if these passages caused offence, at least they'd be hard to ignore. I'd made this calculation when I assumed I'd be reading to a room full of strangers, but given the actual composition of my audience, who was I likely to offend, and who was likely to ignore me? Then I intended to read a long, philosophical passage about language and silence, derivative no doubt, but nevertheless signalling the high seriousness of the author.

Why did I care about signalling Gregory Collins' high seriousness? Why did I want him to look good? Why didn't I, for instance, read some of the book's worst, dreariest, most badly written sections? The simple answer is that I just wasn't that sort of person. Although I harboured some resentment and petty jealousy of Gregory, I had no reason to want the world to think he was an absolute prat. I wasn't a motiveless malignity. More importantly, it was me on the stage not him; I didn't want anyone to think the flesh and blood character they saw before them was an absolute prat.

The reading went as well as it could have, given the circumstances. It was certainly not a difficult audience, although they weren't very warm or responsive either. Ruth Harris stood at the back of the room, fidgety and fluttery, and yet with an enormous beam on her face. In her mind, if nowhere else, she was presiding over another resounding literary triumph, one that I feared might result in her trying to seduce the visiting author. Gregory Collins was enjoying himself almost as much. He was hanging on my every word, sometimes mouthing them along with me. It occurred to me that this was probably the first time he'd ever heard his novel read aloud, and if he'd never struck me as a man who liked the sound of his own voice, he certainly liked the sound of his own words.

Nicola was not enjoying herself nearly as much as these other two, but she looked as though she was deriving some sort of pleasure from the evening, perhaps a perverse one. I didn't for a moment think it was anything as straightforward as watching her boyfriend, or possibly ex-boyfriend, give a good performance. I still suspected it had more to do with some act of revenge she had in mind for later.

In the face of these obviously vested interests I found myself directing the reading increasingly towards the single bona fide member of the public, the woman in the hornrims. At first she wrapped her big coat around her, turned up the collar, closed her eyes, and listened with rapt attention to the smut I was reading out. Then, when I got on to the philosophical part, she unfurled herself, got out a writing pad and started taking notes. That seemed very strange, but then I clicked, oh right, she must be from the local paper, sent to review the event, not a bona fide member of the public after all, but at least Gregory was getting some media attention. I couldn't begrudge him that.

I read for a little over forty minutes. It seemed a long session, but when it was over I was satisfied with my performance. I could have wished for a better and bigger audience but I thought I'd done a good job on behalf of Gregory and myself. Then it was time for questions from the floor. I didn't see there could be many of these.

Ruth Harris pitched in immediately. 'What I'd like to know is how far the novel is autobiographical.'

'Well,' I said, smiling suavely, 'the truth is, I've never actually been embedded in a block of wax.'

She wasn't amused. 'No, of course not,' she snapped. 'I meant the sexual material: the bisexual orgies, the Turkish bath scene, the group sex with the older women.'

These had seemed to me the book's least convincing episodes. I knew very little about Gregory Collins' private life but I was as sure as I could be that he hadn't experienced any of these things first hand. Ruth Harris's mention of sex with older women now seemed to take on a special relevance that I thought it best to quash.

I said, 'You know, there's always a distance between an author's experience and his art; and I think it's good if the exact distance remains mysterious.'

I glanced towards Gregory and saw him nodding in agreement. He liked my answer. Ruth Harris didn't. She asked several more questions designed to plumb the extent of the author's apparent polymorphous perversity. I did my very best to disappoint her.

Then Gregory himself pitched in with a few questions; well, they weren't really questions at all, more self-congratulatory ruminations. 'I'd like to say what a bloody excellent book I think you've written,' he said. 'It's timely and contemporary without being disposable or faddish. And I reckon you've been right clever in setting up an opposition between the clean cold world of the spirit, a world both of knowing and unknowing, on the one hand, versus a world of sensory overload and sexual phantasmagoria on the other.'

He delivered several more 'questions' along these lines, and fortunately they didn't require much response from me. I was briefly tempted to disagree with him for the sheer hell of it, to insist that he'd completely misunderstood the book, but I knew that would be going too far. I simply thanked him for his kind words, as though my natural modesty prevented me from agreeing with his assessment of my genius. I noticed that the woman in the hornrims even made notes of what Gregory was saying, which seemed a bit excessive. I was hoping she'd ask me a question so I could turn my charm yet more fiercely in her direction; another way of irritating Nicola. And I kept expecting Nicola herself to say something, to ask some snotty, lacerating question designed to have me floundering, but she remained silent and self-possessed, her disapproval obvious to me, but to no one else. Perhaps she wasn't there for revenge after all.

I suppose she mightn't have said a word if Ruth Harris hadn't attempted to round things off by saying, 'You've been a lovely audience, and before we let Mr Collins go I'd like to ask you, as a bit of market research, why you're all here tonight.'

She turned to Gregory, who said, 'I'm here because I think Gregory Collins is the most important young writer working in England today.'

Then she asked, 'And what about you ladies?'

Nicola spoke first. I steeled myself. A knowing little grimace lodged itself on her face and she said, 'I'm here because I used to sleep with the author.'

Did that past tense mean that she was never going to sleep with me again? It seemed quite possible, and I was disappointed at how little that disappointed me. It was an answer that seemed to please Ruth Harris, however, suggesting that I, Gregory Collins, was a bit of a rake. She then turned to the other woman, and asked her the same question, and the woman replied, 'I'm here because I hope to be sleeping with the author in the very near future.'

I had no idea whether she meant it, but it was a good line and it might have brought the house down if there'd been a house. As it was, Ruth Harris scowled at her murderously and brought the event to a close. She was now regarding me sourly and, thank God, was no longer offering me dinner.

A part of me thought that Nicola and I should go off with Gregory, and I'd tell her that this was the real author. This might help her see the funny side, at least make her realise that Gregory was no monster and that I hadn't done anything so very terrible. I had no particular desire for reconciliation, but I was vain enough not to want her to continue to think badly of me. The drawback was that this would mean abandoning the woman who'd expressed a desire to sleep with me in the very near future. I could hardly make these explanations while she was present, and I very much wanted her to be present.

But as it turned out, neither Gregory nor Nicola stuck around a moment longer than necessary; and neither of them wanted to be with me. In fact, they left together, and that confused me even more. Had he picked her up on the way to the bookshop? Were they now going off for drinks and flirtation? It hardly seemed likely given what I knew about both of them, but even if they were just walking to the station together, I wondered what on earth they were saying to each other.

Nicola still had no idea who this stranger was. Would she tell him that I was a fraud? Would he then tell her he knew all about it, that he'd set it up, that he was the person I was pretending to be? Would she be as angry with him as she had been with me? And then what? I couldn't imagine and, besides, I had other things on my mind, chiefly the woman in the hornrims. Were *we* about to go off for drinks and flirtation? Well, yes and no. She introduced herself as Alicia Crowe, a name that struck me as utterly unfitting, and said she'd like to talk to me professionally. I assumed she wanted to interview me for the piece I thought she was writing for the local paper, so a few minutes later she and I were indeed sitting in a pub together, having managed to leave a vexed and disappointed Ruth Harris behind, and I was asking the one thing I wanted to know.

'Did you mean what you said?'

She replied, 'Wouldn't it be really shallow to want to sleep with someone just because you liked a book they'd written?'

'Well—'

'I mean it would be almost as shallow as wanting to sleep with them just because they had nice hair or good cheekbones, wouldn't it? Why does anybody ever sleep with anybody? Is it just habit? Or animal instinct? Or to satisfy their own vanity?'

At first I assumed this was a rhetorical question, but she continued to stare at me through the hornrimmed glasses, and it was clear she wanted an answer. I thought for a second of what a handsome couple she and I could make, even more appealing than Nicola and me, but perhaps this was what she meant by vanity.

'I suppose people sleep together because they want excitement, fun, warmth, closeness, comfort, love,' I said.

'Oh yes,' she said, 'they *want* those things, but is sleeping with someone likely to provide them?'

'If you're lucky.'

She nodded thoughtfully, as if I'd given an eccentrically challenging answer.

'You're full of surprises,' she said. 'I didn't think the author of *The Wax Man* would be very interested in warmth and closeness.'

'Trust the teller not the tale,' I said.

She knew I was being glib, and perhaps that surprised her too. *The Wax Man* may have had many failings as a novel, but glibness wasn't one of them.

'I suppose saying that I hoped to be sleeping with the author was a cheap shot. I was using sex to grab your attention. I wasn't really offering to have sex with you. I actually wanted to talk to you about a job.'

I had no idea what she meant. Did she think I was in a position to give her work? Was she offering to be my secretary, my amanuensis? Or did she think I could help her get out of local journalism and into Fleet Street?

'Why?' I said. 'Aren't you happy in your current job?'

'I'm not asking for a job,' she said. 'I'm offering you one. Possibly.'

I brightened up. The prospect of getting out of the rare book trade was very appealing, but then I had to remind myself that she didn't know I was in the rare book trade, that it was Gregory Collins she'd be offering a job to, not me.

'What kind of job?'

'A writer-in-residence.'

OK, maybe she wasn't a journalist after all, maybe she was a college lecturer.

'Yes? Where would I reside?'

She looked at her watch and said, 'Finish your drink. It's still early. There's someone I want you to meet.'

'I'd much rather stay here with you, drinking and talking.'

'There'll be time for that later.'

'Will there?'

'Yes. We could have dinner after you've seen my boss.'

I calculated that by the time we'd seen her boss, then been to a restaurant, it would be getting late and I might very possibly miss the last train home, just like Gregory Collins had missed his last train back to the north. In the same way, I might have to stay over and she would feel responsible and obliged to offer me a bed for the night, and that would open up all sorts of possibilities. Ah, this was the literary life as dreamed of by the unliterary.

'Let me get this straight,' I said. 'You're a journalist or a lecturer or something, right?'

'I'm a doctor,' she said. 'A psychiatrist.'

'Oh,' I said, baffled. 'So who is it you want me to meet?'

'His name's Dr Eric Kincaid. You may have heard of him. He's a genius.'

Naturally I'd never heard of Dr Eric Kincaid, but Alicia, or Dr Crowe as I was now entitled to think of her, spoke of him with such awe that I tried to convince myself I had. On the other hand, if she was to be believed, he had heard of me, of Gregory Collins. She said he'd read *The Wax Man* and was keen to meet me. That seemed unlikely but who was I to question it? I wasn't clear what would happen when I met him. Was he going to interview me for this nebulous writer-in-residence job, or was I being taken there for his entertainment, because I was an interesting case study? Either way, I should have run a mile, but, of course, I didn't. We got a taxi and there I was, travelling with this strange, serious, undoubtedly sexy woman in these unusual circumstances, and it didn't feel bad at all. It felt like another part of the adventure, and one I thought I was still in control of. Regardless of how it ended, it was infinitely more fun than my normal life.

It did occur to me, however, that once these two psychiatrists got together and started talking to me, they might well be smart enough to see right through my act. That threatened to be humiliating, but so what? What did it really matter? I didn't know these people and they didn't know me. I would have welcomed the chance to get to know Alicia Crowe better, but it seemed likely that I'd never be able to hold my head up and see her again after this evening anyway. I had to make the most of her company while I could, and that's why I went along with her plan.

'So where exactly would this writer-in-residence job be?' I asked.

'At the Kincaid Clinic.'

'That's some sort of hospital?'

'An asylum,' she said. 'A nut house. A loony bin. A funny farm. A booby hatch. Don't look so surprised.'

I thought I had some justification for being surprised. I had no idea that asylums employed writers-in-residence, and it sounded like a very tough job.

'Wait till you meet Dr Kincaid,' Alicia said. 'Then everything will become clearer.'

I doubted that, and I wasn't sure this was an area in which I actually craved clarity. I was still enjoying the confusion. The taxi arrived in due course outside an imposing, dignified Victorian building on the outskirts of Brighton. It looked substantial yet severe, rather small for a hospital, more like a converted vicarage or village schoolhouse, and only passingly like my idea of an asylum. The front elevation was complex, all gables and bays, dormer windows and intricately carved bargeboards. It was Gothic, but not horror-movie Gothic. In fact, it looked quite benign and it took a while for me to notice that the retaining wall was a good deal higher than most garden walls, and that the tall cast-iron gates had some heavy-duty electronic hardware keeping them locked. Alicia produced a high-tech little device that she waved in the direction of the gates and they opened automatically. I found this rather impressive and futuristic.

We walked into the grounds and headed for the main entrance of the clinic. I was aware that an asylum at night with locked gates and high walls was the stuff of dark fantasy and bad dreams, yet I felt unthreatened. And when I first stepped inside the vestibule, to the front desk, where a hatchet-faced night nurse looked at us blankly, I was hit by a severe whiteness, a combination of white-painted surfaces and pitiless fluorescent strip light. It was the sort of illumination that drives away shadows and phantoms. And when Alicia took me in to meet her boss, I saw that his office too was wilfully, clinically, bare and bright.

Dr Eric Kincaid was sitting behind a stark metal desk. He was a middle-aged black man. That surprised me, but only a little. It would have surprised me even more if the head of the clinic had been a woman. It would have surprised me almost as much if he'd spoken with a heavy regional accent. He didn't. His voice was thick and deep and grave. If there was a hint of Caribbean lightness to it, he kept it well under control. This was the voice of authority, of the Establishment.

There was a solidity about him, a scale. He carried a lot of weight but he carried it easily, and everything about him seemed padded and rounded. His wrists and neck were thick with fat and muscle. The collar and cuffs of his shirt gripped too tightly, and he pulled at them from time to time, to get some temporary relief from their constriction. His bald head was a polished, dimpled dome, his belly was a globe of flesh that pushed out his white doctor's coat, and his fingers were short, spatulate, competent looking. He exuded calm, dignity, competence, maybe even wisdom: or was I just buying into some familiar myth about the power and charisma of doctors? Did he look like a genius? Well, what did geniuses look like? Like mad scientists, like crazy professors, like Einstein? By these standards he looked all too prosaic.

'Mr Collins,' he said, 'I'm very pleased to meet you at last. Alicia's told me all about you.'

Alicia caught my eye and nodded winningly, encouraging me to go with the flow, to accept what Kincaid was saying, implying that everything would be cleared up later. Had she really told him about Gregory Collins? How would she have had anything to tell?

'Nice to meet you too,' I said.

'I won't lie to you,' Kincaid said, 'I haven't read your book from beginning to end, but I've skimmed it thoroughly and I'm confident we can work together.'

I couldn't imagine where he got such confidence from, and I was sure it was misplaced.

'It's apparent from your writing that you have a firm and subtle grasp on the convolutions of the troubled human mind. Have you spent much time with the mentally ill?'

'Well, I spent three years at Cambridge,' I said.

He considered this remark to make sure I was joking and then he laughed, a laugh that started deep in his belly, then rose swiftly to become a fluting, high-pitched thing. And then Alicia felt she could laugh too. The professional courtesies had been observed.

'I see we shall all be getting on famously,' Kincaid said.

I smiled as distantly, as formally, as inscrutably as I knew how. I suddenly wanted to get out of there as quickly as possible, but I wasn't sure whether matters would be best speeded up by blandly agreeing with him or by saying nothing at all.

'Do you have many commitments, Gregory?'

I said, 'No.' What else could I have said?

'So you could start on the first of the month?'

'I suppose I could,' I said.

'Then let's say you will. It's good to have you aboard, Gregory.'

Aboard? In what sense was I aboard? I'd been expecting, at best, to discuss the possibility of a job, but Kincaid talked as though he thought the deal was already done. He could only have got such an idea from Alicia, and I wondered why she'd wanted that. I was inclined to protest, but I knew it was all irrelevant anyway, and a pleading look from Alicia prevented me from saying anything at all. I didn't want to cause trouble, didn't want her to look bad in front of her boss. So, in as noncommittal a way as possible, certainly without actually saying the words, I let Kincaid think I was agreeing to start work as a writer-in-residence come the first of the month. That wasn't far away but I hoped it was long enough for Alicia to find some means to get out of her self-inflicted humiliation. If she wanted to blame Gregory Collins and say he'd let her down, that would be just fine.

'Very well then,' said Kincaid, 'I'll let Alicia give you the tour of the facilities, and explain the precise terms and conditions, show you your accommodation. You'd be living-in, naturally. You know, you writers are a peculiar breed. Alicia suggested you might be rather resistant to accepting the post, that you might take some persuading, but as ever she was just being cautious. Good. I shall see you next month. You'll be very happy here. Goodbye.'

We exchanged a soft handshake, then I was dismissed and Alicia escorted me out. She had the decency to appear shamefaced.

'You're quite an operator, aren't you?' I said.

'Would you say so?'

'A bit of a con-artist, in fact.'

'Is that so terrible of me?'

'Yes,' I said, 'but it's also quite funny.'

This was clearly, obviously, transparently the moment when I ought to have come clean, when I ought to have said that I was a con-artist too, said I was a Gregory Collins impersonator. Then we'd have laughed about it, seen how ludicrous and impossible the situation was, seen that we were kindred souls, and fallen into each other's arms for one night of improbable, never to be repeated sexual bliss. But I didn't come clean. I remained dirty and deceitful, and for the best possible reason: I wasn't given the chance to be clean.

We had come out of Kincaid's office and Alicia was beginning her tour, but we were scarcely halfway along the clinic's central corridor, a long, low-ceilinged conduit with ten or so identical grey doors leading from it, when one of the doors swung open violently and a demented-looking naked woman emerged and ran towards us. Actually, this was the most naked-looking woman I had ever seen: skinny and bare, ribs and tendons showing through the pale skin, a shaved head, an utterly hairless body, and although her demeanour was certainly wild and threatening, there was nothing but vacancy in the eyes. She was staring at Alicia and me, and despite, in one way, looking as though she had a potent desire to do us harm, in another way I wasn't sure she was really seeing us at all. I had the feeling that in her eyes we could have been any sort of grim hallucination.

'Let's stay very calm,' Alicia said.

I couldn't tell whether she was talking to me or to the crazed patient or to herself, but it was a futile statement. None of us was remotely calm. Alicia talked quietly to the naked woman, calling her by name, Charity, repeating it often and sweetly, trying to placate her, but it was quite obvious to me, layman though I was, that it was doing no good whatsoever. Charity was not being placated. She was getting increasingly upset. She was jumping up and down and her arms were performing weird, uncontrolled semaphore.

'Who's this?' Charity said, pointing at me. 'Some new quack?'

'This is Gregory,' Alicia said. 'He's going to be working here from now on. You'll be seeing more of him.'

It seemed the wrong time to contradict her, to say I wasn't going to be working there. Solidarity with Alicia was all-important. It also seemed like quite the wrong time to say the other thing that had instantly come into my mind, that whatever Charity needed, whatever her mental problems were, a writer-in-residence appeared unlikely to be able to solve them; but I kept quiet about that too. Charity looked at me with uninterested hostility then, swiftly and athletically, made a lunge at Alicia.

What happened next was brief, confused and wholly instinctive on my part. As Charity went for Alicia, I went for Charity; and, as luck would have it, I was quicker than she was. I grabbed her in a smothering sort of rugby tackle. We landed on the cold hard floor of the corridor, though I suppose it was colder and harder for the naked Charity than it was for me, and we wrestled there for what seemed like an indecently long time. My hands were filled with body parts that I had no right to be touching, but I still held on, and even though Charity was fierce and slippery, I was big enough and strong enough to hold her down until I heard the footsteps of two male hospital porters pounding along the corridor. They prised Charity out of my grasp, lifted her up off the ground, and carried her back into her room as though she were an awkward piece of folding furniture, a deckchair or an ironing board. The grey door closed behind them with a weighted gentleness. I expected to hear screams and the noises of a struggle, but no sound came.

'You needn't have worried,' said Alicia. 'She was only dancing.'

'Was she?'

'Yes. It's a religious thing with her. It can get a little Dionysian sometimes but it's never actually harmful.'

Obviously Alicia knew a great deal more about Charity's condition than I did, but I wasn't sure she was right. Charity's 'dance' had looked pretty dangerous to me, and not conspicuously religious.

'You should see her with her clothes on. She's just a hippie at heart.'

'Yes?'

'Well, apart from the hair.'

I was shaken up. Wrestling with a mad, naked woman, even a mad, naked hippie, was not one of the things I'd been expecting on my night in Brighton. The event had been shocking, but so brief and so quickly over that I could almost believe I'd imagined it. I noticed my hands were trembling.

'You need to sit down,' Alicia said. 'Let me show you where you'd live if you were our writer-in-residence.'

I was glad she used the word 'if' rather than 'when', but a part of me didn't really want to see the accommodation. I knew it would make me envious. Whatever it was like, however humble, it would still be infinitely better than my own horrible room in London. What was the point in torturing myself? Yet I couldn't bring myself to refuse. We started to walk.

'What exactly's wrong with the patients here?' I asked.

'They're in an asylum, that's mostly what's wrong with them,' Alicia replied smartly.

'But are they like schizophrenic, or manic depressive or . . . ?'

Actually, that was about as far as I could go with naming varieties of madness.

'What's in a name, Gregory?' Alicia said. 'Words like schizophrenia or manic depression or paranoia, they're just labels, just narrow, reductive terms for things we don't really understand. By naming them we like to pretend we have power over them – like Adam in the Garden of Eden. What we now call schizophrenia we would not so long ago have called dementia praecox. Before that you might have called it being possessed by demons. Perhaps at some time in the future we'll be calling it Kincaid Syndrome, or who knows, Gregory Collins' disease.'

I wondered how it would feel to have a condition named after you. Was that a thing anyone would want? And were they named after the doctor or the patient, the poor bugger who suffered from it or the clever bastard who 'discovered' it? Who were these people? Who was Tourette? Who was Down? What was the name of Pavlov's dog?

'Put it this way, Gregory,' Alicia continued, 'if you were a patient and you arrived here in distress, would you like it if I said, "Ah yes, I know what this is! What we have here is a case of Sydenham's chorea, or Marchiafava-Bignami disease, or Steele-Richardson-Olszewski syndrome." Or would you rather we just helped you get better?'

'Would it have to be an either/or situation?' I said.

'You have so much to learn, Gregory. But it'll be a pleasure to teach you.'

We had left the clinic and were walking through the grounds. The writer's accommodation was apparently outside the main building. I could now see there was quite a bit of land attached to the clinic. There were some neglected flower borders, and then a much larger, overgrown area that ran all the way to the boundary wall. There were structures too: some outbuildings, a cracked and scruffy tennis court, and a dried-up fountain with a chipped cement statue of a mermaid at its centre.

We went just a little further and there, in front of a giant rhododendron bush, was the neatest, quaintest, most appealing little cabin I'd ever seen; the same style as the main building, but its qualities had been distilled and concentrated. It was a structure anyone could have fallen in love with.

'This would be yours,' Alicia said. 'It's always been referred to as the writer's hut. All it needs is a writer.'

Alicia unlocked the door and we stepped inside. The interior smelled musty, like mildewed fruit. The old rattan and wicker

49

furniture was careworn, there was some peeling yellow wallpaper and the overhead electric light provided only a feeble glow, but the place undoubtedly had charm. There was a desk with a typewriter on it, a chair, a frayed carpet, a pot-bellied stove. There was just one room with a sofabed: no bedroom, no kitchen, no bathroom. Alicia explained that I'd have to shower in the main building, just like everybody else, but that sounded like no great hardship. I'd lived with a similar arrangement at college. It wasn't luxurious by any standards, except mine, but to me it was a palace. I sat down on the sofabed, looked around me, and of course I felt tempted.

At that time I had never read Gaston Bachelard's *The Poetics of Space*. If I had, I would have known he described living in a hut as 'the taproot of inhabiting', and perhaps it would have helped me understand why I was so drawn to the place. As it was, I simply started to feel I could all too easily be happy here. This was a nice place in a nice town, and the fact it was located in the grounds of a lunatic asylum seemed like only the slightest drawback. Having Alicia close by, and especially if she was going to be as good to me in the future as she was being at that moment, would be an enormous attraction too. She was sitting close to me on the sofabed and she was gently massaging the back of my neck. She said it would help get rid of my tension. I was prepared for it to take some time.

'So Charity isn't dangerous?' I said.

'No. None of the patients here is actually dangerous, although some of them can be a little frightening.'

'They aren't sex killers or axe murderers?'

'These people are people,' Alicia said, suddenly earnest now. 'That's the important thing to remember. In the old days it was said that asylums were like museums of madness. We like to think the Kincaid Clinic is more like an art gallery or an opera house.'

'And what do you do for them?'

'We do what we can. We use a variety of techniques, some traditional, some experimental; a series of treatments that add up to what we're proud to call Kincaidian Therapy. It would all become clear if you worked here.'

'And what would *I* do?'

'You would help the patients to use language as a bulkhead against madness.'

'Come again?'

'You'd get them to write, that's all.'

It sounded dangerously simple.

'I know what you're thinking,' Alicia said. 'You're worried about the responsibility. That's good. But don't worry. We're not asking you to be a doctor. We're not asking you to deliver a cure; not that we believe in cures, in the ordinary sense. Your job wouldn't be so hard. You'd have enough time to continue with your own writing. We don't want to own you body and soul. I'm sorry I took a few liberties. Sorry I told Dr Kincaid you'd already agreed to take the job. But I like to think of it as an act of creative imagination. If you believe strongly enough that something is true, then the very act of believing *makes* it true.'

I didn't wholly understand why she was so keen to believe that Gregory Collins was going to be their writer-in-residence. True, his book, with its combination of blankness and luridness, might be construed as having some vague relevance to madness, but that hardly seemed reason enough. A more suspicious man would have doubted Alicia's motives, and a more arrogant man might have thought she'd taken one look at my photograph on the back of *The Wax Man* and decided she had to have me. Being neither sufficiently suspicious nor sufficiently arrogant, I just felt confused.

However, as I sat on the sofabed with Alicia's fingers running complex patterns around the nape of my neck, I wasn't much inclined to question her motives. Perhaps I should have been questioning my own. I was starting to think that possibly, just possibly, I might be able to carry this deception a little bit further. I was foolish enough to start thinking I might be able to do a reasonable job of teaching creative writing to a group of lunatics. How hard could it be?

Was this unspeakable hubris? I didn't think so. Those who can't do, teach; and I certainly knew that I couldn't write – didn't even want to. However, the fact was, I'd studied literature for three years at university, I liked good writing, knew it when I saw it, and even had some notion of how bad writing might be improved. Back in those days, in the seventies, many a school would have welcomed an Oxbridge English graduate with open arms and allowed him to teach pretty much anything he wanted, and if I'd been enrolled for a Ph.D. I'd have been supervising Cambridge undergraduates; so surely I was up to teaching creative writing on a funny farm. And, anyway, the job presumably wasn't about turning patients into 'proper' writers. Good and bad probably didn't even come into it. I'd just encourage them, and the doctors, the Alicias and Kincaids of the world, would do the rest. So long as I tried to do a decent job, what did it matter if I wasn't the 'real' Gregory Collins? What was in a name?

And then the obvious flaw in this scheme occurred to me. Even if I was capable of doing the job, even if the clinic wanted me to do the job, I certainly couldn't do it without Gregory's permission, and how could I possibly convince him to give it? And as for what Nicola would say or do . . .

I tried to clear my head of this stuff and concentrate on more immediate matters. My arms had snaked around Alicia Crowe and she had not pushed them away, and then we were kissing with passion, though not quite with abandon. It felt a little adolescent, like the consolation snog at the end of the party, but that didn't mean it wasn't fun.

'You don't have to make a decision now,' Alicia said between kisses, but in some sense I already had.

Then she said it was getting late and she ought to be going, and curiously enough I had no sense of disappointment. I felt sophisticated and worldly and grown-up, and I didn't try to change her mind or make her stay. That would have been juvenile and unsophisticated. I was beyond all that.

'Where do you live?' I asked.

'I have a flat in town but I spend most of my nights here on call. I'm on call now. I have to go in case I'm needed.'

I was impressed by her dedication. And so she went, and I was left in the hut, and I spent the night alone on the sofabed. I slept unaccountably well and when I woke early next morning, I was pleased, though startled, to find Alicia standing over me, and she immediately led me to the front gate, as though sneaking me out of her parents' house, and a taxi was waiting there to take me to the station. Alicia kissed me again, a lot less passionately than she had the previous night, but I had no complaints; it was early and the taxi driver was watching, and as I got into the car I felt a terrible sense of separation and melancholy. The Kincaid Clinic was already starting to feel ominously like home.

'I'll call you,' I said to Alicia.

'I know you will,' she replied.

5

I was only an hour late for work, which I didn't think was too bad considering what I'd been up to the night before, but I knew my boss Julian would think differently, and I knew I didn't have any excuse he'd accept, the truth obviously being the least acceptable of all. On the train back to London I rehearsed stories involving domestic crises, intense but non-life-threatening medical emergencies, failures of the public transport system, even contemplated inventing a wild night of debauchery resulting in a terrible hangover, but I never got as far as delivering my excuses, since the moment I walked into the shop I saw Gregory Collins slumped forlornly at my desk, waiting for me. He was in a terrible state. He looked as though he'd been up all night and he'd obviously been crying.

I looked at Julian sitting at the adjacent desk, expecting him to provide an explanation, but he looked at me, expecting exactly the same. He wasn't happy with my late arrival, and he was even less happy about the unwanted presence of Gregory Collins, but above all else he was intensely embarrassed. A rare book showroom was no place for this kind of emotional display. He waved his hands vigorously at me, at Gregory and at the door. He didn't care what I did, so long as I took this problem out of the shop. Gregory looked up, and the sight of me was all too much for him. His chin turned to soft rubber and he let out a spongy wet moan.

'Let's, er, let's go and get a cup of coffee,' I said.

'Tea,' said Gregory. 'I don't drink coffee.'

We found ourselves in a cramped, crowded, greasy spoon, at a tiny, unsteady circular table that Gregory threatened to knock over with his every clumsy movement. We ordered tea for him, coffee for me and a couple of bacon sandwiches. Gregory was starting to look a little more composed. He blew his nose on a big blue handkerchief. It seemed too banal to ask what was the matter, why he was so upset, so I waited for him to do the talking.

'I thought you were quite good last night,' he said, somewhat to my surprise. I'd imagined we'd be talking about heavier matters. 'I thought your reading wasn't bad at all. Not the way I'd have read it, obviously, but not too bad.'

He had a way of turning a compliment into a complaint, and I was about to say that if he wasn't happy with my performance he should have done the reading himself, but I didn't. I decided to be kind.

'Thanks, Gregory,' I said.

'Disappointing turn out,' he said, 'but I blame that old bird who owned the shop. Couldn't organise a fart in a baked-bean factory.'

'She meant well,' I said, not at all sure why I was defending her.

'It'll be different next time,' Gregory asserted.

'You think there'll be a next time?'

'Who knows? Who knows?' he said enigmatically.

A waitress delivered our bacon sandwiches. Gregory bit ferociously into the white bread and swallowed hard. A bolus of scarcely chewed sandwich lodged in his throat and prevented him from speaking, but at last he got it down and said, 'It's no good, Mike. I can't lie to you. I shagged your girlfriend last night.'

He said it loudly enough that two workmen sitting at the next table looked up from their newspapers and sniggered.

'Nicola?' I said.

'Well of course Nicola.'

'Really?' I said, awed by the wild improbability of what he'd told me. 'Really?'

'We caught the train up to London together and we got talking.'

'Did you tell her who you were?'

'I didn't have to. She'd already worked it out. She's clever. And anyway, one thing led to another and, you know, we went back to her place and did it. It wasn't much cop, and I didn't enjoy it very much, and I reckon she only did it to piss you off, but we did it.'

What was I supposed to do or say? I felt as though only stock responses were available to me, as though spontaneity and real feelings were quite impossible. I knew I was entitled to feel angry, betrayed, hurt, that I was entitled to storm out, to threaten him, hit him, dump the mug of tea into his lap, and in different circumstances I might have done any of these, but as it was, none of them seemed remotely appropriate. Certainly none of them would have come from the heart.

So I said, 'Why did you feel you had to tell me this?'

'Because I believe in being straight with people. I may be a bastard but I'm an honest bastard.'

'Do you want me to thank you? To compliment you on your honesty?'

'I don't know what I want. I suppose I deserve a good pasting.'

'Sorry to disappoint you,' I said.

'It was only a one-off, Mike,' he wheedled. 'It was only crude, bestial sex.'

I'd never successfully associated Nicola with crude, bestial sex, much as I'd tried. I said, 'I need to get back to work.'

I started to get up from the table but Gregory gripped my hand and kept me there. The workmen next to us looked up again, with rising disgust this time, and I sat down quickly, shaking off Gregory's grip, causing the table to list dangerously.

'I'd like to make it up to you,' Gregory said. 'If there's anything I can do, any sort of favour.'

One thing he might have done was say he was sorry, but I'd already sensed that word was no part of his vocabulary. And what right did I have to think apologies were in order? My relationship with Nicola was apparently even deader than I'd thought. I wouldn't ever have claimed to know the innermost workings of Nicola's psyche but I remained thoroughly amazed that she'd slept with Gregory.

'I mean it,' Gregory repeated. 'I'll do anything.'

'Well, I suppose there's one thing,' I said.

Later that afternoon I called Nicola and said I wasn't angry or upset or anything, but I never wanted to see her again, that I was going away for a while and that she shouldn't try to get in touch. She said she understood completely. And then I called Alicia Crowe.

'Alicia,' I said. 'I have a small confession to make.'

'A confession?'

The moment I heard her voice I got a clear picture of her in my head. I saw her face, her hair, her eyes, the glasses, the big red greatcoat, although given that she was at work at the clinic she was hardly likely to be wearing the coat. And I tried to picture her office, smaller than Kincaid's, no doubt, and surely less stark, a few pictures on the wall, a few photographs of near and dear ones on her desk, an interesting house plant or two, maybe a vase of flowers. Was this stupid of me or is it inevitable? Isn't this what everybody always does? When we call home, don't we draw a picture of home in our heads? When we hear a familiar voice on the telephone, don't we always conjure up the owner's familiar face? And when the voice isn't familiar don't we always dream up a face that contains visual equivalents of the qualities we think we detect in the voice?

'I can't stop thinking about you,' I said, by way of confession.

'What does that mean?'

'I suppose it means the Kincaid Clinic has a writer-in-residence.'

'Fine,' she said.

She sounded chillier and less enthusiastic than I'd have liked, but I told myself that was only because she was at work. I had no idea what her situation was there, what precisely her work consisted of, but it was easy to imagine that she wasn't free to whisper sweet nothings into the phone. So I tried to adopt a similarly businesslike tone. I asked her one or two workaday, practical questions about the job, like how much it paid (more than I'd imagined) and whether I needed to do any preparation, whether there was anything I should read or study before I came. But Alicia said she was confident I could breeze through on my native talent, and I was inclined to trust her judgement. She said she'd see me on the first of the month.

Immediately after my conversation with Alicia I handed in my notice to Julian Somerville, although I didn't tell him why I was leaving or where I was going, and he didn't seem at all interested. He said he was sure it was for the best, that he'd already sensed that my heart wasn't in bookselling, and in the circumstances he wouldn't make me work the usual amount of notice. Concocting a story for my parents was harder. Obviously I couldn't tell them the truth, so I said I needed to get out of London to clear my head, and that I'd taken a temporary job as a hospital porter in Brighton. This was an era when a great many people seemed to take temporary jobs as hospital porters; I'm not sure why. My father had thought I was wasting my education badly enough by working in a bookshop, so God knows what he thought of hospital portering, but if my family had one virtue it was that we didn't tell each other what we really thought. It saved an amazing amount of trouble.

All that remained was to tell my landlord I was moving out of his horrible room, and I was set to become writer-in-residence at the Kincaid Clinic. I realised this was, by a very long way, the most reckless, stupid and exciting thing I'd ever undertaken in my life. I felt very proud of myself.

6

It would have been nice to think I looked the part on the day I arrived to take up my post at the Kincaid Clinic. Facially, physically, sartorially, I knew I looked just fine, but in a perfect world I'd have arrived in more style, perhaps in an open sportscar with my luggage packed in around me. As it was, I arrived in the rain by taxi, carrying most of my worldly goods in a holdall and a couple of tired carrierbags. And once the taxi had left – the driver seemed all too eager to get out of the area – I found myself alone outside the locked gates of the clinic, getting soaked, and quite unable to make anyone inside aware of my presence. There was no bell, no buzzer, no way at all that I could see to let anyone know I was there. I'd told Alicia when I was coming, and I admit I was disappointed that she hadn't offered to meet me at the station; even Ruth Harris had provided that service.

In the drenched grey light of a wet afternoon the Kincaid Clinic looked a lot more forbidding than it had when I'd seen it before. More neglected too. I saw there were graffiti on the outer wall. Someone had sprayed 'Nutters this way' in sloppy yellow letters. It didn't look recent and surely it should have been cleaned off by now. As I was thinking this, a passing car slowed down across the road from me, and the passenger, a loutish young lad, wound down his window and shouted, 'What's the matter, mate? Aren't you mad enough for 'em?' before the car drove off in a shriek of wet rubber. Well, yes, I suppose I did cut a fairly mockable figure, standing there in the rain, trying to get someone to let me into the asylum.

Did I know what I was letting myself in for? In the strictly literal sense, obviously not. I didn't know what went on in the Kincaid Clinic, or any other clinic for that matter, and I had only the vaguest idea of what was expected of me, of Gregory Collins. You might well ask how I thought I could possibly get away with it, and I suppose the simple answer is, I never really thought I could, at least not for very long. I assumed I'd be found out sooner rather than later, that someone would put two and two together, or Nicola would expose me, or I'd simply let something slip, and then I'd have to leave the clinic in some shame and confusion. But that would be all right; I'd cope with that. I wouldn't regret it. However things turned out, this was still so much better than the life I was leaving behind. And, besides, there was, or at least I hoped there would be, Alicia.

Questions about madness and sanity were much on everybody's mind in those days. Like everybody else, I'd read some Freud and Jung. Needless to say, only the more colourful stuff, the juicy bits about dreams and phallic symbols and the Oedipus complex, about the collective unconscious and archetypes and synchronicity; and in my ignorance I thought I understood it all. Then I'd read bits of Krafft-Ebing and Havelock Ellis for the sex and perversion; but that seemed acceptable because it looked as though *all* psychology was about sex and perversion. In the same spirit I'd also read parts of Wilhelm Reich, and consequently felt pretty clued up about the connections between sexual repression and political oppression. Call me an idiot.

I'd heard other names too, like Pavlov and Skinner and Adler and Rank, but names was pretty much all they were. I was a little more familiar with R. D. Laing and Timothy Leary, and like many other people I'd been at least partially seduced by the idea that madness might be a beautiful spiritual journey. To be mad, these guys seemed to be saying, was to be unable to fit in with the rest of the tribe, to be unable, or at least unwilling, to go along with the patterns of behaviour that your tribe thinks of as normal. Obviously that could make madness seem attractive, even noble, especially to people like me who had been too young to be real hippies or revolutionaries and had had to content ourselves by growing our hair and arguing with our fathers about the evils of pot. The madman could appear to be in touch with other ways of seeing or being, ways that the lumpen mass and the repressive old bourgeoisie didn't acknowledge or understand.

LSD seemed to fit in here somewhere. It too was touted as some kind of psychic joy ride, a chance to take a day trip to the more garish zones of inner space. Someone I knew at college had dropped a tab half an hour before going in to take his finals and had done surprisingly well. I'd once taken one small dose and while, as advertised, colours and music and lofty thoughts had indeed become a lot more interesting, before very long I was anxious, paranoid, and convinced there was something just horrible lurking inside my wardrobe. It hadn't been dramatic enough to qualify as a bad trip, but it had taught me that my mind was too rickety a thing to start trifling with. That way, I was fairly sure, madness lay.

I had no real experience with the mentally ill, but almost inevitably I'd come across one or two of them at university, people who'd freaked out as exams approached or when their girlfriends dumped them and, frankly, they hadn't seemed to be in touch with any higher truth or reality. They appeared to have exactly the same problems as the rest of us; they just dealt with them in more showy or desperate or self-destructive ways.

And, equally, I knew bugger all about the treatment of madness. I'd heard some horror stories and accepted some received opinions about lobotomies and leucotomies, about shock treatment and dousing people in cold water, about beating them into submission with drugs or inducing insulin comas. You didn't have to be some bleeding-heart liberal to be appalled by that stuff.

Since we were still in the long rain shadow of the sixties I knew there were some flashy and risky therapies being employed out there in the name of revolution and mental health: everything from primal screams to rebirthing to orgone boxes to flotation tanks to group sex. It was no surprise to hear that the Kincaid Clinic employed 'experimental' techniques, but I wondered just how wild these experiments were. I told myself, on no very good basis, that Alicia surely wouldn't be involved in anything dangerous or disreputable. And the mere fact that they were employing a writer-in-residence suggested to me they surely couldn't be doing anything too totally off the wall. If they'd been employing a performance-artist-in-residence I'd have been far more worried.

I'd taken Alicia at her word and not done any specific research about madness and its treatment, but I hadn't felt able to arrive without having read a book or two about creative writing. I'd trawled some bookshops and discovered quite a cache of books that claimed to teach you how to write, and in a few cases to teach you how to teach other people how to write. Some were quite practical and down

to earth, some were just pretentious. Some contained simple suggestions and exercises, others took a more spiritual approach, angled
towards personal growth. None of them was specifically designed for
use in a mental institution, and I suppose I knew even then that I
wouldn't ultimately be able to rely on how-to-do-it manuals, but I'd
bought a couple of them and they were in my holdall and I
considered them a very worthwhile prop.

However, as I stood in the pouring rain outside the Kincaid Clinic,
all this stuff about madness and methodology seemed rather academic. The problem of how to get in was far more pressing. I didn't
doubt that sooner or later someone would come in or go out through
the gates, at which point I'd surely be able to gain access, and if it
hadn't been raining I might have been prepared to wait patiently. As
it was, the rain was getting heavier and there was absolutely nowhere
to shelter, so I looked closely at the gates and, although they were
formidably high, they didn't look utterly impregnable. There were a
number of inviting iron curlicues that could be used as hand or foot
holds if you were of a mind to make an ascent. I reckoned that if I did
that and got to the other side I'd be able to go to the clinic's main
entrance, and find someone to open up the gates so I could bring in
my belongings. It was a bit of a pain, and it obviously shouldn't have
been necessary, but in the circumstances it didn't seem like such a bad
or crazy scheme.

I began my climb, actually a lot trickier than it had looked, since
the rain was making the iron framework slick and I kept losing my
grip. Nevertheless, I managed to get to the top in reasonable order,
but when I swung my leg over to begin the descent of the other side, I
lost my footing, slipped, flailed, and found myself splayed on top of
the gates, one leg and one arm on either side, half of me in the clinic,
half in the outer world, trying desperately to keep my balance. I held
on as best I could, and I may even have called out for help since help,
of a sort, came running.

Two men I'd seen before trotted out of the clinic. They were the
porters who'd taken away the naked Charity after our wrestling
match. They looked businesslike yet sporty, like athletes going out
for a pre-match warm up; but although I recognised them, they
apparently didn't recognise me.

When I saw them clambering up the gates towards me I was at first
rather pleased. Help, I thought, was at hand. But their demeanour,

their body language, and the way one of them shouted, 'Come down from there, you mad bastard!' made me realise they weren't primarily motivated by kindness. They appeared to think I was an inmate trying to escape. They were trying to drag me down as roughly as they knew how. One of them grabbed my ankle and pulled on it heavily. I was flipped over the top of the gate and fell head-first towards the ground, my ankle acting as a sort of pivot, and only by instinctively huddling my arms around my head did I stop my skull making contact with the wet black asphalt of the drive. Instead I landed on my elbows and I lay there winded, unwilling to move, fearing I must have broken any number of bones. A second later the porters were hauling me to my feet, and dragging me inside the clinic. This, I suppose, was what I'd wanted, but again it was not precisely the way I'd have liked to make my entrance.

My belongings, of course, remained outside in the rain. As the porters dragged me through the doors, through the empty waiting area, where my flailing presence caused not the slightest interest to the nurse on duty, one of the porters said to the other, 'They're going to have to electrify that gate before long. Only way to keep the buggers in.' I tried to speak up, tried to say I was attempting to get in, not out, but being shocked, wet and winded I dare say I wasn't sounding very articulate. Certainly the porters treated me as though I was raving incoherently, and I found myself being pulled along the clinic's central corridor, past the line of identical grey doors behind which the patients lived, until we came to a door the porters liked the look of. One of them held it open and the other pitched me inside, into warm, musty, absolute darkness. I heard the door slam and lock behind me.

I was in a padded cell, a new experience, and if I'd ever considered it before I would probably have thought padded cells belonged in the realm of movies and comic books rather than of contemporary psychiatric practice. I tried to stand up, and fell against a thickly quilted wall. In the darkness I could see nothing at all, but I suppose there wasn't much to see. For a very short while I was almost glad to be in the room. At least it was dry. At least I was inside the clinic. At least I wasn't being manhandled by two porters. But this feeling of comparative well-being didn't last long, and I soon started to feel a more natural anger and indignation. At this point there wasn't a great deal of fear, since surely it couldn't be too long before the porters, or someone, would work out that the clinic had one inmate too many. And then I imagined everyone would be full of regret, the porters would get a bollocking from Dr Kincaid, and from Alicia too, possibly. And then I'd be released, apologised to, treated like a lord, in an attempt to make it up to me, and I'd be graciously accepting and forgiving, trying to see the funny side of it. But this expectation soon passed as well.

I stood, then sat, then slouched, then prostrated myself in that padded room for a great many hours. I had lost all track of time before I finally heard a noise outside and the harsh overhead lights were switched on. The room took shape around me: smaller, uglier, more commonplace than I had imagined. There was the scraping of a key in the lock, then the door opened and Dr Kincaid strode into the room.

'Mr Collins,' he said gravely, 'welcome to the Kincaid Clinic.'

No apologies, no offers to make it up to me. I was furious.

'How are you?' Kincaid asked.

Words very nearly failed me but I came up with, 'How the fuck do you think I am?'

'I expect you're feeling a tad anxious, a mite distressed.'

'Very good, doctor,' I said. 'Let me out of here, will you?'

'Soon,' he said, 'but first let's analyse these feelings.'

'Oh, come off it.'

'Bear with me, Mr Collins,' he said, and I couldn't stop him. 'When you first entered this room I'm sure you were angry because you weren't being treated with the respect you thought was your due. But anger is the most volatile of emotions, hard to sustain for any length of time. After that you were fearful of the darkness, the isolation, the unfamiliarity. Some typical fears of the dark may have atavistically gushed forth. But as time passed, these imagined horrors failed to materialise. You were reassured. You became calm. The darkness enveloped you like a friendly cloak, supporting and protecting you. The darkness became a source of strength. You accepted its power. You started to feel tranquil. You felt liberated by the absence of light, of visual clutter. Soon you felt wonderfully at home.'

'Oh did I? Did I really?' I snarled.

'Yes. If you look into yourself I think you'll find that you did, and then you'll understand the wisdom that's at the heart of the therapy we deliver at the Kincaid Clinic.'

'Are you saying this was deliberate? This was a bit of therapy you laid on for me?'

He didn't quite have the gall to pretend this was the case.

'No, not exactly,' he admitted. 'The porters did indeed commit an error, an understandable error in my opinion, but, be that as it may, I want you to see how errors can be turned to psychological advantage.'

'Yours or mine, doctor?' I said.

I thought of launching myself at him and landing a punch on his big, self-satisfied face. It would have felt good. But I didn't. However bad your first day in the new job is you don't stick one on the boss unless you're really looking for trouble. Instead I said, 'Let me out. Now.'

He sighed deeply, as if his bold experiment had collapsed, its failure due to my lack of insight and sensitivity, as though I had failed him. And yet he knew there was nothing more to be done. He accepted that I'd had enough of the padded cell. He opened the door. 'You may go to your hut now,' he said. I was dismissed. My audience with the great man was over.

I decided I'd better go and see what had happened to my luggage. I went through the clinic, through the waiting area, past the front desk where the nurse ignored me again. I walked out of the main entrance, along the driveway to the gates, locked as before, and I looked into the road where I'd left my bags before climbing the fence. Nothing was there. Hardly surprising. Maybe the lads in the car had come by again and nicked them. Something told me I might never see my stuff again. That was a depressing prospect in one way since, apart from a few things I still kept in my old bedroom at my parents' house, it was pretty much all I had in the world. On the other hand, it wasn't as though I'd actually lost very much. All my worldly goods amounted to precious little.

This was an era when many people professed to being unmaterialistic, if not downright anti-materialistic, but I think my profession was more sincere than most. I was prepared to be philosophical about the loss. There were my clothes, for instance. Now, nobody would willingly lose all their clothes but mine were the sort that anybody could lose without too many regrets. People are inclined to think that in the seventies everyone went around in silver jumpsuits, platform boots and glitter jackets, looking as though they were auditioning for

Roxy Music, but I can't say I ever met anyone who dressed like that. Yes, I did own a few of what now seem like archetypal seventies duds: purple loon pants and skinny rib sweaters, and I had a Che Guevara T-shirt, but that was sort of a joke anyway; and, in any case, I didn't wear these things because they were super-fashionable or because I was trying to look 'seventies', I wore them because they were normal and ordinary. I wore them because they were what everybody else wore. And if they were gone they were easily replaceable.

I would have said the same for most of the other things in the bags. There were some books, a few Penguin classics, and the books on how to teach creative writing. I'd be sorry to see them go, but they too were replaceable.

I was sorrier to lose a bottle of White Horse whisky given to me by my father as a sort of 'good luck in your new job' present; and there was a little plastic bag containing enough grass to make three or four joints. These might have been welcome in the long evenings ahead, but what the hell, it was only whisky, it was only dope. These weren't things to get upset about.

My camera had gone too. I wasn't absolutely sure why I'd brought it. I did believe in documenting my life, taking pictures of friends and family, and yet I didn't think I was really going to go round the clinic taking pictures of the inmates. But that made me think of the only truly irreplaceable things I'd brought with me: my collection of photographs, a box full of snapshots showing parties and holidays, weddings, birthdays, me on my first bike, that sort of stuff. It was from this collection that Gregory had extracted the photograph of me for use on his book jacket. There were also half a dozen nude pictures of Nicola, which it had taken me a very long time indeed to get her to agree to pose for. If all these were gone I'd be really sorry; but again, what good would being sorry do?

I went back inside the clinic and at last the nurse looked up at me. 'Problem?' she said.

'My bags were left outside the gate. Now they're gone.'

'Why on earth did you leave your bags outside the gate?' she said. 'Obviously they were going to get stolen, weren't they?'

This was undoubtedly true, yet I couldn't tell whether I was being taunted or humoured, whether the nurse thought I was some pretentious big shot from the big smoke who deserved to be rooked by the humble locals, or whether she thought I myself was some sort of sad bumpkin whose naivety was more to be pitied than blamed. I didn't feel inclined to justify myself by describing my misadventures with the porters and the padded cell, which presumably she already knew about.

Calmly I said, 'If by any chance my stuff turns up, you'll let me know, won't you?'

'Obviously,' she said.

I could tell she wasn't going to be a very warm or forthcoming source of information but she was all I had, so I asked her a couple of things that were on my mind.

'Is Dr Crowe on duty tonight?'

The nurse looked at me as though I was a moron.

'If I had that sort of information, and it's a very big if, then obviously I couldn't give it out to just anyone. Could I?'

'Couldn't you?'

She shook her head regally.

I said, 'And how can I get something to eat around here?'

I thought it was a question that left no room for mockery or condescension, but she looked at me again with the kind of sympathy usually reserved for the offensively feeble-minded, and replied, 'This isn't a hotel, you know.'

'I know,' I replied. Then as sarcastically as I could, I added, 'It's a clinic for the insane. I can see that's a reason for there to be no room service, but I don't see that it's a reason for there to be no food.'

'There's no need to raise your voice.'

I hadn't raised my voice at all. I'd been sarcastic in an intense, quiet sort of way, but I wasn't going to start arguing about the volume of my voice.

'Obviously the kitchens are closed at this time of night,' the nurse said. 'And the food store is well and truly locked. I'd like to help you, but obviously I can't.'

'OK then, how do I get to the nearest pub or burger bar?'

She sneered at me. 'To do that,' she said, 'you'd have to go outside the clinic. And to do that you'd have to climb over the fence. And I don't think you want to do that, do you?'

'Obviously not,' I said.

I set off for the writer's hut, for what was going to be my home for the foreseeable future. For a second I had a vague, unrealistic fantasy that my luggage might, by some act of magic, if not porterage, have found its way there, but you know how it is with fantasies. However, there had been one or two additions to the place since I'd last been there. There was a basket of fruit, a vase of red carnations, and a bottle of champagne. They were arranged, perhaps like a still life, on a little kidney-shaped coffee table in front of the sofabed, and there was an envelope with my name on it. I opened it up to find a postcard from Alicia – a Jackson Pollock painting, black knotted strands against a beigy-grey background. The title was *Number 32*, and on the back were the words, 'Welcome, Alicia'. I found this somewhat cheering, perhaps more cheering than it merited, but I was clutching at every cheerful straw I could find.

I did what I'm sure any real writer would have done in the circumstances: I opened up the bottle of champagne and drank it all. On an empty stomach, I was drunk by the second glass. I ate a couple of pieces of fruit so as not to feel like a complete degenerate, but they didn't do much to absorb the alcohol. By the time, not very much later, I'd finished the bottle, I was ready to fall into a heavy stupor. Which I did.

7

I spent the night asleep on the sofabed, fully dressed. I woke up feeling happier than I had any right to. The sleep had done me some good and I resolved that today would be better than yesterday; after all, how could it be worse? I would start again. I'd challenge Kincaid if I had to. I would take no crap from nurses or porters. I would get what I wanted. I would make sure I was given food and respect and perhaps my own key to the front gate and, most important of all, I would make contact with Alicia.

There was a knock on the door of the hut and it was gently opened by a slight, smiling young man who came in pushing a trolley. He was wearing a peculiar sort of uniform, a high-necked, short-sleeved tunic and loud patterned trousers. In other contexts he might have resembled a chef or a dentist, but in the circumstances, given his scrubbed, hygienic appearance, I assumed he was a male nurse.

'Hello,' he said. 'I'm Raymond. How are you this morning?'

'Not so bad,' I said.

'Sorry about the turbulence. I'm afraid the Kincaid Clinic hasn't been treating you very well, has it?'

At last. This was all I'd been looking for; a bit of sympathy, a hint of apology.

'You can say that again,' I said.

'Can I offer you tea, coffee, a boiled sweet?'

'Coffee, thanks.'

He messed around with a pot and a milk jug and handed me a tiny plastic cup of dense, tepid coffee.

'Care for a bag of salted peanuts with that?'

'Why not?' I said.

He handed them over, and then he presented me with one of those little airline bags containing the odds and sods you might need during a long flight: a comb, toothpaste, a towelette. It also contained a sleep mask and a pair of earphones, which seemed superfluous to requirements, but it was reassuring to be given anything at all.

'It's not much,' he said, 'but it's the least we can do. On behalf of all of us I'd like to welcome you on board and if there's anything I can do to make your flight more enjoyable, don't hesitate to ask.'

I thought he was overdoing the in-flight metaphor a bit, but when I put the coffee to my lips it certainly tasted as bad as anything served by an airline.

Then I heard a woman's voice say, 'I wouldn't drink too much of that coffee if I were you,' and I turned to see Alicia, dressed in her doctorly whites, hornrims in place, clipboard tucked under her arm. She was standing behind Raymond and had placed a firm, restraining hand on his shoulder. He drooped and looked suitably cowed.

'It probably isn't poisoned,' Alicia said, 'but you can't be too careful. Raymond's improving all the time, but he does have relapses.'

The thick, bitter taste lingered in my mouth as I handed the cup of coffee back to Raymond. 'Sorry, Dr Crowe,' he said, and a great weight of subjugation fell on him, and he looked as though he might throw himself at Alicia's feet.

'Take your trolley with you on the way out, Raymond,' she said.

He went without another word, and I was left alone with Alicia.

'God, I'm glad to see you,' I said.

'Are you?'

'Yes,' I said, disappointed. She might have said she was glad to see me too. The last time we'd been in this place there'd been kissing and massage, a great feeling of intimacy and possibility, but Alicia's manner told me there'd be none of that today. She was in professional mode, and although she said she was pleased I'd arrived safely, it didn't seem she was pleased in quite the way I wanted her to be. I also had a sense that she was looking me over and finding my crumpled, rain and mud-splattered appearance a bit of a let down. I tried telling her about my arrival, the gate, the porters, the padded cell, the loss of my luggage, but she wasn't at all concerned.

'Teething problems,' she said dismissively.

'I also lost the books I was planning to use as part of my teaching.'

She was even less interested. 'You'll be fine,' she said. 'Actually, you'll be addressing the patients in about five minutes' time in the lecture theatre, telling them who you are, why you're here, what you're going to be doing with them and so on.'

'I don't know if I'm quite ready for that.'

'Don't worry. They're not monsters. And to make things easier, Dr Kincaid has written an opening address for you. All you have to do is read it out.'

She gave me a dozen densely typed sheets of paper.

'Wouldn't it be better if I told them in my own words?'

'No,' she said.

She probably had a point, since I had no idea what I was going to be doing with them.

'You might decide to take a couple of minutes to familiarise yourself with the lecture before you read it out,' she said. 'Or you might decide otherwise.'

I must have looked discouraged, and Alicia responded by rubbing her hand against my unshaven left cheek. It was a welcome gesture, although I suspected my stubble might only confirm the impression that I wasn't quite spruce enough for the forthcoming event. Then she saw the empty champagne bottle lying on the floor and said, perhaps disapprovingly, although I liked to think a little wistfully too, 'I'd rather hoped we might share that.'

I'd hoped that too, but if she'd really wanted to share it with me then she should have said so on her card, and she might also have been there to welcome me. I tried not to show my irritation. After all, I wanted her to like me.

'There'll be time for other bottles of champagne,' I said.

Her frown suggested she wasn't so sure about that.

'Any chance of a coffee that Raymond hasn't adulterated?'

'You want too much,' she said.

I didn't think that was true, but Alicia wasn't prepared to give me anything else.

'Come on, you can cast your eye over Dr Kincaid's introduction as we walk to the lecture theatre.'

I wondered if I should protest that I needed a wash and a shave, but that all sounded too fussy. Grubby and sleep-creased as I was, I followed Alicia.

Walking and reading simultaneously is never easy, and I couldn't make much sense of the words on the pages. But I wasn't too worried since I suspected this first appearance of mine wouldn't be so much about what I said as about the way I said it, and about the way I presented myself. I would need to appear confident, competent, writerly, like someone who knew what he was doing. This would undoubtedly have been easier to pull off in clothes that weren't streaked with rain and mud, and that I hadn't slept in, but I told myself these things might be used to my advantage, part of an image as an unworldly, rumpled artist. I was making the best of a bad job.

Minutes later I was in a room with the inmates of the Kincaid Clinic. The term 'lecture theatre' seemed a little grandiose given the smallness and meanness of the room. It was no more than thirty feet square. One wall had windows that looked out on sturdy, ragged bushes, the three other walls were bare and had been emulsioned white, though not recently. I was standing behind an unsteady lectern, facing what I couldn't stop myself thinking of as an audience.

There were ten of them, ten patients; I had expected a greater number than that. There were six men and four women, a cross-section, though not a strictly representative one, in a variety of sizes, shapes and ages. They were all white-skinned except for two: a very young, agitated black woman, not much more than a girl really, who was bouncing up and down in her seat; and an older Indian woman sitting placidly beside her, a model of quiet and calm by comparison. These, I would later find out, were Carla and Sita.

I looked the group over, trying to make unthreatening eye contact, trying to make some sort of connection, although I didn't want to stare, didn't want to appear to be too curious about them. They, however, had no such inhibitions. They gawped at me with great interest and some anticipation, as though I was a cabaret act, there to entertain them, although nobody had told them quite what my act was. So they watched me expectantly, as if they thought I might be about to begin juggling or tap-dancing or singing unaccompanied blues ballads. I suspected I was going to disappoint them.

Alicia made introductions. 'This is Gregory Collins, a much-praised author, who'll be working with us from now on. Gregory, I'd like you to meet Anders, Byron, Charles Manning, Raymond, Carla, Cook, Maureen, Sita, Charity and Max. Wake up, Max.'

Max was a plump, sagging, baggy-faced man who had nodded off in the back row. He seemed to be not so much asleep as in a drunken stupor, though naturally I assumed the patients didn't have access to drink. He woke up at the mention of his name and turned unfocused eyes in my direction. He acknowledged me blearily, then looked away, and I was sure it would be no time at all before he was unconscious again.

There's nothing like someone reeling off a list of names to make my mind go completely blank, but I did my best to remember them all. I could attach names to two faces. Raymond, the deliverer of the suspect coffee, was sitting in the front row, just a few feet away from me, gazing up in needlessly respectful awe, and next to him, somewhat less awed, was Charity, the woman I'd briefly wrestled with on my first visit. She was clothed this time, in a hippie peasant smock, although given that her head, and now that I looked more closely, even her eyebrows, were shaved, there was still something very bare and exposed about her.

There were a couple of other shaved heads among the patients. Whether it was a style thing or some sort of medical precaution I didn't know, but even the sanest person can look pretty strange when their scalp and the contours of the skull are revealed. One such scalp belonged to the man introduced as Anders. He was perhaps a little old to be the classic skinhead but even without the exposed skull he would still have been terrifying. He looked menacing, like very bad news. He was vast and pink and his face was puckered up like a fleshy gargoyle. His demeanour seemed to say he'd kill me soon as look at me, and I did my very best not to stare at him, but I must have looked at him just a moment too long, since he curled his bottom lip outwards and downwards at me, and I could see that tattooed on the soft inner flesh were the words, 'F*ck you'. The asterisk was strangely touching.

The other shaved head belonged to a far less threatening character, a floppy, long-limbed man whose bare skull was topped with a little silver helmet moulded out of tin foil. He looked absurd, like a space cadet in a budgetless science fiction movie. This was Cook.

Next to him sat a distinguished-looking older man with silky silver hair, and a crested blazer: Charles Manning. I never learned why people usually called him by both his names, but it suited his fatherly, patrician air. He gave the impression of a country solicitor on holiday, although the effect was sabotaged by the fact that he was bare-chested under the blazer. A ragged crop of somewhat less silky body hair pushed out between his lapels.

He said to me in clear, respectful, friendly tones, 'Do you mind if I smoke?'

I didn't, although I wondered if I was supposed to, whether it was against some rule of the clinic, but before I could say anything, Anders shouted out, 'He doesn't care if you spontaneously fuckin' combust.'

I laughed nervously, as indeed did Charles Manning, and then, since I obviously wasn't going to forbid it, he produced a cigarette, a cocktail Sobranie in pastel yellow paper. He took a lighter from his blazer pocket, handled it skilfully, as a practitioner of close-up magic might, lit the cigarette and inhaled blissfully.

The cigarette smoke drifted across to Maureen, a wide-eyed, bovine, chunkily built, middle-aged woman who was wearing full football kit, claret and blue: West Ham, I was fairly sure. She sat erect in her chair, arms folded across her chest as though posing for a team photograph, but as the smoke wafted into her nostrils she made a great show of coughing and choking.

The final member of the group was a moody, brooding, dandyish young blade, with flowing locks, wearing a sort of frock coat and knee-length boots. He looked like anybody's, or at least any second-rate movie director's, idea of the tortured poetic genius. He was called Byron; not his real name, I assumed.

As a group they were alarming though not, apart from Anders, especially frightening. I certainly didn't think they were the worst audience a lecturer or writer could have. It would have been easy to think of them as a freak show, but I was already smart enough to realise that once I got to know them they wouldn't appear freakish at all, and I hoped therefore they'd also cease to be alarming, cease to be a collection of quirks and symptoms. Chiefly what I got from them on that first day was an overwhelming sense of need. I thought they were looking at me beseechingly, wanting something from me, and I wasn't unwilling to give it, though precisely what it was and whether I had it was a different matter.

Other eyes were on me too. Alicia had taken up a place at the very back of the room, and the two porters who'd heavied me over the night before had positioned themselves on either side of the door, like bouncers. If they felt embarrassed or repentant at seeing me again they were skilled at not showing it. Kincaid was not in attendance, but I suppose that was understandable since he knew exactly what I was going to say. I felt exposed and nervous, and I was glad I had the lectern to hide behind, but I think I managed to give a reasonable impression of a man in control. I smiled winningly but formally towards the faces in front of me, I tried to exude charm and I began to read the text Kincaid had prepared for me.

'Good morning all. My name is Gregory Collins and I'm a writer. You don't know me yet, but over the course of your treatment you will come to know me very well indeed. You will come to trust me, to confide in me, to see that we're on the same side, a vital member of the team that's here to help you get better. This will make you happy.'

I thought this was laying it on a bit thick. Given human nature it seemed absolutely inevitable that some of the people I was facing would not come to trust or confide in me at all. As for making them happy, well, that simply seemed to be aiming far too high. But I read on, 'It is my intention to help you plunge headlong into the wonderful world of language. I shall be asking you to do some writing for me, to express yourself in words on paper. You know, language is a great bulkhead against madness. At first you will find this process difficult and perhaps you will be reluctant, resistant, resentful, but eventually you will start to write, and you will enjoy it and this will become an essential part of the healing process. It will not be easy. It will not be pain-free. As you express yourself and set down your innermost thoughts and feelings you will experience swirling emotions ...'

I glanced up at the patients and thought how unwise it might be to stir up any swirling emotions in them.

'But these emotions will pass,' I read, my voice faltering a little now. 'Writing will become your friend. You will write your way back to sanity. And this will make you happy.'

I was clearly not making anyone very happy at that moment. Ten glum, confused patients looked hopelessly at me. I was no longer in touch with the meaning of the words I was reading but I could hear my voice continuing. 'We will tarry awhile in the groves of prose and poetry,' I said. 'Perhaps some of you will find your inner Homer, your inner Joyce ...'

I felt terrible. I felt I was insulting the patients' intelligence. There were still another eight or nine pages of this bumf to get through. I leaned over the lectern, the way I'd seen some of the more engaging

Cambridge lecturers do, and I made eye contact with the bare-chested old chap in the blazer.

'Hi,' I said. 'Do I remember right, your name's Charles Manning?'

'That's very good,' he said.

'Have you got a light, Charles?'

I knew that he had, and he stood up and passed me his cigarette lighter. He also offered me his pack of cigarettes but I didn't accept. I flipped the head of the lighter, flicked a sharp, concentrated blue flame into life and lowered a corner of Kincaid's pages into it. A band of fire trickled up them, growing, flapping, getting far too hot to handle. When I couldn't hold them any more I tossed them away, dropping them over the edge of the lectern. I looked at my audience and I smiled, as I hoped, wickedly. I thought I had performed a winning bit of theatre, demonstrated that I was going to depart from the prepared script, talk to them as a real person, but in the event I wasn't able to talk to them at all.

The two porters leapt into action, steamed up to the front of the room and started jack-booting the burning paper. They were eager but obviously a little slow, since by the time they got there enough smoke had risen to the ceiling to set off the smoke detectors and the fire alarm. All hell broke loose. The noise from the alarm was of an astonishing, ear-damaging loudness. It scared the wits out of me and it had a profound effect on the patients. They began to express themselves, not through the cool medium of writing, but rather by screaming, laughing, clapping, hooting, and in Charity's case by stripping naked and dancing. One or two appeared to be genuinely upset and frightened by the noise of the alarm and by the violent behaviour of the porters, but for the rest there was something exuberant and joyous in their reactions. They were showing off, playing to the gallery.

At the back of the room was one small locus of calm: Alicia Crowe. She was watching the mayhem as though from a million miles away. She hadn't reacted, hadn't tried to take control of the situation. Now she stood there running a weary hand through her hair, as if she'd seen it all before, and wasn't bored by it exactly, just very tired. Presumably she knew what was coming next.

Dr Kincaid bounced into the room, an ageing but sprightly and dignified super-hero, there at the first hint of trouble. It worked. The moment he entered, even before it seemed possible that all the

75

patients could have seen him, they became utterly calm, or perhaps becalmed. The porters stopped stamping and, coincidentally or not, the fire alarm fell silent.

'Teething problems, Mr Collins?' Kincaid asked.

I wasn't sure whether to pretend the lecture notes had accidentally caught fire (not an easy pretence to sustain since there were witnesses) or whether to admit I'd done it deliberately as an extreme act of literary criticism, as a roundabout way of protesting about the shoddy treatment I'd received on my arrival. In the event I said nothing at all. I nodded and shrugged simultaneously, the two gestures cancelling each other out, and Kincaid didn't bother to ask me what I meant. He looked at the fragments of blackened paper that were now scattered around a wide area of the floor like satanic confetti, and said, 'You will want to discuss this at length later.'

I wasn't at all sure that I would. Kincaid breathed deeply and pulled back his shoulders, creating the effect of having been suddenly inflated, and in a calm, powerful voice he addressed the patients.

'I must confess that I'm really rather angry,' he said in a voice of utter equanimity. 'You will go away now. You will write a piece of creative writing for me, and for Mr Collins. The title of this piece of creative writing will be,' – he had to think, but only for a second; here was a man used to making instant, irrevocable decisions – 'the title will be *The Moon and Sixpence*. When you've finished your work, Mr Collins will evaluate it. Then we can proceed.'

The patients slunk away, broody and resentful, and why wouldn't they be? Their first writing assignment had been turned into a form of punishment, and it was all my fault. And I suppose I was expecting to receive some form of punishment too. I had, after all, set fire to the boss's lecture notes; not nearly as bad as punching the boss, but still, even in such immediate retrospect, not a very mature opening gambit. Already I couldn't for the life of me imagine why I'd done it. Was it to show how wild and subversive I was? That sounded pathetic. I knew I deserved a good bollocking, and in a way would probably have welcomed it.

There was another worry: Alicia. I felt I'd let her down. If she'd been cool to me before, she had every reason to be glacial now. I'd been her choice, and I'd been an instant failure. She had left the lecture room along with the patients and the porters, so that I was left alone with Kincaid. Now would have been as good a time as any for him to deliver a dressing-down, but he only looked at the scrub of burned paper on the floor and said, 'Fortunately it wasn't the only copy.'

8

I went back to my hut. I pulled the ramshackle old chair up to the equally ramshackle old desk, and sat there in silence, facing the redundant typewriter. I had nothing to do at the desk; nothing to write, nothing to read, and I could see this was going to be a problem. I suppose I'm what most people think of as an avid, not to say obsessive, reader. I always have been. I met a few people at university who read more than I did, but not many. If I'm not actively engaged with half a dozen books at any one time I feel guilty and bereft. A train journey without a book to read is absolute torture, and I don't understand how people can just sit there and stare into space or listen to their Walkman, not that there was any such thing as a Walkman in the days when I was at the Kincaid Clinic.

Now, you could argue that this need to read is actually a need not to be left alone with my own thoughts, and although on most occasions I'd disagree with that, my thoughts were certainly hard to live with at that moment, so I set out on a desperate mission to find some reading material.

I went to the main entrance of the clinic, to the waiting area, where I vaguely remembered seeing some newspapers. They were still there and I seized on them hopefully, only to be immediately disappointed. They had been cut to ribbons. Virtually no news item, no article, no piece of text remained intact. I wondered why the clinic even bothered to have the papers there.

The nurse who had been so snotty to me the previous night was still on the front desk. She watched me struggle with the loose strips and flaps of newspaper, and although she was far too miserable to give herself the pleasure of laughing at me, I sensed she was enjoying watching me suffer.

'I'm just looking for something to read,' I said, and instantly regretted it. Why did I feel the need to explain myself to this woman?

'Maybe you should try the library,' she said.

'There's a library?'

'Obviously. Upstairs. The east wing.'

I hadn't thought of the clinic as having wings, and I wasn't sure that in reality it did, but she explained to me, slowly, at length, in terms even an idiot might understand, how to get to the library. I followed them and in due course I came to a door with the word 'Library' on it. I opened it and found myself in a room not much larger than an ordinary domestic living room. It was pleasant enough, had a bay window that gave a view of the grounds, and it had shelves from floor to ceiling that could have accommodated a good few thousand books. But they didn't. These shelves held nothing at all. They were all completely, bleakly empty: just bare stretches of dusty wood, not a book in the place. I felt angry and insulted and bitterly amused. How pathetic, how terrible, and yet how very typical of what I'd so far discovered about the Kincaid Clinic.

Restless and frustrated, I went for a walk around the outside of the main building. As I saw it from different angles it seemed a less and less impressive structure. The front was presentable enough, recently painted and in so-so repair, but that was only a façade, a mask presented to the outside world. Round the sides and back, everything was dilapidated. Chunks of rendering had fallen from the walls and had not been replaced. Drainpipes and guttering clung to the edges of the building, hanging on by their fingertips. Broken windows had been patched up with cardboard and duct tape, and parts of the woodwork resembled flaky pastry. I couldn't help noticing how many locked doors and barred windows there were, but perhaps it was naive of me to expect anything else; this was an asylum, after all.

I turned my back on the clinic and concentrated on exploring the grounds. I investigated the tennis court. There was no net, and clumps of grass and dandelion had split the hard red surface. Elsewhere the fountain with the cement mermaid was full of dead leaves and glass fragments. There were signs that someone was trying to cultivate a couple of borders in the flower garden, but the attempt looked half-hearted. Neglect was rampant, and there was a surprising amount of rubbish and litter about the place, a lot of beer cans and broken bottles, but they didn't look as though they came from the clinic, rather that they'd been chucked over the wall from outside, perhaps by drunken locals, the kind who sprayed graffiti and yelled at me in the rain.

In the far reaches of the grounds there were various out-buildings: a couple of garden sheds, a greenhouse without a single pane of glass intact, and in the furthest corner there was an old metal shelter, like a Nissen hut. It could have been something left over from the war; maybe the Kincaid Clinic had been used to billet army officers. This impression was reinforced by the words 'Communication Room' stencilled on to the outside wall.

The front door of this shelter was wide open, and even though I was reluctant to stick my nose in where it wasn't necessarily wanted I didn't see that any harm could come from looking inside. The interior was gloomy, windowless, bare, but there was a long table set in the middle, with ten chunky, battered manual typewriters arranged on it, and a chair set at each typewriter. Numerous unopened packs of typing paper were also stacked on the table, and although there was no sign that any typing or communicating had gone on here lately, the arrangement suggested all that was about to change. How long would ten mental patients have to sit working at ten typewriters before they produced something worth reading? Not too long I hoped. If I couldn't get my hands on a book or even a newspaper, I would have to rely on what the inmates produced.

I walked back towards my hut and looked up at the clinic. My knowledge of the building's layout was still understandably sketchy but I could work out a few parts of the building, the lecture room, the patients' rooms, the offices. I wondered where Alicia's office was, and as if on cue I looked up and saw her face at a first-floor corner window. She looked away before I could wave at her, so I decided to go up and see her.

Her office door was open and I looked in as I approached. It was not at all as I'd pictured it. It was a poky, inhospitable room, full of tight angles and unusable alcoves, and it was every bit as bare as Kincaid's office. These doctors were surprisingly self-denying. I tapped on the open door and startled her.

'I've come to apologise,' I said.

'Yes?'

'I hope I didn't embarrass you in the lecture room.'

'Embarrassment is of very little medical value,' she said coldly. 'But apologies can be therapeutic.'

'I was nervous.'

'No doubt.'

'I was still pissed off about the way I was treated last night.'

'Yes?'

'I'm sorry,' I said.

'Perhaps I'm not the one to apologise to.'

'Either way, I'd like to try to make it up to you somehow. We could have a drink.'

'You drank all the champagne.'

'Not all the champagne in the world.'

'In any case, you can see I'm working. I'm in the middle of a twenty-four-hour shift.'

'Then maybe I could come back when it ends.'

'When I've finished a twenty-four-hour shift I don't want to do anything except go to bed.'

'That's an option too,' I said.

It was a cheap and easy shot and Alicia wasn't amused.

'This isn't a holiday camp,' she said. 'There's some serious and important business going on here.'

She was trying to dampen my puppyish enthusiasm, and it worked. I did my best to be serious. 'Well, in that case,' I replied, 'if we're being businesslike there's certainly some business I'd like to discuss.'

The prospect of my being businesslike didn't please her much either. 'Yes?' she said.

'Yes. I really need some clothes. Thanks to your goons I don't have any. In fact, I don't have much of anything any more.'

She was no more interested now than she had been earlier.

'The need to apportion blame is understandable, but ultimately futile,' she said.

'What if I went into town, paid for the clothes myself and then you reimburse me?'

This was something of a bluff. I only had a few pounds to my name. The train fare to Brighton had pretty much cleaned me out. I didn't have an overdraft or a credit card. People didn't in those days, at least not people like me.

'So now you want to go into town?' Alicia said.

'Well, yes. But only to buy some clothes.'

'You've been here less than a day, done less than ten minutes' work, if you could call it work, and now you want to go into town. That's not exactly dedicated of you, is it?'

When she put it like that it did make me sound a bit of a skiver, not that, in the circumstances, remaining at the clinic all day would make me any more productive.

'All right then, is there something I ought to be doing here?' I asked. 'Any work you want to give me?'

'What could you possibly do?'

I didn't rise to that one. After all, I hadn't exactly forced myself on the Kincaid Clinic. I was there because she wanted me to be.

'And whether I go into town now or later I'll still need a key,' I said.

'To what?'

'To the front gate. One of those little electronic devices like you've got. Or do you want me to climb in and out every time?'

This made her very unhappy indeed. She simmered with anger.

'Then I could come and go as I please and not bother you,' I added, trying to make the request sound sweet and reasonable, which I thought it was.

'Come and go as you please,' she repeated.

'Only if it didn't interfere with my work here,' I said. 'Naturally.'

'You want to be able to come and go as you please, do you?' she said, and just saying the words made her furious. 'Look, you've already alienated most of the staff, you've created a fire, you've caused distress to the patients, you've demanded money and now you're demanding a key. Don't you think you should slow down a little?'

'I feel as though I've ground to a complete halt,' I said.

'That may be no bad thing. Why don't you go away and read a good book?'

Much as I liked Alicia, and much as I wanted her to like me, and much as I didn't want to prolong the conflict, I couldn't stop myself saying, 'And where would I find one? In the crappy old library?'

'And now you're criticising our library.'

'*What* library? It has no books.'

Alicia had had enough of me. 'Then go away and write one,' she snarled. 'That's what you do, isn't it?'

Was she mocking me? Was she finding me ridiculous as well as annoying? Why wasn't my famous charm working?

'All right. I'll go away. We'll talk later.'

'Good. Fine,' she said, but she didn't sound good or fine, and I certainly didn't *feel* good or fine.

I went away. I was feeling as bad as I thought I could possibly feel. Talking to Alicia had only made things worse. There was something very different about her now. She was no longer the warm, serious, sexy woman who might make someone pack in his old life and start a new one based on impersonation and deceit. Or perhaps she never had been. Perhaps I'd misjudged her all along, and built some trite little fantasy woman in my head. I felt stupid. I felt like going back to her office, confessing everything and taking my leave. Surely they'd open the gates for me in those circumstances.

But I didn't go back to Alicia's office. I wasn't brave enough or desperate enough, not yet. I went in search of food. I consulted the nurse again and asked where I should go to get fed, and she said the canteen, obviously, and she was only mildly unpleasant as she told me how to get there.

The door to the canteen was, perhaps inevitably, locked, but the door to the adjoining kitchen was open. There were no enticing smells issuing from within, but I could hear the rattle of pots and pans, so I looked inside. No doubt institutional kitchens are always bare, scrubbed places but this one seemed unusually stark: white tiles, gleaming stainless-steel surfaces, a bare stone floor. A man was toiling at one of the worktops. He was a patient, the floppy man with the shaved head and the tin-foil helmet, the one called Cook. What was in a name? I was a little surprised to find one of the patients doing the cooking. Was that part of the therapy? It seemed a little too homely and co-operative for what I understood of Kincaid's regime, although I was aware I understood very little.

'What's cooking?' I asked.

Only a little resentfully, Cook replied, 'The usual,' and when I asked him what that meant he said, rather more resentfully, 'Soup and stew.'

'Great,' I said. It sounded boring, but what else could I expect from hospital food? Boring was better than nothing. 'What kind of soup?'

'The usual,' he said again.

'And what kind of stew?'

He brooded and fidgeted and I was expecting him to say 'the usual', but this time he shouted out, 'I don't know. All right? I don't bloody know. Happy now? Satisfied, are you?' and he flounced out of the kitchen.

Even given the temperamental nature of cooks, sane or not, this seemed an over-reaction. Again I didn't think I'd asked an unreasonable question and, more to the point, I didn't see how he could be making a soup or a stew without knowing what kind. I looked into the pot, and I was certainly no wiser. The contents were intensely anonymous. There was a waste bin next to the worktop and I peered into that too. There were a dozen or so freshly opened tin cans nestling in a heap, and I picked one out. It was bare metal. The label had been removed, wasn't to be found in the bin, and all the other cans were similarly naked and free of information.

I went over to a store cupboard and opened the doors to discover hundreds of gleaming tin cans, every one of them stripped of its label. There was no way of telling what any of them contained. I'm tempted to say I stared at the cans in disbelief, but in fact I found it all too depressingly believable. Why in God's name didn't the tins have any labels on them? Had they been bought cheap as part of a defective job lot, flood damaged perhaps, the labels having been soaked off in a deluge at the warehouse? Or was it something more calculated than that, a deliberate ploy to make the patients' lives simultaneously unpredictable yet constant? Then I heard Cook returning.

'Sorry about that,' he said. 'I'm a bit emotionally labile at the moment.'

'I'm not surprised. This must be very difficult for you.'

'Wait till you taste it.'

Half an hour later I did. The canteen was a cramped, low-ceilinged, L-shaped room. There was a hatchway through from the kitchen to the dining room, and one of the porters was serving out the nondescript soup. Each patient went to have his or her bowl filled, then sat down at the refectory table in the long arm of the L. In due course I got my own helping, and although I'd have much preferred to take my food away with me and hide in my hut, I thought it best to stay where I was, to show solidarity, or at least that I wasn't a wimp.

I was willing to sit down with the patients but all the chairs at their table were full, so I had to sit alone in the other branch of the L, on a little raised dais, at what amounted to a high table. I felt even more awkward lording it over them like that. I hoped Alicia or even Kincaid would turn up so I wouldn't be completely alone, but they never arrived. Given the quality of the food it was hardly surprising.

The soup wasn't exactly bad, and it wasn't exactly flavourless. I could taste salt and pepper, sweet and sour, meat and fish, fruit and vegetables, but they all seemed to be equal and opposite, reaching a kind of bland equilibrium, cancelling each other out. The stew, when it was served for the main course, tasted very much the same.

I sat there and didn't know where to look or what to do. Once again I wished I had something to read, not that the patients weren't putting on a bit of a show. Carla, the flashily disturbed black girl, was spilling much of her food down her front, and some of it occasionally went over her shoulder. Anders, the violent skinhead, was attacking his food as though he was in some sort of eating contest, and Max, the man who looked drunk, had fallen face down in his plate.

I tried not to stare, but the patients were certainly staring at me. I could feel multiple pairs of eyes on me and could think of nothing except bolting my food and getting out of there as quickly as I could. Doing some of the worst of the staring was the poetical young man, Byron. I thought of him as young, but in fact I suppose he was pretty much my own age. He had a face that managed to be simultaneously cherubic yet satanic. He had plump, wet lips, a fierce jaw and a headful of black curls. He looked both ravisher and ravished. I suppose he looked a little mad, bad and dangerous to know, though he didn't have a club foot.

When I eventually felt able to leave the canteen, Byron was leaning louchely beside the door and as I passed him he said, not precisely to me though I was sure for my benefit, 'Wasn't it Aristotle who asked, "Why is it that all men who are outstanding in philosophy, poetry or the arts are melancholy?"'

'Yes,' I said. 'I think it was Aristotle. And didn't he also say something about black bile?'

Byron nodded with satisfaction, as though we'd shared a deep intimacy.

These first occasional encounters with the patients were hardly very revealing, yet I assumed they were an important part of the process of becoming acquainted. I knew I couldn't expect too much too soon. And if the patients sometimes deliberately made me feel uncomfortable, that was surely an indication that they were functioning as alert, active people. It was better than having an asylum full of heavily drugged zombies. Kincaid's experimental therapy was obviously preferable to that, though there certainly weren't many clues to what it actually was. The patients were often to be seen going into Kincaid's office, and Alicia's too, and sometimes I'd see the blinds being drawn on the office windows, but what happened after that remained a mystery.

However, the patients were certainly throwing themselves into this writing business. I would see them wandering round the grounds, notebooks and pens in hand, and then they'd go to the Communication Room, and I'd hear distant typing, but they evidently weren't ready to show me what they were producing. Nobody handed over their work, and much as I looked forward to having something, anything, to read, I didn't press them.

I didn't speak to Kincaid at all for a good long while after the débâcle in the lecture room, and when I occasionally saw Alicia I tried to keep our conversations brief. They had a tendency to end in tears. One day she arrived at my hut with a bundle of clothes for me, and I was inclined to take this as a friendly gesture, until I looked at the clothes. They were my own, the ones that had been in my missing holdall, although I noticed that the Che Guevara T-shirt wasn't among them.

'Where did you get these?' I demanded ungratefully.

'What's the matter? Aren't they good enough for you?'

'They're mine.'

'Of course they're yours. I've just given them to you.'

'But they were always mine. Where did you get them?'

'We have our sources.'

'Where's the rest of my stuff? My books? My photographs? Where are they?'

'If you really want to know, I found these clothes.'

'Found them?'

'Yes. They were in the bushes. Some local boys apparently threw them over the wall.'

'You were going to give me clothes that someone had thrown over the wall?'

'So you don't want them?'

'Yes, I want them. And I want a lot more besides.'

'Gregory, you're behaving a little hysterically.'

'No, I'm not.'

'Trust me, Gregory, as a doctor, I can say most certainly that you are.'

'I thought you didn't like labels.'

That got to her.

'I'm going to leave now,' she said. 'We can talk about this later. Or we can not.'

And that was pretty much my life for the first week. I ate and slept. I wandered the grounds. I had ambiguous little encounters. I did 'nothing'. The days weren't so hard, but the evenings could be tough to get through. Drink and drugs would no doubt have helped, but I now had no access to them and, in truth, I had never had any great appetite either. Sometimes I was dismayed at just what a clean-living lad I was. I certainly wished I still had my books, or even a radio. They would undoubtedly have helped pass the time, as would a television, but there was no set in the clinic, no television room, and you'll realise what an utterly different and alien age we were living in, if I tell you that didn't seem remotely odd to me.

Mostly I'd sit in my hut feeling inert, bored, lonely, feeling like I might have made a terrible, stupid mistake; and I'd listen to the night noises, to the creaking trees, the flurries of unidentifiable wildlife, the distant traffic. And I'd look up at the clinic, at all the lights that blazed constantly, and sometimes I'd watch Kincaid's office window, and see the man himself, pondering, pacing restlessly, then suddenly getting a bolt of inspiration and darting to his desk and furiously jotting down notes.

And one night, as I was thinking about Kincaid, and wondering what he'd done to give Alicia such a high opinion of him, he was suddenly there at the door of the hut. I hadn't heard him approach, and I was aware how slack and vacant I must have appeared, what an idle, good-for-nothing employee, yet he looked at me kindly, and that threw me.

'You won't mind if I step inside your hut,' Kincaid said.

Why would I have minded? And how could I have stopped him if I had?

'How's it going?' he asked. I thought about telling him the truth, but before I could open my mouth he said, 'Don't tell me. I'm sure I can guess. You're feeling inert, bored, lonely. You think you might have made a terrible, stupid mistake.'

I was impressed by his savvy.

'Also,' he said, 'you're not sure you're up to the job. You're not even sure you know what the job is. You feel lost. You feel becalmed, a little frightened. You don't know what you're doing here. You're not even sure who you are at this very moment.'

He was right, of course, and in other circumstances I might have been disturbed or infuriated by that. Generally, I didn't want people to know so much about me, didn't want to be so transparent and commonplace, but at that moment, feeling that somebody understood was quite reassuring. Then Kincaid said, 'Don't worry. This is all perfectly fine and normal,' and I was aware of a certain relief at knowing I was experiencing things that were within acceptable bounds.

'Really?' I said.

'Yes. I find you sitting here all alone, doing nothing as it were, wishing you were doing something, not knowing what that something should be, and I understand your pain. But I tell you this: doing nothing is absolutely the best thing for you at this time. It isn't easy to be a blank sheet of paper. Freeing yourself from fear, desire, thought, ambition, action; these are worthwhile and noble goals. If you succeed in the attempt you'll be the most useful member I've ever had on my team.'

I stared at him, blankly I'm sure, and I had nothing at all to say.

'Excellent,' he said. 'You've also seen the importance of freeing yourself from speech, from response. Well done.'

And then he went again. The visiting genius disappeared into the night and I was left unsure whether he'd been dispensing wisdom or absolute bullshit.

9

The layman (and there weren't many men more lay than I was when I first arrived at the Kincaid Clinic) could be forgiven for not knowing the difference between coprophilia, coprolalia and coprophemia; so let me clarify.

Coprophilia is literally the love of faeces; and I've got nothing much to say about it other than it's disgusting and twisted and I don't want anything to do with it. But the other two are far more interesting and relevant.

Coprolalia is literally 'faecal speech', a condition, a bit like Tourette's Syndrome, where the patient can't help but let rip with a string of obscenities, regardless of where he or she is: in the supermarket, in the church confessional, at the Brahms recital. Some textbooks will tell you the patient actually plays with words the way a coprophiliac plays with faeces; which again isn't very attractive and not at all sexy. Coprophemia, however, in the right circumstances, can be both.

Coprophemia involves the use of obscene language as part of sexual arousal. At its most extreme it's a destructive perversion, where the dirty language becomes more important than the sex itself, but in a milder form it's a harmless enough little kink, a sexual extra. But as I say, I wasn't remotely aware of these distinctions and definitions when I first arrived at the Kincaid Clinic, and if anyone had told me they were distinctions that were going to have any importance for me, I probably wouldn't have believed it.

Anyway, it was Friday night. My first week of employment, if not strictly of work (since I'd done sod all), was over, not that its being over made any appreciable difference to the atmosphere or the activities of the clinic. I'd had my talk with Kincaid and I'd gone to bed, not because I was tired, but because I could think of nothing better to do.

I lay there, willing myself to go to sleep, but unable to as my mind milled the same old stuff – what was I doing there? should I confess? and so on – and naturally enough I got to thinking about Alicia. I wasn't exactly having sexual fantasies; that would have been too easy, too unambiguous. I still feared I'd made a fool of myself over this woman. For whatever reason, she had wanted me to take the job at the clinic and she'd used her charm, for want of a better word, to get me there. Charm, don't you hate it? But once I'd arrived, the charm had stopped. That may or may not have made her a bad person but it certainly made me a complete idiot. I felt hurt and a bit used, and yet I still wanted us to get on. And what else did I want? Sex? Love? A relationship? The meeting of two soul mates? Well, why not? I wouldn't have turned down any of those things, although I knew it was presumptuous to demand them, perhaps even to hope for them. I'd have settled for company, warmth, someone to talk to. So, for one reason and another, Alicia was much on my mind, and then suddenly she was there.

Perhaps I'd gone briefly to sleep after all, because I didn't hear my door opening or closing, but I was suddenly awake and in pitch darkness, and I heard Alicia's voice say, 'Is there room for another one in there?' Then she giggled. She was no longer using the steely, combative, medical tone I'd become familiar with in the last few days. It was the old Alicia, the one I thought I knew.

I fumbled to turn on the bedside lamp and Alicia said, 'I prefer it with the light off,' which in other circumstances might have been a small disappointment, but I was so glad to have her there at all, so surprised and pleased, that I couldn't possibly object. She sat down on the bed and I reached out a hand to touch her. My fingers made contact with her rib cage. It was bare. Her body was warm and smooth and I could feel a regular rhythm rising and falling under the skin. My hand moved down her flank, to her hip and her leg, and I discovered she was completely naked.

'So, are you going to fuck me?' she asked.

This was by some way the most surprising thing she'd ever said to me.

'Well, yes. Sure,' I replied.

I heard her exhale. It was a gentle, approving sound.

'And will you be kissing my breasts and making my nipples stand on end, and then are you going to eat my pussy, and will you press your mouth and nose against it, and will you lick my clitoris until I'm all drenched and dripping, and then are you going to take your big fat cock, and shove it in me, first in my mouth and then in my cunt, filling me up? And are you going to ram it home, ram it in and out, until I shriek and scream and claw your back and then are you going to pump your hot, creamy cum right into me?'

It was the first time I'd been asked a question in quite those terms, but that was because I'd never had sex with a coprophemic before, not that I even knew the word at the time.

'Well, when you put it like that . . .' I said.

I suppose I had always known that pornography was largely a way of telling, rather than a way of being or doing. It's not what you do, it's the way you describe it (although I suppose some activities, coprophilia for instance, would be obscene however poetically you described them). But in general the sexual act is much the same whether it's being described poetically or euphemistically or lubriciously. There was nothing remotely poetic or euphemistic about Alicia's vocabulary. I could tell she was excited by these dirty words, by her own use of them, and I was excited too, though I think I was as excited by her excitement as I was by the words themselves.

I pulled her into bed and began to kiss and stroke her, and she said, 'Tell me what you're going to do to me,' and that threw me a little. For one thing, I wasn't quite sure that sex was necessarily a thing that one person 'did' to another. I preferred to think it was a thing two people did together, call me a pathetic old liberal if you will.

For another, I felt suddenly rather innocent. No doubt Cambridge had a lot to answer for. In those days the university contained seven men for every woman, and that created problems for everybody. Yes, I'd managed to find girls who'd wanted, or at least hadn't refused, to go to bed with me, but none of it had ever been very richly erotic. Mostly what we'd done was put our heads down and hoped for the best and, even after university, much the same had applied with Nicola. It had all been normal and healthy, and very straightforward, and really rather tame. Nobody had ever asked me to talk about what I did or I was going to do; and certain girls had only been prepared to have sex with me on condition that we didn't talk about it at all, before, during or after. I wanted to give Alicia what she wanted but I felt extremely reticent. I wasn't entirely lost for words, and I wouldn't say that I was shy exactly, but I felt I somehow lacked the vocabulary.

'I'm going to give you a good screwing,' I said ineptly.

'And how exactly are you going to do that?'

'I'll put my penis in your vagina and then—'

'No,' she said, a little irritated but not angry, at least not yet. 'You're not going to screw me with your penis. You're going to fuck me. You're going to put your smelly old cock in my steaming hot cunt.'

'Right,' I said, and I endeavoured to do my dirty linguistic best. I used the terms, the words and phrases and pornographic constructions that Alicia favoured and demanded, but I feared I mightn't be doing it convincingly. At times I felt like I was improvising bad dialogue in some hideous theatre workshop. Fortunately Alicia had enough dialogue, or I suppose in the event monologue, of her own.

'Yes, that's right. Oh, that's fucking good. Shove it in. Let me feel your dirty, hairy balls slapping against me. Oh, you filthy, dirty fucker.'

And so on, for quite a long time at very high volume. She let out the occasional grunt and shriek, but mostly she remained highly verbal, highly articulate.

Partly it was encouragement. She was egging me on to new acts, new heights or depths, and in a way it was similar to giving me a set of instructions, telling me what to do, telling me what she needed done. I had no objection to that. It's nice when women tell you what they want. And partly it was a commentary, describing, in the lewdest terms possible, what we were doing, and although, therefore, the commentary and the acts were inseparable, the pleasure she was taking in the words seemed somehow independent of the acts themselves. I was glad she was having such a profound reaction to what we were doing, and yet I couldn't help feeling there was something rather unspontaneous about her responses. I felt she wasn't so much improvising as quoting, and that her words came from some pornographic book of love that she had memorised from beginning to end.

I didn't disapprove of this exactly. Sex, I knew even then, was largely a matter of repetition. We know what we like, that's why we keep doing it, and although we all think we enjoy novelty, a completely novel sexual experience seems unlikely after a point. If you haven't done certain things by a certain time in your life the chances are you probably don't want to. Certainly coprophemic sex with Alicia was quite a novelty for me, but I kept getting the uneasy feeling that Alicia's reactions, her performance, if you prefer, didn't have all that much to do with me.

I wasn't a complete robot. I was doing more than just obeying orders. I was my own man, and yet when a woman is telling you to suck her breasts, lick her clitoris, stick your tongue up her anus, it would take a very contrary man to insist on doing something different. And indeed, Alicia's commands (or demands) were so encyclopaedic, there was very little I could have done that she hadn't already covered.

And after I'd 'filled her up with my giant load of hot, filthy, steaming cum', to use Alicia's phrase, we lay together in a welcome silence. When your partner has exhausted the possibilities of every sexual obscenity, it's hard to know what to say next. And the truth was I didn't need to say anything. I was perfectly happy lying there in the dark, with my arm around Alicia, not saying or doing anything. And I wondered if this was what Kincaid meant about freeing yourself from speech and response. I even remembered what he'd said about my time in the padded cell, how darkness and silence could be reassuring and supportive. Of course my experience of the padded cell would have been rather different if Alicia had been in there with me, and lying with Alicia now wasn't 'doing nothing' in the sense that I'd been doing nothing in the writer's hut for most of the past week. Nevertheless, it occurred to me that Kincaid might possibly know what he was talking about. Then I realised how vile it was to be lying in bed with Alicia while thinking about Kincaid. I tried to clear him out of my mind.

Then Alicia spoke. She said, 'This never happened, right? I was never here. We never had sex. Nobody must know: not Kincaid, not the staff, not the patients, not anybody. If anyone suspects, I'll deny it with my dying breath. If you ever tell anyone, I'll call you a liar, say you're making it up, weaving some sick little fantasy about me. Right?'

'Right,' I said.

'Good,' she said, and she softened, she curled into me and was again her warm, affectionate, maybe even loving, self. I wondered how long this could possibly go on.

IO

I don't know if Alicia and I literally slept together that night. I know that I fell asleep while she was in my bed, and I know that when I woke up she'd gone, so perhaps she never slept there at all. I also know that while I slept I dreamed of being in bed with her, and by the morning everything about the whole episode had taken on an utterly dreamlike quality.

I was brought abruptly into consciousness by a knocking at the door of the hut. I sat up, saw that Alicia wasn't beside me and in a way I was glad. Even though I didn't feel quite as intensely about secrecy as she apparently did, I didn't much want to be found in bed with her by any of the people likely to be knocking at my hut.

I got up and opened the door a couple of inches to see Raymond peering in at me. 'Would you like any duty free, sir? Only joking.'

I stared at him fuzzily. This time he had no trolley, he wasn't offering coffee, and as I opened the door an inch wider I saw he wasn't alone. Accompanying him were the other nine inmates of the Kincaid Clinic. They stood in a silent, straggling line outside the hut. Some looked at me hopefully, some beseechingly, some with unconcealed excitement, some couldn't look at me at all. Anders, of course, looked at me as though he wanted to beat me up. But all of them seemed to be attaching an unnatural importance to being in my presence. That was when I looked at my watch. It was six in the morning.

'What on earth do you want from me at six o'clock on a Saturday morning?'

For a time nobody spoke, but after a painfully prolonged silence Raymond was nudged forward and took on the role of spokesman. 'We've brought you a little something to read,' he said.

A cardboard box was handed along the line, as though it were a fireman's bucket, and was deposited on the threshold of the hut. The top was open and I could see it was full of paper, or rather typescript. The patients were delivering the week's work, ten versions of *The Moon and Sixpence*. I was impressed, indeed amazed and daunted by their immense productivity. There had to be a thousand pages or more in there, at least a hundred pages per patient. That wasn't just prolific, that was manic; well, what a surprise. Reading it all was going to be a big job, even if it was one I'd been looking forward to.

'Thanks,' I said. 'Thanks very much. I'll get back to you as soon as I can.'

'We could taxi around out here until you've read it,' Raymond said.

'No. You wouldn't have liked it if I'd stood over you while you wrote it, would you?'

There was general consent that I'd said something reasonable and the patients started to withdraw, going off in a solemn, mournful procession. I should probably have gone back to bed, resumed my dreams of Alicia, but this boxful of writing had me hooked. I got dressed and got ready for work. I felt good. Here at last was something to do. This was what I was here for.

I took the pages out of the box and separated them, arranged them into individual works, as it were. This was harder than it might sound. The pages weren't numbered, and not all of them had very clear beginnings or ends; but using common sense, intuition, and noting the different typewriter faces, I did my best.

Then I began to read. I didn't just sit down at the first page and systematically read my way right through to the end, since I was far too eager to get an overview of the types and varieties of writing. I picked a page here, an opening paragraph there, a couple of random sentences elsewhere. I got a taste, a flavour, a sense of things to come. But then I did indeed go back to the beginning, not that there was a beginning *per se*, and studiously, thoroughly, conscientiously, read and then reread the complete works.

Here was a version of God's plenty; most of it having absolutely no relevance to the title *The Moon and Sixpence*, for which I was somewhat grateful; although oddly enough there was one piece that seemed to make a pretty good stab at retelling the story of Charles Strickland and his adventures in Tahiti. I say 'seemed' because my memories of the original weren't very fresh, Somerset Maugham being almost as unfashionable then as he is now.

The other pieces were more obviously 'creative'. There was a childhood memoir about growing up in a softer, more bucolic age, a time with fewer cars, less crime and better weather. There was a strangely subdued erotic fantasy about a naive teenage girl who's invited to an English country house, a place much like the Kincaid Clinic, where she meets a family of eccentrics who engage her in elaborate but really quite mild and harmless forms of sexual activity.

There was a continuous stream of consciousness, a hundred or more pages: unparagraphed, underpunctuated, unmediated and strangely unrevealing meanderings about love, pain, despair, that sort of thing. Another piece recounted, at floaty length, the deeply spiritual joys of dancing naked.

There was an account of a football match, written in painstaking, mind-numbing detail, recording every move, every pass, every tactic, every disputed decision, every mood swing demonstrated by the crowd. It took about as long to read the piece as it would to have watched the match, although perhaps that was the point. It had a certain lumbering, anal power, but it was remarkably little fun to read, although I knew I wasn't there just for fun. More entertaining was a story set on a Boeing 747 where the pilot comes down with an attack of food poisoning and the plucky air steward has to land the plane on a tiny volcanic island and does so with dignity and aplomb.

One of the most curious and, surprisingly, one of the most readable pieces consisted of a list, rather a long list, of 'interesting facts': the world's most prolific playwright was Lope de Vega; in 1873 Mark Twain patented a self-pasting scrapbook; the Amazon river has one hundred tributaries; Morocco was the first country to recognise the United States; and so on. Another piece, one of the shorter ones for fairly obvious reasons, was an endless series of anagrams, about the 'avarice' of 'caviare' and the 'long leases' of 'Los Angeles', and 'Alfred' who 'flared'. Parts of it were very clever, but it really made no sense at all. The anagrams didn't add up to anything. They were just anagrams.

Only two pieces struck me as genuinely disturbing, which I suppose is to admit that they were rather well written. One was a first-person account, a confession I suppose, from a woman who had got so angry with her baby that she'd picked it up by its feet and held it out of a fourth-floor window, and with her free hand tossed a coin to decide whether or not she was going to drop it. The coin came up heads, the baby fell to its death.

The final piece seemed genuinely psychotic. It was a description of a murder: the pursuit, capture, stabbing, mutilation and anatomically precise dismemberment of a young female victim, in the car-park of a pub called the Moon and Sixpence. I wasn't quite stupid enough to assume this was describing events that had actually taken place, or even that the writer wanted to take place, but to have described these events at all suggested to me that the writer was potentially sick and dangerous, although at the same time I knew I might be over-reacting and over-dramatising.

It took me far longer than it should have to realise that none of these pieces had the writer's name on it. That seemed odd. You might have put it down to modesty or lack of ego, but I felt it implied something more than that. I wasn't ready to start finding conspiracies, but presumably the patients must have got together and agreed to remain anonymous. I tried telling myself this was no bad thing, that it would allow me to come to the texts without prejudice. But who was I kidding? Even if I didn't want to become involved in some banal guessing game, it would have been unnatural not to want to know who'd written what.

Some assumptions were inevitable. You tend to think you can tell a man's writing from a woman's writing, an old person's from a young person's, the writing of the spectacularly insane from that of the more discreetly insane. But other, larger, assumptions offered themselves too. Surely Raymond had written the piece about the emergency plane landing. Surely Maureen, the woman in the football kit, had written the account of the football match. Surely Charity had written the piece about dancing naked. And if I'd had to guess who'd written the piece about the sexual violence in the pub car-park, I would certainly have gone for Anders.

But the moment I thought these things I also thought that perhaps I was being too facile. Perhaps a man like Anders who oozed violence so effectively in person mightn't have any need to write about it. Maybe this violent fantasy had been written by one of the quieter, more harmless-looking people – the quiet ones always, allegedly, being the worst – or perhaps it had been written by a woman trying to exorcise her worst fears. Similarly, in a less dramatic way, just because you dressed in football kit didn't necessarily mean you wanted to write obsessive accounts of football matches. Maybe it meant the opposite. And again, if you spent a certain amount of your time dancing naked, perhaps you didn't need to write about that either. If you can't judge a book by looking at its cover, you probably can't judge mental patients by their literary output. But what then *could* you do with that output?

Well, you could spend a whole weekend poring and agonising over it. You could make notes and annotations. You could mark the bits you liked best. You could jot down suggestions for how things could be said more simply or more clearly. Without getting too pedantic about it you could correct a little spelling and grammar. And all of this I did.

Naturally, most of the writing didn't deserve or benefit from this length and depth of reading, but I thought I owed it to the patients to treat their efforts with the utmost respect. And besides, having been so idle and restless all week I was inclined to let the work take up as much time as possible.

I concentrated long and hard, but there were one or two distractions. Raymond came by at intervals to ask if I needed pillows or blankets, and Cook, in his tin helmet, brought me bowls of soup and stew. From time to time I was aware of being watched. Patients would position themselves some distance from the hut so they could look at me through the windows, trying to see how I was reacting as I read their efforts.

I did my best to show I was treating the job with the right degree of commitment and high seriousness, that I was reading thoroughly, intently and yet not too critically. But these weren't easy concepts to communicate non-verbally, and sometimes it was actually quite hard to read at all while aware of being watched. I became very self-conscious and lost all sense of how I might normally behave or appear while reading. I became someone who was performing the act of reading.

A far more important and welcome distraction was Alicia. I was not distracted by her actual presence, alas, not by the flesh and blood woman, that would have been too much to ask, but thoughts about her and the night we'd spent together were distracting enough. I kept reminding myself that she had come to my hut, that we'd had sex, that it had been great, if quirky, and maybe its quirkiness was part of its greatness. I had got what I wanted. Actually, I had got far more than I had hoped or bargained for, but perhaps good sex is always like that.

And I found a lot of questions drifting into my head. I wondered if what Alicia and I had done 'meant' anything. Did it mean she liked me, that she'd come to my hut again? Would that be regularly? Once in a while? Every night, whether I wanted it or not? Did that mean that my life at the Kincaid Clinic was going to be a lot more tolerable and enjoyable from now on? Or was it going to be more difficult and problematic? Did Alicia want the same things from me that I wanted from her? And did I have the slightest idea of what I really wanted, anyway?

These weren't merely rhetorical questions, but I knew there was no point in trying to answer them. For the time being I would have to live with an amount of uncertainty, and that didn't seem so terrible. The mere possibility of a future that involved more Alicia, more sex with her, more intimacy with her, was enough to sustain me, at least for now.

By the end of the weekend I had completed my first seven days at the Kincaid Clinic. It had been a tough week in all sorts of ways, but I'd got through it, and by Sunday evening, satisfied that I'd dealt properly with the first batch of patients' writing, I felt I wasn't in such bad shape. The future looked possible.

And then Kincaid came to see me again, and even that didn't seem too bad. Whereas on his previous visit my desk had been completely bare, it was now stacked with a thousand or so pages of typescript. I looked like I was doing something.

'How quickly life can change,' Kincaid said, as he stepped into the hut. 'You're pleased it's such an impressive trawl.'

'Well, there's certainly plenty of it,' I said. 'Want to read some?'

He appeared to be debating with himself whether this would be a useful strategy, but I already suspected what the outcome was going to be.

'No,' he said, 'I don't think that would be entirely appropriate. I might be invading your territory. I'm keen to know what the patients are up to but . . .' more studied rumination, then, 'I think it would be better if you simply wrote me a report.'

'Yes, I could do that,' I said, 'if you think you can trust me to analyse it properly. I'm no psychologist.'

'I trust you totally,' Kincaid said, and he was about to retreat, but I didn't let him get away that easily. 'There is something I'd like your professional opinion on,' I said, and he couldn't resist that. 'None of these pieces has the writer's name on it.'

'Did you tell them to put their names on?'

'I didn't tell them anything. You did.'

Another man might have thought I was accusing him of something or other, forgetfulness at the very least, but not Kincaid. He said, 'You know, this is interesting. I think what we might be seeing here is a manifestation of the patients' group mind.'

I didn't know what that was, and I suppose it would have been easy enough to ask him what he meant, but I couldn't be bothered. I didn't want to give him another opportunity to show off.

'I'll bear that in mind,' I said. 'Though I can understand why they wouldn't want to put their names on some of it.'

'How so?'

'Somebody is writing some very sick stuff, violent murderous fantasy, dangerous stuff.'

'Dangerous?'

'Well, needless to say, I'm not so naive as to think he, or I suppose possibly she, has actually done or is going to do what he, or she, describes, but if that's what's going through his, or her, mind then—'

'Then what?'

'Then I think we should keep an eye on him or her.'

'Yes, Gregory, we do keep an eye on our patients – that's why they're here.'

I felt nicely humiliated.

Kincaid said, 'I don't think you need worry, Gregory. After all, they're only words on paper. Sticks and stones, they're not.'

'Well yes,' I said, 'but—'

'But me no buts, Gregory. Perhaps the person writing these violent fantasies is doing so simply in order to worry you, to manipulate you, to make you have this very conversation with me.'

'I can see that,' I said.

'In which case we surely have a duty not to be manipulated, not to worry, not to have this conversation.'

I wasn't sure about that. I couldn't help thinking that if the writer of the piece committed some horrible sex crime, in or out of the clinic, now or later, it wouldn't be much defence, neither legal nor moral, to say, 'Oh, we didn't worry because we thought it wasn't sticks or stones.'

'Up to a point,' I said, but Kincaid had already lost interest in me and our conversation.

He rumbled throatily. 'So you'll let me have the report on my desk at nine o'clock tomorrow morning,' he said. 'Then you'll see the patients and deliver your judgement of their work. Don't feel you have to be too gentle with them.'

And he was gone. I was left with the prospect of a report to be written and a class to be faced; two things to be daunted by, yet surprisingly I was undaunted. If Kincaid wanted a report by nine o'clock then he'd have one. It would be short, well-written and with a certain good humour and common sense about it; quite unlike the pages I'd spent the weekend reading. And as for seeing the patients and delivering a judgement, well, I preferred to think it would be more of a group discussion. I wouldn't be standing in judgement on them, wouldn't be giving them marks out of ten. It would be a getting acquainted session. I'd ask a few questions, get them to talk about what they'd written. I'd ask them to do some reading aloud. The time would soon pass. It would be like being back at Cambridge. Sort of. I thought I could cope with that.

II

On the stroke of nine next morning I was knocking on Kincaid's office door and I had in my hand a neatly typed one-page report on the patients' outpourings. Kincaid summoned me in and I stood by his desk as he read the report, which told him what I've told you, that the writing was variously manic, depressive, obsessive, naive, self-referential, obscure, compelling in one sense, repellent in another. I couldn't help saying that I wondered if a title like *The Moon and Sixpence* hadn't had a stifling effect on the patients' creativity (although given that few of them seemed actually to have referred to the title, this probably wasn't a very telling criticism). And I ended by saying I thought it was far too early to report anything at all with any certainty. Kincaid's attention as he surveyed the report was intense yet cursory, as if he might be employing skills he'd learned on a speed-reading course.

'It's quite well-written,' he said as he finished. 'And there are one or two telling phrases, but frankly, given your considerable literary gifts, I suppose I'd expected more in the way of critical appraisal and value judgements.'

'You mean whether or not I liked any of it?'

'I mean whether or not it was any good.'

'Good in what sense?'

'In the sense of publishable.'

'Publishable?'

I was taken aback. Did he really think there was some literary genius locked away behind one of the clinic's grey doors? Did he think they were likely to come up with something really good the first time out? And did he really think a writer was the best person to know what was and wasn't publishable? Most writers, I suspected, had only the vaguest idea. Perhaps what he really needed was a publisher-in-residence, someone like Nicola.

I could only say, 'I think it's still early days yet.'

'I know it's early days,' Kincaid agreed, 'but if a man can't envisage a future, then he may have no future at all.'

I wasn't sure if this was true or not, but I was soon back in the lecture room with the patients. It was just them and me this time. No porters were in evidence, Alicia was not poised at the back of the room, and to some extent this felt like a welcome vote of confidence. I could be trusted not to burn the place down.

I'd abandoned the lectern and arranged eleven chairs into a circle. It evoked memories of group therapy sessions I'd seen depicted in films, and perhaps also of King Arthur's round table, a way of saying there were no favourites here, and possibly no leader. The patients sat uneasily, fidgeting, preening, slumping, in accordance with their differing conditions.

I'd separated what I took to be the individual pieces of writing, and arranged them on the floor in the centre of the circle. 'I'd like you to begin by retrieving your own work,' I said. It was a fairly lame and obvious ploy, but I thought it was worth a try. It didn't work in the slightest. Nobody moved. All ten sat there in inert silence. I was annoyed. I'd done my bit, spent the weekend wading through this verbal swamp of their making, and now they were refusing to play the game.

I remained in my chair and said nothing, thinking this was indeed just a game, a bluff to see who could sit it out longest, and I thought I ought to be able to play the game every bit as well as they could. I was wrong. They had the strength of numbers, madness and perhaps practice on their side. When I couldn't take it any longer, I said, 'How about you, Charity? Surely this must be yours.'

I picked up the nude dancing piece and offered it to Charity.

'Must it?' she said, and she twitched her top lip at me. How dare I make such a cheap, easy assumption? Her hands stayed in her lap and she refused to take the sheets of paper I was holding out to her.

'How about you?' I said, addressing Sita, the Indian woman. 'Which one of these is yours?'

She looked at me serenely and said absolutely nothing.

'She doesn't speak,' Raymond said by way of explanation.

'Never?' I asked.

'Not so far, anyway.'

There was obviously a whole bundle of problems lurking here, and this didn't feel like the moment to go into them. I turned rapidly to the woman in the football kit. Today she was wearing a canary yellow shirt. Norwich City, I thought.

'Then how about you, Maureen?' I said. 'Is this your account of the football match? If it is, you should be proud. It's a very good piece of writing.'

She was unmoved, so I turned, not without anxiety, towards Anders.

'Is this yours?' I asked, and I offered him the pages describing the violent rape and murder. He looked at me as though he might well do me some physical harm, but not now. For the moment his hands remained where they were, bunched into meaty but unmoving fists.

'In fact,' I continued to lie, becoming more transparently desperate, 'there's some wonderful writing here, things that any writer would be pleased to have written. I know I would. I'm surprised nobody wants to take credit for it.'

They weren't falling for any of this, and when I said, 'So, would anybody like to read aloud what they wrote? Or something they didn't write?' I knew I was flogging an absolutely decaying horse. I embarked on a series of increasingly hopeless questions. Had they enjoyed doing the writing? Had any of them written before? Did anybody have a favourite author? All of these were equally useless. Nobody said a damned thing. I felt like some idiot student on teaching practice. I found myself at the centre of a ring of sullen, obstructive silence. I'd had enough.

'Well, if there's nothing more to be said, then there's no point trying to say it,' I muttered.

I started to leave, and then gradually, slowly, the patients got up from their seats, moved into the centre of the circle and began to pick up pages of manuscript from the floor. At first I thought I must have made some sort of breakthrough, that they were taking what they'd written, but that happy delusion didn't last long. They were clearly not taking their own work since they would grab a single sheet here, a couple of pages there, a handful elsewhere. And when they had what they considered enough they didn't return to their seats. They stood ruminatively for a while, holding and shuffling the sheets of paper they'd salvaged, and then, with a shared purpose, they all simultaneously tossed them energetically, intently yet playfully, into the air.

Once the pages were airborne they became much more desirable, much more fascinating to the patients. They tried to snatch them as they fell, diving to catch them before they hit the floor, then tossing them up again. Sometimes two people would make a grab for the same bit of paper, and then a little tug of war would ensue. Some patients clasped handfuls of paper to their bosoms, rubbed their faces with them. Others kicked pages around the floor as though they were dancing in piles of fallen leaves.

All this was done wordlessly, but not exactly silently. It was accompanied by what seemed to me rather predictable madhouse noise: whooping, screaming, hysterical laughter and so forth. The patients were ignoring me completely by now, and I stood hopelessly at the centre of all this frantic paper-orientated mayhem and I felt utterly dispirited.

And when, much as before, the porters came running in, adding to the chaos, and when Alicia came and viewed the scene with great weariness, and when Kincaid also eventually arrived and instantly put a stop to it all, I had a terrible feeling, not only that history was repeating itself, but that it might continue to repeat itself endlessly, indefinitely, that it would always be like this. I'd be constantly losing control, Kincaid would be constantly bailing me out, for ever and ever, or at least until such time as I couldn't face it any more and walked out, or until Kincaid fired me. One or other of these options surely couldn't be far away.

Kincaid commanded the patients, 'Go away again, and write something else. This time your project is to be entitled ...' He displayed a rare moment of indecision and said, 'Oh, I don't know. Mr Collins will give you a title.'

I was speechless, my brain was dry. I was being asked to perform the tiniest creative act and the task was beyond me. After a long, though hardly pregnant, silence, and for reasons that I couldn't fathom, I found myself saying, '*Heart of Darkness*'.

Kincaid was well-pleased with my choice, but the patients didn't react to it at all. They simply shuffled off leaving the crumpled and abandoned manuscripts behind them. Kincaid and I stood together for a moment.

'I'm really sorry about this,' I said.

'I know you are,' he said.

'If you want me to resign I will.'

'Why would I want that?'

'Why wouldn't you?' I asked.

He narrowed his eyes a little, to appear shrewd and powerful, as though he was looking into my inner self.

'Because I have faith in you,' he said. 'Perhaps more faith than you have in yourself. I know you, Gregory. I know you're no quitter. You'll give me another week. After that you can do what you like, but I know you and I know you'll give me another week.'

'Oh, OK,' I said weakly, but I wasn't really sure I meant it.

12

Left alone in the lecture room, I found myself on my knees, collecting the manuscript pages together, smoothing them out, trying to make a neat pile of them, and when I'd done that I took them up to the library where I set them on one of the empty shelves. At least the place now contained some reading matter.

I stood in the library and experienced a whole cocktail of emotions. Did many people drink cocktails at that time in the seventies? Perhaps not. Perhaps that was a craze that came later, and in any case this was a cocktail that was likely to disagree with even the strongest stomach. I wanted to cry, to run away, to run to Alicia's arms, to smash something. I felt useless, a complete failure; and the fact that Kincaid didn't want to get rid of me only made me feel worse. I was grateful for his indulgence but I was ashamed to need it. Surely if you were no damned good at something you should admit it and move on to something else. Besides, I wasn't even sure I could last through another week. Then two rather strange, encouraging things happened.

The first was a visit from Raymond. I heard the rattle of his trolley in the corridor outside the library. Raymond's face appeared at the door, looking cheerful and perhaps as though it might be wearing a little make-up. I let that pass. He wheeled himself and the trolley into the library, and he was followed by Carla, the young black girl. She dawdled across the room and pressed herself against the window, leaning her forehead on the glass and looking out at nothing in particular.

Raymond made no acknowledgement of her presence, but said, 'You don't have to believe everything Alicia Crowe tells you.'

My first reaction was to take this as an insult against Alicia, and I wanted to come to her defence. Nobody was going to accuse my Alicia of being a liar, but Raymond added mildly, disarmingly,

'There's absolutely no reason not to drink the coffee. It's not going to poison you. Really. I never poisoned anybody. All right, so I put a little prussic acid in the water supply on the aircraft. But I knew I'd get found out before anybody drank it. And I wanted to get found out. I had to convince everybody I was mad, didn't I?'

'Did you?'

'Yes. I know that's what lots of them say around here. But in my case it happens to be true. I needed to get away. I'd made some powerful enemies up there as I jetted back and forth across the skyways. They were out to get me. I knew that if I could get locked up here I'd be safe. It's worked very well so far.'

'Apparently.'

'But I wouldn't poison you. What would be the point? What would it achieve?'

'Well,' I said, 'it might reinforce the impression that you're actually mad.'

This amused him. 'Very good,' he said. 'I can see you're going to enjoy your time here.'

There was no answer to that. The coffee certainly looked and smelled appealing enough, and my instincts somehow told me I could trust Raymond, at least to the extent of believing that he didn't want to poison me.

'Tell you what,' he said. 'Why don't we get Carla here to be your official food taster? I love Carla. I wouldn't hurt her for the world.'

Before I could consider the offer, Carla had sprung into life, hopped and skipped across the library and was drinking a cup of hot black coffee. She attacked it like a wine taster, running it round her mouth before swigging it down. Then she froze, did a double take, grabbed her stomach with both hands. Her face buckled in agony, she fell to her knees, and I realised she was playing at being poisoned, doing a comic turn that involved gurning and squawking and writhing around in an embarrassingly poor mime of someone in their death throes. She ended the performance twitching in a foetal position on the floor, but by then I had stopped watching, and was drinking my own cup of coffee, convinced it wasn't toxic.

'Oh, you're quite the frequent flier, aren't you?' Raymond said.

I found myself feeling oddly well-disposed towards both him and the idiotic Carla, who had now picked herself up and was doing extravagant calisthenics in front of a run of empty shelving. I am always amazed at the way the smallest things can be responsible for making the most major changes in people's emotions, but as Raymond wheeled his trolley out of the library, giving a little curtsey as he went, the prospect of another week at the Kincaid Clinic seemed, for some reason, not nearly so daunting.

Then the second thing happened: the telephone rang. I looked around the library in surprise. I hadn't even been aware there was a phone in there, and I was amazed to find an old Bakelite model shrilling out from under a chair in the corner. Even so, I just ignored it at first. I didn't think it could possibly be for me, and it would surely stop before too long. But it continued to ring and at last I felt obliged to pick it up. A voice I recognised as the nurse's said, 'Phone call.' And I said, 'For me?' And she said, 'Obviously for you. You're Gregory Collins, aren't you?' There was a fizz of static on the line before I was connected. In that second I thought perhaps it was Kincaid, having changed his mind about giving me the sack. But it was Gregory Collins, *the* Gregory Collins.

'It's me,' he said. 'Bob Burns.'

Call me unimaginative and given to stereotyping, but the moment I heard his voice I pictured pinched northern terraces, pinched northern faces, miners walking home through grainy, high-contrast streets, the whites of their eyes staring out through blackened faces, their hands full of pickaxes and caged canaries. I wondered if Gregory might be calling to wish me well, to ask me how the job was going, but he was far too self-absorbed for that.

'I'll not beat about the bush, Michael. I've had a letter that's a bit disturbing.'

I didn't imagine Gregory could be more disturbed than I was at that moment, but I asked, 'Who from?'

'Dr John bloody Bentley.'

'Oh,' I said. It surprised me that Bentley would be writing to any of his old students, and it seemed especially unlikely he'd have written to Gregory Collins. But Gregory reminded me, 'I sent him a proof of my book, remember?'

I did, but only vaguely, and it didn't seem reason enough to merit a phone call.

'I was asking him for a quote for the jacket,' Gregory said. 'But the bugger never replied, so I thought he probably didn't believe in that sort of thing, and like you said at the time, it probably wouldn't have done me much good anyway, but now he's written to me.'

'Has he given you a quote?'

'I'll read you the entire letter,' Gregory said. 'It's not long. "Dear Collins, Thank you for sending me the advance proof copy of *The Wax Man*, which I have now, a little belatedly, had a chance to read. I can assure you it will be warmly received at my next book-burning party. Sincerely, Dr John Bentley." What do you think of that?'

In the way that you can find yourself laughing even when you have nothing to laugh about, I found myself chuckling at Bentley's letter.

'It's no laughing matter,' Gregory said. 'Don't you think it's shocking?'

'I don't think it's very surprising if that's what you mean.'

'But don't you think burning books is a bloody fascistic thing to do?'

'Of course. But I also think the letter's probably an example of Bentley's famous Cambridge wit.'

'How's that?'

'I think it's a joke, Gregory.'

'You don't think he's going to burn my book?'

'Oh, I think he probably is.'

'Then how is it a joke?'

Explaining jokes is a futile business at the best of times. In my current frame of mind I thought that explaining one to Gregory Collins was likely to drive me to despair. Not the longest of drives.

'OK, it's not a joke,' I said.

'So don't you think I should denounce him?' Gregory asked.

'Denounce?'

'Tell the university authorities. Or write a letter to the *Times Literary Supplement* or something.'

'No, I don't think so. I don't see what that would achieve, especially given that you burned your own book at one of his parties.'

'That's different altogether. A bloke's allowed to burn his own stuff, like Freud – he destroyed all his letters and notes 'cause he didn't want to make it too easy for the biographers, but that's a bit bloody different from when the Nazis burned his works.'

'Yes, it's different,' I said, 'and I can see why you mightn't like it, but I don't think you've any choice but to put up with it. If you get into a fight with Bentley I can't see how you're going to emerge from it without looking silly.'

'You think I look silly?'

'No, in general, I don't think you look silly, and I think it would be best if you stayed that way.'

'It's a rum business,' he said.

I wondered what he'd been expecting from me. Perhaps he thought that since I was the one who'd tried, totally unsuccessfully as it turned out, to embarrass Bentley at our book-burning party, I was going to be an ally in trying to attack him on some dubious moral grounds. The truth was I didn't care about Bentley any more, didn't care much at all about the people I'd known or the things I'd gone through at university. It all seemed a million years ago and a million miles away.

'Why don't you do something subtler?' I suggested. 'Like making him a character in your next book?'

'There may never be a next book,' Gregory said, and he drifted into a moody silence. Then he asked, 'What do you think Nicola would say?'

'Something pretty snotty, I'd guess.'

'Would you mind if I gave her a bell and asked her professional opinion? I haven't seen her since, you know, that night.'

I knew I had no say in the matter, no right to object or even have an opinion, and yet some dim, dormant part of me minded a lot. I didn't want Nicola and Gregory cosying up, discussing matters of literature and conscience behind my back. But naturally I had to say, 'What you and Nicola get up to is your own business.'

'Good,' Gregory said. 'I thought you wouldn't mind, but a bloke's got to be careful. I wouldn't want good mates like us to fall out over a bird. Right you are then, I'll keep you informed.'

I could tell he was about to hang up, and suddenly I was furious with him. He was such a self-centred bastard, so completely without interest in anyone other than himself. Even if he didn't care about me or my job or my well-being, wouldn't simple curiosity have compelled him to ask how things were going at the clinic? I didn't intend to open my heart to him, but I decided that while I'd got him, I'd make use of him.

'I need some advice,' I said.

'From me?' I was glad he showed the appropriate amount of surprise. 'If it's about writing—'

'It's about teaching.'

'Great. That's what I do best.'

'So tell me, how do you do it? How do you stand up in front of a class of ten people—?'

'Only ten?' he said. 'If I had a class with only ten in it I'd think I'd died and gone to heaven.'

'Yes, but these are adults and they're mad,' I said.

He wouldn't concede that this made any difference.

'Anyway,' I continued, 'how do you get them to respond? How do you get them to speak? How do you keep control? How do you make them respect you?'

'I don't know,' said Gregory flatly. 'You just do.'

It was a more useless answer than I could possibly have imagined. 'And what do you do if your first class turns into a cross between a paper chase and a rugby scrum?' I asked.

'In my school they'd get a bloody long detention.'

'Mightn't work in my position.'

'And I assume you don't have corporal punishment?'

Nobody had actually told me we didn't, but I was making the same assumption. 'Right,' I said.

'Mmm, mmm,' I could hear him brooding, trying to come up with something. It was a painful procedure for him. When I'd just about given up hope of him saying anything at all, he finally replied, 'Well, some people say you should be yourself when you're teaching, but I think that's asking for trouble. If you try to be yourself they'll have you. I think you need to be someone else. Anyone else.'

'But I *am* being someone else!' I whined. 'I'm being you.'

'Are you though?' he said heavily. 'Are you really?'

I thought I understood what he meant. I was pretending to be Gregory Collins, but in name only. When I'd stood in front of the patients I'd been all too depressingly, and all too vulnerably, like the real Michael Smith. I hadn't had an act; and that had been the problem.

'OK, yes,' I said, 'I can see that.'

'And I'll tell you something else,' said Gregory. 'If a useless chuff like me can succeed as a teacher then someone like you has a duty not to fail.'

'You know, Gregory,' I said, 'I think you might be right.'

I said I'd give the Kincaid Clinic another week, and this time I meant it.

13

In one way I could see that this second week was likely to be more of the same; more enervation, more feeling like a spare part, but it differed in this respect: throughout the first week it had been possible to have some optimism, to hold on to the quaint belief that there might be something to look forward to. Now I knew what was coming. I knew the patients were entirely likely to deliver more of the same old rubbish, and I didn't have a clue how I was going to deal with it. All right, I could follow Gregory's advice and adopt a persona, but I wasn't sure exactly where that would get me, or for that matter where it would get the patients.

They were now rather more in evidence than they had been the previous week, both in the clinic and around the grounds. I saw them wandering through the corridors, sitting by the dried-up fountain, on the couches in the reception area; and every time I saw them, they were carrying writing pads, apparently locked in agonies of creativity, and then I'd see them scurrying into or out of the Communication Room, a name that now seemed to be submerged beneath multiple layers of irony. When the patients noticed me, some of them still often looked at me with resentment or hostility, or sometimes in a way that seemed simply crazy, but once in a while I sensed them regarding me with what felt more like sympathy, maybe even pity, as if I was the sad, hopeless case and they were the concerned, perhaps condescending, visitors, as if they were just passing through and I was there for keeps.

I spent long hours in my hut doing nothing. Sometimes Charity would dance by. Sometimes Max would stagger past, looking drunk. 'How are you, Max?' I'd ask. Occasionally Maureen would stroll past too, still in her football kit, but carrying a spade and a hoe. And once in a great while somebody would actually stop and have a conversation.

The first was Byron, he of the poetic good looks. He asked me a lot of questions about my background, education and qualifications, which it would have been easy to regard as hostile, but I chose not to regard them that way and told him as much of the truth as I thought I could get away with.

'Yes,' he said, 'I thought you must be a Cambridge man. I was at Oxford myself. The difference always shows. We must have a good long chat about literary matters before long.'

That didn't sound so terrible, and I almost found myself looking forward to it. Byron seemed the sanest of the patients by some way, and I wondered how and when his madness might manifest itself; perhaps in a long chat about literary matters? I also wondered which of last week's pieces he'd been responsible for. None of them seemed to show the benefits of an Oxford education, though, unlike Byron, I wasn't sure I would have spotted such an influence.

Meals were much as before, grey, tasteless, homogenous, but Cook now talked to me too. 'Sorry about the other day,' he said. 'I was feeling a bit paranoid. But wouldn't you?'

'It can't be easy when you don't know what's in the cans,' I agreed.

'Well, the best things never are easy,' he said. 'And it's not as if I absolutely never know. Like for instance, tins of anchovies look different from tins of corned beef. Baked bean cans have a certain look to them. You can always spot a tinned suet pudding. But when it comes to tinned new potatoes as opposed to tinned pineapple chunks, or tinned kidney beans as opposed to tinned savoury mince, it's anybody's guess.

'And anyway, I think there's something really symbolic about it. Because, when you think about it, life's like a tin can without a label, isn't it? You want to get into it but you never know whether you'll like what you're going to find.'

'That's sort of true,' I said.

'I realise I should say something about my name,' he said. 'Cook's a funny name for a cook you might say, but why not? Even funnier name for someone who isn't a cook, if you think about it.'

I tried not to think about it.

'And I also realise you must be wondering why I'm wearing this helmet made of tin foil.'

Actually, I wasn't. I could already guess. I'd heard enough about schizophrenia to know that sufferers often believe they're receiving messages from distant, and usually malign, sources, that they're hearing voices, that they think they're having instructions put into their heads by aliens or MI5. I suppose this particular manifestation of madness must only have appeared when people began to understand something about radio waves. Prior to that, the notion of messages being projected through the ether would have been meaningless, although I suppose demons and spirits could have done something similar. The foil helmet, I suspected, was a shielding device to protect Cook's mind from these evil broadcasts.

And so, predictably, disappointingly, it proved. Cook explained at tedious length, in crippling detail, about these messages he was receiving, about their source, their bad influence, their compelling persuasiveness, how there was an underground cell, consisting of disenchanted Huguenots and Rosicrucians, living in Hayward's Heath, who had built a machine, a cross between a printing press, a steam engine and a pinball table, that was being used to control and torture him. When I couldn't stand to hear any more I said, 'Maybe you should write about it.' But as I made my getaway I knew this was a stupid thing to have suggested.

Cook confirmed what I'd suspected all along, that whereas some mad people may no doubt be special and interesting, it isn't the madness that makes them that way. The madness is quite separate from the specialness. People who are boring when they're sane don't suddenly become more interesting just because they're mad. And this was obviously true of their writing too. Boring people wrote boring things. Boring mad people would write boring mad things. If writing was a means of self-expression (and I was certainly game to argue that it wasn't; I mean, did Dante write the *Divine Comedy* because there was something he was dying to get off his chest?), then obviously it would be the medium for certain mad, dull people to express the true mad dullness of their natures. Perhaps I should have known this before I started work at the Kincaid Clinic.

In general, life was now rather regular and calm. Nothing much disturbed the slow rhythms of the clinic, although there was one night when I heard the sound of loud, beery voices coming from immediately outside the clinic's boundary wall, as though a group of drunks was out there having a party. A bottle got smashed, there was a lot of swearing and in other circumstances I might have felt vaguely threatened. But I realised how safe I was there in the clinic. What were a few drunks going to do? Climb the wall and break in? Let 'em try.

The noises had stopped by the time Charles Manning came by. He was dressed as before, blazered and bare-chested, a pastel cigarette pressed between his lips.

'Need a light?' he asked, and I laughed and said no.

Casually, he then said, 'I suppose you're here for the sex.'

I wasn't quick enough to come up with a reply.

'Everyone knows,' he continued, 'if you can't get crumpet in a mad house, you'll never get it anywhere.'

Something told me this might very well be true, and yet the idea that the patients were enjoying a frisky sex life seemed both improbable and distasteful.

'Is that why *you're* here?' I asked, trying to make a joke.

He looked insulted but he was determined not to be provoked, nor to answer my question.

'They're at it like rabbits,' he said. 'Like goats and monkeys. In twosomes and threesomes and foursomes and moresomes. Hetero and homo, plain and fancy, bi and tri, onanistic, inverted, orgiastic. You'd be surprised.'

I agreed that I would. Now, I wasn't so gullible as to take this at its face value, but Charles Manning was a reasonably plausible narrator and I worried he might be telling at least some version of the truth. It depressed me no end.

'I try to stay above it all,' he continued, 'but I admit there are moments when I let my defences down. I'm only made of flesh and blood. Hot flesh and pulsing blood and wet mucous membranes—'

'Does Dr Kincaid know about all these goings on?' I interrupted. I thought it was a reasonable question, one likely to connect Charles Manning with some sort of reality and stop his flow of free association.

'I rather think he does,' Manning said with lumbering irony. 'Given that he's usually there watching, making notes, standing in attendance, cajoling, encouraging, arranging his charges into tableaux vivants, posing in their midst, buck naked, his penis raised like a conductor's baton, although clearly of somewhat different proportions. So yes, I think he probably has some knowledge of what goes on. Yes, I do.'

I wasn't sure I believed that at all.

'And Dr Crowe?' I asked gently.

'Oh yes, she knows what goes on.'

'But does she . . . attend?'

Why did I ask that, given that I couldn't possibly have trusted any answer I received? But Charles Manning was more perceptive than I'd have given him credit for. 'I don't think you want to know the answer to that question,' he said, and I agreed. 'No, I'm not here for the sex actually,' he said, now adopting a frank and man-to-mannish tone. 'It's a long story, but in round terms all you need to know is that I'm not mad at all. You see, I was working in the film industry. I was a projectionist. Responsible job. Bringing enlightenment and entertainment to the masses. Lord, I loved those old pictures, the Ealing comedies, the Edgar Lustgarten mysteries, the Pathé Newsreels. They don't make them like that.'

'No,' I agreed.

'These days they're full of violence, which I can take or leave, and sex, which frankly I can't bear. They kept sending all these dirty movies for me to project, all these bosoms and buttocks and flanks and so forth, many of them continental. You know what I'm talking about.'

'Yes,' I said. '*Emmanuelle* showed for a whole year at a cinema in Cambridge while I was there.'

'Precisely. And the more I complained the worse it got. They were trying to get rid of me, make me resign, but I wasn't having any of that. Where was I going to get another job at my age, what with the unions and the unemployment and the strife and the emancipation of women and so forth? So I put on an antic disposition – that's a Shakespearian allusion, you probably spotted it, I like the Olivier version best myself. Yes, I pretended I was mad. They can't sack you if you're insane, it's company policy. So they decided I needed looking after, sent me to this place, very decent of them in a way, though they had no choice in the matter, of course, I saw to that. Damned if they did. Damned if they didn't. So here I am. The wife's a bit cheesed about it, but she's adjusting. And you see, all I have to do is sit it out here until popular tastes change, till people abandon all this sex and so forth and return to good old-fashioned storytelling, and fun for all the family, Mary Whitehouse and Lord Longford and so on. Then they'll come crawling back to me, saying you were right all along, Charles, old egg, have your job back, have a whopping great pay rise, and why don't you join the British Board of Film Censors while you're about it? Good plan, I think.'

'Well, yes,' I said.

'Also,' he said, 'I'm suffering from anal castration anxiety, which is a lot like common or garden castration anxiety but it's been displaced into the anal area through regressive distortion. A lot of so-called "toilet phobias" go along with it, fear of falling into the bowl, fear that some worm-like creature will crawl out of the S-bend and lodge itself in my anus and burrow into my gut and eat me up from the inside. Not that there aren't times when being rid of the whole genital apparatus seems like quite a desirable option. But anyway, I'm dealing with it, thanks to Dr Kincaid.'

He looked at me expectantly, but whatever his expectations were, I failed to live up to them.

'Do you think I should write about it?' he asked.

'I think you've got to go with your instincts,' I said, sincerely hoping that his instincts would lead him elsewhere.

Charles Manning stared at me with the kind of contempt I felt I richly deserved. He bowed and withdrew and I was left alone in my hut feeling like a complete fool. I had no reason to believe that he was telling the truth about the sex life of the clinic, and perhaps I had every reason to believe he was lying. It was certainly possible he was trying to confuse me, to 'psyche me out' as we might have said in those days. But the fact was, I still had no idea what Kincaidian Therapy was, except that it involved doing something or other in an office with the blinds drawn. Was that significant? Did orgies come under the general heading of experimental techniques? I certainly hoped not.

I'd be lying if I said the second week just flew by; no week that consisted of inactivity interspersed with bad meals and conversations with the insane was ever going to slip by on gossamer wings, but it passed less painfully than I might have expected, and certainly much quicker than the previous week had. I stopped making a fuss about my lost belongings, I stopped worrying about trying to get a key to the front gate and I stopped worrying about doing nothing. And I did my very best to stop worrying about Alicia, but that didn't quite work.

I'd been hoping our night together might have made us better friends; I certainly wanted to see more of her, but I sensed she was keeping her distance. In the simple physical sense she certainly wasn't at all conspicuous around the clinic, and on a couple of occasions when I went to her office I found the door locked. And as for sex, well, who knew whether last Friday night's fun and games would ever be repeated? Not me. It would have been great if I could have run into her in the clinic and she had said something kind or encouraging or reassuring, but in her absence I suspected the worst: that she thought of it as a one-night stand, a moment of madness (her madness not mine), never to be repeated and never to be referred to again.

When I did at last see her again, chasing after her as she went from the clinic to the Communication Room, I thought it best to appear professional, to discuss some topic that related to the business of the clinic. I said, 'I've had a few conversations now with patients and I'm a little confused.'

She looked at me as though I was precisely the sort of man she expected to be constantly confused.

I said, 'They're always shooting me some line about not really being mad, or not being mad in quite the way they appear to be, and I'd like to know whether or not they're telling the truth.'

'In many cases so would we,' Alicia said.

'But you must have done some tests. You must have some case histories. There must be some files.'

'Yes, there are. In Dr Kincaid's office. In the filing cabinet. Under lock and key.'

'And I think it might be really good if I saw them.'

'You do, do you?'

'Yes. Don't you?'

'No,' she said. 'If you have someone read a file, a text that purports to describe a patient, and then introduce them to that patient, there's an unfailing tendency to find what the file's told them is there. You find what you expect to find. You trust what you read, what someone else has written, rather than your own observations. It's something to do with the hegemony of the written word. A fair amount of research has been done on this stuff.'

'I can sort of see that,' I said.

'You should rely on your own observations.'

'But how are my observations going to tell me whether Raymond ever really tried to poison his passengers, or whether Charles Manning was really a cinema projectionist?'

'You use your judgement,' she said.

'Couldn't I use my judgement after I've seen the files?'

'Gregory, I've tried to be polite. The fact is, I don't think someone who's been here no time at all and whose skills remain at best unproven should be given the complete run of the place. I don't think a mere writer-in-residence should be given free access to highly confidential medical and psychological data that he may not have the wherewithal to interpret. I don't think someone in your position has any right to be so bloody demanding. End of discussion.'

And it was. I hadn't even got as far as mentioning the orgies, and perhaps it was just as well. If she could get that angry about files, how angry would she get about sex? And yet, come Friday night, sure enough, perhaps strangely enough, certainly happily enough, Alicia came to my hut just as she had the week before. And it was in many ways a repeat performance. What people blithely refer to as 'the physical side' was just fine. All the touching, the kissing, certainly the penetration, even the orgasms (not quite simultaneous, but close enough for beginners), took care of themselves. It was the verbal side I still had trouble with.

I had the sense that I was playing not a sexual game, but a word game, the rules of which Alicia knew much better than I did. It was a game she'd been playing for years, a game she'd invented; and although she was keen to have me as a player, she wasn't prepared to give me access to the rule book. So I had to learn as I went along. I tried to stay within the spirit of the game, but inevitably I infringed some of the subtler by-laws from time to time, committed the odd foul, said the wrong thing.

Alicia kept up her stream of obscene consciousness, and I joined in where I thought appropriate, echoing her words and sentiments. She'd say something like, 'Stretch my cunt with that fat throbbing cock of yours,' and I'd say, 'Yes, open your cunt for my fat throbbing cock,' and this sort of thing, while not exactly displaying wild creativity on my part, worked just fine.

However, there came a moment, well actually a period of some minutes, when Alicia was not speaking at all. It was preceded by her saying, 'Now feed that fat piece of meat into my mouth so I can run my tongue under the foreskin and taste the cum leaking out,' which I did, and which she did, but it meant I then had to invent some new dialogue without any help from her. So I said something like, 'That's right, swallow that slimy monster, you filthy slut,' but that didn't work at all.

Alicia freed her mouth, pulled away and said, 'I'm perfectly happy to swallow the slimy monster. And I'm perfectly happy to act like a filthy slut, to *be* a filthy slut, but I don't want to be *called* a filthy slut. Got it?'

'Oh, OK,' I said. I could well understand why a woman wouldn't want to be called a slut, although given some of the things Alicia had called me, it seemed unnecessarily delicate. I had imagined we were in an area where notions of verbal nicety had been lifted. Call me a fool. It made me realise just how much I still had to learn about the game.

But we got through it, brought the game to a satisfactory conclusion, and as we lay together afterwards I felt relaxed enough and comfortable enough to say the wrong thing again. I asked Alicia, not very romantically perhaps, 'Are the patients here allowed to have sex?'

I felt her body tense up and she said coldly, 'Why? Which one do you want to have sex with?'

'Nobody. That's not what I meant. I only want to have sex with you.'

'Not that hippie girl, Charity?'

I was still finding it hard to think of Charity as a hippie, but I certainly didn't want to have sex with her.

'Not Sita, maybe?' Alicia suggested.

'I'm not even sure I know which one Sita is.'

'The Indian woman who never speaks,' she snapped. 'Or is it Max, maybe? Perhaps your tastes run in that direction.'

'Don't be disgusting,' I said.

That was meant to be a joke, to lighten the mood a little, but it scarcely worked. I found it hard to believe that Alicia was genuinely angry with me. I knew better than to tell her I thought she was being ridiculous, but I really did find it incomprehensible, and I wondered whether it made Charles Manning's story more credible or less.

'What brought this on, anyway?' she demanded.

'Charles Manning said something about orgies, that's all,' I said.

'And that makes you envious, does it? You'd like to participate? You feel like you're missing out?'

'No, I don't feel like I'm missing anything.'

'Good. Because you're not. Believe me.'

It sounded knowing and portentous but I didn't know what she meant. I was also aware that she hadn't answered my original question about whether or not the patients were allowed to have sex. Alicia's technique of becoming angry in order to avoid answering questions was crude but highly effective. It made me increasingly reluctant to ask her anything at all.

Come the morning, as the previous week, she was not there. It was Saturday, and again I was woken unreasonably early by a knock at the door of the hut and I opened up to see the line of ten patients. The ceremonial handing over of the week's work took place, and there I was stuck with another thousand pages or so of typescript.

As before, I spent the weekend being driven to distraction by all this mass of bad, bad writing. There were more meaningless anagrams: I read about 'absinthe' in 'the basin', about a 'military terror' in the 'territorial army'. There was more childhood reminiscence, more quasi-religious rambling, another account of a different (but not really so very different) football match, more supposedly amazing facts: that the mosquito has forty-seven teeth, that 90 per cent of American teenagers suffer from acne, that on 4 July 1776 George III wrote in his diary, 'Nothing of importance happened today'.

There was some nonsense about the world being like a beehive, another 'confession'; this time the writer claiming to have suffocated his or her grandmother to end her sufferings from terminal cancer. There was a foul and violent account of life in a women's prison with male guards who used the inmates for various scatological and sexual ends before murdering them. Did I assume this was written by Anders? Well, yes, I did actually. And I assumed that an obsessive account of a woman shaving her legs, her armpits, her pubic area, her head, her forearms, her eyebrows, her toes, and so on, was written by Charity. I also thought it reasonably likely that the rather well-written, if pointless, retelling of Conrad's *Heart of Darkness* was written by Byron. Of course, I knew I might be wrong about all this.

These were certainly hasty and potentially misguided assumptions, but I didn't much care any more. I'd had enough.

I was a lot less thorough in my reading this time. What did it matter? What was I supposed to get out of this torrent? What was I supposed to read into it? I found myself looking out of the window. I found my mind wandering far and wide. I found myself thinking about Alicia, about my future, about the job I'd given up at the bookshop, about my parents, about nothing. There were times when I realised I'd been staring at a page for ten minutes or more, and taken in nothing whatsoever; and I didn't care. My mind had been made up for me. I was leaving.

On Sunday evening Kincaid came to the hut again to ask me how it was going, but not to listen to my reply, and to tell me something I entirely expected, that he wanted a report on his desk first thing Monday morning, and that I'd be 'confronting' the patients shortly thereafter. I told him this was no problem.

At nine next morning I was in Kincaid's office handing over my report. Once again it consisted of just one page. In fact it consisted of just one sentence, of just four words: 'These people are mad.'

Quite a lot of work had gone into that sentence. I had considered various synonyms and euphemisms. I'd toyed with adding adjectives or qualifiers. I'd contemplated using a well-chosen and tellingly placed obscenity, but in the end I'd decided the simplest solution was the best. Kincaid looked at the single sentence for rather longer than he'd looked at the full page of writing I'd presented him with the previous week. Then he said, 'I shall have to think about this.' That was fine by me since I didn't much care what he, or anybody else, thought.

I went to the lecture room where the circle of chairs was set out and all the patients were already in place. The porters had been posted by the door this time, no doubt in anticipation of renewed mayhem, and Alicia had installed herself at the back of the room. Was she there as my guardian angel, to stop me getting myself into further trouble, or was she a spy for Kincaid? Once again, I didn't care. I took my place on the single empty chair, balanced the heap of manuscripts on my lap and looked at the faces of the patients: violent, vacant, angry, hostile, as might be the case. I didn't know precisely what I was going to say, but I certainly knew the gist, and the moment I opened my mouth the words started pouring out, sounding remarkably articulate and considered.

'You know,' I said, slapping the bundle of manuscripts, 'this is a pile of crap. It's rubbish. It's pointless, worthless. It's a waste of your time to write it. It's a waste of my time to read it. I don't know why you're doing it. I don't know if you're doing it out of some deep psychological need, or just to piss me off, but if it's the latter then it really gets the job done. I'm totally pissed off with it.

'Which is not to say this writing isn't very revealing. I'm sure it is. But it doesn't reveal anything we don't know already. It tells me that you people are, how should I put this ... mad. It tells me you're insane, crazy, raving, demented, deranged, psychotic, bonkers, wacko, screwy, cracked, gaga, barking, doolally, tonto, meshuga, bananas, loco, mental. It tells me you're a bunch of lunatics, nutters, maniacs, fruitcakes. It tells me you've got a few screws loose, that you're off your heads, off your trolley, round the bend, round the twist, that you're not playing with a full deck, that you're one volume short of the complete works.

'And the truth is, if I have to sit in that hut week after week, day after day, reading what you've written, then I think there's every chance I'll finish up as mad as you lot, and that's a price I'm not prepared to pay. So what I'm going to do is take this bundle of verbal excretion back to my hut and I'm going to put it in the stove and burn it. And then I'm going home.'

And with that I left the lecture room, taking the typescripts with me, and I did indeed go to my hut. I didn't really intend to burn the patients' writing, and I wasn't sure why I'd said I would; for cheap dramatic effect, I suppose. But I was absolutely serious about going home, or at least going somewhere that was not here. I dropped the pages of writing on to the floor by the stove and that was that. I was done. I was ready to go. I had no bags to pack. I looked around the hut to see if there was anything worth stealing, as an act of petty revenge or as a souvenir. There was nothing I wanted. I left the hut and started to make my bid for the outside world, but as I slammed the door shut, Alicia came striding towards me.

'Is that what you call using psychology?' she asked, and she sounded a good deal less angry than I'd been expecting.

'I'm sorry about all this, Alicia,' I said. 'I'll explain everything to you some day, but right now I have to get out of here.'

'I don't think that's an option.'

I couldn't understand what she meant. Was she going to attempt to hold me to my contract or something ridiculous like that, perhaps threaten to have the porters lock me up again?

'They're still there,' she said. 'The patients are waiting for you. They won't leave the lecture theatre until you've been back and talked to them again.'

'I don't have anything else to say to them.'

'Come now, you're the wordsmith, as you've proved.'

'That doesn't mean I have anything to say.'

'You'll think of something,' she said, and she kissed me on the cheek, and placed her hand on my arm and pulled me back to the lecture room. I didn't know why she was doing it. I could see no point in it at all. As I walked into the lecture room again all ten patients were sitting there much as I'd left them, but the moment they saw me they broke out in noisy, enthusiastic, only somewhat insane, applause. I had absolutely no idea what they were applauding, and my confusion must have been obvious. Byron, who had apparently been made spokesman, stood up and shook me by the hand.

'That was very good,' he said. 'Thank you.'

'I don't know what you're thanking me for,' I said.

'For being honest, for one thing,' said Byron. 'A lesser man would have read all this crap we've produced and told us it was interesting or promising or even good. You told us it was crap. We liked that.'

'Did you?' I said.

'Oh yes, and in the same way, a lesser man might have said that our writings showed that we were a little confused, or a little disturbed or a little disorientated. You told us we were carpet-chewers. We liked that even more.'

'Why do you like to be called mad?' I asked.

'Because that's what we are, and that's why we're ready to make a deal.'

I glanced over at Alicia. Was Byron really in a position to make deals? Alicia's knowing nod and smile suggested that he probably wasn't, but that I should hear him out nevertheless.

'What sort of a deal?' I asked.

'Well, first of all, obviously, that you don't leave.'

'No,' Raymond chimed in, 'don't deplane at this time.'

'What's the rest of the deal?'

'We'd like you to help us get better,' said Byron.

'To improve our talents with due care,' added Charity.

'But we know things can't go on quite as they have been,' Byron said. 'For one thing, we don't want to be told what to write about. We don't want to be given titles. We want to be free to express ourselves in any way we see fit.'

'I thought you'd been pretty much doing that already,' I said.

'Oh no. We can express ourselves much more freely than we have been doing.'

This sounded like a very mixed blessing.

'And we still have to insist that we don't put our names on the work. Anonymity is very important to us.'

'You're saying you just want to be free to do whatever you like without any interference from me, and without even putting your name to what you've done?'

'That's it, Gregory,' Byron said.

The others made assenting noises, including a drunken belch of agreement from Max.

'Then I'm not sure why you need me at all.'

'Hey, Gregory,' said Cook, 'don't start feeling persecuted.'

'We find you inspiring to have around,' said Charles Manning.

'Like a muse,' said Byron.

'Or a mascot,' said Maureen.

I didn't want to fall for any of this. 'And what do I get out of this deal?' I asked.

'Well, I don't pull your fucking head off, for one thing,' said Anders, but he said it rather amiably.

'The deal,' said Byron, 'is that we're nice to you.'

Nice is such an odd word, a word it's hard to take very seriously, one that's lost most of its colour, if not its meaning; and yet it's a word everybody uses. Oh sure, novelists, journalists, broadcasters, people who are supposed to care about words, they don't use it, but the rest of the world uses it all the time. We use it about people, 'He's such a nice guy'; about objects, 'Nice shirt, Mike'; after sex, 'Mmm, that was nice'. And so on. It's a blunt word, imprecise, blurred; but that's part of its virtue and we all know what it means. The idea of people being 'nice' to me was very appealing indeed at that moment.

'Give me five minutes to think about it,' I said, and I went away and thought for considerably less than five minutes. It felt good to be wanted. The fact that the people doing the wanting were inmates of an asylum didn't make much difference. I didn't entirely take their reasons for wanting me to stay at their face value. I didn't really believe they wanted me as a muse or a mascot. On the other hand, not being much of a conspiracy theorist, I wasn't of a mind to see anything very sinister in it either.

I stayed. You know I stayed. If I'd left we'd be at the end of the book already, and you can see we're nowhere near. I went back to the lecture room and told them they had a deal. Alicia smiled at me. I liked to think she looked more pleased than anyone.

'There's just one small condition,' I said. 'You have to let me out of the clinic for the rest of the day.'

14

They didn't like it, none of them, not the patients, nor Alicia, nor Kincaid; but what could they do? They either let me go for the day or they let me go for ever. With rather more ceremony and solemnity than I thought appropriate, Kincaid used his electronic key to let me out of the clinic. The tall metal gate slid back, I stepped outside and the gate shut behind me. I was out and, in some senses of the word, free, but that included the freedom to return, which I intended to do once I'd completed a bit of business in town.

The clinic was six or seven miles outside Brighton, so walking there was out of the question, and if a bus ran along the road there was no sign of a stop. So I hitchhiked, and it was much easier than I'd have imagined. Frankly I wouldn't have stopped for me. What kind of person picks up someone hitching outside a lunatic asylum? Answer: a good-natured old chain-smoking plumber in a big white van with a heap of pipes, cisterns and boilers crashing around in the back. He asked no questions, made no conversation and dropped me off in the centre of town.

I didn't get down to business right away. I wandered around doing the sort of things you do in Brighton. I walked along the sea front, went through the Lanes, looking in the windows of antique shops. I went on the pier and, with what little money I had, I bought fish and chips, then washed the grease away with a pint of bitter in a dark pub that had a rattlingly loud jukebox. Someone kept playing 'I'm Not In Love' over and over again, a song that had already started to sound dated, but I found it reassuring. I always hate it when you see a movie or read a book and it's trying too hard to give a period feel so that everything is absolutely from that time: all the cars, the clothes, the music, the houses, the furniture are precisely, quintessentially 'seventies'. It's never like that. In the 1970s a lot of people were still driving sixties cars, sitting on fifties furniture, living in forties houses. Clothes and music are obviously more temporary and contemporary, but not everybody consulted *Vogue* or *Melody Maker* and instantly adopted that week's trends. Styles seep in and they don't erase everything that went before; they're more a sort of semi-transparent veneer, an overlay that only gradually makes the past invisible.

I enjoyed my day in Brighton, but I wasn't sure I was enjoying it quite as much as I ought to be, and I had the sense that I was forcing myself to have a good time, so I decided I'd better do what I'd come for. I went to Ruth Harris's bookshop. It was harder to find than I'd have imagined but I located it eventually and fought my way inside. It was every bit as full of books and as empty of people as when I'd been there for the reading. Ruth Harris greeted me with surprising warmth. I wasn't certain she'd even remember me, but she did, and fortunately she seemed to have forgotten, or at least remodelled, important elements of the night of my literary début, and I felt that was going to be to my advantage.

'It was rather a good night, as I recall,' she said. 'The crowd was small but very enthusiastic, very knowledgeable.'

She made a pot of tea and we talked and I turned on the charm. I explained why I was back in Brighton, that I was living there after a fashion, told her in vague terms about what I was doing at the Kincaid Clinic, and even though I could see she found the idea of a writer-in-residence at an asylum faintly ridiculous, she was still impressed. Possibly she liked the idea that I wasn't some self-indulgent scribe who worked solely to satisfy my own ego. I was out there doing good, helping those less fortunate. Again I was encouraged.

I asked her if she'd read any good books lately, but she said she never found time to do any reading these days, being far too busy running the business. So I asked how business was, and she said it was fine, but I could tell she didn't mean it and I didn't think she really expected me to believe it either. A glance at the place confirmed that business wasn't fine at all.

I told her I'd once been a bookseller myself, although knowing her stated aversion to literary first editions I didn't say exactly what kind of bookselling I'd done. The fact that I'd worked in London impressed her, and I looked around the shop as though giving it some serious professional scrutiny, which in a sense I was. Obviously nobody likes someone telling them how to run their business so I used my softest manner and said, 'You know, in a way I think this shop may be too good.'

'Oh yes?' she said, not quite as easily flattered as I'd hoped.

'Yes,' I said. 'You've got some very good stock here, quality in depth, but I wonder if possibly there are just too many good things.'

'Can you have too much of a good thing? she asked.

'You know, Ruth, I think you can. Sometimes a bookshop can be so full of good things that you can't see the wood for the wood pulp.'

I might also have said that in certain other cases a bookshop could be so full of crud that a person couldn't even get in the door, or walk round the shop, or turn a corner without demolishing a pile of books, but I was being kind.

'So what do you think I should do?' she asked. 'Burn some of the stock?'

I laughed falsely and said, 'No, no, but there are other possibilities.'

'Such as?'

I took a deep breath, hoped my charm was working at maximum throttle, and told her there was a library up at the clinic that was desperately in need of books. I said it would be an act of great charity to help the clinic, but that charity could work two ways, and once her stock had been streamlined, once people could actually see what she had for sale, business was sure to improve. I also said she'd have my undying gratitude, though I wasn't entirely sure I wanted her to have that.

'Well,' she said, 'you may have a point about some of the stock not being as accessible as it might be.'

'And this need only be a loan,' I said. 'Once you've sold some of your remaining stock and you've got more room in the shop you could have the books back.'

I had a feeling this could be years away. I knew I was asking a lot, but I thought what I was saying was actually true. Ruth Harris would have nothing to lose under this arrangement. And it wasn't as though I was demanding any of her premium stock – in fact, I wasn't sure she had any premium stock.

She scrutinised me carefully. It seemed she wasn't altogether unwilling to do me a favour but she was weighing up what she might be able to ask in return.

'Oh, all right,' she said. 'If you're willing to spend the afternoon in the shop sorting through the stock, then I suppose that would be all right. You're a very persuasive young man.'

'And then I'll need you to take me and the books back to the clinic,' I said.

'You do drive a hard bargain, dear boy.'

I don't think I'd ever heard anyone outside of a Noël Coward play use the term 'dear boy'. I was amused to be thought of as dear and as a boy, though I didn't want Ruth Harris to find me too dear or too boyish. No doubt I was exploiting her, but it was a gentle form of exploitation and it was in a good cause, and when she patted me on the bottom at various times in the course of the afternoon I didn't feel I could complain.

By the end of the day we had a Volvo-load of grubby, unloved books packed into boxes and ready to be taken to the clinic. The load wouldn't by any means be enough to fill all the library shelves, and it was scarcely enough to have made much of a dent in the chaos of Ruth Harris's shop, but it was a start.

In a perfect world I'd have returned triumphantly to the clinic with a fine selection of classics ancient and modern, a range of reference books, encyclopaedias, atlases, dictionaries, books of poetry, a smattering of history and philosophy, a cookery book or two for Cook; and then a few potboilers and ripping yarns for the long evenings.

As it was I found myself to be the purveyor of a heap of drek that was heavy on dated showbiz biographies, cowboy novels, bodice-rippers, car manuals and chemistry textbooks. Ruth Harris offered to throw in a copy of *The Wax Man*, since the pile left after the reading hadn't reduced at all, but I declined. No point asking for trouble. She drove me back to the clinic, and I was aware of her becoming increasingly uncomfortable as we got near. She may have been vulnerable to my charm but she still found the Kincaid Clinic a bit creepy.

'You should be careful they don't lock you in there and throw away the key,' she said and gave a theatrical shudder.

'They don't like me *that* much,' I said.

Alicia was waiting at the gate when I returned. I was surprised, and was wise enough not to think it was because she'd missed me. She used her electronic key to open up, and we drove inside. Ruth Harris looked daggers at Alicia, then got out of the car, sprinted round to the tailgate and began energetically unloading the boxes. Her enthusiasm was surprising, but then I saw her real enthusiasm was to be gone. The moment the boxes were out of the car, she planted a conspicuous wet kiss on me and she was back behind the wheel ready to go. I didn't mind that in itself, since I'd spent more than enough time in her company, but I hoped I wasn't going to have to tote the books up to the library all by myself. If the patients were going to be nice to me, here was a great way to start. Alicia brandished her electronic key, the gate opened, the Volvo accelerated away, and the gate slid shut again. I was back. The *status quo* had returned, almost.

'What have you done?' Alicia asked.

'Got some books for the library.'

'What kind of books?'

'All kinds,' I said.

She peeled back the flaps on the nearest box and looked inside. 'Oh my God,' she said, before running off in a panic I couldn't possibly comprehend. I didn't understand it any better when she returned with Kincaid. He looked at me with exasperation and pity.

'The first thing I want to say, Gregory, is that I'm not angry with you. If anything, I'm angry with myself. Before we go any further I need to look at these books you've got. You'll be kind enough to bring them to my office.'

He swept off and I was left with Alicia. I'd made *her* angry again and I had no idea how.

'I didn't think there was much point having a library without any books,' I said, trying to justify what seemed to me to need no justification.

'You have so much to learn, Gregory,' she said, and she followed Kincaid.

Unaided, I carried the first two boxes up to Kincaid's office and set them down in front of him and Alicia. They didn't accept them with any noticeable grace, and from Alicia's expression you might have thought I was carrying in boxes of raw sewage.

'Is it because Dr Kincaid is black?' Alicia said.

'What?'

'You perhaps feel resentful that a member of a dark race has dominion over you.'

I was not stupid enough then, and I'm certainly not stupid enough now, to believe that I'm entirely free from prejudice, racial or otherwise, but as far as I could see, such problems as I'd had with Kincaid weren't about race. Also, in the current situation, it seemed he was having more of a problem with me than I was having with him.

I said, 'I don't think so.'

'So,' Alicia replied thoughtfully, 'is it simply the fact that he's an authority figure?'

Yes, I did have the odd problem with authority, but who doesn't? The best reply I could come up with was, 'I don't think filling the library with books makes me that much of a rebel.'

Kincaid and Alicia conceded that as a hypothetical argument this had merit, but they continued to behave as though I'd done something terrible. Kincaid started pulling books out of the boxes and sent me to fetch a second load. By the time I got back, the contents of the first two boxes were spread across the floor and Kincaid and Alicia were picking up books at random and scrutinising them.

'Is this a good book?' Alicia asked.

She held up a book called *Lone Riders of the High Mesas*. Its cover showed snaggly cowboys, anthropomorphic cacti, a yolky yellow sunset.

'I've never read it,' I said.

'Even so.'

'You can't judge a book by looking at its cover,' I said. 'And beggars can't be choosers.'

These old clichés made me feel comfortably reassured, and only offended Alicia mildly.

'To be fair to you, Gregory,' Kincaid said, 'there is a psychological concept, rather outmoded these days, called bibliotherapy.'

'Yes?'

'Using texts as a therapeutic tool,' said Kincaid.

'But surely, Dr Kincaid,' Alicia butted in, 'those texts must be very carefully selected by the therapist for each specific patient. We can't simply take pot luck.'

'You mean patients can't just read whatever they want?' I said.

'Of course not,' Alicia insisted. 'They might want something that would exacerbate their condition. Supposing you were a belonephobic and you read the *Naked Lunch*?'

'Belonephobic?'

'Fear of needles,' she explained.

'Well, if I was a belonephobic I suspect I'd give *Naked Lunch* a fairly wide berth,' I said.

'But you wouldn't know what it was about until you'd started reading, would you?'

'Maybe not, but the moment I started I'd know and then I'd stop. That's the great thing about books. If you don't like what you're reading you don't have to carry on. It's not like being strapped into your seat in front of a film with your eyes and ears pinned open. You just close the book and it stops.'

Kincaid didn't want this debate going on in his office and he waved me away to fetch a third load of books. When I got back this time I thought he must have gone mad. He appeared to be systematically mutilating the books, tearing off covers, ripping out pages, while Alicia looked on admiringly.

'What's going on?' I asked.

'Dr Kincaid is making sure the books are fit for consumption by the patients.'

'Censoring them?'

'Oh come on, Gregory, don't be pathetic,' Alicia sneered.

'Then what?'

Kincaid broke off from his page tearing. He looked irritated.

'I suppose it's time,' he said.

'Yes,' Alicia sighed, 'I suppose it is.'

'All right, Gregory,' said Kincaid. 'Apparently this is the moment when I need to explain the basis of Kincaidian Therapy to you.'

From looking irritated Kincaid became suave, perfectly at ease, the public man. He knew exactly what he was going to say to me. Perhaps he'd said it many times before, to individuals and groups far more knowledgeable or sceptical or hostile than me. And Alicia, who must surely have heard it many times before too, gave the impression that she never tired of listening to these wise words.

'I shall be speaking in layman's terms for your benefit,' Kincaid said.

I took note of the insult, but what was I going to say, 'No, no, please talk in medical jargon that I don't understand'?

'Let me ask you, Gregory,' he started, 'what do you see when you look out of the window?' He held up his hand to make sure I didn't answer. 'It's a question you might answer in any number of ways.

You might say you see the grounds, the tennis court, the writer's hut. You may see one or two of the patients, or a member of staff. Perhaps you see trees and sky. Perhaps you see sunshine or clouds. It probably all looks very familiar to you by now. Perhaps you see nothing remarkable. You might look out and say you see nothing at all.'

I wouldn't have said that, but I didn't contradict him.

'But what happened when you went into town today? You saw things of a different order. You saw advertising hoardings, cinema posters. You may have looked in a shop window and seen television sets. You might well have seen a newspaper or magazine. You might have seen some boy wearing a T-shirt with the image of a pop star on it. You obviously went into a bookshop and saw any number of jacket designs, illustrations, author photographs. The number of images you saw in the outside world was infinitely greater than the number of images you could see in the clinic.'

'I think I get the point,' I said.

'I wonder if you do. Let me put it another way: how many madmen have you seen in your life? And how many madmen have you seen on television or in films? How did you know they were mad? Could you tell simply by looking? Did they have wild hair and rolling eyes? What were the signs? Did they dress like Napoleon? How do you know what Napoleon looked like? Have you ever seen Napoleon in the flesh or have you only ever seen pictures?' He stared at me, demanding an answer. 'Well, have you?'

'No, of course I've never seen Napoleon in the flesh.'

'But if you'd come in here wearing the hat, your hand tucked into your tunic, we'd all have known you were dressed as Napoleon and we'd all have known you were mad. We would have read the signs, the semiotic, if you will. Am I making myself clear?'

'Well, up to a point,' I said.

'Look, Gregory, I have no desire to be biblical, but the truth is we're talking about images here, graven images. Not false images of God, but false images of the world. The human environment is awash with created images, and they get in the way. They cause confusion. People are bombarded with pictures, photographs, illustrations, cartoons, comics, films, television. And in some cases, in all too many cases, this bombardment is literally driving people insane.'

He smiled with grim satisfaction.

'It wasn't always like this,' he continued. 'Once you saw what you saw. You saw what was there. There was the thing or there was nothing. The world was the world. It was itself, not an image of itself, not a cheap copy. And quite simply things were better then. People were healthier, happier, saner. And why? To put it crudely perhaps, because what goes in must come out, you only get back what you put in. Looking at my patients I see that their output is scrambled. But why wouldn't it be when their input is similarly scrambled?

'Our mission at the Kincaid Clinic is simple yet not at all easy. What we have to do is control the input, stop the flow of images. Turn off the tap. Let the dog see the rabbit. The real rabbit, not a picture of the rabbit. Am I making myself clear?'

'I think so,' I said.

'What we have here are ten patients displaying divergent forms of madness. What they have in common is that they've all seen too many images. As a first principle, therefore, we protect them from these sources of madness.

'We're not against visual stimulation *per se*, you understand. We don't object to our patients looking at the view from a window, but we don't let them look at paintings or photographs of views from windows. It's fine for our patients to look at flowers, but not at still lifes of flowers.'

'Or at the labels on tin cans,' I said, as a little something fell into place.

'Quite. So we create an environment that is free from images. No television, no films, no picture books, no glossy magazines, no flowery shirts or wallpaper, and so on.'

'And newspapers with all the photographs cut out.'

'You're very observant. I suppose that goes with being a writer. Now, I have been accused of philistinism,' Kincaid said. 'But that won't stick. We aren't against the visual arts, just against the *representational* visual arts. Anything Islamic is no problem whatsoever. Jackson Pollock, absolutely fine. Rothko perhaps. Hockney definitely not. Colour Field certainly, portraiture most certainly not; the Cubists I'm not so sure about, but I think it's better safe than sorry. And frankly, what's a little philistinism in the cause of such a great good? And, in any case, this is where you come in.'

'Yes?'

'Yes. It seems to me that the dilemma I've outlined here is at the heart of *The Wax Man*. No?'

I grunted non-committally, allowing that this might be one possible interpretation.

'You see, the most obvious objection to Kincaidian Therapy is that it is simply protectionist. It keeps the patients away from images and this brings about a great improvement. But when they return to the outside world they're back where they started. We have to do something to make them less vulnerable to images, to give them a way of protecting themselves. We need to use language to do this: language, the last great bulkhead against this anarchy of images. We stop the input of images, we substitute an input of language. Then we reverse the poles; we get the patients to create a bulkhead of their own, through their own writing. Yes?'

'A bulkhead,' I said.

'I knew you would understand.'

Did I understand? I wasn't sure if I did or not. I was well aware of my ignorance in matters psychological, and yet this description of Kincaidian Therapy sounded like pretty thin stuff to me. I didn't say that, naturally. And I didn't argue. I wouldn't have known how.

'I know what you're thinking,' Kincaid said. 'You're thinking it all sounds too good to be true. Trust us, Gregory, before long you'll come to see that's the whole point.'

'Yes, you will,' Alicia agreed.

'Good,' I said.

'Yes, very good, Gregory,' Kincaid added. 'I knew the concepts of Kincaidian Therapy wouldn't be beyond your grasp.'

Was he mocking me? I couldn't tell any more. Like any good liberal I was uncomfortable with the deluge of pap that issued from what we then called the mass media. A few of us had read Marshall McLuhan, and tried on the notion that the medium was the message and that our society was about to be retribalised, but to the limited extent that we understood what he was on about, I don't think many of us really took him very seriously. Even if we loved certain types of rock music and movies and television, most of us still thought the world was getting crasser and more absurd by the minute, and that the mass media, image-laden as it was, had a lot to answer for.

So yes, it did sound as though Kincaid might be on to something. Sort of. The diagnosis didn't sound unreasonable. On the other hand,

Kincaidian Therapy sounded suspiciously like rather a grand name for what amounted to no more than staying indoors and turning off the TV set. And, apparently, for tearing the jackets off books, and ripping out all the illustrations.

As for whether a few creative-writing exercises from me were going to be enough to enable the patients to protect themselves in the wicked, illustrated world beyond the clinic, I had my doubts. A part of me was extremely relieved that Kincaidian Therapy didn't involve anything more sinister, that it didn't involve orgies, for instance, but I did wonder if I'd been told the full story, and I certainly still wondered what the patients got up to in Kincaid's office when the blinds were down, and in Alicia's too, for that matter.

'You'll need time to digest all I've told you,' Kincaid said. 'You'll want to repack the books I've already dealt with and transfer them to the library while I continue with the rest.'

I wasn't sure I wanted to do that at all, but I did it. The work was hard and tedious but I was happy to get out of Kincaid's office and out of his presence. What Kincaid had just told me was surprising and yet somehow terribly obvious. Perhaps I should have worked it out for myself. Why hadn't I noticed the complete absence of images in the clinic? I felt the way I did when I was first told about sex: it was strange and improbable and yet it seemed to explain everything. But then, as you thought about it some more, it became stranger and more improbable than ever and it raised at least as many questions as it answered.

One of the most obvious questions that came to mind, regarding Kincaidian Therapy rather than sex, was whether or not the ten inmates of the clinic had seen more images than anybody else. If the whole world was being driven mad by too many images, then why were these ten *particularly* mad? Why wasn't all the world universally and equally mad? Surely madness had more diverse and complicated causes than this. And if a single diagnosis seemed suspect, how much more suspect was a single form of treatment? But then again, what did I know?

It was late in the evening before Kincaid had mutilated the last of the books and later still before I'd transported them all to the library. I got them out of the boxes and put them on the shelves in no particular order. I'd sort and alphabetise them the next day, maybe even get a patient or two to help me. I wondered if one of them would want to take on the role of librarian. I was knackered by the time I'd finished, but I sat down at the library table, looked up at the filled shelves and I felt a certain amount of pride. I'd done a good job. Obviously the books were a strange collection, made stranger by having pages torn out and covers removed, but they were much, much better than nothing.

I was about to go to my hut and turn in for the night when I looked out of the library window and saw something going on in the garden. It was Kincaid. He had built a little bonfire out of the pages and jackets that he'd torn from the books, and he was standing in front of a small, flapping pyramid of flames. He looked massive and sinisterly majestic. He was agitated yet gleeful, moving from foot to foot, as if he was about to start dancing round the fire. I looked at him and for a moment I thought he might be quite insane. And then I dismissed the thought, telling myself I'd seen far too many bad movies.

15

I woke up next morning feeling good, and not without reason, I thought. Life seemed all right. I'd decided to stay at the clinic. I'd struck a deal with the patients, or at least they'd struck a deal with me, and I'd been told what Kincaidian Therapy was.

These were all reasons for feeling good, yet I think the main reason was that I had something to do. Today I would organise the library. Perhaps it was pretty dull of me to find that a source of pleasure, but compared to the inaction of most of the last two weeks it felt like a hell of a lark. And it was a means to a very desirable end. Once I'd sorted the books I'd be able to read some of them. Even in that swamp of fourth-rate and mutilated volumes I would surely find something that could distract and entertain an obsessive reader like me, and this would make my life better still.

I spent most of the day classifying and alphabetising the books. I enjoyed the sheer laboriousness of the job and let it take longer than it need have done. I didn't ask anyone to help me, and nobody volunteered, but when the task was virtually finished Byron and Anders arrived in the library. The occasion had elements both of a university tutorial and of a visit from a Mafia boss. The two dons. They looked around the library, seemed unsurprised and unimpressed by what I'd done, and then Byron languidly demanded of me, 'Who's your favourite author?'

It was an unexpected question but I answered it truthfully and said, 'Shakespeare.'

Anders gave a thick, sinusy snort, indicating a free-floating contempt that I didn't think had much to do with my actual answer. Perhaps he might have been less contemptuous if I'd said Harold Robbins or Jackie Collins, but I doubted it. Byron was more accepting.

'Not a bad answer,' he said. 'Obvious but not bad. Least favourite?'

'Harold Robbins?' I offered. 'Jackie Collins?'

Anders snorted again, but this time it contained no hint of literary criticism. It was just a snort.

'Anders isn't much of a reader,' Byron said. 'But he's quite a writer.'

'Aren't you all?' I said.

'Some more than others, but I know what you mean,' Byron agreed. 'So Kincaid's told you all about his therapy.' I wondered how he knew that. 'What do you think of it?'

I'd been happy not to think about it at all while I was arranging the books. It was too difficult and begged too many questions. I may have been a good reader but I was a very average thinker. So I didn't know what to reply to Byron and, in any case, I wasn't sure if it was absolutely ethical or sensible to discuss these things with the patients, so I said, 'I think it's very interesting.'

I was not surprised by Anders' snort.

'You've read I. A. Richards' *Practical Criticism*?' Byron enquired.

'Well, I've looked at it,' I said.

Practical Criticism is one of those books you can easily feel you've read even if you haven't. Back in the 1930s Richards presented his Cambridge students with plain texts of certain poems. He didn't reveal the titles or authors and he didn't provide any critical or historical information, simply asked the students to read the poems and write down their responses. It sounds pretty old hat today, but I gather it was quite revolutionary at the time. The poems, along with extracts from what the students wrote, as well as Richards' responses to both, make up the book. The poems' titles and authors are revealed on the last page, printed in reverse, like mirror-writing.

What the project seems to have proved is that it's possible to think almost anything at all about any given piece of writing. People think great poems are rotten, that rotten ones are great. Different people will find the same poem utterly lucid or utterly impenetrable. They'll disagree about whether a thing is original or hackneyed, whether it's boringly Christian or paganly immoral; and so on.

I had indeed read the book at college but I probably hadn't read every word, and I was sure I'd forgotten much of it. I suspected Byron was just the sort of smart alec who'd pick up on the gaps in my knowledge and memory, and argue with me. That's why I only admitted to having 'looked' at it; that gave lots of room for denial and backing down. I didn't want a literary wrangle with Byron at that moment. I also hadn't the slightest idea what this had to do with Kincaidian Therapy.

'Richards talks about visualisation,' Byron said. 'Some people, he reports, read a piece of writing and "see" in their mind's eye a series of precise and vivid visual images. They see Wordsworth's daffodils, they see the albatross around the neck of the ancient mariner, they see the stately pleasure dome and so on. They'll tell you they enjoy writing for its ability to call up these images. They make that a touchstone of what good writing is.'

I did more or less remember this and I nodded as sagely as I could manage.

'But,' said Byron, 'Richards argues that these images needn't necessarily have anything to do with the poem itself. They may have far more to do with the individual psychology of the particular reader. Readers may "see" the images of daffodils or albatrosses or pleasure domes that they already carry in their own heads. The writing calls up the pre-existing image, like pulling a file out of some mental filing cabinet. The actual piece of writing may be irrelevant. These kind of readers see what they want to see.

'And I'm only mentioning it because it seems to me this could play havoc with Kincaid's theory, don't you think? There he is trying to protect us from images, yet the process of reading and writing may be a means of *creating* images.'

This was an objection I hadn't got around to considering, though I liked to think that given enough time I probably would have.

'But simultaneously,' Byron continued, 'Richards tells us that when certain other people read they don't summon up visual images at all. For them the word cow doesn't call up an image of a specific, individualised cow, it merely creates in them certain feelings, notions and attitudes that the actual perception of an actual cow would produce. I'm paraphrasing here, naturally.'

'Naturally,' I agreed.

I was aware of Anders stalking up and down behind me, paying no attention to Byron, but browsing through the books I'd just arranged on the library shelves, pulling them out, riffling through them, slamming them back in what I thought was likely to be the wrong place.

Byron continued, 'Richards says that whereas a visual image is a copy of a thing, that is a representation of a single cow, a word can simultaneously and equally represent many vastly different cows. So it's just possible, isn't it, that what Kincaid might be doing in his therapy is trying to move us away from the single, individualised representation inherent in created visual images towards the more universal truth contained in words.'

Well yes, just possibly he was, but if so then why hadn't he said so? Why was it up to a Byron to make the case that Kincaid's theory had some sort of intellectual rigour to it? And actually I wasn't sure that Byron was right. I wasn't sure that's what Kincaid was doing at all. I suspected Byron was giving Kincaid credit for being a good deal cleverer than he was. Byron looked at me quizzically, the way my tutors often had at university, trying to elicit some sort of informed response from me, a response that hadn't always been forthcoming.

'Does that sound reasonable?' Byron asked.

'Yes, it sounds reasonable but—'

'And did he mention Rothko?'

'Yes, he did.'

'But I'll bet he didn't say that Rothko's paintings have been described as television for Zen Buddhists, did he?'

'No, no, he didn't.'

Anders stopped his browsing, riffling and slamming and plumped his wide buttocks down next to me on the library table.

'Why don't you admit it?' Anders said. 'You think Kincaid's a cunt who doesn't know what he's doing.'

'No, I—'

'You see now, that's a very interesting example of what I think Richards had in mind,' Byron said. 'When Anders used the word cunt you probably didn't actually summon up a mental picture of a particular set of female genitals, did you?'

I wasn't sure if this was a very interesting example or not, and I certainly doubted that it was what Richards had had in mind. True, I hadn't visualised a single set of female genitals but neither had the word summoned up the feelings, notions and attitudes that the actual perception of an actual set of female genitals would have produced. I suspected we were dealing with some other issue here, but I felt unable to see which. I considered saying something about Plato and tables and shadows on the walls of caves, but decided against it.

'I suppose the only real question is whether or not Kincaidian Therapy actually works,' I said.

Anders snorted again, before saying, 'Yeah, just look around you. Every fucker here's so happy and healthy, aren't they?'

Well no, they weren't happy and healthy, but why would they be? They were in the clinic, in the middle of their treatment. If the therapy had completely done its work they wouldn't have been there at all, would they? They'd have been released. I was in no position to say whether or not the therapy was working. I hadn't been there long enough. I hadn't seen how bad the patients were before the treatment started.

'Anders is a bit miffed because he's missing his favourite television programme,' Byron explained.

'Yeah, I'd kill to see an episode of *Bless This House*,' said Anders. I smiled nervously.

'Could I ask you both a personal question?' I said.

'You could try,' said Byron.

'Why are you here?'

'Nothing like starting with the big ones, is there?' Byron said.

'I meant why are you here at the Kincaid Clinic.'

'We know what you meant,' said Anders.

Byron and Anders looked at each other deferentially, each happy to let the other have the floor, but Byron's deference was more formidable, so Anders said, 'See, I'm a crook. Right. A hard man. You can tell that, obviously, just by looking at me. Got into a bit of bother with the Old Bill and also with some geezers down Peckham way. I had to scarper. Sharpish. I convinced the doc that I was having trouble with my nerves, and here I am. I reckoned this was the safest place to lie low till it's all over with.'

This sounded plausible enough, and yet the way Anders told it, it didn't sound remotely convincing. He must have sensed my scepticism.

'All right,' he said, 'I'll give you the other version. You know in *Zen and the Art of Motorcycle Maintenance* where that cunt Pirsig looks in the mirror and he can't work out why it is that his image is reversed left to right but not top to bottom, and it's such a big fucking philosophical wobbler that he goes crackers over it? Well, a very similar thing happened to me.

'I'm in this after-hours dive in Stepney and this cunt comes up to me and says, "What can go up a chimney down but can't go down a chimney up?" Then he pisses off and leaves me to think about it. So I think about it for hours, days, weeks. I go right up the pictures. I wander the streets, thinking about it, doing my head in. When they eventually find me, I'm a crazy man, my clothes are in rags, filthy, soaked in my own urine, and I'm beating my head against a wall. Literally. So they reckoned the Kincaid Clinic's just the gaff for me.'

'The answer's an umbrella, incidentally,' Byron said. 'We wouldn't want you going the same way.'

This sounded infinitely less convincing than the lying-low story. In fact, I assumed Anders was probably joking, or at least mocking me and my desire to know anything about him. I was tempted to laugh, but I imagined that laughing at Anders was a risky business.

'Right,' I said seriously, but I must still have sounded unconvinced.

'Something the matter with that?' Anders exploded. 'Isn't that good enough for you, you cunt?'

'Yes, sure,' I said, 'It's fine—'

'You think there are some good reasons for being mad, and some bad reasons? You think my reasons aren't up to snuff? That it?'

'No, no, I'm not saying that.'

'I should fuckin' hope not.'

Anders prised himself off the table and turned his back to me. I couldn't believe he was really as angry or as offended as he sounded. I thought he was just doing it for effect. But it was quite a useful effect.

'And how about you, Byron?' I asked warily.

Byron ran a long, fine-boned hand through his hair and said, 'I have absolutely no idea why I'm here.'

It was a bafflingly opaque answer, but not a bad one, and certainly a satisfyingly final one. I didn't ask any more questions. The three of us stood there for some time in a little lacuna of silence, as though we were three actors in a play who'd delivered all our lines perfectly but were now waiting for some cue, some off-stage sound-effect or fanfare of incidental music that the technical crew were unable to provide. Finally Byron said, 'As a matter of fact my favourite author is Shakespeare too.'

'Same for me,' said Anders, though I assumed he didn't mean it.

For a moment, just a moment, I pictured, nay visualised, William Shakespeare. We all know what Shakespeare looks like: the bald head, the goatee, the ruff, perhaps an ear-ring. I was summoning up a kind of generalised schoolbook portrait, and I wasn't sure how historically accurate it was, but that was certainly my idea of Shakespeare. Was this merely pulling a file out of some mental filing cabinet, or was the word creating for me many vastly different Shakespeares?

And what if Byron and Anders had claimed Pushkin or Thomas Mann as their favourite authors? Images of Pushkin and Mann obviously existed, but as far as I was aware I'd never seen any of them. I had no idea what these authors looked like. Nor for that matter had I ever read a word by either of them. So what did their names conjure up? Were they just names? Just words? Words detached from visual images? Was this what Kincaid had in mind? I felt very weary.

'Have you got anything here by Shakespeare?' Byron asked, waving at the library shelves.

'Afraid not.'

Byron and Anders grunted in unison.

'But there's plenty of other good stuff,' I said. 'Help yourself.'

I don't think they believed me, and they left the library empty-handed.

16

And so began the easiest, most stable and probably the most enjoyable phase of my time at the Kincaid Clinic. I felt, however naively, however unjustifiably, that things were going to be all right, at least for a while. I still had no doubt that sooner or later someone would realise I wasn't Gregory Collins, that I might even feel the need to confess all even sooner, but that would be all right too. What would be would be. In the meantime I would survive. I would work. I'd do my best for the patients, whatever that might involve. I would read what they wrote. But first, of course, they had to write it and give it to me. Until then I could sit in my hut with a more or less clear conscience and read something from the library. This felt like a great step forward.

I began by reading *Lone Riders of the High Mesas*, determined to find in it some of the literary merit that its now missing cover had suggested to Alicia it didn't possess. It was probably the first cowboy novel I'd tackled since I was a kid, and maybe it was my mood, or simply because I was so starved of reading material, but I actually thought it was fairly entertaining. I decided I'd recommend it to the patients, maybe get them to write a cowboy story of their own. Why not? It would be a welcome change from their own obsessions. Then I remembered that they were now free to write whatever they chose, whatever that meant.

After *Lone Riders* I planned to read a couple of detective novels, a travelogue about the Sudan, and a love story with a motor-racing background set in and around Brooklands in the 1920s. None of these looked as though it was going to be a great book, and not all of them promised even to be good reads, but I was looking forward to them a lot. They would help to pass the time, keep my mind ticking over, involve me in acts of the imagination, however humble.

But in the event, I still didn't feel able to sit in the hut all day, every day, reading and indulging myself. I had to try to be useful. I wanted to make myself available to the patients, to get to know them better and allow them to get to know me. Some patients were more forthcoming than others. Charity, Raymond, Charles Manning, Byron and Anders, had revealed themselves one way or another, though to what extent I was seeing their true selves was debatable.

Next I got to know Maureen a little. On the surface she was one of the clinic's less intriguing specimens, and I was perhaps a little ashamed of the way I judged her as boring and not worthy of attention. She was just a fat woman in football kit. How interesting could that be? And when I discovered that she was also the woman who did such gardening as got done around the grounds, that didn't make her seem much more appealing. In those days, gardening struck me as a woefully middle-aged, tedious activity, the kind of hobby your mother had. Yet, in a curious way, Maureen's very lack of appeal, and my initial inclination to dismiss her made me that much more determined to befriend her.

I came across her working at a flowerbed with a rake in her hand, although she used the rake clumsily and looked very unsure of herself. On seeing me she became desperately self-conscious and hugged the rake to her stomach as though she thought I'd come to take it from her and tell her she was doing it all wrong. I smiled mildly and tried to appear benevolent.

'Hi,' I said. 'How's it going?'

It was a simple, polite question that required a simple polite answer. 'Fine' would have sufficed. But at the Kincaid Clinic we were not in the realm of the simple and polite, and so Maureen pivoted her head in slow confusion and replied, 'Very, very, very, very badly.'

I hoped it was the gardening that was going badly rather than her life or therapy, and strangely enough my hopes were fulfilled.

'I'm having a bit of trouble with seed,' Maureen said.

'Seed?' I enquired. I was treading carefully. Thoughts of orgies were not entirely absent from my mind.

'I've got these seeds, you see,' she replied, and she showed me three tiny foil envelopes. I was relieved. 'I know what seeds they are. This one's poppies, this one's hollyhocks, this one's heart's-ease. I know what they're called but I don't know what they look like.'

'Don't you have the seed packets?'

'Of course not,' she said, and I realised why not. Seed packets show pictures of the flowers that the seeds turn into. Kincaid was running a tight ship.

'Don't worry,' I said, trying to sound reassuring. 'They never come up looking the way they do on the packet.'

I spoke with moderate confidence about this, since it was something my mother often mentioned. She was always trying to grow things and being disappointed at the results, but Maureen was not reassured.

'But do you know what these flowers look like? Can you describe them for me?' she asked.

'I'll try,' I said. 'But you must know what poppies are like.'

Maureen shook her head.

'You know,' I said. 'Poppy day. Flanders Field. They're red and sort of flat and floppy. With a black centre. Big seed head. Opium. You must know.'

'Yes?' Maureen said, clearly meaning 'No'.

I realised that my verbal invocation of the natural world might be lacking, but I was doing my best, and I couldn't believe she didn't know what poppies looked like.

'Perhaps I used to know but now I've forgotten,' she said wistfully. 'I've forgotten so much. Are they tall?'

'Tallish,' I agreed, wanting to sound positive, 'but nowhere near as tall as hollyhocks. Those things can be as tall as a man.'

Maureen looked stunned by this idea, as though she were imagining some monstrous flora from outer space. I tried to say there was nothing outlandish or threatening about them, that hollyhocks were very English, very traditional, very friendly, but that only confused her further. She now looked at me as though I was speaking a foreign language.

'So what about heart's-ease?' she asked.

'Now there you have me,' I admitted. I had absolutely no idea what heart's-ease looked like. 'My mother would know. I'll ask her next time I speak to her.'

'Mothers,' Maureen said glumly and I knew better than to ask. But I didn't have to. 'I don't have a mother.'

'I'm sorry to hear that.'

'I used to have one but she died.'

'Sorry.'

'I killed her actually. It was an accident. I think it was. We argued. All the time. She said I was wasting my time hanging around football grounds. Not fit to be her daughter. Suddenly there was a knife in my hand. Then everything went red; like I was surrounded by Arsenal shirts or Manchester United or Barnsley. Then I came here. I think that's what happened. I can't remember. I'm sorry. I probably shouldn't have told you.'

'Probably you shouldn't,' I said, and she looked duly chastised.

I must say I didn't believe her. Why? I suppose because she sounded too glib about it, didn't provide enough detail, didn't bring enough emotional weight to her account. Besides, she just didn't look the type. I knew that was naive of me, but I also thought that a genuine mother-killer would surely be locked up somewhere a lot more secure than the Kincaid Clinic.

'Tell you what,' I said. 'I'll see if there are any gardening books in the library.'

I couldn't remember whether there were or not. If so, they had no doubt once contained illustrations. These would now be gone, and the likelihood of the books containing simple verbal descriptions of flowers seemed a slender one. Perhaps Maureen sensed this. She said, 'I suppose I could just sow the seeds and wait and see what happens.'

'That might work.'

'Then again it might not,' she said.

I agreed that was true too, and as I left her she was spading great lumps of earth in a furious, purposeful manner as though she might be digging a grave.

17

Not all my encounters with the patients were so informal. Sometimes I actually seemed to be involved in the work of the clinic. Kincaid had decided to show me just how effective Kincaidian Therapy was, and so I was sitting in his office looking at some genuine Rorschach ink blots. I'd never seen any before. They were on big white cards and they came in various rich, saturated colours. I'd always imagined that any old blots would do, but no. Apparently there are ten specially designed, standardised blots they show to all patients so that results can be equally standardised.

As I looked at the cards, I was trying very hard not to 'see' anything lurking in them, but that was next to impossible. I saw rabbits and insects and devils. I refused to wonder what this meant and I certainly wasn't going to tell Kincaid what I was seeing. Not that he would have been interested. I wasn't the subject of study here.

'I want you to listen to a recording,' he said, and he slipped a tape into a little cassette recorder.

I heard Kincaid's voice on the tape, thin and metallic now, stating a time and date, some months earlier, and saying he was about to start an interview with Max, the man I had come to think of as our resident drunk.

'Just as a matter of interest,' I asked, 'where does Max get his drink?'

'An addict will always find a way,' Kincaid said enigmatically. Then the Kincaid on tape said, 'I'm now showing Max the first inkblot. What do you see here, Max?'

Max's voice sounded slurred as he said, 'I see a spider. Well, maybe not so much a spider, maybe more like an iceberg, or a car crash, or two men having a sword fight, or a small explosion in a fireworks factory, or an organ, not a church organ or a Hammond organ, but an internal organ, a spleen or a pancreas or something like that.'

Kincaid listened to the tape and from the look on his face you'd have thought he was hearing one of the more tragic monologues from world literature.

'I see a golf course,' Max's voice continued, 'an underground cavern, torn upholstery, boxing gloves, a punctured car tyre, wood grain, a tractor pulling a plough, fingerprints, a kind of hat, a cheese grater, the inside of an old valve radio, a carburettor, an orchid, Siamese twins, a man carrying a wedding cake.'

On the tape Kincaid's voice asked, 'Do you *really* see these things, Max?'

'Yes. Don't you?' Max replied.

'No,' said Kincaid. 'I don't, as a matter of fact.'

'So are you implying I'm not really seeing them either?'

A good point, I thought. True enough, I found it hard to believe that Max or anybody else could really look at those cards and see boxing gloves or icebergs or Siamese twins. Actually, I thought he was just taking the piss, but I also thought that when you're encouraging a patient to see things that by definition aren't 'really' there, it's a bit churlish to then question what he says he's seeing. It also occurred to me that what Max pretended to be seeing might be every bit as psychologically revealing as what he was actually seeing.

Kincaid stopped the tape. 'You find it as depressing as I do,' he said, and I didn't contradict him. 'But now let's see the Max of today.'

At some secret, silent cue Max walked into the office. We had only spoken in passing but he was familiar enough to me. I'd seen him staggering or slumped or sleeping at various locations around the clinic. He was unshaven now, unwashed, his clothes were creased and stained, and his shoulders were heavily flecked with what appeared to be sawdust. He was trying to walk steadily, to look as though he was in control, the way drunks sometimes do when confronted by authority. He sat down with great formality although I could detect a lack of alignment in his eyes, a looseness in the way he placed his hands on his knees, and I thought Kincaid must surely be able to detect it too.

'Now, Max,' Kincaid said. 'I'd like you to look at this ink blot.'

He held up the first card and Max stared at it for a long time, his mouth twisting until he said, 'No, I can't see anything in that one.'

Kincaid held up a second card and Max stared hard again, as though he was really trying to make something out, to find some hidden image or message, but he just couldn't do it.

'No, nothing there either,' he said.

Kincaid beamed as he held up a third card. Max stared longest of all at this one, until it seemed to me his eyes lost their focus completely, as if he'd drifted off in some alcoholic reverie and forgotten what he was supposed to be doing, but he pulled himself together and said, 'No, doctor, I don't see a thing. Sorry.'

'There's nothing to be sorry about,' said Kincaid excitedly. 'Nothing at all.'

I found myself in a state of some disbelief. Could this procedure be quite as simplistic as it seemed? Could Kincaid really be so gullible? Seeing images in the blots was 'bad', not seeing them was 'good.' Could that genuinely count as proof that Kincaidian Therapy was working? The old Max on the tape saw images in the blots and that was a sign of his madness. The new Max in front of me saw nothing, so he must be sane. Please!

Then Kincaid held up the fourth card. Max stared once again, and this time looked pained, as though he might be experiencing severe stomach cramps. But at last, apparently much against his will, he had to let it all out.

He said, 'All right, all right, I admit it. I see truffles, waterfalls, shaving brushes, human ears, stampeding buffalo, piles of dirty laundry, circuit boards, brown-paper packages tied up with string . . .'

Kincaid gathered up the cards and put them face-down on his desk. The session was over. Kincaid's face signalled disappointment yet also a stoic, if wounded, bravery.

'How did I do, doc?' Max asked brightly. 'How many did I get right? Have I won a goldfish?'

This was proof enough to me that Max was still taking the piss. If I'd been Kincaid I'd have been tempted to abuse my position and given Max a few unnecessarily painful injections and maybe a course of fierce laxatives, but Kincaid was a true professional. He said, 'You can go away now, Max, while Mr Collins and I evaluate these results.'

Max put one foot in front of the other, heel to toe, swaying a little, and repeated the procedure as many times as were required to get himself out of the office.

'Interesting, yes?' Kincaid said, once he'd gone.

'I suppose so,' I said.

'Max hasn't been entirely freed from the bondage of images, but compared with his condition a few months ago he's improved remarkably.'

I didn't want to argue with Kincaid, yet I couldn't stop myself saying, 'But wasn't he just drunk?'

Kincaid looked at me condescendingly.

'Max has many problems,' he said. 'Alcohol is his rather pathetic way of coping.'

'And what happens when he starts seeing pink elephants?' I asked.

Kincaid was no better at spotting my cheap jokes than he had been at spotting Max's piss-taking. 'Then I'll know I've failed,' he said solemnly.

Soon after, I came across Max again, in a less medical setting. He was lying beside the path that led from the Communication Room to the dried-up fountain. His eyes were closed, mouth open, legs curled under him in a position that would have been excruciating for anyone who wasn't anaesthetised by drink. I couldn't just leave him there, so I shook him awake and said, 'Would you like me to help you get back to your room?'

He flickered back to consciousness and nodded. My motives for helping him weren't entirely altruistic. I had quite a curiosity to see how the patients lived. This would be a way of seeing inside one of their rooms.

I got Max into the clinic and to his own front door. We both hesitated on the threshold and I wondered if perhaps the patients' rooms were forbidden territory, but nobody had told me so, and Max said at last, 'Won't you step inside for a night cap?' It was four in the afternoon, but I said I would.

I had no picture of what Max's room would be like; and however hard I'd tried I'd never have imagined the reality. I stepped inside and it was for all the world like entering a tiny, perfect replica of a rustic English pub. There was a free-standing wooden bar in one corner. Behind it were bottles and glasses and optics, an ice bucket, a row of tankards, and in front was a single wrought-iron, marble-topped pub table with three chairs around it, and one of the chairs was occupied. Sita, the silent Indian woman, was sitting there, staring placidly into a glass of colourless liquid, her white muslin sari trailing to the ground, where it hung in an expanse of sawdust.

'You've met Sita,' Max said by way of introduction. 'Our resident enigma.'

'Hello, Sita,' I said, though naturally she didn't reply.

'Just because Sita doesn't say anything doesn't mean she's got nothing to say,' Max insisted.

'Doesn't it?' I asked.

Max was surprised by my question, and he appeared to be giving the matter intense, if brief, consideration before he said, 'Oh all right, maybe it does mean that.'

Sita sipped her drink. Although I got the feeling she'd been there a good long time, she didn't look remotely drunk, and when her eyes acknowledged my presence they were clear and lucid. I was surprised to find her there at all. If I'd been asked to speculate about who among the patients might be a secret drinker, or a boozing companion for Max, Sita wouldn't even have crossed my mind.

I looked around at the pub paraphernalia on the walls, nothing figurative, no hunting scenes or sporting prints, but there were lucky horseshoes, antique carpentry tools, some brewing equipment. I'd seen many less convincing attempts at creating an olde worlde pub atmosphere.

'This is amazing,' I said.

'You won't tell anybody about it, will you?' said Max. 'This is just our little secret.'

I said that was fine by me, but I found it hard to believe we were the only ones in on the secret. How could you possibly set up a replica pub in your hospital room without anyone knowing?

'Where do you sleep?' I asked, noticing that there was no bed in the room, not in itself so very surprising since it would undoubtedly have spoiled the pub effect.

'Where I fall,' Max said. Yes, well that explained the sawdust on the shoulders. Then he adopted the style of a genial pub landlord. 'What's your poison, Gregory? Will you be having the usual?'

'I don't really have a usual,' I said.

'Well, I usually serve whisky,' he said, and he slopped whisky into a thick-bottomed glass for me. 'This'll soon have you feeling frisky.'

I looked at the whisky bottle. The label had been largely scraped off, perhaps because of its pictorial elements, but enough of it remained to be identifiable. It was White Horse. 'Is this your usual brand as well?' I asked.

Max shrugged. It was all the same to him and he poured himself a drink much larger than mine and launched into a convoluted story about some occasion when he was drunk in Leith. I wasn't really listening, since I was wondering if this bottle of whisky was the one that had been in my missing holdall. There was clearly no way of telling. White Horse wasn't exactly an uncommon brand, and even if we'd been dealing with some rare single malt the evidence that this bottle was mine would still only have been circumstantial. But I thought it was a bit of a coincidence. And I thought too that if my whisky had survived, then maybe some of the rest of my stuff might also have survived; in which case, where was it?

'Where do you get the booze from, Max?' I asked.

'I have my lines of supply,' he said mysteriously.

'Go on,' I said.

He hesitated, but then decided I was an ally or at least not a squealer, and said, 'Let's just say some of the natives around here aren't entirely unfriendly.'

I thought of the lads in the car and the ones who partied outside the boundary wall. I could see they might have an ambivalent attitude towards the inmates of the Kincaid Clinic. They might consider them contemptible nutters, they might spray graffiti on the outer wall, but they might also take a certain delight in supplying them with booze, and who knew what else?

Max and I joined Sita at the table and I sipped my whisky. It felt wicked, and certainly subversive, to be drinking in the afternoon in a mental hospital with two of the patients, though Max and Sita treated the occasion casually enough.

Max said, 'I suppose you want me to tell you why I'm here.'

I said I did. I thought it would save time.

'I'm remodelling my consciousness through alcohol. It's a kind of auto-psychosurgery if you like.'

'Yes?'

'I imbibe alcohol. I annihilate some brain tissue, create a few cellular modifications, remould some cortex, incinerate a few circuits and synapses, strew some litter on the mesocorticolimbic pathway. Sounds a little crazy perhaps, but I know what I'm doing.'

'Does Kincaid know what you're doing?' I asked.

'No,' said Max, 'He thinks I'm depressed. He thinks I'm using booze as self-medication.'

'And he thinks that's all right?

'So long as I keep away from those nasty old images he's happy as a sand boy.'

Suddenly Max leapt to his feet and started viciously stamping the floor. At first I thought he was having a fit, but no, there was method here. A spider was scuttling through the sawdust, a real spider, not some alcohol-induced hallucination, I was pleased to see. Max stamped the spider to death and carried on stamping long after the creature was reduced to a black smear. It was manic and alarming but Sita sat through it unmoved. Perhaps she was used to it.

'I feel better for that,' said Max. 'I hate spiders. It's not a phobia or anything. I just hate them.'

'How long have you been doing this consciousness-remodelling of yours, Max?' I asked.

'Years,' he said. 'And years.'

'Is it working?'

'I still need a lot more data,' he said and poured us both another drink. 'Do you think I should write about it?'

'If it's what you want to write about.'

'What else do I have? Aren't you supposed to write about what you know? And what else do I know about?'

I was going to say I wasn't absolutely sure people should only write about what they know, since most people know so little, when I became aware that Sita was pointing at something on the floor. I looked and saw, with some amazement, that as a result of Max's stamping, the sawdust had been shuffled around, and by chance had formed itself into a human profile, one that looked quite passably like Kincaid. We all stared and sniggered childishly before Sita got up and very decorously brushed away the face with the hem of her sari.

18

And then there was the patients' writing. I was prepared for this to get better under our 'new deal'. I thought that maybe the previous awfulness had come about because they felt too constrained or pressured. True, they didn't seem to have paid very much attention to the two titles Kincaid and I had given them, but there might still have been some sense of being told what to do, and perhaps that had inhibited them. Maybe they had things they really wanted to say that could only be said in their own ways and in their own time.

But I was also prepared for the writing to become worse. I was ready for the patients' outpourings to be even more mad and maddening, to be even fuller of irrelevance and banality. By the mid-seventies the notion of 'letting it all hang out' hadn't been utterly discredited but it had already started to sound as much a recipe for disaster as for liberation.

In either case, whether the writing was better or worse, I was also expecting, and certainly hoping for, a drop in output. There had been something frantic about the production in those first two weeks, and I thought that was probably because the patients were trying too hard. Perhaps they'd been determined to impress me, or more likely, writing was a novelty for them and they'd thrown themselves into it with the energy that can accompany any new fad. Now that some of the novelty had worn off they'd surely settle down and write less.

Wrong. It wouldn't be true to say that nothing changed at all, that the writing went on exactly as before; for one thing, I didn't get the Saturday-morning knock followed by the bulk delivery. Instead the writing came to me piecemeal. I'd find a couple of dozen sheets of typescript left outside my hut, or I'd go into the library and find a densely typed sheaf of paper waiting for me. Nobody ever gave me their work directly, never put it straight into my hand, and I had to accept this since no doubt it was done to preserve their precious anonymity. But apart from the method of delivery it was pretty much business as before.

The writing was all basically, intrinsically, amazingly, more of the same. It seemed to be neither better nor worse, neither freer nor more inhibited, neither more nor less psychologically revealing. It was just the same. So there were more spiritual ramblings, more confessions, more sex and violence, more amazing facts. There was another account of a football match – Bolton Wanderers o, Notts Forest o – a real nail-biter apparently; another fairly accurate retelling of a well-known work of literature: *Macbeth*, in this case. There was stuff that looked like experimental prose. There was a tale of bitter, unrequited, ungrammatical love. There was a piece about the glory and wonder of trees; there was a day in the life of a candle. There were also more anagrams – one of which revealed that 'Kincaid' was an anagram of 'acid ink', and if I'd been on acid that might have seemed wonderfully significant, but I wasn't, so it didn't.

By any reasonable standards it was all absolutely dreadful; not uniformly dreadful, I suppose – some bits must have been better than others – but after I'd read a certain amount of this stuff my notions of good and bad, of better and worse, became extremely fogged. It felt as though I was dealing with the worst kind of slush pile (not that I had any personal experience of slush piles), and as such my first inclination was to reject it all.

And yet, perhaps because I couldn't reject it, because rejecting it would have been as inappropriate as it would have been meaningless, I found myself slowly coming, not to like it exactly but at least to tolerate it. And as more and more writing arrived every day, I came to appreciate that there was something irreducible about it. It was what it was, and that gave it a certain stature and dignity.

So I started to accept it, to welcome it en masse. I started looking forward to each new delivery, each new instalment. It wasn't like looking forward to the next episode of a serial, or following the adventures of a set of characters and wanting to know what happens next; it was more like looking forward to the morning newspaper. By definition you never know precisely what's going to be in the paper, but at the same time you have certain realistic expectations which are, by and large, fulfilled. The patients' writing ceased to surprise me, yet became an essential part of my routine, of my daily life.

Then I began to develop a curious fondness for it, although I could see that fondness was in some ways irrelevant too. Regardless of how I felt about the writing, regardless of its qualities, I still had an obligation to deal with it, to talk to the patients about it, to do something with them and for them. In a perfect world I might have preferred to sit them down individually and have one-to-one tutorials with them. I saw myself playing the part of the groovy young academic: hip, approachable, willing to talk about rock lyrics; that sort of thing. But, inevitably, this wasn't possible. Since nobody would own up to having written any particular piece of work, group discussions were the only option.

We would congregate in the lecture room, I'd select a piece of the patients' writing more or less at random, then choose someone to read it. The law of averages suggested that once in a while somebody must have ended up reading a piece they'd actually written, but nobody ever admitted it. Raymond, Charity and Charles Manning were probably the best of the readers, whatever 'best' meant in this context. Byron, for all his poetical looks, was surprisingly poor. Carla, predictably, was completely hopeless. She was quite incapable of reading what was put in front of her, and sometimes just made it up as she went along, which sounds like it might have been interesting but it never actually was. And Sita, of course, never read anything at all. I asked her to, gently and without pressurising her, but she just stared at me silently with those big, dark eyes and said nothing.

Once a piece had been read aloud, we'd talk about it in a very detached, abstract, practical criticism, I. A. Richards sort of way. We'd discuss what we thought the author 'was trying to say', how the language was used, how the metaphors and imagery worked, if they worked, and if not why not. Then we'd talk about how the piece might be improved, how it could be tightened up or made more effective. We talked about structure. We talked about vocabulary and register and sometimes about the origins of words. This makes it all sound rather serious and literary and highbrow, but you have to remember we were in a lunatic asylum.

We were in the lecture room, in our circle of chairs, and I handed Maureen a text and asked her to read it out. She wasn't keen at first – they never were – but the piece didn't seem to present any particular problems. She read that the zip fastener was invented in 1893 by W. L. Judson of Chicago, that St Albans is named after St Alban, that

Tallulah Bankhead's father was a congressman and her grandfather was a senator, that Baron Georges-Eugène Haussmann rebuilt Paris in the 1860s, that peach melba was named after Dame Nelly Melba, the Australian Nightingale, that the Norwegians get rid of rats using slices of white bread coated with lye and syrup, that Chesterfield Football Club is nicknamed the Spire-ites, that Benjamin Franklin invented the rocking chair, that only seven of Emily Dickinson's poems were published in her lifetime, that at any given moment there are eighteen hundred thunderstorms taking place in the earth's atmosphere, that underground ice-houses were known in China as early as 1100 BC. And much more in similar vein.

When Maureen got to the end of the piece she sat down and I said, 'Well, what do we all think of that?'

'It's crap,' said Anders.

'No, it's not crap,' said Raymond judiciously. 'But it's not great.'

'I wouldn't give it more than five,' said Charles Manning.

'I wouldn't give it more than a hundred billion,' said Carla.

'I like it,' said Cook.

Several others agreed that they also liked it.

'Yes, I liked it too,' said Maureen. 'I enjoyed reading it, especially the football reference.'

'All right,' I said, 'I suppose that could be one reason for liking a piece of writing, that it relates to our own interests and obsessions. What other reasons might we have for liking it?'

'I don't know what it means to like or dislike a piece of literature.' It was Byron talking. 'We don't judge literary texts. They judge us.'

This put a bit of a damper on proceedings, until Anders said, 'I liked it because it was fuckin' funny.'

'You just said you didn't like it!' Cook protested quietly.

'I said it was crap. I didn't say I didn't like it. There's a time and a place for crap.'

'What did you find funny about it?' I asked.

Anders shrugged and Raymond leapt in with, 'It's funny because it's so true.'

'But is it all true?' Charles Manning asked. 'I'm not sure I believe there are eighteen hundred thunderstorms going on at any given moment.'

'Yes,' Cook agreed, 'and I'm not sure about Benjamin Franklin and the rocking chair.'

'Does it matter whether or not it's true?' I asked.

'What?'

'Maybe that's the point, maybe that's the joke,' I suggested.

They looked at me baffled, and in truth I couldn't see where that line of thought was taking me, but then Byron pitched in at full strength.

'I think Gregory is talking about indeterminacy here,' he said. 'Unreliable narrators, the lie that tells the truth.'

'Would you like to say more about that?' I asked, knowing that he would.

'What I think the narrator is trying to do in the piece is set up a dichotomy between the created world and the observed world, between fact and fiction. The language is unemotive and yet the things described are dramatic and resonant. It tells us that the world consists of zips as well as saints, of lightning as well as peach melbas. There's an oscillation between the banal and the numinous; and perhaps the point is that there is no opposition here. Not only can poetry be made out of anything, poetry already exists *in* everything; there's no such thing as an unsuitable subject for art.'

'You've said a mouthful,' said Max, stirring out of his alcoholic doze.

'It's heavy,' said Charity.

'So is he right?' Cook asked. 'Is that really what it's about?'

I was tempted to say, don't ask me, ask the person who wrote it, but I'd said things like that before and it had never got me anywhere. So I said, 'If that's what Byron gets out of it, then that's what's in it.'

'What I get out of it is the desire to get naked and dance like a dervish,' said Charity.

'You'd get that out of reading *Exchange and Mart*,' Maureen said.

'What I get out of it is the desire to pull some fucker's head off,' said Anders. 'That's only a personal interpretation, obviously.'

'I get the desire to pull my *own* head off,' said Carla.

And so on.

I had no doubt that the patients were often toying with me, playing up their own madness, to see if I was capable of coping with it and, somewhat to my surprise, I soon found that I was. I wouldn't swear that I developed a new persona exactly, but I certainly found a means of not giving too much of myself away. I stopped being frightened of Anders. I stopped being disturbed when Charity tore her clothes off, just as I stopped being made to feel uncomfortable by Sita's ominous silence. I ignored the silliness that Carla demonstrated, just as I ignored Max's drunkenness and Raymond's increasingly ornate use of make-up and his tendency to wear odd items of women's jewellery. I dealt with what they gave me to deal with.

Sometimes we talked more generally about writing, although it soon became apparent that the more general the topic, the more room there was for madness and idiocy. On one occasion Carla asked me, 'How long is a short story?'

'How long is a piece of string?' I replied, foolishly as it turned out.

'Two foot six,' she replied with great certainty.

'No,' I said gently. 'I mean, yes, all right, *some* pieces of string are two foot six, but the point I'm making is that stories, like pieces of string, can be any length you like.'

Carla ploughed her finger-ends down her cheeks, giving the subject far more intense consideration than I thought it deserved.

'No,' she said, sounding troubled, 'a piece of string can't be *any* length. It can't be a million miles long, for instance, because no string factory would ever be able to manufacture it, and no lorry would ever be able to transport it, and just imagine the size of the ball it would make, and what shop would ever stock it and who'd ever buy it, and—'

'All right,' I said, 'I accept that a piece of string couldn't be a million miles long.'

'And it couldn't be a millionth of a millimetre long either, because—'

'I get your drift,' I said.

'So you were wrong when you said a piece of string could be any length. So you were probably wrong when you said a short story could be any length.'

'Yes,' I said, 'I was wrong.'

'So how long is a short story?'

'Two hundred and fifty words,' I said.

'No,' said Carla. 'I think you're wrong about that as well.'

That was one of my amazingly naive attempts to get the patients to write at shorter length. I thought that if I could get each of them to write, say, just two hundred and fifty, or five hundred or even just a thousand words a week, life would be much easier for all of us. But it didn't work, not at all, not in the least. The words continued to come as thick and fast as ever: scores of pages every day, a thousand or more every week. It was overwhelming, but in a way I had to admire it.

Kincaid still had me writing regular reports on what was being produced. I did my best to make it sound interesting or significant, and I'd occasionally quote a good line or phrase that had somehow crept in. I didn't offer any opinions about the mental health of the writers, I thought that was Kincaid's business, not mine. I also occasionally suggested in the reports that the best way for him to find out what was being written was for him to actually read some of the damn stuff, but he was always too busy or too grand or something. He said he trusted me.

My relations with Kincaid were never easy, but we found a way of rubbing along together, or at least of leaving each other alone. And he could still surprise me with small acts of understanding, and even concern. On one occasion he said he'd been worrying that he hadn't seen me write anything 'creative' since I'd arrived at the clinic. He hoped that working with the patients wasn't affecting my 'true vocation' as he put it. I assured him that being at the clinic had absolutely nothing to do with it and I came up with some lame, but not entirely unconvincing, guff about an author needing to lie fallow from time to time. Kincaid listened with unexpected interest. Tales of the literary life fascinated him.

'I can't lie to you, Gregory,' he said portentously, 'the truth is I do have certain literary ambitions. I'm working on a little something at the moment; that's what I do in my office in the evenings. Perhaps you've seen me pacing back and forth in the throes of composition.'

I admitted that I had.

'I envisage a trans-genre, not to say transgressive work that's part autobiography, part scientific treatise, part prose poem. I see it as a synthesis of art and science, east and west, the conscious and the subconscious—'

'Right,' I said, and I was aware of my head nodding tensely, a tight-lipped smile on my immobile face, pretending to be intrigued by this literary prospect.

'Don't look so worried,' Kincaid said, 'I shan't ask you to read it and give me your opinion.'

He laughed modestly, and once again I was pleased by his grasp of psychology. The idea of having to read and comment on something

Kincaid had written was daunting. At the same time I felt vaguely insulted. Would my opinion have been so worthless in his eyes? Did he regard himself as so possessed by genius that my comments would have been irrelevant to him? Well yes, I suspect he did. And for a moment I thought I ought to offer, perhaps demand, to be given a chance to read his great work in progress; but then I thought no, wait a minute, maybe he's using even cleverer psychology than I thought, manipulating me to read it when I really didn't want to. Life with Kincaid was never simple, although sometimes I suspected I was making my own complications.

Life with Alicia continued to have its complications too. By day she was the cool, not to say frosty, not to say hostile, medical practitioner. I was still not clear what she did to, or for, or with, the patients. They went into her office just as often as they went into Kincaid's, but I had little idea what they got up to in there since Kincaidian Therapy, as I currently understood it, seemed largely to involve doing very little. But I was prepared to accept that my knowledge was patchy, my understanding imperfect and certainly Alicia always seemed to be in the middle of doing something vitally important.

I would still occasionally make businesslike enquiries about the workings of the clinic. I wondered, for example, why the patients never received any visitors, why none of them ever received any mail; and in a tone that suggested I was a cretin Alicia told me there had once been a time when the clinic encouraged visitors, but they'd always arrived wearing floral dresses or ties with gun dog motifs or Mickey Mouse watches, and this visual chaos would set the patients back weeks or months. The same applied to letters; they'd arrive full of doodles and drawings, containing family snapshots, with stamps on the outside that depicted the Queen and who knew what else. All this was a horror and an intolerable risk, and apparently totally obvious to anyone with half a brain.

I didn't much like the way Alicia treated me at these times, but later she would make up for it. She would come to my room and be warm and sexy and extremely dirty-mouthed, and she expected the same from me. At times this coprophemia, as I only much later came to know it, seemed a shade rigid and formulaic, a bit too much like hard work, but I didn't complain. The glass was definitely half full rather than half empty. On the other hand, I did sometimes feel confused about what was actually going on between us, and then I'd ask some different stupid questions such as, 'Are we having a relationship, Alicia?'

We were in my bed, with the lights inevitably turned off, and I heard Alicia's laughter in the dark and then she said, 'What do you mean by relationship?'

'I mean the same as everybody else does,' I replied, thinking this wasn't a bad answer.

Alicia can't have thought it was too bad either, since she said, 'Yes, we're having a relationship. We all have relationships with everyone we meet. How could it be otherwise?'

'But what kind?' I insisted. 'We're not "going out" together, are we, because we only ever see each other here in the clinic, and we're keeping it a secret. So obviously we're not "dating" or "courting" or anything like that.'

'Courting. That's a quaint word, the kind of word your mother might use.'

'All right,' I admitted, 'I don't suppose I want us to be courting.'

'Then what do you want us to be doing? And why is it important to you that we put a name to it?'

'It's important to know where we stand. At least it's important to me to know where *I* stand.'

'You want to know whether we're boyfriend and girlfriend, whether we're lovers, or slaves of passion, or just people who have the occasional friendly fuck, is that it? You want to know whether we're serious, whether we're an item, whether we're committed, whether you're spoken for.'

'Is that so unreasonable?' I asked.

'And once you've put your label on it, everything will be all right?'

Her condescension annoyed me and I thought it was my turn to be angry. 'Look,' I said, 'I'm getting really pissed off with this talk of "just words" or "just labels". I don't think words are so terrible, and it seems to me a label's a pretty useful thing. It means you can tell the difference between a bottle of beer and a bottle of arsenic, for instance.'

'That's always assuming someone's put the correct label on the bottle,' she said, apparently thinking she'd made some infinitely subtle point.

'Well *obviously*,' I replied, may even have shouted. 'Obviously I don't want you to tell me I'm your "soul mate" if all you think I am is some quick shag. I don't want you to lie to me.'

'You're not a quick shag,' she said. 'You're a long, slow, delicious, lingering shag.'

'That's very flattering, Alicia, but you're evading the issue.'

'Yes, I am. And don't think I'm unsympathetic, Gregory. You want me to say a few simple words that will tell you where you stand – one word if possible.'

'You make it sound as though I'm asking for the world.'

'Asking for the *world*, asking for the *word*. A Freudian would make plenty out of that.'

'Thank God you're not a Freudian,' I said.

'You know, Gregory, sometimes you talk too much.'

I thought this was a bit rich coming from Alicia, but she then very effectively stopped me speaking. She wrestled herself into a position above me and firmly lowered her genitals into my face. I couldn't talk, but she could. And while I lapped and licked and probed and tongued, she delivered an incredibly filthy, dirty monologue about what a filthy, dirty man I was. I was in no position to argue.

19

I know it'll sound strange and suspect if I say I began to feel at home in the Kincaid Clinic. The implication would seem to be that anyone who feels at home in a lunatic asylum must be a lunatic, but I'd challenge that. Most doctors and nurses presumably feel at home in hospitals but that doesn't mean they're sick. Zoo keepers must feel quite at home in their zoos but that doesn't mean they're wild animals, does it?

Not only did I *feel* at home, I wanted to *stay* at home. My need to have my own key to the front gate, my desire to be able to come and go as I pleased, didn't so much disappear as become irrelevant. I got to the stage where I didn't know what I'd have done out there. Would I have gone shopping? Gone to a pub? To the movies? To a bookshop? All these things started to seem rather pointless to me.

I realised that in an important way I too was on the receiving end of Kincaidian Therapy; at least its broader tenets. Just like the patients, I was cut off and protected from the world of created images. And although that could feel odd at times, I got used to it surprisingly quickly. I found it strangely soothing, and I had to consider the notion that there might be more to Kincaidian Therapy than I'd first thought. I was also cut off from much else besides: from news, from politics, from world affairs, from pop music and television and sport, but that felt like no loss at all. What was I missing? What was going on in the world at that? Well, there were problems with unions and terrorists, the American bicentennial, Labour prime ministers coming and going, songs like 'Fernando' and 'Save Your Kisses For Me', television programmes like *Love Thy Neighbour*, movies like *All the President's Men*. Even at the time these things seemed a bit passé, a bit *seventies*.

I wasn't a complete hermit. It wasn't as if I had absolutely no dealings with the outside world. For one thing, I did phone my parents from time to time, but you know how it is with parents, you keep having the same conversation year after year, decade after decade. They asked me how things were going with the job and I said, 'Fine' and that was as much as they wanted to hear. I did ask my mother what heart's-ease looked like and she did her best to describe it, but I didn't learn anything I could pass on to Maureen. My mother would ask me if I'd found a 'nice girl' yet and I said I was still looking.

Very occasionally the dealings went the other way and the world came to me. For instance, I was enormously surprised one day to get another phone call from Gregory Collins. Given my situation you might think he'd have been on my mind all the time, but actually I felt as though his was a voice from an entirely different time and place.

'I've been reading about Ted Hughes and Sylvia Plath,' he said without preamble. 'Apparently, back in 1962, she decided to cast a spell on him. Literally. So she went to his desk, got some of his manuscripts, and bits of dandruff and fingernail clippings and stuff, and she made a bonfire out of them and danced around it, chuntering devilish curses.

'Now I reckon this begs a few questions, the main one being why Ted Hughes let his desk get in such a disgusting state. Anyway, whether the spell worked or not is debatable, but Hughes had the last laugh, not that he's much of a laughing boy from what I hear. After Plath committed suicide, he made a bonfire of his own and burned the final volume of her journals. He said he did it to protect their children, but most people reckon the journals had Plath's version of what a bastard he'd been to her. And you know, if that was the case, I don't think you can blame him. Which of us wouldn't have done the same? Posterity be buggered.'

'Hello,' I said. 'What can I do for you?'

'I just wondered how you were getting on,' he said, and I knew something was wrong. Gregory would not have been calling out of such straightforward motives.

'I'm fine,' I said, playing along. 'I took your advice. Sort of.'

'I'm glad,' he said, though he didn't sound glad. 'One thing I'm calling for is to tell you I've decided against making a complaint about Bentley.'

'Good,' I said.

'Yes.' Gregory added hesitantly, 'I had a word with Nicola and she told me it was a daft idea.'

How very like Nicola, I thought. I'd never heard her use the word 'daft' but she certainly knew daftness when she saw it, and was always quick to denounce it.

'Good,' I said.

'She's really got it in for you though, I'm afraid.'

That didn't surprise me much, but I didn't want to be told it by Gregory, and I certainly didn't like the implication that the two of them had been discussing me.

'I tried to put in a good word for you,' Gregory said, 'and I hope it helped a bit, but basically she wasn't having any of it.'

The idea that Gregory wanted to be my champion was deeply unattractive, and the idea that he thought he might be able to change Nicola's opinion of me was just laughable, not that I found myself laughing. And I felt even less amused when he said, 'Tell me about Nicola.'

'Tell you what?' I asked, although I knew I didn't want to tell him anything at all. He'd slept with her more recently than I had, and he had the great advantage of being on speaking terms with her, which I certainly wasn't; that should have told him something.

'Let me put my cards on the table,' he said. 'Fact is, I know I'm an ugly git and I don't get many chances. But I think I might be in with a shout when it comes to Nicola. What do you reckon?'

'A shout?'

'Do you think she'd go out with me?'

'If you don't know, I can't tell you,' I said haughtily.

'Oh, but you can. You know women. And you know Nicola. Am I the sort of bloke she'd go for?'

'She went for you all right that night in Brighton.'

'But that was just sex. I'm after more than that.'

'Aren't we all?' I said.

'And I don't want to make a chuff of myself.'

A few months ago I would never have dreamed that Gregory was 'in with a shout' with Nicola, but then I'd never have thought he was likely to have a one-night stand. So it appeared I knew nothing about either of them. If he wanted to pursue her I wasn't going to try and stop him, and if he fell on his face and made a 'chuff' of himself, well, that wouldn't surprise me and it wouldn't exactly break my heart either.

'Go for it,' I said. 'Follow your heart.'

'Really?' he said, and he sounded happy in a boyish, uncontrived way that made me feel rather small. 'That's bloody great. You've bucked me up no end. And this means I have your blessing, right? You won't hold a grudge if me and Nicola start courting. All's fair in love and war, may the best man win and all that gubbins, right?'

'Yes, all that gubbins,' I said.

'You're a mate, you really are. I appreciate this. If there's anything I can ever do for you in the future ...'

I found his gratitude embarrassing. I felt I had done nothing for him. I certainly wanted to do nothing, and at that time I couldn't imagine I'd ever want or need him to do anything for me. I wished he hadn't called. It felt like an intrusion.

The world could intrude in other ways too. I had a sense that the locals were getting louder, rowdier, more out of control. They'd congregate invisibly but very audibly, outside the boundary wall. I'd sit in my hut and hear laughter, shouting, girls squealing in delight or feigned terror, and then cans, bottles, a few stones would be lobbed over the wall into the grounds. It wasn't every night by any means, and it still didn't feel especially threatening but I had a sense that it was happening increasingly often, becoming more and more of a pain in the neck.

Then one night some of the perpetrators became visible. Half a dozen young men came and stood at the front gate of the clinic, peering into the grounds as though into a monkey house. They looked younger and much more harmless than I'd pictured. They might even have been sixth-formers on a dare, but their callowness didn't make them any more welcome. I wondered why the porters didn't appear and clear them off.

Most of the time there would have been nothing for them to see, but their very presence made all the difference. I understand it was always like this. In the days when asylums were open to the public, those inmates who gave the most convincing displays of madness were the ones who received the biggest rewards from visitors. And so, in a way, it was at the Kincaid Clinic. Carla decided to put on a show for the watchers at the gate. She went and talked to them and did a fairly good impression of a gibbering, drooling mad girl, and the boys were duly provoked and entertained. They gave her a can of lager. And when Charity arrived and started dancing naked they got rather more than they'd bargained for.

There was nothing truly indecent about Charity's nudity, and her dancing was that of free-form expression rather than of a strip show, not least because of her shaved head, but the boys found it much more confusing and far harder to deal with than Carla's more obvious lunacy. They gawped in silence, and when she danced right up to the gate and started interacting with them they were extremely cowed. Nevertheless, I felt I had to do something to try to protect Charity, not least from herself.

I went to the gate, told the boys to clear off before I called the police, and I draped an old shirt of mine around Charity's shoulders. I don't know that the lads were especially fearful of my anger, but at least they knew that the show was over, and I led Charity back to her room.

'I suppose you want to come in,' she said.

In a way I did. Having seen Max's room I was keen to see others. They surely couldn't all be quite as fancy as Max's, and Charity's room proved to look pretty much like your typical hippie girl's pad. It was packed with stuff: clothes, scarves, sandals, scented candles, a hookah, peacock feathers, bunches of dried flowers and pine cones. The air was clotted with the smell of old joss sticks and musk oil. It was an extreme version of a lot of girls' rooms I'd seen at college.

There was a portable mono record player on the floor, a Dansette (pitifully uncool in those days, though soon to be beguilingly retro), and there was a stack of records beside it, but the records were without their covers, just slices of black vinyl in plain inner sleeves. They looked paltry and denuded, denatured by being separated from their cover art: none of Hendrix's electric ladies, no zipper on *Sticky Fingers*, no plastic window on *L. A. Woman*. I suppose Charity would have been all right with the Beatles' *White Album* although there might have been problems with the record label and its image of an apple.

I'm never sure I believe people when they say that nudity has nothing to do with sex. I suspect it always has *something* to do with sex. Certainly I felt uncomfortable to find myself behind closed doors with a female patient who was naked but for a shirt, especially given Alicia's accusation that I wanted to have sex with Charity. I stood awkwardly at the centre of the room. There were no chairs and it didn't seem right just to plonk myself down on the bed. Charity had no intention of making me feel comfortable.

'Got any drugs on you?' she asked.

'No!' I said.

'I thought as much. You know, if I have one complaint about Dr K, it's that he doesn't give us enough drugs.'

'Oh?'

'And even when he appears to be giving us enough I sometimes think they're mostly placebos. He gets all these free drugs given to him by the drug companies—'

'Does he?'

'Oh come on, don't be naive, Greg. This whole place is funded by drug company money.'

'Is it?'

'How else do you think it survives? On love? On government subsidy?'

I hadn't thought about it. I hadn't been much concerned with the clinic's finances. And even if I'd wanted to know about the Kincaid Clinic's workings I got the feeling I'd have had a hard time discovering much. If I couldn't get access to the patients' case histories, I was hardly likely to get financial information.

'I never thought about it,' I answered.

'That's because you're an artist, I suppose,' she said, and I wasn't sure if she was being contemptuous or not. 'All I'm saying is Kincaid gets given all these free drugs and he keeps them to himself, and I think it's a rip off. That's why I have to make a deals with the local boys.'

'Deals?'

'I dance for them and they supply me.'

She opened her hand and revealed a stash of pills and tablets, like a handful of shiny, multicoloured insects.

'They just gave you these?'

'Right. Not bad for a little dance work. Dancing may be spiritual but it has its material side too.'

'Why do you need drugs?' I asked.

It was a naive question even for me, even for then. This was a time when the whole world was starting to need drugs: to get high, to come down, to stay calm, to stay thin, to stay in control, to wake up, to doze off, to make friends, to make deals, to show you were made of the right stuff, to insulate, to meditate, to fornicate. And soon there would be all those people who didn't need any reason at all.

'I need more drugs to be more sane,' Charity said.

'Yes?'

'God is drugs,' she insisted.

'I don't know about that,' I said.

'Well, I don't care about your opinion. Timothy Leary says that modern psychology is based more on worrying about what the neighbours think than on anything else. Isn't that a terrible condemnation?'

'Seems like you get along fairly well with your neighbours,' I said.

'You're so conventional, Gregory. Even your name sounds straight. Gregory Collins. It sounds like a name from the past. The future's going to have a different name. Want to smoke some dope?'

'Is that all right? I asked.

'It's against the law of the land, if that's what you mean, but it's not going to kill you.'

'I mean what if Dr Kincaid finds out?'

'Fuck Kincaid,' she said.

'I've heard that some people do,' I said, vaguely paraphrasing a line I remembered from the movie of *Cabaret*.

She gave a laugh that already sounded stoned.

'Maybe you're not such a straight after all,' she said.

She dug in a plastic bag and produced a fat, ready rolled joint. She lit it, inhaled once herself and handed it to me. I hesitated, but only for a moment. If I was prepared to drink with Max, why shouldn't I smoke dope with Charity? If I was the wild subversive guy I sometimes thought I was, surely I should ingest a few illegal substances. We sat down on the bed, keeping a safe distance between us, and I took a couple of deep drags. It tasted like mild, ineffective stuff.

'Sometimes I think cosmic consciousness is the only gig worth playing,' Charity said. 'Spiritual growth is the only therapy worth thinking about.'

Grudgingly I admitted that might be true. To the limited extent that I thought I knew what spiritual growth was I would probably have welcomed it, but I wasn't actively seeking it out. It seemed to me the world was far too full of people who were looking for wisdom, truth, ultimate solutions, and I was amazed and depressed at how easily they found all these things.

'We're all looking for guidance,' Charity said. 'We all need like a guide, someone who'll reawaken the divinity inside us.'

'Someone like the Pope,' I said.

We both giggled at that one. Maybe the dope was better than I thought.

'I mean a real holy man,' Charity said. 'A guru. Maybe a shaman.'

'You think you're going to find one around here?'

'Why not? The gates of Eden may be wherever you look for them.' She stared at me a little too hard and said, 'Couldn't you be a guide?'

I was stoned enough to think she might be serious.

'No, not me,' I said. 'I've got nothing to teach anyone. Except for creative writing. And even then—'

'But that's just what I'd expect a really great spiritual teacher to say.'

'I'm just a writer,' I lied.

'But writing's a spiritual discipline, isn't it?'

'In a way—'

'And God's like this bestselling creative writer, isn't he?'

'No, I don't think so,' I said.

'Yeah, yeah,' Charity said. 'A lot of people want to say God's dead but what if he's like a writer who's run out of plots, or he's got writer's block? Or what if maybe he's not dead, but, you know, he's just gone nuts?'

The dope was working wonderfully, so well that not only could I follow what Charity was saying, but I also had a profound, if free-floating, sense of its significance, of the way in which it seemed to explain everything about writing and God and the workings of the Kincaid Clinic. Things in the room were looking sharper and brighter, the peacock feathers were shivering with a cold, metallic light.

'Do you believe in free love?' she asked me and I froze a little.

'"Free love" is a term I've never been able to use except in inverted commas,' I said.

She looked at me sadly. 'I don't think you're a bad guy, but you're too armoured and too much in your own head. And that's why you can't believe in free love.'

I wasn't sure whether that was true or not, and although I

recognised 'armoured' as a Reichian term I didn't altogether know what it meant, and I wasn't sure Charity did either. I replied, 'All I'm saying is that I don't think free love is so much a question of belief as of temperament.'

'Now you're just using words,' she said, as though this was the final condemnation.

'The rumour is there are already quite enough believers in free love here in the clinic.'

'Who told you that?' she demanded. 'Charles Manning?'

I didn't deny it.

'Poor old Charles. Yeah well, that's the myth the straight world has about the insane, right? They're crazy so they can have all the sex they want and it doesn't matter, whereas the sane people are repressed and shut down and militarised and they only have it on Saturday nights if they're lucky, and that's supposed to be healthy. Free love is the sanest thing anybody's ever come up with.'

AIDS, of course, was not on anybody's mind at this point, although the horrors of venereal disease and crabs and hepatitis still seemed well worth avoiding if at all possible, to say nothing of unwanted pregnancies.

And then, belatedly but not unexpectedly, Charity started to explain herself. She said, 'I don't belong here, you know. I'm not crazy. It's my family; that's where the problems always come from. Always. They're rich, they hate me, I'm an embarrassment to them. They call me an exhibitionistic nymphomaniac. But I'm just looking for attention and love, and I'm looking to take a few drugs and get in touch with the spiritual forces. They can't deal with that. OK, so I have a religious vision once in a while, I like to dance sky-clad, I see the face of God in a puddle or a patch of shadow or something, but what's so bad about that? They think it's dangerous. God and sex and drugs are too much for them. They want me out of the way, so they pay the bills for me to stay here. That's cool with me, like it's a health club or a finishing school. I like it here, but I don't belong.'

'Nobody seems to think they belong here,' I said.

'Yeah well, some of us are right about that and some aren't. You can fuck me if you want, Gregory. It'd be really cosmic.'

She let the shirt drop from her shoulders.

'No thanks, Charity. I'm sure that would get me into all sorts of trouble,' I said, and I woozily dragged myself up off the bed and started making slow, stoned progress towards the door, across a floor that seemed to be made of marshmallow.

'Hey, Gregory, don't be a drag. Don't make your excuses and leave.'

I didn't flatter myself that Charity really wanted to have sex with me. Either she was just trying to embarrass me or she was just stoned or she was just a nymphomaniac. None of these cases required me to do anything. However, her professed belief in free love did sound like possible circumstantial evidence for Charles Manning's assertion that the clinic was a hotbed of sexual activity, and although I still saw no real proof of this, I found it was on my mind a lot more than I wanted it to be. I made my excuses and left.

20

I realise parts of my account make it sound as though the whole clinic was a continual seething mass of sex, drugs and alcohol, but it didn't feel that way to me at the time. I still spent a large part every day just reading, either the patients' work or the limited treasures from the library. And when the patients came to talk to me they often had perfectly chaste concerns. Byron would talk quite rationally about literature, although he never read anything from the library. I suspect he thought the books there were beneath him. Raymond, now usually to be seen wearing white gloves and vermilion lipstick, might come and tell me about some of the more exotic tourist sights he'd seen on his stopovers. Cook might tell me that someone had been putting ideas in his head and that he now thought the world was like a colander or a book of matches or a pizza. Some of these encounters were tedious, but I didn't complain. I liked to be available for the patients. I didn't try to be all things to all people, but I did what I could.

I was in my hut one day when I detected a burning vegetable sort of smell. Then wisps of smoke drifted by, then sheets, then choking clouds of bleached grey smoke filled the hut. I got up from my desk and stood in the doorway looking out across the garden and saw the smoke came from the far side of a rhododendron bush. I went to investigate, but I knew what I'd find. Nothing more sinister than Maureen burning some garden rubbish. She'd made a small unruly bonfire out of branches, weeds, grass cuttings, all of them suspiciously green and unwilling to burn. She and Raymond stood looking at the bonfire unhappily.

'How's it going?' I asked.

'Not so good,' Maureen said, sounding both sad and puzzled.

Raymond fanned some smoke away from his face with a gloved

hand and muttered, 'They say there's no smoke without fire, but we're not so sure.'

He had a point. There was no gleam of flame visible anywhere in the heap of smouldering rubbish.

'Everybody likes a good fire,' said Maureen. 'Everybody likes to see the flames dance.'

'You know what we like best about fires?' Raymond asked.

I feared it might be something sexual, or something about air crashes or destruction or the cleansing power of flame, but I said, 'Tell me.'

'We like the faces,' Maureen said. 'We like it when the flames have died down and you're left with the embers and you stare into them and you see things: faces and animals and footballers and things like that.'

'And air crashes,' said Raymond.

'Yes,' I said, 'I suppose we all like that.'

'But do we all see the same things,' Maureen asked, 'or do we just project what we have in our own minds, you know like the old ink blots?'

Yes, I said, I knew all about the old ink blots. We stood peering into the heart of the smoking pile. There was still no sign of a flame and I think we all felt a disappointment.

'You won't tell Dr Kincaid that we see images in the fire, will you, Gregory?'

I said that I wouldn't, any more than I'd have told him about Max's replica pub, or Charity's dope-smoking. I was pleased the patients thought of me as an ally, that they confided in me rather than Kincaid, although I wasn't sure what this was likely to do for their mental health.

'I think it's probably all right to see faces in the fire,' I said. 'I don't see how you can help it. I don't think it can be all that bad for you.'

Maureen and Raymond smiled at me but I wasn't sure what their smiles meant. At the time I liked to think it showed that they believed me and found my words reassuring but later I began to wonder if what they were really saying was, 'How would you know? You're only a writer.'

They were wrong about that, of course, I wasn't a writer, but I was trying to do my best. True, there were times when my best seemed miserably inadequate, times when the writing, which continued to arrive in the same dauntingly vast quantities, didn't seem to be getting any better, and neither as far as I could see, did the patients. And yet, and yet ... Sometimes it really did seem to me that the work was starting to add up to something, though I couldn't have said what, not a work of art, not a body of writing, not a thing you could show to anyone and say, look at this, this is good, this has quality or value or meaning. What then? Well, sometimes I wondered if it really did amount to a gestalt, a group mind as Kincaid had suggested, or at the very least a picture of madness at this time in social and cultural history.

But this notion wouldn't always hold either. There were other times when I felt I was wasting my time as well as everyone else's, times when I thought, at best, I was just there helping the patients pass the time, keeping them out of harm's way, distracting them. And all I was doing when I put their writings in the library was collecting waste paper.

I was walking in the grounds when I heard a voice, unmistakably Anders', though he sounded softer, more constrained, more intimate than usual and he was involved in describing something or other.

'Yes,' I heard him say, 'there's a Spanish galleon, and a double-decker bus, and a rhinoceros, and a map of Italy, or maybe just a boot, and there's a rolled leg of pork, and waves on a beach, and a dressing table, and oh fuck, that does feel good.'

You might have guessed it was someone casting their eyes over more Rorschach blots, but that seemed an unlikely activity to be taking place out of doors. It also sounded like Anders was enjoying it far too much. I was curious to see what he was up to, and although he wasn't someone you wanted to disturb or intrude on, after listening to more of his monologue, 'An armchair, a dolphin, a lightbulb, a pygmy, a lung, a trumpet, and oh Jesus ...' I decided to take a look. Fortunately I could hide behind another rhododendron bush and peer through its foliage.

At first I could see only a part of Anders, the lower half, but that was in some ways enough. He was lying on his back and his trousers and underpants were down, leaving him naked from waist to ankle. I could see chunky, hirsute legs, scarred knees and also his penis, chunky certainly, though not hirsute or scarred, and it was being nonchalantly fondled by a fully clothed Sita.

I experienced a number of contradictory, ambiguous emotions. The first one was surprise. I had never watched people having any sort of sex before, and it felt horribly intrusive. But at the same time I felt almost pleased, as though I'd discovered or proved something. It wasn't by any stretch of the imagination an orgy, but it was definitely something.

Anders continued to talk, slowly, in this meandering yet precise, free-associative way, and Sita stroked his penis in a complementary though not identical rhythm. 'A pheasant, a meringue, a sledgehammer, an ear, a Christmas tree,' he said, and then in quite a different tone added, 'Christ, Sita, you're doing a bloody good job down there.'

I moved as surreptitiously as I could, to a position where I could see Anders' face. I wanted to see what he was looking at. The back of his head was resting on the grass and his eyes were staring straight ahead of him, up into the sky, into space, at nothing. But then I saw the sky was full of clouds that a lively breeze was ruffling and remoulding. Anders was describing what he saw in them. 'A castle, a pillow, a loaf of bread, an isthmus ...' I studied the clouds and I could see what he meant, sort of. Yes, there was definitely one formation in the sky that looked quite like a castle, a loaf of bread and so on. I probably wouldn't have 'seen' these things if I hadn't heard Anders naming them, but they were definitely, in some sense of the word, visible; in some sense of the phrase, there to be seen. What, if anything, they had to do with sex I had no idea.

Anders continued to speak, though he now was talking more quickly and with less precision, 'A helicopter, a petrol pump, and a, you know, a fish, an octopus, one of those ... oh Christ, I'm coming ...' which he duly did, after which he slid into a deep silence. Sita let go of his penis and wiped her hand on the grass; not very flattering to a man, I'd have thought.

I retreated. My tread was tentative, since I assumed the post-orgasmic Anders would be rather more alert than the pre-orgasmic one, and I imagined he might have specially violent impulses towards peeping Toms. I was so busy trying to creep away that I didn't see Charles Manning until I'd nearly walked into him. I was startled. He was not.

'Sometimes it's good to watch, isn't it?' he said.

'What?'

'The human imagination is a deep, fecund source of erotic images, but sometimes it isn't enough.'

'What? I said again.

'Personally,' he continued, 'I'd say I've lived a fairly full sensual life. It's certainly provided the fodder for a goodly amount of self-abuse. And yet there's nothing like a bit of fresh, real-life stimulus for recharging the erotic batteries. One's own fantasies are necessarily limited. To catch a glimpse of someone else's reality is jolly arousing, even if Anders isn't precisely the man I would most like to have striding through my erotic reveries.'

I stopped myself saying 'what' again. Instead I said, 'Well, Charles, if there are all these orgies of yours going on there must be no end of visual stimulation for you.'

He looked at me rather less pleasantly than usual. 'Oh you're smart, aren't you? I know what you're trying to do. You're trying to make me believe I'm seeing things. You think I'm making it up. You think I didn't see Sita giving Anders a hand job, is that it?'

Maybe he didn't say 'hand job'. I think it wasn't a term we used much in those days.

'No, Charles,' I said. 'I'm not saying you're hallucinating. I saw the same thing you did – Sita and Anders, doing God knows what exactly. But I've never seen any of these orgies you talk about.'

'And only seeing is believing?'

'Well in a way, yes.'

'Although sometimes you can't believe your eyes. And sometimes your eyes deceive you.'

'Well yes,' I agreed.

'Tell me, Gregory, what do you do when you masturbate?' he enquired.

'What?' I knew exactly what he'd said but it seemed best to pretend I hadn't understood.

'I'm not enquiring about physical technique,' he said. 'I'm interested in whether you run, as it were, dirty films in the cinema of your imagination. And are you the star of these films? A supporting actor? A spear-carrier? And are these mental films reruns or remakes or sequels of events you've actually participated in, or are they scenarios you'd *like* to participate in, or scenarios you couldn't *possibly* participate in, but enjoy thinking about, nevertheless? And who's in the cast? Is it Marilyn Monroe and Sophia Loren and Julie

Ege, or is it the girl from the corner shop or your old gym mistress or the Queen?'

'I don't really want to share my masturbatory fantasies with you, Charles,' I said. 'It's nothing personal.'

Charles Manning looked understanding but troubled.

'You see, I'm wondering whether it's bad to have these fantasies,' he said, 'to run these pictures through my mind. I'm frightened they might be ruining all the good work Kincaidian Therapy is doing for me.'

I couldn't tell whether he was really concerned about this or not, but I thought it was best to say, 'I don't know. You should ask Dr Kincaid.'

'Or Dr Crowe,' he said slyly.

That offended me. I didn't want him discussing his masturbatory fantasies with Alicia, and he obviously knew that; yet at the same time I realised I was being absurd. Alicia was a grown woman, a doctor, a professional; she was hardly going to be harmed by answering a few questions about sex from one of her patients.

'Yes, why don't you,' I said.

'And what if I find I'm having masturbatory fantasies concerning Dr Crowe herself, or about Dr Crowe and you, or Dr Crowe and you and Dr Kincaid and Sita and Anders all together in a kind of sexual snarl-up?'

'Then I think you should go and have a cold shower,' I said primly.

'And tell me,' he said, 'what role do you think visualisation plays in coitus?'

'Oh please, Charles,' I said, but that didn't stop him either.

'I've never been sure of the morality of picturing one person while you're having sex with another. It seems at best distasteful, at worst an act of betrayal. But supposing your current partner doesn't arouse you sufficiently? What if you have trouble sustaining an erection? You need to stay hard in order to please the one you're with, and so you begin to think of someone else or perhaps of many others. Your arousal is renewed. The erection remains, the act of coition is satisfactory, you've pleased your partner. Who's to say it's such a bad thing?'

'Not me,' I said dismissively. I was too young to consider this an issue worth thinking about.

'Then there's the other side,' Charles Manning said, 'when you need to slow yourself down, when you're in danger of coming too soon. No point trying to visualise in those circumstances. I did briefly try fantasising about women I didn't find attractive, but it never worked. Once the blood is up, all women are attractive, all women are arousing. Some people suggest doing mathematical problems or thinking about sports results, but again those methods never worked for me either. You want to know what works for me?'

'Not really,' I said, though I knew it would do no good.

'Reciting poetry,' Charles Manning said. 'To myself. In my own head, not aloud obviously, that would undoubtedly spoil the moment. But if I turn my mind to Kipling or Vachel Lindsay or T. S. Eliot, they slow me down very effectively indeed.'

I. A. Richards, or at least Byron, might have wanted to ask Charles Manning if he ever visualised poetic images as he recited, whether he saw boots or the Congo or ash on an old man's sleeve; and whether it was the images or the words themselves that delayed him. But I didn't ask that question. I simply said, 'Surely there aren't many occasions when you need to sustain yourself or slow yourself down, are there, Charles? You told me you weren't here for the sex.'

'There are all too many,' he said sadly. 'All too many.'

'Maybe you should write about it,' I suggested.

'Oh no, Gregory. Some things are far too precious to write about. Now, if you'll forgive me, I'll retire to my room so I can pollute myself before the memory of Anders and Sita loses some of its sharpness.'

I had no desire to detain him. Returning to my hut I found the memory of seeing Anders and Sita anything but erotic. I wasn't disgusted or offended, but I had the feeling that I'd seen something I shouldn't have seen, that I didn't want to see. I liked to think I'd watched them not out of any voyeuristic impulse, but out of simple curiosity. I'd heard Anders' voice and I'd wanted to see what he was up to. I wanted to know what was going on in the clinic. Was that so odd or so terrible?

One thing apparently going on was a general, steady undermining of the principles of Kincaidian Therapy. Kincaid was trying to keep out the images but they kept creeping right back in, via sawdust or flames, drugs or clouds or masturbatory fantasies. The subversive in me was quite content with this. You wouldn't want the head of the clinic to be able to wield absolute power, would you? At the same time, if Kincaidian Therapy was to be given a chance, the patients should surely be trying to stick to its tenets. Sometimes it was almost as if they wanted to stay sick. I wondered why they could possibly want that.

21

All too often as I tell the story of my time at the Kincaid Clinic I'm struck by how slow and stupid I seem to have been. I don't think I should necessarily have known from the beginning exactly what was going on around me, since parts of it remain fairly inscrutable to me even now, but sometimes it does seem reprehensible that I didn't worry more about how little I knew. Such discoveries as I made were forced on me rather than sought out. For instance . . .

Alicia and I were with Kincaid in his office where he was about to conduct a session with Carla. She came into the office, sort of skipped, sort of stumbled, tripped over the edge of a non-existent carpet, then made an attempt to sit down on a chair, but she missed the seat by a foot or two and performed a pratfall, like a physical comedian of the old, unfunny school. Kincaid and Alicia took no notice of the pantomime. Having picked herself up, Carla managed to take up a position on the edge of the chair, but her knees flapped back and forth as she opened and closed her legs, her fists clenched and unclenched, and her features now adopted a series of extreme, rapidly changing expressions, as if she were engaged in exercises designed to limber up the facial muscles.

'Hello, Carla,' Kincaid said to her.

Carla abruptly straightened in her seat as though invisible strings had yanked her upright. 'Och, hello, doctor,' she said in a thick, foolish, unconvincing Scottish accent. I was already finding this spectacle both profoundly irritating and profoundly embarrassing. I'd seen enough of Carla around the place to know she was an habitually silly girl, but in the close confines of Kincaid's office the effect was much more concentrated and much less tolerable.

'Do you know what day it is today, Carla?' Kincaid asked her.

'Christmas?' Carla asked all dewy-eyed.

'No, Carla, I think you know it's not Christmas.'

'Then is it Mother's Day? Or St Swithin's? Or Fat Tuesday? Or Maundy Thursday? Or the seventh Sunday in Michaelmas? Don't tell me, doctor, I really want to guess this one.'

'It's Monday,' Kincaid said.

'No,' Carla said sweetly and sadly, 'I'd never have got that.'

'Do you know who this is, Carla?' and he nodded towards me.

Carla tossed back her head, and her face was gripped by an agony of concentration. 'Is it George Harrison, the quiet one?'

That was near enough for me, and considering that when Kincaid then asked her who the prime minister of England was and she said Zsa Zsa Gabor, it was perhaps surprisingly close. Kincaid pointed at the clock on the wall, a plain, robust circular face with big, clear numbers that showed eleven thirty.

'Now, Carla,' said Kincaid, 'if I asked you what the time was, I think you'd tell me it was midnight or seven o'clock, or a quarter to two, wouldn't you?'

Carla stared at him in amazement, an expression that was replaced a moment later by a sneer.

'And if I raised three fingers,' Kincaid continued, 'and asked you how many I was holding up, you'd tell me it was one or two or four fingers or perhaps even seventeen, wouldn't you? And if I asked you to give me the name of a country, any country, you'd say umbrella or apple or fuselage or any word in the dictionary except one that was the name of a country. I'm right, aren't I? I'm not misrepresenting you here, am I, Carla?'

She turned in my direction and looked at me in all innocence, as though this was news to her.

'Now, in the old days,' said Kincaid, and it seemed that Kincaid's explanation must be for my benefit rather than for Carla's or Alicia's, 'we might have described Carla's condition as *malingering*. It's a word that doesn't sound very scientific, yet for a long time it was perfectly serviceable. If you were a murderer trying to prove you weren't responsible for your actions, or a soldier trying to get out of the army, you would behave as absurdly, as insanely as possible, and try to convince the doctors you were mad. If you succeeded they'd let you go.

'We have a bigger choice of vocabulary these days. Today it would be all too tempting to look at Carla and say, ah yes, here we have a factitious disorder, a form of hyperkinetic catatonia, an hysterical pseudodementia, a Ganserian twilight state or, if you will, a form of buffoonery psychosis, although, of course, these are merely words, merely labels.'

'That's right,' Alicia agreed.

'The premise is,' Kincaid continued, 'that if Carla is only pretending to be mad, then there must be a sane reason for that pretence. But what could that reason be? Carla is not accused of any crime. She's not trying to get out of military service. Her family life is stable. By a great many touchstones Carla would seem to be quite sane. In fact the only indications that she isn't, are her displays of malingering. I believe this is what people have started to call a *Catch 22* situation.'

Kincaid's way of talking about Carla as though she was either absent or unable to understand what was being said about her made me very uncomfortable. It seemed disrespectful, as though the girl's presence, perhaps even her existence, was irrelevant, that she was just a guinea pig, a piece of data. Not that it bothered Carla. She was staring at the ceiling now and tugging at her left nostril.

'Surely,' Kincaid said, 'no sane person would pretend to be mad. Does it therefore follow, that if there's no reason there's no pretence? Obviously we can't take the patient's word on these matters. To believe that a patient is mad simply because she says so would be as absurd as to believe she was sane simply because she said that.'

'I think I get the point,' I said.

'I thought you would,' said Kincaid. 'I knew you'd respond to this little linguistic-philosophical conundrum. I think it will stay with you and give you food for thought in the days ahead. It might make the basis for a short story or a prose poem. Do you write prose poems?'

'Not lately,' I said.

Carla was now looking alert and baby-faced and her head was swivelling back and forth.

'Perhaps you'd like to ask Carla one or two questions yourself,' Kincaid suggested.

A malingerer or not, psychotic or not, I had no real desire to speak to her. It was obvious that whatever I asked her she was going to give me some lunatic reply. What would be the point?

But then Alicia said, 'Yes, go on, Gregory,' so I thought I'd give it a go.

I tried to appear caring and concerned, but not gullibly so, and I said, 'Carla, what would you do if Dr Kincaid said you were well enough to leave the clinic?'

Kincaid and Alicia both nodded to show they thought I'd asked a good question, while Carla began to chuckle, then laugh, rocking mechanically like one of those laughing policemen you used to get at the seaside. The motion slowly subsided and she said, 'I'd put my head up my arse.'

Kincaid looked at me smugly and sadly. He was pleased. I was proving something he already knew to be true.

'Like to try another question?' he said.

I couldn't imagine that the content of the question mattered much but I asked, 'Read any good books lately, Carla?'

'No,' she said.

A straight answer. To my enormous surprise, I seemed to be doing something right.

'Seen any good films?'

'No.'

'Watched any good television?'

'No.'

'Been to any good orgies?'

I don't know why I asked that. It just slipped out. And I knew that Carla's reply would prove nothing, indicate nothing, but I was still interested to hear what she said, and I was equally interested to see Kincaid and Alicia's reactions, both to the reply and to the mere fact that I'd asked the question. Their faces showed nothing I could read, slight frowns that might be taken to indicate that I'd asked a less good question this time, but not much more than that.

Very quietly and simply Carla said, 'Yes, I have actually. Would you like an invitation to the next one?'

I thought it was a rather clever reply, although naturally I didn't think it meant anything. Carla laughed at her own answer, and I found myself laughing too, though I suspected we were laughing at different things. Kincaid and Alicia didn't join in, and Kincaid had apparently had enough of my questions, since he didn't allow me to ask another.

'I can see you're struggling, Gregory, and I can't blame you,' he said. 'You see, we have another word for what Carla is displaying. Pathomimicry. That is to say, Carla is mimicking pathologies she does not have. She is, if you will, adopting the image of someone else's illness. And I think you'll agree with me that this penetrates to the heart of what we're dealing with at the Kincaid Clinic. Carla has not only seen too many images *per se*, she's seen too many images of madness.'

I wanted to say, wait a minute, where did she see these images? In the Kincaid Clinic? But Kincaid didn't give me a chance to speak. He said, 'I think it might be good for all of us to sit in the dark for a while.'

I could'nt believe he'd said that. He got up, pulled the blinds down and turned off the office lights. The four of us sat there in silence and darkness for what seemed an absurdly long time. Was this really Kincaidian Therapy in action? Was that all that went on in these sessions? Sitting quietly with the lights off? When he reckoned we'd all had enough he dismissed us.

Carla went her buffoonish way, and Alicia and I walked along the corridor towards her office.

'Why in God's name did you ask her a thing like that? About the orgies?' Alicia demanded.

'I don't know,' I answered honestly.

'It doesn't take much to get these patients worked up, you know.'

'I wasn't trying to get her worked up.'

'Then why did you say it?'

'I guess I'm just a natural subversive. We creative types tend to be that way, you know.'

'Are you completely obsessed by sex?'

'Well—' I said.

'And what is this thing you have about orgies? What do you want to do? Watch? Participate? Or do you want to watch *me* participate?'

'What?'

It came as absolutely no surprise to find that Alicia had a much livelier sexual imagination than I did, but for a fleeting second I was able to hold a horribly titillating image of Alicia at the centre of some sort of sexual scrum, surrounded, compressed, skewered by naked lunatics.

'No, I don't want that,' I said.

'You'll find doctors, mostly in America, mostly in California actually, who'll tell you that the only good therapists are the ones who fuck their patients.'

'Well, I don't think I'd want to have anything to do with that,' I said.

'Wouldn't you?'

'No.'

'Not even in your fantasies?'

I wondered if Charles Manning had been talking to her.

'Well, fantasies are fantasies,' I said, 'but no, I still don't think so.'

'Oh, I think you could manage a little fantasy for me, couldn't you, Gregory?'

We had come to her office, and she pulled me inside. She slammed the door behind us, though I noticed she didn't lock it, and then she drew the blinds to darken the room, just as Kincaid had. It wasn't the kind of pitch blackness that usually pertained when Alicia and I had sex, but it served well enough.

'Right,' she said. 'Fuck me. Fuck me like some fierce, drooling lunatic would, with your fierce, drooling, lunatic cock.'

'Oh, OK,' I said.

I did my best to oblige, though in the main I was one of those *mute*, fierce, drooling lunatics. On this occasion Alicia didn't seem to object to my silence. She was verbose enough for both of us. And when it was all over, as we were lying together on her office floor with a chair leg pressed into my flank, Alicia said to me, 'That was very good. You make a very convincing lunatic. Rather more convincing than some of the ones in the clinic.'

Was that meant to be a clue? Was Alicia trying to tell me something about what was going on in the Kincaid Clinic, something that should perhaps have been obvious from watching Carla's behaviour? I had always known that none of the patients was quite what he or she seemed. Some were perhaps, in Kincaid's terms, malingering. They were exaggerating or even inventing symptoms. They wanted to appear madder than they really were, but I knew that didn't mean they were completely sane. Just because someone claims to be adopting an antic disposition doesn't mean they aren't antic. Others were making great claims for their sanity, but in ways that tended to confirm their madness. When they told me their stories, when they made their confessions, their claims to madness or sanity, did they really think I believed them? Did they even want me to?

And something else occurred to me. I remembered how everything had changed at that session in the lecture room at the end of the second week, right before I threatened to walk out of the clinic, right before the 'new deal'. It embarrassed me to think of it now, to recall my easy, knee-jerk response, when I'd abused the patients and told them how crazy they all were. But they'd liked it, and maybe that was the whole point. The moment I called them insane they became very happy, as though they'd won, as though they'd managed to convince me, as though their performances of madness had worked. I felt very foolish, very gullible.

So then I entertained another possibility. I tried to imagine what it would mean if all the patients were actually perfectly sane. What if they weren't mad at all, but for one reason or another they'd decided to appear that way in order to be admitted to the Kincaid Clinic? It was easy enough to imagine reasons for them doing that: reasons to do with wanting to feel protected, of finding the real world too difficult a place. It would be a pretty eccentric thing to do but it wouldn't necessarily mean they were mad. Once they'd convinced Kincaid of their madness and secured a place in the clinic they were therefore happy enough, they'd proved their point, but they still needed to display madness from time to time in order to avoid being pronounced sane, and sent home again. And they displayed it especially well in their writing.

This had some profound consequences for Kincaidian Therapy. For a start it meant that the patients' 'madness' had nothing to do with exposure to images. If their madness was all simply mimicry then both cutting off the flow of images and building this legendary linguistic bulkhead were a complete waste of time. The writing was not a means of alleviating their madness, but an opportunity for them to show it off.

I would have liked to talk to someone about this, and although I didn't feel I could ask Alicia directly, since I was fairly certain she'd fly into a rage, I did get up the courage to say, 'If I wanted to prove to you I was completely sane, how could I do it?'

'You couldn't,' she said. 'And I wouldn't want you to. Only the truly demented need to go around proving how sane they are.'

Yes, that sounded coherent and yet it didn't quite satisfy me. I suppose I was looking for a beautifully simple answer. I wanted all the patients to be completely mad or completely sane: either/or, yes or no. And I recalled a writing exercise that I'd come across in one of the lost textbooks I'd brought with me. The teacher asks the students to write down five true statements about themselves, and then a sixth statement that's a lie. Then the others in the group try to identify which is which. The point of the thing is to show how easily fact and fiction can blend together. The book also warned that there's always some clever dick in the group who tries to sabotage the exercise by writing five lies and only one truth or writing all lies or all truths. I wondered what kind of mayhem the patients would make of it, if they'd been prepared to write to order, which of course they weren't.

I spent a lot of time sitting in my hut, wandering round the grounds trying to think this thing through, wishing I had someone I could discuss it with, and I wasn't getting anywhere. I was thoroughly preoccupied and as I walked past the clinic's front gate I was only dimly aware of the car parked outside, and I took no notice of the woman who got out until she'd come right up to the gate and was shouting at me. And it still took me a moment to realise it was Ruth Harris, owner of the bookshop.

'Hello, handsome,' she called to me. 'How's business?'

'Oh, hello, Ruth. Business is just fine,' I said. Yes, I needed someone to talk to but Ruth Harris wasn't the one.

'Mine too,' she said. 'It turns out you were right. Since I got rid of some of the dead wood things seem to be looking up a little.'

'Glad to be of help.'

'So I wanted to thank you. How about letting me buy you dinner?'

'Thanks, Ruth, but no, I can't.'

'No?'

'I'm very busy. The patients need me.'

'I need you too, Gregory.'

She was joking, but it was one of those spiky, awkward jokes.

'I'm very flattered,' I said, 'but I can't.'

'Well, I'm not going to beg, Gregory.'

'Good,' I said.

I couldn't tell if she was really offended or not, but she pretended to be in quite a huff. 'I was going to give you a little something,' she said, and I looked embarrassed, and she added, 'Don't worry, it's only a *very* little something.'

She handed me a small, scruffy padded envelope that obviously contained a book. Books were always welcome, but I thought I had no need of another one at that particular moment. I thanked her without even bothering to see what book it was.

'You have to open it,' she implored.

I opened the padded envelope and looked in. Ruth Harris had brought me a thin paperback dictionary of psychology.

'Well, thanks very much.'

'No, no, you're missing something,' she said, and she jabbed her finger towards the cover of the book to point out the name of the author: Dr Eric Kincaid.

I admit I was surprised, but not totally. It was only to be expected that a man with Kincaid's professed writing ambitions might already have written a book. I slipped it into my pocket, pretending to be grateful, and Ruth Harris twittered on a while longer before wishing me the best and returning to her car.

It wasn't until the evening that I thought again about Kincaid's dictionary of psychology, when the obsessive reader in me reasserted himself. So, despite all the other more pressing and intractable things I had on my mind, I inevitably found myself thumbing through the book. According to the blurb it was 'written for the general reader', and reading a couple of entries confirmed this to be true. I was pleasantly surprised. Given Kincaid's propensity for the grand statement, the dictionary seemed amazingly simple and clear. I thought it was actually well written. I found myself lingering over the entries for depression, schizophrenia, nymphomania; the easy stuff that everybody thinks they know about without really knowing anything at all. Then I found myself reading the weirder stuff: the Funkenstein test, hellenomania, memory cramp, bdelygmia (look 'em up). There was no entry for Kincaidian Therapy. And eventually I looked up some of the specific conditions I'd come across at the clinic: alcoholism, mutism, anal castration complex, paranoia, exhibitionism, pathomimicry.

They were all there, all clearly and concisely described. It was amazing. If you'd had the book and the relevant patient in front of you, you'd have been able to make a perfectly sound diagnosis. It appeared that the inmates were textbook cases. Kincaid's dictionary might have been describing the current population of his clinic. Just to make sure this wasn't the case I turned to the front of the book and checked the date of publication. I was relieved to see this was the paperback edition of a hardback that had been published some years previously. Surely none of the patients could have been here that long. I jumped to the hasty conclusion that even though madness appeared to be wild and formless, it had the habit of fitting itself around some fairly rigid templates; when you've seen one case of polyglot neophasia you've seen them all.

But that assumed that the patients were actually mad. What if they weren't? If the patients were actually (in some sense of the word) sane but, for whatever reasons, wanted to appear mad, what could be a better guide to feigning madness than a dictionary of psychology? And if you specifically wanted to convince Dr Eric Kincaid of your madness, why not match up to his particular definitions and observations? Could it really be that the patients were acting out Kincaid's script? Could it be that he was having his prejudices about madness confirmed by people who were trying very hard to confirm them?

It felt as though a light bulb had gone on above my head, a weary old image for brain activity, I admit. I was wary of adopting a grand theory, and of finding it so easily. I wasn't sure what it meant, what its implications were, but it seemed to fit the case. It sounded crazy, but that was precisely why it made sense. Did that in itself sound crazy? And what should I do about it? Should I go running to Kincaid, and tell him what I thought, that he was wasting his time, that the patients were deceiving him, playing with him, and that he was too stupid to see it? I knew how that would go down. Even if it were true he'd be the last person who'd want to hear it, and he certainly wouldn't believe it. Wouldn't he think *I* was crazy? Perhaps I should start with Alicia.

And that was when I learned the difference between coprolalia, coprophilia and coprophemia. The dictionary fell open at the right page and there it was. Coprophemia, in Kincaid's words, is: 'filthy speech, scatalogia, perhaps a paraphilia in which the patient uses obscene words and phrases as a means, or at least a major component, of sexual arousal.' Yep, that was an accurate description of Alicia's bedroom antics. Antics indeed. Oh fuck.

Now, it seemed to me that being a coprophemic was by no means synonymous with being mad, but the fact that it was there in the dictionary at all gave me pause. I'd thought Alicia was just a little wild, but it appeared there was a psychological word for it, that it was a recognisable disorder. Did that mean she was crazy? Oh fuck again.

I had a bad night. I didn't know whether I was right or wrong about anything, and I certainly wasn't sure that I wanted to be right. I didn't sleep. I couldn't think. I knew I couldn't talk to anybody. I spent the night feeling as though my head was being turned inside out like an old woollen bedsock; not a condition that Kincaid's dictionary had any word for. But round about daybreak, light finally dawned.

I thought of a way of finding an answer, an easy answer, I hoped, and perhaps only a partial one, but one I reckoned I could trust, one that relied on textual evidence, on the written word. I still had a touching faith in that. I decided I was going to break into Kincaid's files and read the patients' case histories. That might not tell me absolutely everything there was to know but it would surely help prove or disprove my grand theory.

I began by thinking I might try to break into Kincaid's office in the middle of the night, but I soon saw that wouldn't work. Kincaid's sleeping quarters were right next to the office. He'd be bound to hear me. The middle of the day, in working hours was a much better bet, but a distraction was needed, a way of getting Kincaid out of his office and getting me in. I also needed some means of opening the filing cabinet.

I decided to engineer a small crisis. I went and talked to Maureen while she was gardening. I wanted to see what tools she had and whether any of them could be used to jemmy open the filing cabinet. The best I could find was a small but sturdy pair of secateurs, not exactly the perfect instrument for the job, but I picked them up, apparently absent-mindedly, and slipped them into my pocket when Maureen wasn't looking. Then I talked to her about gardening, about what a menace birds could be, always eating the seeds and pecking at seedlings the moment they came through. I knew this via my mother. Perhaps what was needed was a scarecrow. She liked the idea a lot, and decided she'd make one at once.

I offered her a pair of my jeans and an old shirt and, leaving her to it, I sauntered up to Kincaid's office, asked him if he was busy, then in a *faux*-casual sort of way asked him whether he thought sculpture constituted graven images. He most certainly did. Then how about scarecrows? No different, he said. So I suggested he might want to pop down to the garden and see what Maureen was up to; and he fell for it. He swooped out of the office and I found myself alone, impressed by the success of my simple scheme. I felt simultaneously scared yet reckless. The need to know what was in those files had become unbearable.

I went over to the filing cabinet, jammed the point of the secateurs ineptly in the gap above the top drawer, and tried to lever it open. The metal bent and buckled but the lock remained intact. I tried again, no more expertly than before, and that was when I got caught – by Anders. He was standing in the doorway of Kincaid's office, smiling delightedly.

'A bit of breaking and entering,' he said. 'Nice one. Need a hand?'

He looked like a man who was far more used to opening locks than I was, so I handed the secateurs to him and he enthusiastically jammed them into the cabinet, as though he'd been doing it all his life, as I suppose he probably had. The lock snapped and the drawer sprang open to reveal a row of thick manila files. I felt I was on the threshold of something very, very important. That was when I got caught for the second time – by Kincaid. He'd quickly lost interest in Maureen and the scarecrow and had returned to his office.

I was lost for words; there wasn't a thought in my head, no excuse I could come up with. I'd been caught red-handed and I was ready for the inevitable worst; but Anders, much cooler in a crisis than I could ever have hoped to be, was immediately on top of the situation.

'All right, doc,' Anders said to Kincaid. 'You've got me bang to rights. You can't get away with nothin' in this place. A bloke tries to practise his craft and do an honest bit of thieving, and straight away he gets nabbed at it by the bloody writer-in-residence. I ask you. Then before I can worm me way out of that one, the boss hisself shows up. Maybe I'm just not cut out for a life of crime.'

'Is this true?' Kincaid asked, though whether of me or of Anders wasn't clear.

'Are you calling me a liar, you fucking arsehole?' Anders demanded, and for once I found his sudden fury rather appealing, or at least useful. Whether it was real or feigned I was glad of it since it drew attention away from me. He fondled the secateurs lovingly as if he wanted to use them on flesh.

'Why?' Kincaid asked gently. 'What did you expect to find in the filing cabinet?'

'Pictures,' Anders said, and his mouth trembled sluggishly and tears began to trickle from his eyes.

'Oh, Anders,' said Kincaid, 'you still have such a long way to go.'

Anders' head sagged. 'Will you go with me, doc? Will you?'

'I'll try, Anders, I'll certainly try.'

Anders appeared to find this unbearably moving. He meekly handed over the secateurs, which Kincaid received as though they were a thoughtful gift, an apple for the teacher. He patted Anders' shoulder in a manly fashion.

'Just as well you were here, Gregory,' said Kincaid.

I had no idea if he meant it, whether he'd believed Anders' story or not, but if he hadn't believed it then I couldn't think why he was pretending he had. Equally, I had very little idea what reason Anders could have for taking the blame. Did he simply like me? Did he want to protect me, or was he doing it for dark reasons of his own, to put me in his debt? Either way, I was no nearer to getting my hands on the patients' files, and since Kincaid would now be guarding them even more carefully, the promise of textual evidence had receded considerably. I felt I'd acted pretty ineptly.

Later that night I sat in my hut, still trying to tease out all the implications of what I thought I'd discovered. Then I heard some familiar rustling sounds outside. And when I smelled smoke I assumed it was Maureen doing some late-night gardening, getting rid of garden rubbish as before, maybe seeing some flames this time. I thought I'd go and have a word with her, apologise for the business with the scarecrow.

I found her, and sure enough she was burning rubbish; but not just garden rubbish. She'd created a large bonfire, and the outer layers did indeed consist of twigs and clippings, but I could see that at the centre of the bonfire, was a stumpy heap of manila files: the patients' case histories. And sitting on top of the fire, like a Guy Fawkes, was the now abandoned scarecrow.

'What are you up to?' I asked her as gently as I could, though I wasn't feeling gentle.

'He made me do it.'

'Kincaid?'

'Who else? The devil?'

I stood watching the fire, and I thought of the line from Heinrich Heine, 'Whenever they burn books, they will also in the end burn people,' and I looked at the scarecrow who was turning black and folding in on himself, and I couldn't help thinking he looked an awful lot like me.

22

'But Maureen claims that Kincaid *told* her to burn the files,' I insisted.

'She would say that, wouldn't she?' said Alicia. 'She's insane. She's a pyromaniac.'

'Is she?' It was news to me. I'd seen her burning a bit of garden rubbish but that hardly seemed synonymous with pyromania.

'Isn't that just a word?' I asked.

'Let's just say she has pyromaniac tendencies, shall we?'

I agreed that we would say that. We were in bed together, and although we were in darkness, as usual, it was one of those rare moments when we were actually talking to each other rather than performing other verbal gymnastics. Alicia was seeming extremely sane.

She went on, 'I don't even understand how she was able to get at the files. Weren't they locked away in the filing cabinet?'

'The filing cabinet had been broken open.'

'By Maureen?'

'No, by Anders.'

'Why would he do that?'

I could have repeated Anders' own version about him searching for pictures, but I wanted the story to sound more convincing than that. 'Habit?' I suggested. 'Maybe he's a man who likes breaking and entering.'

She didn't find that psychologically very plausible either. 'It's very odd,' she said.

'Aren't there copies of the files?' I asked. 'Duplicates?'

'Don't be ridiculous. If the medical profession kept duplicate copies of every bit of paper it produced, nobody would ever find anything.'

'But the information in them must exist in some other form, surely?'

'If it's in a different form, then by definition it's different information.'

'But presumably you and Dr Kincaid between you could reconstruct the files.'

'Presumably we could. But why would we want to? We already know what we know. What would be the point?'

'Maybe so that other people could share what you know.'

'You, for instance.'

'Yes,' I said, 'but not only me.'

'How about this for an option, Gregory? Why don't *you* reconstruct your own version of the files? Why don't you write down what *you* know? It would be every bit as valid as what Dr Kincaid and I might do.'

'That's surely not true,' I said. 'There are all sorts of things I don't know about them.'

'And so you want to believe in some external authority, some files, some case histories, some text that will solve everything, remove all doubt, tell you everything you need to know. It sounds simultaneously naive and fundamentalist to me, Gregory.'

'Does it?' I asked. I really wasn't sure any more.

'Yes, it does,' said Alicia. 'You know, the ability to live with an amount of doubt and uncertainty is a fairly reasonable definition of maturity and mental health in my book.'

I wanted to feel mature and mentally healthy, and it certainly appeared that I had no choice in the matter. The files were gone, and it was entirely my fault. Who knew whether they'd really have contained the great doubt-quenching revelation I'd been hoping for, but any such revelation would now have to come from some other source.

When Kincaid eventually talked to me about it he took a different line from Alicia. He stuck to the story that he'd had no part in the burning of the files and, given how upset he seemed, I was at least somewhat inclined to believe him.

'This is a great blow,' he said. 'Documentation is very important in our work. As a writer you understand that.'

'Well, yes,' I said.

'But there may be something good to be salvaged, and I think you'll soon see what. You'll see that we have at our disposal another, far more telling form of documentation.'

'We do?'

'The patients' own writing,' he said triumphantly.

'Oh, right,' I said, but I'm sure I didn't sound convinced. Given the nature of the patients' writing, and its strenuous anonymity, I couldn't see how it was any sort of equivalent to, or replacement for, files and case histories.

Kincaid saw I was perplexed and said, 'Gregory, I think it's time to publish.'

'Publish?'

'Yes, Gregory. I want to see the patients' literary efforts in print. A thickish volume: a preface from me, an introduction from you, an afterword by R. D. Laing or some such. It would be a sort of anthology to show how the clinic's work took these mad people on a literary journey into sanity. It would look good on both our CVs. And it would do the clinic no end of good when it comes to applying for grants.'

'Are you sure we're ready?' I said.

'We've got many thousands of pages cluttering up the library. Don't tell me we don't have enough material.'

'We have the quantity, yes, but—'

'Come, come, Gregory. You submit it to a publisher and they publish it. I don't know precisely how these things are done, but I'm sure *you* do. You're the professional. You must have your contacts.'

'I suppose,' I said.

'Good. Then I'll leave you to sort out the chapter and verse, and I look forward to the publication party. These things don't normally take very long, do they?'

I couldn't believe Kincaid's grasp on the way publishing worked was quite as slight as he pretended, and I wondered if this was his way of taunting and torturing me. Perhaps he knew I'd been trying to get into the files and he was saying, all right, if you think the written word is so meaningful, let's see if you can give some meaning to the patients' outpourings.

'You'll find Alicia and I and the patients are right behind you on this one,' he said.

He was right. Alicia came to me again that night and said she was delighted at what I was doing for the patients, that she was proud of me. The patients seemed proud too. Word of what I had apparently agreed to do was already all round the clinic. Raymond's coffee deliveries became more frequent. Max slipped me a half-bottle of rum. Charity rolled me some of the fattest joints I'd ever seen. Byron offered me words of literary encouragement, and Anders said if there was any little problem I was having he'd be happy to sort it out for me. I thought I'd better do something.

I was aware that this was a distraction from the real problems I'd been wrestling with, about the patients, about Alicia, about the point of Kincaidian Therapy, and I was also aware it might be a smokescreen. Yet I found myself welcoming the distraction. If I could neither prove nor disprove anything about the patients' madness or sanity, it might be as well to get on with something else. I would be mature and healthy, and live with doubt, as Alicia had recommended. And even if I was taking that recommendation from someone who might not herself be an absolute model of mental health, that was all right too.

My knowledge of the publishing world was hardly encyclopaedic, but one thing I was sure of, you couldn't just bundle up this mass of writing, the raw material that rested on the library shelves, send it off to the publisher and hope for the best; well, you could, but it would be sent straight back, probably unread.

It needed editing, though I wasn't sure what form that editing should take. Even though I'd come to think of the writing as some vast continuum, that didn't mean it was utterly homogenous and indivisible. Some bits were definitely 'better' than others. There were pieces that stood up on their own as memoirs or interior monologues or fantasies or even, at a pinch, as experimental short stories. I saw that it might indeed be possible, with judicious editing, to put these pieces together and form an anthology that was no worse than many collections of new writing by new writers.

The disadvantage of doing it that way was all too obvious. Whatever else these pieces were, they weren't simply new writing by new writers. Whatever doubts I might have about the authenticity of the patients' madness, it was obviously impossible to send this anthology off into the world and expect it to compete on equal terms in the world of literature. If the patients were mad, even if they were only pretending to be mad, the anthology had to show that. It had to show the insanity, the mania, the obsession, the sex, the violence, the banality – the whole works.

And if that was the case, I should try to make the selection as genuinely representative as possible. Choosing the 'best' stuff therefore seemed inappropriate. A true picture of what was going on in the clinic would of necessity include much that was tedious and repetitive and downright incompetent. But that raised other objections. I didn't want this anthology to be just a freak show, the literary equivalent of going along to Bedlam to gawp at the amusing lunatics. I knew I had a job on my hands.

I went to the library and spent the whole of the next week reading and rereading, arranging and rearranging, ordering and reordering the vast textual resources at my disposal. Very little of it was quite as I had recalled. My mind had played odd little tricks. The stuff that I'd thought of as being rather good now seemed nowhere near as good as I remembered, while some of the stuff I'd initially imagined could be dismissed out of hand, didn't seem too bad at all.

I organised the writing into piles all around the library. I began simply enough with groupings of yes, no and maybe; but I soon found the maybes were becoming far and away the biggest group. I found it hard to reject anything, hard to accept anything. I tried some thematic groupings: divided the writings into those about sex, violence, childhood, time, mortality, fantasy, obsession. But these categories refused to hold. Everything was related to everything else. There were fantasies about sex and violence, pieces that fretted about time and mortality, pieces that were obsessed with childhood.

I started to worry about my own prejudices too. If I only included pieces I liked, I might be turning the selection into a picture of my own tastes. That was no good. And was I being unfair? Perhaps I liked some patients' writing better than others. How would those patients feel who were under-represented or even omitted from the anthology altogether? Would it make them hate me? Would they take some sort of mad revenge? For a moment I thought perhaps I should just offer each patient twenty or thirty pages of the anthology and say, 'These pages are yours, do what you like with them.' But that obviously wasn't going to work either, not given their continuing desire for anonymity.

I began to wonder whether some sort of arbitrary sampling mightn't be appropriate, that I should just take sections at random, perhaps using some mechanical means of selection, dice maybe, and slam them together to make a collage or cut up. It could certainly be construed as fair, and the finished article would no doubt be convincingly experimental and demented. No, that didn't seem good enough but, then again, neither did anything else.

By the end of the week chaos had overtaken both the library and my head. My thoughts were as shuffled and as disarrayed as the mass of paper now strewn all over every part of the library shelves, floor, tables and chairs. I no longer felt able to make any judgements, literary or otherwise. I was too close. Everything seemed to be of a piece. Yes, some bits might briefly seem better written or more coherent than others, but what did that mean? What were the values I was attaching to good, better and best? Wasn't I imposing my will, my narrow ideas of what constituted sanity? I was striving for clarity, for coherence, but after a while that seemed meaningless too. Maybe incoherence was the *whole point*.

Time passed, words swirled around me. I drank lots of coffee, got wired, smoked a little dope to smooth off the edges, drank some of Max's rum to make myself feel more relaxed. None of it did much good.

When Kincaid eventually stuck his head round the door late one night I was confused, cranky, manic and just about ready to admit defeat, but I knew he wouldn't let me do anything so pathetic. He expressed his continuing, unshakeable confidence in my abilities. He looked at the mass of disorganised paper and said, 'Yes, this is a learning experience for me. You're showing me how form comes out of chaos.' I wanted to hit him. He must have sensed this, or at least detected some frantic, weary desperation in me, and he added, 'You know, Gregory, you shouldn't be too proud to ask for help.'

The man was right again. I decided to call Gregory Collins.

23

What else was there to do? As I had quite effectively proved to myself, I was no editor, no anthologiser and, in reality, as far as I knew, neither was Gregory Collins, but who else could I turn to? Nicola? Dr Bentley? Oh sure. So I decided I'd ask Gregory to help me. I'd ask him to take a look at the patients' work. And if he found the material as intractable as I did, then all well and good, we'd tell Kincaid that this whole anthology idea was a bad one and we'd put it behind us. It would be admitting failure. It would be disappointing quite a few people, but at least if we admitted defeat together I wouldn't look like such a complete loser.

I called Gregory at his school, and explained myself. He was flattered to be asked, and unnaturally excited at the prospect. The school holidays were about to start and he was driving down to London to spend a couple of weeks with Nicola. Things were 'champion' between them. He told me this rather less sheepishly than I thought courtesy demanded and I was a little surprised too to find he was either a car driver or a car owner. He looked like a man with public transport written all over him. Anyway, he said it would be simple enough for him to drive down to Brighton for the afternoon and cast his eye over the material for this putative anthology.

I tried to describe the vast quantity of writing and its capacity to provoke despair, but I couldn't make him understand, and after a while I stopped trying. If he really thought he could just breeze in and assimilate this whole mess in one afternoon, he had a shock coming. We set a date for his visit. I asked him to indulge me and to get there as early as he could, just in case the job proved to be bigger than he was anticipating, and grudgingly he agreed.

Now I had to invent a fake identity for Gregory. Alicia, of course, had once been in the same room as him, at the reading I'd done in

Ruth Harris's bookshop. They'd never spoken, never been introduced, and I had the feeling she might not remember him at all, but to be on the safe side I kept the name he'd invented for himself then, Bob Burns. If Alicia started asking questions about how I now came to be friends with someone who had then been a complete stranger, I could either say that we'd become friends since the reading, or even, if I needed to get wildly inventive, that he'd been a friend all along and I'd planted him in the audience to say nice things about me. But Alicia was neither inquisitive nor suspicious. I explained to her and to Kincaid, and eventually even to the patients, that this was a friend of mine who had unfailing literary judgement, and who was kind enough to come along and help me. Nobody doubted me. Kincaid said it was no bad thing to have a second opinion, but he warned that I shouldn't be too easily influenced by an outside source, that I should ensure the project remained 'ours', by which I assumed he meant 'his'.

News of the impending arrival of 'Bob Burns' produced a flurry of creativity in the patients. In the days before his visit they produced a further few hundred pages, pages I could barely bring myself to read. They were about to become Gregory's problem.

He arrived in his car exactly on time. Kincaid was there at the gate waiting to let him in. I was a bit miffed at this, considering the ignominy of my own arrival. Wouldn't a few hours in a padded cell have been as perfect a welcome for Gregory as they had been for me?

Why did I feel hostile towards Gregory? It was easy to think of reasons, not all of them very good ones, and none of them very noble. Perhaps I was resentful that he could do what I couldn't; that he really was what I was only pretending to be: a writer. And now I would owe him something. He was doing me a favour by coming to the clinic. I had every reason to be grateful to him, and gratitude is the most difficult and troubling of emotions. And then there was Nicola. Did I wish I was spending two weeks in London with Nicola? No, definitely, positively not, and yet I still didn't much like the idea of her spending two weeks with Gregory. It wasn't that I thought, If I can't have her then nobody can; I just thought that Gregory shouldn't be the one to have her. He didn't deserve her. He wasn't good enough.

The situation was only made worse when I saw that Nicola seemed to be having some beneficial influence on him. I saw he looked less like a nerd than he used to. The hair had grown and been styled, the clothes weren't so conspicuously unhip. He still didn't look like anybody's Prince Charming but he was much improved.

Before he'd even got out of his car he said to me, 'Nicola sends her love.'

'Really?' I couldn't believe she would have sent me anything so warm and unequivocal.

'Really,' he said. 'She's not bitter, not any more.'

'That's nice.'

'Her job's going well, and she's been promoted. She's an editor there now, and things are great between her and me, so she's got nothing to be bitter about, has she?'

I wanted to say that she never did have anything to be bitter about, that only I was entitled to be bitter.

'Yes, well, send her my love in return,' was all I said.

'I'll do that.'

Gregory was introduced as Bob Burns. He exchanged pleasantries with Kincaid and Alicia, then I led him through the clinic up to the library. He showed no curiosity as he passed through the building, showed no uneasiness at finding himself in an asylum, but as we walked I was aware of patients lurking in corridors and stairwells and doorways, pretending they were just there by chance, just happening to catch a glimpse of my pal the littérateur, the man who had the power to transmit their work to a waiting world.

It was with a peculiar, perhaps a perverse, pride that I showed Gregory into the library. Even an unemotional, dour Yorkshireman like Gregory would surely be impressed by the sheer quantity of paper, the sheer number of words he was going to have to deal with. But Gregory saw it all set out, spread out on the library shelves and table and floor, and he showed no signs of being impressed or surprised or challenged by the size of the task ahead. All he said was, 'What I need you to do is fetch me a big pot of tea, and keep it coming at regular intervals. All right?'

'All right,' I said grudgingly.

He sat down at the library table, without taking his coat off, and he started to read the first page that happened to come to hand. I could see it was one of the more disgustingly violent pieces, and I was about to explain that this maybe wasn't the ideal place to start. But Gregory hushed me and said something about not wanting to have his primary response tainted, and after that his concentration was so awesomely fierce it was as though I, the library, the clinic, the world, had ceased to exist for him.

I went off to the kitchen to get some tea. Raymond and Cook were there already, and they fell over themselves to brew a fresh pot. I thanked them and took it up to the library. And that's how it went for the rest of the day. Gregory read and I served as his waiter. It was probably as good a role for me as any. What else would I have done? Sat and watched him read?

As I came and went I would always find a patient or two who just happened to be strolling past the library, sometimes even listening at the door, though I was baffled as to what they could be expecting to hear. Even Kincaid couldn't keep away and he asked me if there was anything my friend needed. Like what? 'Oh,' said Kincaid, 'a cushion, secretarial help, a massage, ear-plugs, an extra reading lamp.' Irritated by this concern, I assured Kincaid that my friend had a frugal, monkish disposition: he liked silence, isolation, a hard chair, a bright overhead light. I felt like Gregory's minder, his public relations man, his pander. These roles were far less appealing than being his waiter.

I saw, on my visits, that Gregory's progress through the pages was awe-inspiringly fast. I wondered if that was what came of being a schoolteacher and having to read dozens of boys' history essays. I was impressed by his concentration and his work rate. Even so, it was obvious he had much more than a day's work on his hands.

At five in the afternoon he said, 'I'm supposed to be meeting Nicola in London at half past six. I'm not going to make it. Would you ring her for me?'

'No, Gregory,' I said. 'I think it should come from you.'

'But I'm engrossed.'

'Trust me. She won't want to hear it from me.'

Puzzled at my assessment of the situation, but willing to believe I knew more about these matters than he did, Gregory made the phone call. I stood some distance away and pretended not to be listening, but I heard him say things were very exciting and it was obvious he'd have to stay overnight. If Nicola raised any objections to this plan, and I assumed she would, Gregory did not respond to them.

When he came off the phone I said I'd go and see about fixing up a bed for him, but he said no, that wouldn't be necessary. He intended to continue reading right through the night. If he got too tired he'd cat-nap at the table for an hour or so, then wake up and carry on. He led me to believe he spent many nights like this at home, up all night reading history books, partly as teaching preparation, but mostly for the sheer fun of it.

I last looked in on Gregory at a little after midnight, to tell him I was going to bed and he was on his own as far as further pots of tea were concerned. Earlier in the day he'd scarcely looked up as I'd entered or left the room, but now he gazed at me with an affection that made me uncomfortable, and he said, 'There's some bloody good stuff here,' and then he hesitated, considering whether he should say the thing that was really on his mind. He decided he would. 'I want to thank you, Mike,' he said. 'You're a right good pal.' I was deeply embarrassed and that seemed a suitable note on which to turn in for the night.

Next morning I took a fresh pot of tea to the library. When I got there Gregory was still sitting at the library table, much as I'd left him. His eyes looked a little red, but he was wide awake and excitedly alert. He had dealt with every piece of manuscript, read every bit of writing, and arranged the pages into beautifully neat, regular stacks, and he was looking at them with a benevolent, satisfied gaze. There was an air of smug modesty about him. He had an important verdict to deliver.

'Well?' I asked.

'I need to see your boss,' he said.

I took this as a big insult. Was I just the hired help around here? Was his judgement too grand to be shared with me?

'No,' I said. 'Anything you can say to Kincaid, you can say to me.'

'All right,' he said. 'I was going to tell him I think you've done a brilliant job of inspiring this writing; I think you've probably shown some genius, in fact.'

Now I felt bad, and yet I suspected that he'd deliberately planned it so I should feel bad.

'If it was up to me,' he continued, 'I'd say let's publish the whole bloody lot, exactly as it is, in all its sprawling majesty, don't change a word. But knowing the publishing trade I suppose it'll have to be trimmed down, made more palatable. But we mustn't grumble. We don't live in a perfect world. And I'd be right proud to do the job of trimming.'

'So you think it's publishable?'

'Of course. Nicola will publish it.'

'Will she?'

'If I tell her to publish it, she'll publish it.'

He said it with a ruthless pride in his own power. He was a man who could get things done, make things happen, make his girlfriend do what he wanted. Why did that annoy me so much?

We went along to see Kincaid and Alicia, and Gregory talked about 'the work' as though its importance lay somewhere between *Ulysses* and the Dead Sea Scrolls. He insisted that his role would merely be that of midwife, that the honour was all mine, that he intended to interfere as little as possible, simply to make sure the baby came out whole and healthy. He said he didn't even want his name on the finished book. He was happy for it to say, 'Edited by Gregory Collins'. Kincaid and Alicia were duly impressed by this selflessness, and by the promise of all the good work he was going to do for them, all the literary strings he was in a position to pull.

I was obviously a little less impressed. Yes, I was glad he thought the book was publishable, glad that he'd taken on a job I'd discovered I wasn't able to do, and I was pleased that he thought, or at least said, that I'd displayed a kind of genius, but I was still pissed off to be reminded of my own inadequacies. Why wasn't I a man who could get things done, make things happen? Why did I need Gregory to do them for me, and through an old girlfriend of mine, as it happened. I felt I was a person more entitled to connections and power and string-pulling than Gregory was.

I like to think I managed not to display any of this irritation and jealousy. The four of us, Kincaid, Alicia, Gregory and I, did a lot of smiling and handshaking and saying what we took to be the right thing. Then we loaded up Gregory's car with the whole mass of manuscript. A few patients gathered, wanting to know what was going on, and Kincaid told them he believed he had assured their place in history. Alicia gave them a more prosaic, more detailed explanation, and this made them very happy indeed; a little too happy, it seemed to me. Word spread and resulted in the kind of giddy excitement that I thought was all too likely to end in tears.

Once Gregory's car was loaded I experienced the terrible feeling that I was losing something very valuable and personal. I knew this was unreasonable. This writing was not in any sense 'mine' and it wasn't being lost. It was making its first step towards being found. Barring a car crash, car theft, Gregory not being up to the job he'd set himself, Nicola not being quite as pliant as Gregory thought she was, her company going bankrupt, and so on and so forth, the manuscript was on its way to its public. Still I couldn't help feeling sorry to see it go. I had grown attached to it, to its physical presence.

I tried not to think of this moment as the end of anything. As soon as possible I would convene a meeting with the patients, insist that writing was about process, not about finished product, and I'd get them writing again, begin a second accumulation, volume two maybe. And yet, in retrospect, I now think it would have been much better to accept that this was indeed an end. It might even have been an ideal moment to call it a day. I could have said my job was finished, and left with my head held high. That would have shown some style and integrity. The only problem with this bright idea was that I had nowhere to go. Was I supposed to get another writer-in-residence job in some other nut house? I felt these were few and far between, and probably I had the only such job in the whole of England. Was I supposed to go back to bookselling? Retrain as something else? As what? My career options, my life options, seemed ruinously, laughably limited.

Perhaps, more tellingly, if more reluctantly, I would have had to admit that I was actually happy at the Kincaid Clinic. I had a job, a wage, somewhere to live, a girlfriend of sorts, and if I didn't precisely have friends or a social life, at least there were ten patients I got along with reasonably well. It wasn't the perfect life, but it was *a* life, as much of one as I'd ever had at university, far more of one than I'd had in London. For the first time in a long time I realised I had something to lose.

24

Gregory Collins had been so certain, so blithely, immodestly confident he could do what he'd promised, that I almost wanted him to fail. Almost but not quite. Now that the idea of publication had been put into all our minds, I wanted it as much as anyone else. Kincaid talked as though it was a foregone conclusion, and the patients took his word for it. I was the only one who had any concerns about the difficulties of getting a book published.

But Gregory didn't fail. It took a little time for the publishing machine to gather momentum. I tried to imagine Gregory persuading Nicola, then Nicola persuading her bosses, of the project's viability; but her company was small and eccentric enough for decisions to be made quickly, and much sooner than I could have anticipated we received a formal letter from Nicola confirming that her company wanted to publish a selection of the patients' work. They had an unexpected empty spot on their forthcoming list and this anthology was just the book they needed to fill it. This meant things would have to move fairly swiftly, which I thought was good; a taste for delayed gratification not being one of the patients' strong suits.

I was delighted but surprised. I never thought it was going to be that easy. The letter went on to say that a draft contract would be sent in due course. Kincaid would be able to sign it on behalf of all the patients, since as head of the clinic he was acting *in loco parentis*. We were told it would be a standard contract and I didn't doubt it. Nicola surely wasn't going to rook us. Later there would be a cover design for us to approve, and in the meantime Kincaid and I were to buckle down and get on with writing our introduction and foreword, detailing our philosophy and methods. No more than that was required of us. We could leave all the donkey work to Nicola and 'Bob Burns'.

I did wonder how Nicola felt about all this. Given how angry she'd been about my original impersonation of Gregory it seemed hard to believe she'd happily decided to publish a book that was built around that impersonation, but a number of possible explanations presented themselves. First, that the anger had simply worn off. That's what anger does sometimes, and how long can you perpetuate a grudge against an old boyfriend you never cared all that much about in the first place? A second explanation might have been that Gregory was indeed the Svengali he claimed to be, that one word from him was enough to make Nicola do his bidding. That didn't fit with my reading of either of their characters, although I knew that my character-reading could be pretty wayward. Another, perhaps more plausible, explanation presented itself: that Nicola's desire to publish the book didn't have anything to do with her feelings for me or for Gregory. Maybe she simply thought this was an interesting project, a worthwhile one, even a profitable one.

The letter from Nicola made the patients very happy. What's more, it made them behave relatively sanely, and that worried me a little, because it seemed that doing the writing hadn't had that effect at all. It was only the prospect of seeing it in print that appeared to have done them any good, and that didn't seem right. The relationship between cause and effect felt out of kilter. Perhaps this was publication therapy rather than writing therapy. Perhaps that was all you needed to do to cure people of their madness – just offer to publish what they wrote. But this, of course, assumed they'd been mad in the first place. To the extent that I still didn't know whether the patients' madness was phoney, I equally didn't know whether their newfound (comparative) sanity was phoney either.

Gregory was not troubled by these things. I received lots of correspondence from him. I knew he was the sort of person who wouldn't undertake this project lightly, but even so I was surprised by his intensity. He sent me letters, memos, pages of notes, detailing the progress of his editing. He saw myriad possibilities, he spotted great literary themes and parallels in the work; one letter of his invoked Jung, Pindar and both John Fords. Although I was pleased that he was keeping me informed, I had the feeling these communications weren't really for my benefit, but rather for the benefit of future scholars who might want to know precisely how he'd gone about his task; a feeling that was confirmed when he informed me he was keeping carbon copies.

At the end of every bit of communication, Gregory wrote in large energetic letters, SEND ME MORE, and the patients were only too happy to oblige. Every day a new pile of writing would appear; and every couple of days I'd bundle it up and send it off to Gregory. I never dispatched it without first having read it, but I no longer gave it the sort of attention I once had. There seemed no reason to. This writing was no longer mine. It belonged to Gregory and to the world at large; at least some of it did, the parts that Gregory would edit and approve and include in the anthology. The patients knew this as well as I did, and now they treated me as little more than a messenger through whom they could gain access to Bob Burns.

If anything the writing became even more manic. In person the patients may have behaved with a new restraint, but on paper they raved more extravagantly than ever. There was hideous sex and violence, idiotic confessions, paranoia, mystical druggy outpourings, castration anxiety, crazed word play, retellings of *Gawain and the Green Knight* and *Black Beauty* – the whole shebang. They were playing to a new audience, and Gregory just lapped it up. Each new batch of writing raised him to higher levels of excitement, and sometimes that worried me too.

I suppose it was because when you got right down to it I wasn't sure I shared his lofty estimation of the writing. I wasn't sure it was really as good or as fascinating as he was claiming. I liked it well enough, felt attached to it, but that was for personal reasons, and I thought that Gregory's claims for it were at best excessive and over-optimistic, at worst pretentious, ridiculous and just plain wrong.

Was this sour grapes? Was I angry because Gregory could detect literary quality where I'd only detected insanity? Did it piss me off that he was a better 'literary critic' than I was? I suppose the simple answer had to be yes. I could partly console myself by saying that I'd been too close to things, that it was easier for an outsider to come in and see them more clearly; but that didn't mean I wasn't pissed off. But neither did it mean that I wanted the book to fail. I didn't. I wanted it to be good. I wanted Gregory to be right, even though I didn't think he was.

I couldn't express my doubts to anyone; certainly not to Gregory or Kincaid, and not even to Alicia. Things had been going very well between her and me. She still wouldn't admit we were having a relationship or anything like that, but her nocturnal visits had become more frequent and she was hardly ever angry with me these days. We continued to have highly verbal sex in which I was increasingly called upon to play the part of a sex-crazed lunatic. Was that a bit sick? No doubt it was, but what was I supposed to do? Say to Alicia, 'I'm sorry, but I can only have normal, healthy, conventional sex with you.'? If I'd survived her initial fury I'd never have survived her demands that I define normal, healthy and conventional.

There was only one occasion when Alicia really disturbed me. It was night. I'd been up in the library looking for a book to read. By this time I'd pretty much exhausted the resources of the Ruth Harris selection, so it took me a while to find anything. I finally settled on a biography of General Gordon. When I got back to my hut all the lights were out, and that seemed odd because I was sure I'd left them on. I thought maybe a fuse had blown. But then I saw the door was wide open and I'd definitely closed it. Someone had obviously entered the hut and turned off the light, and I naturally wondered why, and whether they were still there in the dark. Something told me they were. I stood at the open door and listened.

I could hear movement, the heavy sigh of the mattress on my sofabed, a regular, sexual rhythm; and I heard a voice, a familiar one, Alicia's, and she was saying things (or at least variations on things) I had heard her say before: coprophemic utterances, dirty talk, obscenities, words of profane sexual encouragement. 'That's right, that's right you filthy fucking lunatic, lick my cunt, suck it, devour it, stretch it, stick your tongue in, your fingers, stick your whole hand ...' And much more in a similar vein. And who, I wondered, was being sexually encouraged? I ran through an entire cast list of possibilities: all the patients, both male and female. Which one would she have chosen? Or maybe she wasn't with just one; maybe there were three or four of them in there, both sexes, all persuasions, all enjoying the pleasures of Alicia's filthy mouth. Maybe she was at the centre of one of Charles Manning's orgies.

Now wait a minute, hold on, I thought. This was getting out of hand. Alicia was supposed to be the one with the over-active imagination, not me. But in any event, whatever the cast, she'd seen fit to bring them back to my bed. Why had she done that? Was that meant as the final insult, the ultimate slap in my face, and was that some extra turn on for her?

I tried to think of what to do or say. I couldn't come up with anything rational. I didn't feel entirely in control of myself. On automatic pilot, angry yet vulnerable, scared yet reckless, I stormed into the hut, switched on the overhead light, ready for the disgusting pornographic spectacle in my bed. But I was disappointed, or rather I was extremely pleased, since it seemed the light had chased away all the filthy images, all the sexual demons. Alicia was quite alone in my bed, between the sheets, apparently naked but completely covered, and she was masturbating and she was addressing her filth to the empty air above her. Her eyes, freed from their hornrims, squinted in the light. She was surprised to see me but not embarrassed. 'Turn the light off. Get in here and fuck me, you madman.' I did as I was told.

Afterwards she explained that she'd crept into my bed in order to surprise me, but as she waited there alone and naked, she'd started thinking about me, picturing what I'd do to her when I arrived, and that had got her aroused, so she'd had to start masturbating and verbalising. And as she'd said those dirty words she'd been imagining me as the lunatic in bed with her. I decided to believe this and be flattered by it.

However, when the next batch of writing arrived it contained, if not precisely a transcript, then a very fair reconstruction of the coprophemic monologue Alicia had delivered to the empty hut that night. My first reaction was to be furious. Someone had obviously been eavesdropping, stealing Alicia's words. A part of me wanted to convene an emergency meeting of the patients and like some old-fashioned headmaster demand to know who was responsible and keep everybody there until the culprit confessed. But, inevitably, I didn't. I didn't even tell Alicia about it. I knew I wouldn't be able to discover the scribe, and any attempt to do so would have made me look ridiculous. I did, however, take some small revenge. This was the one bit of writing I didn't pass on to Gregory.

When I had the next meeting with the patients I found myself looking at each of them in turn, wondering which of them had written down Alicia's words, but it was an old and frustrating game and I soon abandoned it. These meetings had now become a bit perfunctory, if not entirely superfluous, yet I didn't feel we could not have them. I'd have been left with absolutely nothing to do. We no longer discussed individual pieces of writing but addressed more general topics.

'Is it OK just to write down your dreams?' Raymond asked.

I assured him there was a rich tradition of dream literature, though I also warned him that dreams were always a lot more interesting for the dreamer than for the poor sod who had to read them.

'The world is like a dream,' said Cook.

'But aren't dreams really images?' Raymond insisted.

'In a way,' I said.

'So aren't dreams really bad for us? Kincaidian Therapy is trying to keep us away from images but our subconscious minds keep supplying new ones.'

I didn't have an answer to that one, and was glad when Byron stepped in. 'Raymond has a point,' he said, 'but in this case I'm not sure there's a very clear distinction between the conscious and the subconscious mind. For instance, I find myself looking forward to our book being published. I imagine what it will be like to hold a copy, I try to envisage how it will look. I'm creating images for myself that I don't think are so very different from dreams.'

'And what about when you're tripping?' Charity said. 'And the trees turn into snakes, or people's faces turn into Frankenstein masks?'

'And what about when I imagine something coming up out of the toilet and biting off my penis?' said Charles Manning.

'And what about the idea that language derives from pictograms?' Byron offered. 'If that's the case then it's hard to see that words are any different from pictures at all. Isn't it?'

'I really don't know,' I said. 'You'll have to ask Dr Kincaid.'

That shut them up.

In order to keep them down to earth I suggested they try to come up with a title for the anthology. This led to further intense activity, though I hesitate to say 'creativity' since a lot of the things they suggested were either terrible or just plain stupid. *War and Peace*, for example, *Bonkers Outside Brighton*, *Much Madness is Divinest Sense* (borrowed from Emily Dickinson, I believe), *Draining the Ego* (a reference to Freud), *All Our Own Work* (maybe some irony there, maybe not), *I Spit in the Face of My Mother*, *Tales from the New Bedlam*, *Kincaid and After*, *Make Mine Mandrax*, *Mind Readings*, *The Footballers*, *Narm Saga* (which I could see was an anagram of 'anagrams'). There were plenty more where they came from and I duly passed them on to Gregory, in the reasonable certainty that he wouldn't be using any of them. In one of his letters Gregory told me that after much brainstorming and many sleepless nights he'd decided on *Disorders*, a title that, perhaps surprisingly, we all felt we could live with.

For my part, I now had to come up with a foreword, something that purported to explain what I'd been up to all this time. I had to do some writing. I kept it exceptionally brief. My role, I said, had simply been to give the patients the freedom to write whatever they wanted, and the results were here for all to see. This seemed uncontroversial and in every sense undeniable. I would leave the grandiose waffle to Kincaid. He appeared to work long and hard on his introduction but when it came it was only a very slightly reworked version of the lecture he'd tried to make me deliver to the patients on my first day, the one I'd burned. Perhaps he thought it was unimprovable. Gregory declared himself happy with both our contributions, though they clearly didn't excite him in the way the patients' writing did.

We were sent roughs of the jacket design. Over the years I've talked to a lot of authors and I've learned they seldom really like their book covers. Given the large number of hands involved in *Disorders*, it was even less likely that we'd all be happy. Some of us were inevitably less unhappy than others. I'd suggested using a Jackson Pollock painting, maybe the one from the card Alicia had used to welcome me on my first day, *Number 32*, but it was reckoned that the Pollock estate would be far too difficult and expensive to deal with, so some lad in the publisher's art department had knocked up a drip painting and that's what they were using. I thought it was all right, if a little nondescript; the lad in the art department was no Jackson Pollock. Kincaid got a mite fretful that if you stared at the design and squinted you could make out what looked like faces in the bottom left-hand corner, but first Alicia and I, and then all the patients assured him this wasn't the case and he relaxed a lot.

The existence of a title and a jacket design spurred the patients to even greater heights of productivity, but I knew this couldn't go on for ever. Sooner or later a line would have to be drawn, and Gregory or Nicola or somebody in the publishing company would have to say, enough is enough, for better or worse it's finished, it has to go to the typesetters and printers. And sure enough such a day did come.

Gregory informed me, in a long self-regarding letter, that his mighty labours were at an end. He had worked night and day, editing and shaping, cutting and pasting, arranging and rearranging, ordering and, yes, disordering. His eyes hurt, his brain hurt, his fingers were bleeding from paper cuts, but finally the noble and heroic task had been accomplished. He now intended to take himself to bed for a couple of weeks to recover. I wondered how this was going to affect his teaching. Across the bottom of the letter was written, SEND ME NO MORE. That was the *real* end of an era.

25

The time between the contents of the book being finalised and the finished product appearing was a difficult one for all of us. Once I'd told the patients that Bob Burns had instructed me to send no more of their work they stopped writing immediately and completely. I thought this was strange, and probably not very healthy. They'd written quite happily when there had been no suggestion of publication, so why should they stop simply because this anthology was now full; an anthology which, however you looked at it, contained only a fraction of their output? I tried to encourage them, said how much I wanted to read more of their work, but it was no good. I didn't have that kind of power over them any more.

I expressed my worries to Alicia but she didn't share them. She said it was fine for creative artists to remain fallow after they'd finished a project, to wait for the creative reservoir to fill up again, just like I was doing. I was alarmed that the patients were now being described as 'creative artists' but I thought maybe she was right. Perhaps they'd exhausted themselves, burned themselves out. And even if she was wrong there was no way I could force them. Besides, I'd read my Sam Beckett. I knew that silence was every bit as articulate as utterance, that the act of non-writing was every bit as expressive as the act of writing, arguably more so; it just left me at a bit of a loose end, that was all, looser than ever. I was left doing a lot of thumb-twiddling, as indeed were the patients.

Released from the time-consuming burden of writing they were now free to display some of the more colourful symptoms of madness. Raymond had time to come up with a whole new look involving blue sparkling eye-shadow, ox-blood lipstick and strings of pearls, and he flapped around advising us to fasten our seat belts because it was going to be a bumpy ride. Charity's dancing was as nude as ever but now more intense and spiritual, she claimed. She also said she saw the face of Buddha in a plate of stew that Cook had concocted. Cook meanwhile had decided that the world was like a crossword, an anagram, a code, a secret language, like a metaphor, like a simile.

Byron had started wearing a cape and had a tendency to wander around, looking tortured and poetic, while Anders could often be found punching trees or kicking the boundary wall. Sometimes I wished he'd kick Carla. She'd become completely unbearable, flopping and tumbling about the place, and shouting gibberish. Maureen tended her garden but it didn't bring her much joy. Various things were now fully grown in her flowerbeds but she didn't know which were weeds and which were flowers. She said she wished she'd just made a football pitch instead. Even Sita looked less calm than usual, though she remained as silent as ever.

I came across Byron and Max on the tennis court one day, playing tennis not only without a net, but also without racquets and balls. They were just miming a series of serves, lobs and volleys, and this seemed a pretty harmless activity to me, but Kincaid got terribly worked up about it. The way he saw it, Byron and Max were pretending to see things that weren't there, creating, as it were, invisible images, which were even worse than visible ones. You could see why he'd want to put a stop to it. And then there was the penis incident.

Even the most heterosexual of men, even the ones who've led sheltered, modest lives that don't involve many visits to gyms or nude beaches, still find they see a lot of men's penises. You don't have to go out of your way, don't have to seek them out or stand and stare at them, but you still see them. And this is to say nothing of all those penises in art and pornography which, again, even the most discreet of us can't help seeing once in a while. But however familiar you were with penises you would still surely have been taken aback by the small brown-paper package I found outside the door of my hut one morning.

There was an experiment done in the early seventies where some feminist educator went around finding groups of women and taking photographs of their pussies and then showing them the pictures. The big discovery was that most of these women couldn't identify themselves. They didn't know what their own pussies looked like, and this said lots about repression and patriarchy, about not being in touch with their own bodies and so forth. I suppose there was a good point being made here. Certainly I think most men know what their own penis looks like. On the other hand, if some man came along offering to take photographs of your penis I don't think you'd be terribly likely to call him an educator.

So I opened the package and found it contained what looked for all the world like a severed human penis, and although I didn't in the ordinary sense of the word 'recognise' it, I was fairly sure I knew whose it was, or had been. I felt certain this was Charles Manning's penis. I'd never given any thought to what his penis might look like and it was certainly no longer in its natural state, yet this thing in the package fitted the bill. Besides, surely Charles Manning was the only man in the clinic likely to have done such a thing.

I must have had all these thoughts in a rapid, compressed fashion since the instant I saw the severed penis, I passed out. Passing out is such a useful narrative device. It's a jump cut, a leap forward, a way of getting things done without having to live through them or go into detail. Not in this case. When I came to I was still in my hut, the severed penis was still in front of me and, not wanting to pass out again, I ran from the hut screaming for help, looking for a doctor.

I found Alicia. I was too frantic to speak coherently. I gestured towards the hut. I may possibly have shouted something about penises and severing, but it wouldn't have been very lucid. Alicia went into the hut, saw the penis still lying on the desk and she screamed horribly. She thought it was mine. I still can't really believe she thought that. True, she had never actually seen my penis in broad daylight, but surely she knew me better than that. Did I look like the sort of man who'd chop off his own penis? And if I'd actually done it, surely I'd have been covered in blood. Perhaps she wasn't thinking rationally. But at least she didn't pass out. She stayed and she looked more carefully and she employed her medical training. Not only was she able to work out that the penis wasn't mine, she was able to see that it wasn't human at all. It was only a dog's penis. She was greatly relieved, as was I when she told me.

We never discovered who'd put it outside my door, and we never found the dog, poor mutt. We didn't even try. It was just something to be shrugged off, something that could have been much worse. And yet it seemed to me things had come to a very peculiar pass when you were relieved to find a dog's penis left outside your door.

And then there was the day that Max got drunker than I'd ever seen him, and climbed up on to the parapet that edged the clinic's roof. By the time I knew what was happening, everyone from the clinic, Alicia and Kincaid included, had gathered at ground level and were staring up at him. He was tiptoeing along the edge, knees bending, arms flailing, like a man on a tightrope.

'I hope the silly fucker falls and breaks his neck,' Anders said, not unpredictably.

'Perhaps that's what he's trying to do,' Maureen said, and called out to Max, 'Don't do it. Don't jump.'

'He's not going to jump,' Byron said. 'It's just a cry for help.'

I had no idea whether Max really intended to throw himself off, but he looked so drunk and uncoordinated I thought he might easily do it by accident.

'If the daft cunt wants help all he's got to do is ask for it. He's in a hospital,' said Anders.

I thought this was a genuinely perceptive remark, though it went unacknowledged, not least by Alicia and Kincaid. The nurse arrived carrying a bed sheet and tried to find takers who would each grab a corner to hold it out like a fireman's blanket. I reckoned this was pretty sensible and well-organised of her, but finding three others who shared her good sense proved impossible.

'Maybe he's sleepwalking,' somebody said.

'Maybe he's having a psychotic episode.'

I didn't think there was any need for these various, ingenious explanations for Max's behaviour.

'He's just drunk,' I said, not with any great sense of urgency or triumph, but I found my analysis didn't go down too well.

'Just because he's drunk doesn't mean he isn't sleepwalking.'

'Just because he's drunk doesn't mean he isn't making a cry for help.'

I wasn't going to argue with anyone, but it seemed to me that walking on roofs or parapets is just one of those things people do when they're drunk, something they'd never dream of doing when sober. Nevertheless, I thought we ought to try and get him down.

'You should go up there,' Raymond said. He meant me. 'You're good with words. You can talk him down.'

I hoped this remark would sink into the general clutter of unhelpful suggestions and be ignored, but I found it was being taken seriously, being discussed as a damn good idea, and before long it was accepted as the obvious, not to say the only course of action, and I was being touted as the one man who could bring Max down safely. I didn't find this collective confidence remotely flattering and I didn't really think I was likely to get the job done, but when I saw that even Alicia was joining in the consensus, I went with the flow, or at least with the line of least resistance. I hoped I wouldn't actually have to go out on the roof. There was a dormer window not far from the parapet. It would be possible to go up there, stick my head out the window and talk to Max from a position of safety.

'How are you, Max?' I asked when I got up there.

'I'm fine,' he said. 'I'm drunk.'

'Why don't you come in, Max?'

'Why don't *you* come out?'

'Because I'm scared I might fall off. Just like I'm scared *you* might fall off.'

'I won't fall off,' he said with blurry confidence. 'There's a minor deity who protects the truly pissed and incapable. Come out here.'

'But I'm sober so I won't be protected.'

'That can be changed,' he said, and he waved a chunky half-bottle of whisky at me. 'Come on, I hate drinking alone.'

The prospect of a good slug of whisky was actually quite attractive, though by no means attractive enough to draw me out on to the parapet.

'I've got a rotten head for heights,' I said.

'Oh yes, any excuse not to drink with me,' Max said. 'It's all right, I understand. Why would anybody want to drink with me? I know I'm a bore. Nobody loves me. Nobody would care if I fell off this roof.'

'Not true,' I said. 'Look at all the people down there. They care.'

'No they don't. They're hoping I'll fall off. It'd make their day.'

'Well, *I* care, Max,' I said.

'Then come out here and have a drink with me.'

I know that drunks are manipulative and self-serving, but knowing it doesn't really make any difference. I felt I had to go out there with him. Awkwardly, warily, I hauled myself out of the window and on to the parapet. I thought I heard a gasp from the onlookers but that might have been my imagination. I had no intention of doing anything gasp-inducing. I didn't even stand up. I planted my bum on the parapet and sat with my legs dangling into space, my hands gripping the edge as tightly as they could.

'You've earned a drink,' said Max and he lurched over and handed me the whisky.

It took quite an effort to prise my fingers loose from the edge of the parapet to take the whisky bottle, but I was in need of courage, of having my nerves steadied. The first mouthful didn't do much, so I took another.

'Things look very different from up here, don't they?' Max said.

Well, yes. They looked terrifying. The ground appeared to be a million miles away. 'Different,' I said, 'but not necessarily better.'

'Everything looks better after you've remodelled your consciousness a little,' Max said.

Obviously I hadn't done enough remodelling. The faces that looked up at us were hard to read but I knew Max was right; as a spectacle, as a drama, this episode was going to be far more satisfying to them if one or both of us tumbled from the roof. I was determined not to give anyone that satisfaction. I sat very still, made no sudden moves, while Max made nothing *but* sudden moves.

'Why don't you sit down?' I said. 'You're making me very nervous.'

'Oh well, I can't be responsible for your nervousness, can I?'

'Yes,' I said. 'You're entirely responsible.'

'Oh?' said Max, and this was an entirely new thought. He didn't like the feeling of responsibility and he looked as though he felt bad about it. I, however, was starting to feel a little better. The benefits of the whisky were kicking in: a warmth, a glow, an unjustified feeling of moderate well-being.

'You're probably wondering why I'm out here on the roof,' Max said.

'Because you're drunk?'

Max looked at me and seemed disappointed. 'I sometimes wonder if you're as thick as you pretend,' he said.

'I'm sure I am,' I said.

'I'm here because it's as good a place as any,' Max said, as though this explained everything.

'I can think of better places,' I said.

'All right, yes, I suppose I can think of better too: Harry's Bar, the Deux Magots, the Moon Under Water. But within the Kincaid Clinic, at least until they open a cocktail lounge or a snug, this place is as good as any.'

'If it's as good as any, then why not come inside?'

'You have so much to learn, Gregory.'

'That's what everyone tells me.'

Max offered me the bottle again. There was now only a little left in it. I drank half of what remained and passed it back for him to finish off. He drained it, then fished in his pocket and produced another bottle. 'When I stated that one place is as good as any other,' he said, 'what I meant is that we're all in hell, each in our own personal versions of hell that accompany us wherever we go. Alcohol doesn't get you out of hell, but it occasionally deceives you into believing that you're only in purgatory.'

'I'm sure you don't really believe that,' I said.

'Why would I say it if I didn't believe it?'

'I think it may be the drink talking,' I replied.

'You want to see something?' he asked.

When you're sitting on the roof of an asylum with a drunken inmate and he asks you if you want to see something, you tend to be a little hesitant. There are so many things he might want to show you that you just wouldn't want to see, especially after the penis incident. So I said, 'Possibly', and he put down the whisky, frugged up to the other end of the parapet and came back cradling something in the crook of his left arm.

'What have you got?' I asked.

He turned towards me and I saw he held a bird's nest. He carried it in both hands, as delicately as his lack of motor co-ordination permitted, and he offered it to me. I hesitated again. Why on earth would I have wanted it? Then I saw what it contained. There were four tiny birds sitting in the hollow of the nest. They were naked and their ragged open beaks looked bigger than their bodies. They seemed embryonic and macabre, and they were screeching at me, at the world, with a shrill impotence. I still couldn't see what I'd want with them, so I refused Max's gift and he took a couple of steps away from me.

'Shouldn't you put them back where you got them?' I said.

'Why?'

'In case you drop them.'

'I'm not going to drop them.'

He reached into the nest and plucked out one of the noisy little things, as though it were a bite-sized morsel of dough. He weighed it in the palm of his hand for a moment, and then with a whip of his arm, flung the baby bird out into darkness, off the roof. There was a horrible thin splat somewhere below, out of sight, but this time the onlookers didn't react.

'What did you do that for?' I demanded.

'No reason,' he said, and he picked out a second little creature.

'If it's for no reason, then why do it?'

He considered this. 'OK, then I guess it must be for a reason.'

'Oh come on, Max, stop it.'

'Stop what?'

He hurled the second bird down at the ground. There was another distant impact.

'Don't you think it must be kind of satisfying,' Max said, 'to be one of these birds? You're sitting there in your nest when godlike fingers grab you, raise you up, spirit you away; then you're flying through the air, you have a feeling of exhilaration, speed, wind. Then contact. Then nothing. Oblivion. That sounds OK. It sounds better than *my* life.'

'Nobody's killing you though, are they, Max?'

'Aren't they? Aren't they? I think I've been wrong all this time. I thought I was drinking in order to remodel my consciousness. Now I think I was doing it because I really was depressed, like Kincaid thought. Alcohol sometimes helps, but not always. Sometimes it just makes everything worse. But I have a new therapy. Killing things. That never fails to make me feel better.'

I was angry, not only because I disapproved (in a wishy-washy liberal way, no doubt) of cruelty to animals, but because I also disliked the pleasure Max was taking in that cruelty, more so since he was using his own condition, his own anguish, as a justification.

'I don't know what you're so upset about,' Max said. 'They're only birds. It's not as if they had souls or anything.'

'It's not about souls,' I said.

'Then?'

I found myself saying something I knew was going to sound

absurd. 'If the birds were trying to kill *you* then I'd try to stop them, just like I'm trying to stop you killing them.'

I was imagining some sort of Hitchcockian scenario with flocks of flappy scavengers appearing out of a clear sky and swooping down horribly on Max's cranium.

'You'd try to save me, would you?' said Max. 'And how'd you do that? By *reasoning* with the birds? Or did you have some sort of physical intervention in mind?'

The truth was I didn't have anything in mind at all, yet when Max made a move to fling the third bird off the roof, I found myself standing upright, taking a couple of shaky steps along the parapet towards him, determined to *do* something, and I did manage to get half a hand on his throwing arm. It wasn't enough. Despite my intervention the bird was thrown, much as before, but because I'd grabbed Max's arm the throw was less powerful than the previous two. The descent was slower, the impact less of a splat, the death perhaps less instantaneous. Not at all what I'd intended.

Down below the patients were getting restless. Even if they couldn't make out exactly what was happening up on the parapet, they knew some kind of conflict was in progress. This stirred them powerfully.

'Be careful, Gregory,' Alicia called out, and I was touched.

'One left,' Max said to me. 'Are you going to fight me for it?'

I didn't suppose I was. Standing upright on the parapet was already more than I'd ever bargained for. I had no intention of getting into a fight, not up there in those conditions where the loser, or even the winner, might fall to the same fate as the fledgelings.

'We don't have to fight,' I said. 'Why don't you just put the nest back and stop behaving like a twat.'

That surprised him, and maybe it surprised me. I'd gone up there to reason with him, not to abuse him, but the situation had brought out the Anders in me.

'Do you really care about this?' he said.

'I suppose I do.'

'You care more about this bird than you do about me?'

I'd had enough of Max's self-pity.

'Oh fuck off, Max. Stop being pathetic.'

'You're right. I'll stop being pathetic.'

He took a step towards me and I thought he might be about to call it a day and climb in through the window, but that wasn't what he had in mind at all. He handed me the nest and then he walked off the roof. It was brilliantly undramatic. He simply took a step into the air. I was so taken aback, so horrified, that I almost lost my own footing. But not quite. I wobbled, then sat down on the parapet, holding on with one hand, clutching the nest with the other. The single remaining fledgeling squawked up at me and didn't seem even slightly grateful.

At ground level, all hell was breaking loose. I hadn't seen Max's fall. I'd been too scared, too concerned with self-preservation, to watch. Now I looked down and saw that he hadn't made it to the ground. There'd been no fatal impact, scarcely an impact of any kind. Anders had been there for him. Anders had not only broken Max's fall, he'd actually managed to catch the drunken sot as he fell, and he was now holding him in his arms, *pietà* style. It took all of us a long, frozen moment to see what had happened. Even Anders seemed not to be quite sure what he'd done or how; but then he clicked, and the moment he realised he was cradling Max, he said to him, 'If I ever catch you doing anything like this again I'll break your fucking neck,' and he let him drop to the ground. Max landed heavily and stayed there, looking surprisingly comfortable, like any drunk who's found a good place to crash out. Anders walked away in disgust.

Kincaid squatted down beside Max, ran his hands over him, frisking him for a pulse and broken bones. He found the former and not the latter, so he stood up and turned away. Nothing here was worthy of his attention.

'Is he all right?' I called down.

'He'll live,' said Kincaid, sounding disappointed.

A handful of patients gathered up Max and carried him inside the clinic. The rest dribbled away, like the last stragglers at a party broken up by the police. I felt left out, and was experiencing a sense of anti-climax, feeling both guilty and foolish. I wondered where Alicia was.

'The drink must have relaxed him, cushioned his fall,' Kincaid shouted to me. 'It does, you know.'

Usually yes, but now in my own case the effects of the alcohol had worn off completely. I was not relaxed. I felt paralysed. I wasn't sure I'd ever find a way down from the roof. I didn't know what to do with the bird's nest.

'You'll probably want to stay up there for a while,' Kincaid called. 'You'll have a lot to think about.'

It was true, I did. I asked myself why the patients were behaving this way. Well, you could have claimed that the process of writing had been incredibly therapeutic, so the moment it stopped, the patients went crazy again. But I didn't really accept that. I thought it was more about attention. While the patients had been writing, they'd been given loads of attention, first by me, then by Gregory. Now that the writing had stopped they needed to draw attention to themselves in other ways. But the publication of a book is another way of gaining attention, and I hoped that when the book came out they'd calm down again.

I suppose there must have been page proofs or galleys but I never saw them. I saw nothing until the finished copies and I think I preferred it that way. A box of twenty books was duly delivered to the clinic just before publication. Kincaid seized the box as though it were a bomb that needed defusing. Only when he was sure that the box and the books were all they seemed, did he distribute the copies, doling them out, one to each of us, like some medical Santa Claus. The patients formed a celebratory, self-congratulatory scrum, but I didn't feel able to join them. I took my copy and retired to my hut with it.

Once I was alone I found myself weighing the volume in my hand, staring at it, sniffing the paper and binding, then placing it on the desk, setting it in different positions and at different angles, trying to see it as others might see it. I thought it looked handsome enough, authentic enough, like a real book, and yet I was aware of a nagging and shameful sense of disappointment. At the time I found this inexplicable but with hindsight I've concluded it was because although it was a perfectly real and presentable book, the thing we'd been waiting for all along, it was still *only* a book, just a single object in a world of other objects. I had wanted it to be more special than that. I had wanted it to be unique, to glow with a sort of heavenly light.

Things only got worse when I tried to read it. Despite all the correspondence Gregory had sent me, I had only the vaguest sense of what the book would actually contain. All its contents would surely be familiar to me, since I had read them so to speak at source, but I had only a patchy idea of what Gregory had finally included, and really no idea at all how the material had been arranged or structured. Shall we just say I was even more disappointed?

For all Gregory's fine words and professed hard work, it appeared to me he'd done a pretty sloppy job. It wasn't so much that he'd taken pieces at random, a strategy that I could see had some validity to it, but rather that he'd wilfully chosen some of the patients' least good work. The book seemed to be a series of unconnected, not to say disconnected, lumps of scrappy, ragged prose. Most of them were very short indeed and rather crudely hacked about. Stories started and stopped in mid-flow, occasionally in mid-sentence and with no apparent rhyme or reason. Then, to make matters worse, there was no logic to the arrangement, no patterning, no shape, no interesting juxtapositions. Yes, it was in some sense representative. There was sex and violence and anagrams and football matches and true facts and spiritual ruminations, but the examples he'd chosen weren't the best ones. It was just a mess. What in God's name did Gregory think he was up to?

Now that I looked at this shoddy finished product I was absolutely sure I could have done a better job myself – I certainly couldn't have done a worse one. Why had I been so feeble as to think that Gregory was any better than me? I felt angry with myself as much as with him. Why hadn't I had a bit more self-confidence, a bit more arrogance?

And yet I knew I had to put these feelings behind me, or at least keep them to myself. Bitching about the editing could only make me look bad and, besides, I didn't want to spoil everybody else's fun. Kincaid and Alicia, the patients, even the porters and the nurse weren't experiencing any of my ambivalence. They were all totally in love with the book. They thought it was wonderful, simply wonderful. The jacket was great, the paper it was printed on was great, the typeface, the endpapers, the glue, all were towering achievements of British publishing. Everyone was besotted with the mere existence of the book. And somehow that made it easier for me to put my doubts, my literary objections, aside. I just smiled at everyone and told myself that perhaps it was enough to cherish the *idea* of the book without even having to think about its reality or its contents.

In retrospect, I find it hard to remember what I thought would happen once *Disorders* was published. I suppose most people who have books published entertain fantasies or even, God help them, expectations that their books will become instant hits, will top the bestseller lists, that they themselves will become stars, be interviewed by all the right newspapers and magazines, that they'll be invited on to radio, even TV. Being on TV was a much, much bigger deal in those days than it is now.

My own hopes and expectations were different. My first intuition was that the book was all too likely to fall into the bottomless pit of neglect that consumes so many books. I thought we'd probably get a couple of short reviews, perhaps one in the local paper and another in some respectable but small circulation literary journal, and that would be the extent of it. I imagined these reviews would be friendly. Even if the reviewers hated the book, which I now thought they had every right to, they were surely going to be kind, weren't they? It would take a very hard critic indeed to badmouth the inmates of the Kincaid Clinic. Why kick an author when he or she was already incarcerated in an asylum?

In many ways I would have been happy with this limited reception, since I was well aware that the more publicity the book got, the greater the likelihood of my exposure, and I still very much didn't want to be exposed. I knew it would have to come sooner or later, but I kept saying to myself, not now, not yet.

It appeared that Kincaid was also conspiring to maintain the book's decent obscurity. To nobody's surprise, he had decreed that the patients needed protecting from the excesses of the mass media. They wouldn't be allowed to do any of the usual publicity activities, even if they were invited to. There'd be no going off to do interviews, no bookshop appearances, no readings, no visits to local radio stations. He wasn't going to let them go out in the world to be blitzed by created images. Bulkhead or no, they still weren't ready for that.

The book's first mention in print had been in a trade magazine, noting that Gregory Collins, author of *The Wax Man*, that highly promising, if undoubtedly flawed, first novel, had now edited a collection of writings by the mentally ill. The tone suggested the book was an interesting and worthy project but not one to set the literary world alight.

The clipping came through the post with a compliments slip initialled by Nicola and, to my surprise, more soon followed. The real reviewers got to work, and things started to happen. My expectations had been pitifully modest. The book was reviewed far more widely and in far more prestigious places than I could possibly have imagined. I'm not pretending we were up there competing with Anthony Burgess and Iris Murdoch, but a lot of literary editors seemed to think this was a book to be taken seriously, a book that mattered. More than that, reviewers actually liked the book, liked it a lot more than kindness to the mentally ill would have demanded or accounted for.

Of course, opinions weren't uniform, and the book didn't receive universal unadulterated praise. At least two reviewers raised doubts about the morality of the enterprise. They saw a problem in parading the outpourings of the insane, but even they concluded that on balance the inherent worth of the writing prevented the book from being merely a freak show. None of the reviewers doubted that the book was at the very least a fascinating literary curiosity; but one or two suggested it was more, that it was a significant piece of writing, a sprawling, collaborative, avant-garde masterpiece.

One reviewer began by apparently agreeing with me, saying that being mad doesn't make you interesting, and it certainly doesn't make your writing interesting, but he went on to say that *Disorders* was a good book precisely because the patients *were* interesting, and so was their writing, and that Gregory Collins had done a great job of inspiring, editing, even 'healing' the patients. I thought all these reviewers were out of their minds. Why couldn't they see what a pig's ear Gregory had made of everything?

When the reviews arrived in the post, I would convene a meeting of the patients and read out the day's arrivals. I felt like the village storyteller or town crier. The patients gathered round and hung on every word, responding passionately to each note of praise, to each hint of reservation or criticism. When I'd finished reading there'd be much discussion, much textual analysis, many attempts by the patients to read between the lines, to draw out hidden or veiled or subconscious meanings. I guess they were behaving just like authors.

Kincaid would sometimes sit in at these sessions and he was as beguiled as anybody. He regarded every approving word as a vindication of himself and his methods. He never acknowledged that I had been even remotely instrumental in the creation of the book and I found this infuriating, but I knew that I'd have looked pathetic if I'd started trying to assert my own importance. When, in the vaguest way, I hinted at this to Alicia, she had no idea what I was talking about. 'But your name's on the front of the book, isn't it?' she said.

When we were in bed together I was still required to say a great deal. The publication of the book and its observable success had made me even more desirable to Alicia. Now, when we had sex, I was still required to play the madman, but the game had changed, so that I had to be a *literary* madman; madness and artistic endeavour being so closely linked, she assured me. I would pretend to be a successful author (quite a challenge to my acting skills), but one on the brink of insanity. Alicia would be an adoring fan, hoping she could pull me back from the abyss by having sex with me. 'Tell me about all the hundreds of literary groupies you've fucked with that big dirty prick of yours.' It was hard work, keeping up the level of invention and filth that Alicia required, but I did my best, and since she never complained I assumed I must be doing something right. Did I think this was normal and healthy? No, of course I didn't, but if a woman can't be allowed to indulge her sick fantasies in a writer's hut, where else is she going to do it? On paper?

The book continued to get coverage, and not only on the book pages. It became apparent that we had what some might call a highly exploitable book on our hands, but given Kincaid's strictures it wasn't easy to see just how we were going to exploit it. That was when Nicola became increasingly involved. She said there were any number of newspapers eager to send interviewers and photographers to meet the multiple authors of *Disorders*. All she needed was a date and a time. Kincaid was having none of it. Possibly, he said, he might be prepared to allow one very carefully vetted journalist into the clinic to conduct a short interview under his own watchful eye, but a photographer was out of the question.

Nicola grudgingly reported this back to the papers who misinterpreted it as a desire to preserve the patients' anonymity, in which case they were prepared to be obliging. They were willing to photograph the patients in silhouette, or from some angle that left them unrecognisable. But Kincaid said that wasn't the point at all, and once editors were faced with the prospect of an unillustrated article they cooled off considerably. I thought this wasn't absolutely logical of Kincaid. His therapy was about keeping patients away from images, not away from cameras, but I suppose it was fair enough to think that once they'd been photographed they'd want to see the results, and that could threaten all sorts of mayhem.

Then the papers said, OK, we won't photograph the patients, we'll just photograph the editor and the doctor: Collins and Kincaid. I sensed that Kincaid was tempted by this prospect. He wanted attention and recognition, yet he resisted. If the patients weren't to be photographed then neither were we. This seemed even less logical, though for my part I was obviously relieved. Having my picture in the national papers was the one sure way of blowing my cover. I complimented Kincaid on his integrity.

There was talk of sending a radio crew to the clinic to make a documentary, and that sounded harmless enough, but Kincaid didn't want that either. As with visits from the patients' relatives, there would be too many uncontrollable factors; all those old problems with flowery shirts and patterned ties and someone might even have a visible tattoo.

Nicola eventually went ballistic. She called the clinic and did her nut with Kincaid, demanding to know what he was playing at, why he was being so obstructive, whether he was serious about this book or not. Didn't he want the book to sell, to be read, to reach as big a public as possible? I believe she may even have accused him of dilettantism.

I admired the way Kincaid stood up to her, but in the end, and even though I had my own reasons for not wanting to be part of a publicity circus, even though I didn't think the book was nearly as great as everybody else did, I still felt Kincaid was being needlessly obstructive. Alicia joined in too. Here, she said, was a great opportunity for Kincaid to prove wrong all those pygmies (that was the word she used) who'd said he was a trifler, who'd dismissed his work as trendy and shallow. I wondered who'd said this, where and when.

It was hard to tell which of these pressures Kincaid finally bowed to, but in the end he agreed that something ought to be done.

'Very well,' he said, 'I know what we'll do. We'll have a literary evening.'

26

Kincaid's notion of what constituted a literary evening, like his notions of just about everything else, were pretty much his own. Since the patients couldn't go out into the world, then the world, or at least a small bit of it, would come to the Kincaid Clinic. He regarded this as quite a concession.

An invited audience of twenty or so carefully chosen individuals was to be allowed into the clinic for a single occasion. This group would contain literary journalists, members of the psychiatric profession, some academics and a few of the clinic's trustees. It was to be a low-key affair. The visitors would be given a tour of the facilities, they'd hear a brief lecture by Kincaid, then the patients would give a short reading from *Disorders*.

My role in all this was unspecified, and if Kincaid had had his way it would probably have been non-existent. He certainly didn't want me to address the invited group and tell them what I'd done with the patients; he didn't want me to be around at all. He even suggested I might like to take the evening off and go into town.

My reactions were understandably ambivalent. There was every reason for me to keep out of harm's way, to avoid showing myself, and yet I was angry to be left out, elbowed out, of the proceedings. I felt I had to fight my corner. I had to find a discreet but vital role for myself. I decided I would take charge of the patients' reading.

I told Kincaid that I wanted 'to be there for the patients', to organise their part of the event, help them decide what they should read, to guide them, to rehearse them; then on the night itself to keep their spirits up, reassure them, give them their cues and keep them calm and coherent through what might prove to be a difficult occasion. Kincaid grudgingly conceded that it was a job that needed doing. Alicia, by contrast, found it touchingly modest. She was really liking me a lot at this time.

And yet the more I thought about it, the more I reckoned that the role I was designing for myself was by no means a trivial or menial one. The patients would indeed need some help, and I was willing to give it to them. The prospect of the reading filled them with excitement and anxiety, and I thought there was a new disingenuousness about their reaction. They seemed not to be play-acting. They had some trepidation but they really wanted to do it. This public appearance promised to be as validating for them as it was for Kincaid and his therapy.

As Carla said to me, in one of her more lucid moments, although with how many layers of irony I couldn't quite be sure, 'If we're good enough to read to an audience then we can't be complete nutters, can we?' I decided to take this at its face value.

The question of who would read what was apparently going to be a tricky one. In the past I'd been the one to pick out pieces of text and assign which patient should read them aloud. I knew this wouldn't be good enough now. The patients had started to care. They only wanted to read the 'best bits' as they put it, the parts they thought had special literary merit, the parts that suited their voices and personalities. If anyone had asked me I'd have said that thanks to Gregory some of the very best bits weren't in the book at all, but I continued to keep that to myself. There was a moment when I thought this process of selection might finally tell me who had written what, not that I cared very much about that any longer, but it didn't do that at all.

For instance, Anders was keen to read the obsessive passage about the woman shaving her body, a very early piece that had somehow made it through the editing process. Carla said she wanted to recite some amazing true facts. Raymond wanted to read an account of a football match. Byron claimed not to care what he read, just so long as he was the last to perform. A good few of them wanted to read passages about sex and violence. They reckoned these were the most dramatic and compelling, the ones most likely to create audience response. That was undeniable. No doubt the spectacle of various asylum inmates reading out accounts of sex murders would have a certain power, but I didn't think it was going to be much of an advertisement for the benefits of Kincaidian Therapy or for the book.

I tried to be gentle with them, to guide them into creating a short, varied, sane programme, but perhaps I was hoping for too much, and perhaps I was overestimating my powers of persuasion. But we did arrive at a selection, a running order, that seemed, to me at least, to show the patients and their writing in a sympathetic and not entirely unrepresentative way. It was eccentric and obsessive, occasionally repetitive, occasionally impenetrable, not without sex and violence, not always entirely healthy, but not repellent either, not laughable, not simply insane.

I knew that in all this we were doing a further act of editing, selecting only from Gregory's selection. We were creating a kind of sub-anthology, making something new. And that felt good. I was finally showing some creativity. We did a couple of read-throughs and they went pretty well, though I was aware that things could change when a live audience was brought into the equation.

I wondered if Nicola would be a member of that audience. It was surely common enough for publishers to attend events like these. And it occurred to me that Gregory might also find a way to be there, just as he'd been at the reading in Ruth Harris's bookshop. Both prospects filled me with horror. However, a little while before the event, I received news that neither of them would be there, for the unimpeachable and entirely staggering reason that they would be getting married that day. To each other. I was dumbfounded.

We were at a time in history when all sorts of people claimed not to 'believe' in marriage, although this lack of belief often lasted no more than a couple of years after they'd left college. People relented because they wanted to make their mothers happy, because they wanted to have children, because they saw certain tax advantages. Some people thought of this change in belief as a cop out, as buying into some dusty, hypocritical old values, though I was never one of these. I found it hard to believe there was any great ideology at stake here, but I was still surprised when anybody I knew announced they were getting married. However, Nicola and Gregory's announcement was a surprise of a different order.

The news came in a rather apologetic letter from Gregory, informing me of the wedding and telling me I wasn't invited. If he'd had his way, he said, I'd not only have been present, I'd have been his best man. The prospect sent my head reeling. Just what kind of fool *was* Gregory Collins? Fortunately Nicola had had the ordinary good sense to veto the idea. Inviting the bride's ex-boyfriend to a wedding might just about be permissible in certain circumstances, but having him as best man was just plain stupid. When said ex-boyfriend and potential best man is currently working in an asylum pretending to be the groom – well, no need to catalogue the objections.

The absurdity of Gregory's desire to have me there distracted me a little from the less spectacular, though no less real, absurdity of the wedding itself. I found it all but impossible to believe that Nicola would marry Gregory. Sleeping with him, going out with him, that was bizarre enough, but marrying him, that was just incomprehensible.

What people 'see' in their partners is always inscrutable, but again, Nicola and Gregory's case created a new level of inscrutability. In one way, it was easy to see why Gregory might want to marry Nicola. She was much the best he was ever going to get, and in my opinion she was far better than he deserved. But that only made more urgent the question of why Nicola wanted to marry Gregory. It's not unknown for beautiful women to marry unattractive men – Jackie K and Aristotle O spring to mind – but these things are generally explained by money or power or the urge for a father figure. These didn't seem to apply in Nicola and Gregory's case.

I also think that the very beautiful often distrust their own beauty and seek out its opposite. But I didn't think Nicola was quite beautiful enough to need a man who was quite so unbeautiful as Gregory. So what were the other options? That Gregory was great in bed? No, that didn't bear thinking about and even in those days I knew that marriage has very little to do with what goes on between the sheets. Maybe Nicola was pregnant, but that was no reason to get married either. It would just be making a bad job worse; Nicola wasn't that silly. So maybe she was doing it to piss off her parents. That seemed a bit extreme. To piss me off? No, I didn't flatter myself that much.

So what other explanation offered itself? The only one I could think of was that it had to be about Gregory's writing. Maybe Nicola was smitten with his creativity, his literary pretensions. Maybe she thought he was a genius. Maybe. Just maybe.

I found myself thinking about their forthcoming wedding far more than I wanted to, and I wondered why. Was I jealous? Well possibly, although not, I'd insist, because I wanted Nicola for myself, but rather because I wanted someone to want me the way Nicola apparently wanted Gregory. I suppose I was envious of people who had a relationship that wasn't merely sexual and that didn't only happen on certain nights and largely consist of weirdish sex, as mine did with Alicia. I didn't want to get married to Alicia or to anyone else, but I was still sufficiently bound up in society's mores that I'd have liked to have someone who wanted to marry me. Naturally, I didn't say any of this to Alicia.

I certainly had plenty of other things to keep me occupied, but on the day of the reading I kept thinking about Gregory and Nicola, wondered if they were married yet, wondered if Gregory was making his speech, wondered who he'd found to be his best man. And when the twenty or so invitees arrived at the clinic for the literary evening, in a special bus that had picked them up at Brighton station, I kept thinking of them as wedding guests. An absurd notion; they didn't look remotely like well-wishers, and neither did they much look like people out for a literary evening. They looked more like sober, uncomfortable tourists who had signed up for a mystery tour with a disreputable travel firm and were now regretting it. They were a serious, strangely homogenous bunch; a lot of suits, a lot of distinguished silver hair, and as they got off the bus it was surprisingly hard to tell who was who, which were the psychiatrists, which the academics, which the journalists, which the trustees.

Kincaid and Alicia were waiting for them, ready to shake hands and exchange pleasantries. The porters were there too, like a guard of honour, as were Byron, Maureen and Sita, judged to be the most presentable and least volatile of the patients. I kept my distance. I was watching from the library, peering out of the window, a little nervous and still a little resentful at being excluded. But then someone I knew got off the bus, someone who made my exclusion seem not only tolerable, but a stroke of infinite good fortune. It was Dr John Bentley, my old Director of Studies, the man who'd hosted the book-burning party at which I'd first met Gregory Collins.

I leapt back from the window. There was no way he could have seen me at that distance but I still felt the need to hide. My heart was doing a drum solo, my palms were wet, my ears felt unaccountably hot. I stood there trembling lightly, trying to think through the implications of Bentley's presence.

In one way it probably wasn't so surprising. Bentley was a scholar, he read books, he kept an eye on what was happening in literature. He mightn't be the first person you'd invite to such an event, yet he was by no means the last. But surely there could be nothing accidental about his presence. He must have recognised the name Gregory Collins both as someone who'd burned a manuscript at his party, and also as the writer of *The Wax Man*. He'd been in correspondence with the author, for God's sake, and if he was as good as his word he'd even burned his book. That in itself would have made his presence problematic enough, even if I hadn't been involved in this ludicrous deception.

I didn't know if Bentley had ever seen a finished copy of *The Wax Man*, complete with dust jacket and author photograph of me. I thought it was reasonably unlikely. Gregory would have sent him a plain, unjacketed advance proof copy of the book. Therefore he was presumably expecting to meet the real Gregory Collins at this event. The moment he laid eyes on me he'd know everything. What would he do then? He would surely do what anyone else would in the circumstances, be they literary critics or journalists, scientists or trustees, or anything else. He would stand up and say this man is an impostor, this whole thing is a sham. The sky would come tumbling down around all our ears.

As I've said throughout, I knew this deception couldn't go on for ever. I knew a day of reckoning was on its way, and I knew that day would be painful and shaming; but Bentley's presence promised to make it painful and shaming in ways I had never imagined.

I told myself I could deal with my own humiliation, but what I really cared about were Kincaid, Alicia and the patients. Whatever resentments I felt towards Kincaid, I had no desire to make him a complete and public laughing stock. How could he be taken seriously if he couldn't tell the real Gregory Collins from an impostor, and that went for Alicia too, since she was the one who'd recruited me. And as for the patients, insane or not, malingerers or not, this was potentially their moment of triumph. I didn't want to let them down. So I desperately hoped I could hold things together just a little bit longer, a couple more hours until this 'literary evening' was over, until the visitors had gone. After that it didn't matter; then I'd be willing to be exposed and vilified, and drummed out of the clinic. But how was I going to get through those essential couple of hours?

Chiefly by hiding, I hoped. I'd remain a back-room boy. If I could manage to show my face to the patients while keeping it out of sight of Bentley, I thought I might get away with it. Just about. Maybe.

I left the library and took a slinking, circuitous route to the small office next to the lecture room, which was where the patients were already congregating, using the place as a dressingroom, although with the exception of Raymond, who'd somehow managed to obtain a pair of glittering false eyelashes, a candy floss wig and an air hostess's tartan uniform, they weren't doing much dressing up. They were tightly wound, however, pacing or twitching or being uncharacteristically vivacious, but none of them was tenser than me. Anders even came over and said, 'I don't know what you're looking so tense about. You don't have to go out there and read this crap.'

That was true and it gave me some small cause for optimism. I stayed with the patients for the hour or so it took Kincaid to welcome the visitors, lecture them and give them the tour of the clinic. I wanted to be a reassuring presence, and I demonstrated some breathing exercises I'd learned in my days of amateur dramatics.

Then we heard the visitors coming along the corridor and entering the lecture room. The office door opened unexpectedly and Alicia came in, saw me looking terrified and said, 'Are you all right?'

'First-night nerves,' I said.

Perhaps she thought this was a good enough explanation, perhaps not; either way there was no time to discuss it. She told us the patients were needed 'on stage'. Alicia escorted them out of the office. Sita was going along with them even though she wasn't reading, so I remained behind, alone, as nervous as I could ever remember being.

Once everyone was settled in place in the lecture room, I crept along the corridor and listened at the door. I couldn't see anything, but I could hear every word. It started well enough. Maureen read a bucolic piece about growing up in rural Lancashire in the 1900s. Then Anders delivered the shaving passage, then Raymond read a description of a football match. His outfit didn't really fit with his account of pincer movements, long balls and crunching tackles, but I thought he got away with it. They all read well, just as we'd rehearsed. Sometimes they sounded hesitant, sometimes they gabbled a little, but in the main they were excellent, better than lots of authors I've heard reading their own work.

Cook read a short and really very complicated passage full of puns and word play and anagrams, that came across like sound poetry or surrealist glossolalia. It was fine. It even got a couple of laughs. Then Charity read a piece about a sex murder in a nunnery. This was a bit of a test. I'd convinced her to leave out some of the gorier parts, and certainly it was no worse than large swathes of what passes for serious literature these days, but at that time, in front of an audience of the moderately great and good, it made me very nervous. But she got away with it too. She was good. Maybe some people in the audience were shocked, maybe some thought it was inappropriate but by the time Charity sat down I could tell the audience was on our side. We were now a little over halfway through the programme and I was almost able to let myself relax.

I knew that the actual reading was only part of the story. I was just as worried about what some of the patients might do when they weren't reading, when they were just sitting there 'doing nothing'. Mightn't Charity think this was a perfect opportunity for allowing her God-given body full exposure, mightn't Carla decide to indulge in some fierce pathomimicry, mightn't Anders dislike the way someone in the audience was looking at him? Well, undoubtedly they might have, but mercifully they didn't. They held themselves together. They stuck to the script. The event was developing an intensity that was impressive and undeniable.

Charles Manning read a slightly dull piece about the London blitz, but dullness was fine by me. I would settle for that. And Carla, as she'd requested, read out some 'interesting' facts about submarines and tapestry-making and wildlife in Kenya. This was dull too, and I feared she might try to enliven it by screaming or writhing on the ground, but no, and there was a surprising charm about her delivery, like the presenter of an uncondescending children's TV programme. There was a little more sex and violence as Max, in a voice that was only slightly slurred, read a lurid passage about white slavery, and again I hoped nobody was offended.

The end was in sight, or at least in hearing. Byron was reading what I knew to be the final piece – I'd let him read one of the confessions, one where the author claimed to have dropped the bomb on Nagasaki, since I thought it would be a good finale and yet nobody could mistake it for a real confession. He read very well, better than he normally did, in a way that made it seem accusatory and moving, but also somehow satirical. Then it was over and the audience broke out into prolonged, genuine applause. We'd made it. There were tears in my eyes. I ran back to the office to be there when the patients returned in triumph.

They were as moved as I was. 'We fuckin' killed 'em,' said Anders, as they ran into the room. I found myself being hugged and kissed and shaken by the hand; and some way off I could hear Kincaid in the lecture room, addressing the audience again, blowing his own trumpet.

The applause started again, and Alicia stuck her head round the door to say that the patients were needed for a 'curtain call'. They didn't need asking twice, but as they returned, Charles Manning, Anders and Maureen each grabbed bits of me and started to pull me along with them. I resisted, tried to fight them off, tried to assert my natural, if violent, modesty, but as I struggled other patients joined in, clamped down on me so that eventually I was immobilised, helpless, and I was carried bodily into the lecture room as though I were a mascot.

They set me down in front of the audience. I kept my head lowered, and my eyes averted, but it was too late now. Raymond was saying, 'The man to whom we owe everything, our pilot through these turbulent skies: Gregory Collins,' and there was more applause and I knew it was all over. There was no longer any way of hiding myself. I looked up at all the faces. There, leading the applause, clapping louder than anyone, was Dr John Bentley, his face twisted in sly, impish glee.

I couldn't imagine what was going to happen next. What would Bentley do? How would he destroy me? I felt inert, and for a while nothing very dramatic happened at all. I was swept along as we all piled out of the lecture room into the canteen, where Cook had set up a necessarily plain buffet. The notion was that patients and visitors would now mingle informally before Kincaid drew events to a close and the guests were loaded back on the bus. This session in itself had always threatened plenty of scope for disaster but now that Bentley had seen me, I had a pretty good idea what form that disaster would take. I thought it was only a matter of time.

In the way that you never quite know how you're going to react to stress I found myself at the buffet table, stuffing myself with anonymous, flavourless sandwiches. The condemned man was eating a hearty plateful of finger food, white bread spread with who knew what. I became aware of Charity and Anders standing next to me, watching me intently. 'Case of the munchies?' Charity asked.

I knew I sounded most unlike myself as I said, 'Charity, whatever happens, how ever all this turns out, believe me, I did my best.'

Anders snorted at this piece of cheap sentiment and Charity's look was as blank as I might have expected. Neither of them knew what I was talking about, but Charity's big wide eyes showed soft, slow-moving concern.

'Are you in trouble, Greg?' she asked. 'Want us to pray for you?'

I couldn't reply because I felt someone's fingers gripping my forearm, and I turned to see that Dr Bentley had laid hands on me and was steering me from the canteen, through the open back door, to the world outside. I didn't resist. What would have been the point? We walked in silence until we came to the dried-up fountain. I sat down on the cold, rough lip and Bentley positioned himself at an appropriately detached distance. We made an odd couple sitting there in the shadow of the cement mermaid.

'Well, Michael,' he said.

'Well, indeed,' I replied.

Bentley laughed. The bastard was finding this funny. 'You present me with something of a problem,' he said.

'Do I?' I couldn't see what his problem was at all. I just wanted him to do his worst and get it over with.

'Do you have anything to say in mitigation?' he asked.

I shook my head.

'No extenuating circumstances you'd like me to know about? No claims of diminished responsibility?'

I shook again.

'I find your reticence disarming,' he said. 'I had thought you might argue that even though you're not the "real" Gregory Collins, you do appear to have done a fair job of harnessing the creative abilities of these . . . lunatics.'

He was right. I might once have argued something like that, but it sounded very flimsy now that he said it. And the word lunatic seemed needlessly cruel.

'I suppose,' he said, 'a corollary of that argument might be that since the patients obviously admire you so much, and since you've clearly done them, in some sense of the word, "good", then discovering that you were a fraud might be detrimental to their continuing mental health.'

'That's an argument,' I said.

'And yet,' said Bentley, 'I think we owe it to the patients not to treat them as children or simpletons. If they've been victims of a deception they surely have a right to know.'

'Yes,' I said. 'I'm sure they do.'

'What then of Dr Kincaid, Dr Crowe and the Kincaid Clinic? Their reputations might be severely damaged if you were exposed.'

'Yes,' I said.

'It might seem vindictive of me to enhance my own reputation at the expense of theirs.'

It had never occurred to me that Bentley's reputation was at stake here, yet now that he mentioned it I could see it might be some tiny feather in his cap to be the man who'd exposed a literary and psychiatric hoax, even if he'd only done it by the purest fluke.

He continued, 'You might also argue that there would be those who'd accuse me of acting out of even worse self-interest, who'd say I was revenging myself for the occasion when you burned my book. For that matter I suppose you might also argue that I wouldn't particularly want my book-burning parties to become common knowledge.'

'I suppose I might,' I said, though I wouldn't have.

'Equally,' he said, 'I suppose one might argue that since you're a member of college, one of my former students, the scandal your exposure would create might be a worse evil than the one you've perpetrated, and might reflect exceedingly badly on the college and on me. You might think I had a duty not to destroy a college man.'

'That never occurred to me,' I said. I knew Cambridge colleges looked after their own, but I'd never felt I was one of their own.

'However, if at some later date the truth came out and I appeared to have been complicit in the deception, then the scandal and the ignominy would be far worse.'

'I understand,' I said, but somehow I didn't think all these filigrees of logic and consequence were very necessary or relevant. I didn't think Bentley was really trying to decide on a course of action. I thought he was just showing off his brain power, torturing me slowly and exquisitely before doing what he surely had to do. And so he went on.

'Now some would certainly say that the exposure of a fraud, be it literary or otherwise, is a universal good, and the very least that scholarship might aspire to. We scholars are supposed to love truth. And yet for those of us who are scholars of *literature*, truth is rarely quite so cut and dried. Art may aspire to tell the truth, may indeed do so, but it tells it via a series of illusions, deceptions, confidence tricks. Perhaps all artists are charlatans. Not that I think you're claiming to be an artist, are you, Michael?'

'No,' I said.

'So what, ultimately, am I saying?'

I wished I knew and I certainly wished he'd stop prolonging the agony. He did that thing where you make a little church out of your fingers then press them against your lips. Very prudent and professorial. Very corny.

'What I seem to be saying is that while there are indeed some persuasive arguments for exposing your little fraud, and even though I find the arguments *against* exposing you somehow specious, I nevertheless find myself having a great deal of sympathy for you. And I can't help wondering why that is.'

Neither could I.

'Why?' he asked himself. 'Why do I feel inclined to help you? Could it really be simply because I like your face?'

I can think of worse reasons, I thought, but I didn't say that aloud.

'Another reason,' Bentley said, 'might be that I like jokes. And I have to admit this is rather a good joke.'

Well yes, there was his taste for Warhol's *Empire State* but that seemed to be something altogether different.

'I suppose what I'm really saying,' Bentley said, 'is that at this moment I'm confused. I don't know what I'm going to do at all.'

'No?' I said.

'No. But once I've decided,' he said, 'I'm sure you'll be one of the first to know. Until then, what can I say? Keep up the good work.'

He stood up, bristled slightly, turned his back and started walking towards the clinic. I remained immobile. It seemed to be over, at least for the moment, although the threat would continue to hang over me, and that would certainly be a punishment, though not necessarily punishment enough.

27

I know what I should have done. The moment the evening was over, once Bentley and the others were back on the bus, I should have gone along to Kincaid and confessed everything. The game was surely up. I'd had a good innings. I could have retired, not undefeated exactly, but at least on my own terms. I could even have just disappeared.

So why didn't I? Oh, all the usual reasons: pride, inertia, cowardice, sex. It was all too difficult. I was scared. I didn't want everyone to know what a fraud I was. I didn't want people to hate me. I didn't want Alicia to stop liking me and having sex with me.

And I admit there were moments when I hoped I was wrong, that the game wasn't up, that something would happen to change everything and make it all right. Perhaps Bentley would decide not to do anything after all. Or perhaps he'd be run over by a bus. Perhaps some crazed undergraduate would slaughter him. Stranger things had happened in Cambridge. Or maybe Anders knew a good hit man I could employ. Or perhaps I should do it myself, set up some elaborate alibi at the clinic and then sneak off to Cambridge and kill Bentley in his rooms.

But no, in general I didn't really think any of these would happen. I was sure Bentley would tell all. Maybe not immediately but very soon, and no doubt in some clever, clever way. And that only made these last moments, these last days, all the more precious. I didn't want to leave. What would I gain by confessing? I would hold on as long as I possibly could. I hoped for another night or two with Alicia.

Kincaid's literary evening was heralded as a great success, not least by Kincaid. He was even more full of himself than usual. Oh well, that would change soon enough. The patients were pleased with themselves too. They'd been so good, so in control on the night of the reading, it was hard to know what to do with them next; not that

I was exactly in a position to start any new projects. I felt a great fondness for all of them. I'd be sorry to lose them and I hoped they'd be sorry to lose me.

The waiting was tough, and now more than ever I found myself becalmed and powerless. I kept thinking about Nicola and Gregory. I wondered how the wedding had gone, whether she'd looked beautiful in white, whether she'd even *worn* white, whether it had been a grand affair, where they'd gone on honeymoon. I certainly wondered how long it would last.

While I was sitting in the hut the next night, thinking of these things, waiting for fate to do its worst, I heard a kerfuffle outside. I peered out and saw the porters struggling with someone who was trying to climb in over the front gate. It was reminiscent of my own ignominious arrival, though I couldn't immediately think who, apart from me, would be crazy enough to want to get into the Kincaid Clinic. Perhaps it was some restless native up to no good.

The porters dragged this new arrival down to earth and started to give him a good kicking. Booted feet were making repeated solid contact with the victim's torso. He was trying to curl up in a ball to protect himself, but the porters weren't allowing that. They opened him up, rolled him on to his back for ease of access, and then I was able to see his face. It was Gregory Collins.

I ran from my hut and shouted at the porters to stop kicking him, which perhaps a little surprisingly they did, but by then Gregory had also stopped moving. He was flat on his back, legs together, arms spread. It was probably a good thing that Charity couldn't see this.

'What the fuck is the matter with you two?' I shouted at the porters. 'You could have killed him.'

'We wouldn't have killed him,' one of them replied, as though defending himself against charges of professional incompetence. 'We know what we're about.'

Apparently they did. Gregory started to move. He writhed and moaned and looked distressed, but he was still undoubtedly in the land of the living, and then I noticed he was wearing a morning coat and a grey silk waistcoat – wedding tackle.

'Oh God, Bob, what happened?' I said, rather pleased that in the circumstances I'd remembered to use his false name.

He sat up a little but gave no sign that he was capable of standing. He said, 'She left me in the lurch. At the church.'

He laughed at the way his tragedy had been reduced to this familiar, predictable doggerel. I couldn't help feeling sorry for him, yet it seemed, on second thoughts, not so much tragic as simply inevitable, although I suppose all tragedies have an inevitability about them. Nicola had finally seen the error of her ways; better late (very, very late) than never.

'They were all there,' Gregory groaned. 'All Nicola's friends and family. Some of the teachers from my school. My family. They'd come a long way, all done up like shilling dinners. And I'm standing there like a lummox and the organist's playing bloody *Jerusalem*, and her father comes in on his own and says he thinks he'd better have a word with me in private, old chap. He called me old chap. I knew what he was going to say. She'd changed her mind. Who could blame her?'

'I'm really sorry, Bob,' I said.

'That's very good of you, Greg,' he said carefully.

Now he did stand up and that made him look markedly less tragic. The hired wedding suit didn't fit him. It was too narrow in the shoulders, too long in the sleeves. The waistband of the trousers formed a tight equator under his plump gut, and yet the trouser legs were vast and wide and billowed in ruffs around his ankles. He would have looked silly enough in any circumstances, but the beating from the porters had pulled him even more laughably out of shape. His hair stood on end, his tie was hoist somewhere under his ear, and his attempts to look dignified and brave only completed the comic effect.

I told the porters I'd take care of him from here and I helped him to my hut. I was touched, though nevertheless flabbergasted, that Gregory had come to me in his hour of need. If I was the one who'd just been stood up at the altar I certainly wouldn't have turned to Gregory. Who *would* I have turned to? I had no idea.

He sat on my sofabed, patting his body to make sure he was all there. I felt truly sorry for him. I knew I was going to have to tell him all about Bentley, the literary evening and the impending doom, but the moment would have to wait. Seeing him like this, knowing that Nicola had dumped him in the most humiliating way possible, knowing that Bentley was lurking in the outside world ready to do his worst to me, I also felt we had a surprising amount in common.

'I don't blame Nicola,' Gregory said glumly. 'I blame myself.'

When one person turns up at the church and the other doesn't, it seems to me that blame can only be directed one way. It was uncharacteristically generous of Gregory to admit any fault.

'After all,' he said, 'she did catch me in bed with one of the bridesmaids.'

'What?'

'Well, actually, two of the bridesmaids.'

'What? What, Gregory?'

'It didn't mean anything. I was just living out my dirty little fantasies. I thought it was better to do it than to write about it. Get it all out of my system the night before the wedding. But Nicola caught me at it. So I don't blame her.'

I looked hard at Gregory and I didn't believe a word of it. Finding one person prepared to have sex with Gregory Collins seemed preposterous enough. Finding two, who both happened to be bridesmaids, who would do it with him the night before the wedding, stretched plausibility too far for me. I assumed he was making it up. So if this alleged scene of debauchery hadn't really been played out, then Nicola obviously couldn't have caught him at it. So either she'd had other perfectly good, perfectly understandable reasons for not turning up at the church and Gregory was using this story as an excuse; or just possibly he hadn't been stood up at all. Perhaps he was the one who'd chickened out and run away. That made sense to me too; that he had finally realised the impossibility, the inadvisability, the sheer insanity of getting married to Nicola. That seemed infinitely more likely than this other nonsense. Still, I didn't challenge him. Why bother? He'd got his story and as far as I was concerned he was welcome to stick to it.

'You know Gogol?' Gregory asked.

'The author?' I said. '*Dead Souls, The Overcoat, The Government Inspector.*'

'Very good, Michael. He wrote *The Diary of a Madman* too.'

'Right,' I said.

'Well, when he was young he had a poem privately printed, called *Hans Kuchelgarten*. It got two stinking reviews, so he took back all the unsold copies and burned them. Only three copies had actually been sold so it was more or less the whole bloody edition. Anyway, he got over it and years later he had a big hit with *Dead Souls*. Right off he started writing the sequel, but it didn't go very well. It took him the best part of ten years and he still thought it was rubbish.

253

Meanwhile, he got sick with all these psychosomatic illnesses, and they gradually turned into real illnesses, and eventually he realised he was going to die and his great sequel wasn't any bloody good, so ten days before he snuffed it, he burned the bugger in an open fireplace. What do you think of that?'

'What do you want me to think?'

'I'd like you to think I'm part of a great tradition.'

'Anything you say, Gregory.'

'I want in,' he said passionately.

'What?'

'I want to stay here. I want to become an inmate. I want some of that Kincaidian Therapy. I want to write.'

Oh my God. This was far, far too much. There were so many reasons why I didn't want Gregory there, and I still couldn't face telling him all of them, so I simply said, 'That would be a real mistake.'

'No, no, it wouldn't,' said Gregory. 'You see, what's going on is that I'm being persecuted. Somebody somewhere is writing a book about me, not just about my past but about my present and my future as well, and I've got no choice but to do what's written in the book, to live out this life story, written by somebody else. Can you imagine what that's like? So obviously what I need to do is stay here, keep my head down, pretend to be somebody else until I work out where this book's being written and then I track down the author, make him hand over the book, and then I burn it. Right?'

His eyes opened very wide and he gave a smile that showed all his teeth, and he seemed to be giving a reasonably convincing portrayal of a crazy person. And I just thought, Fuck it. What did I care? What did it matter? We were so near to the end, what possible difference could it make?

'Whatever you say, Gregory.'

'Best call me Bob from now on.'

I took him to see Kincaid and Alicia, and they regarded his arrival with much more nonchalance than I did. Kincaid was still in high spirits from the success of the literary evening and was feeling omnipotent. Another difficult case, no problem. Gregory was still Bob Burns as far as they were concerned, so I tried to explain things by saying that Bob had been working too hard editing some illustrated books, and Kincaid just loved that. And Gregory rambled on about his wedding and threesomes with bridesmaids and books being written about him, and both Kincaid and Alicia agreed that the clinic was the best possible place for him.

'But where are we going to put you, Bob?' Kincaid said. 'The clinic has ten rooms and ten patients. The library and the Communication Room are obviously out of the question, and we have a writer very much in residence in the writer's hut, so I wonder where you'd be most at home. I know. I think we'll give you a couple of days in the padded cell.'

Why did I find that so satisfying? Why didn't I try to protect Gregory a little? Was it just *Schadenfreude*? Sadism? Did I want Gregory to suffer the way I had? Well yes, all the above, plus the fact that it would at least keep him out of harm's way for a while. And to be fair, he went happily enough, accepted it as part of the therapy, nodded gullibly as Kincaid spouted some guff about the welcoming, enveloping darkness. I said I'd see him soon. The porters took him away and I was left alone with Kincaid and Alicia.

'Our little literary evening is bearing fruit already,' Kincaid said proudly. 'Tomorrow afternoon two of the trustees are coming back to the clinic for a top-level meeting. I have high hopes. An academic called Dr John Bentley will be joining us too. I don't expect you'll want to be there.'

Before I could say anything, Alicia interrupted. She was on my side now. 'Please, Dr Kincaid, I think Gregory has every right in the world to be there. In fact, I insist on it.'

Kincaid obviously didn't enjoy tangling with Alicia any more than I did. He made a little moue of acquiescence, and I said, 'Great. I wouldn't miss it for the world.'

28

There were six of us at the meeting in Kincaid's office. I sat on 'our' side of the table along with Kincaid and Alicia, while on 'their' side were the trustees, two silvery-haired, grey-suited doctors, one male – a Dr Gutteridge, one female – a Dr Driscoll. They looked like people you could trust: substantial, decent, tough-minded without being cruel, the kind of people you'd be happy to have operate on you. They explained, though quite for whose benefit I wasn't sure, that they combined a truckload of medical, administrative and financial expertise. They were there to judge us, or rather they had already done so and were now about to deliver that judgement. They had both apparently been present at Kincaid's literary evening, though they looked completely unfamiliar to me.

The last member of the sextet, the final judge, and the hanging judge as far as I was concerned, was, inevitably, Dr John Bentley. He'd walked into the office at the beginning of the meeting and looked me firmly, though quite inscrutably in the eye. His gaze had revealed nothing of his intentions. But then, as he sat down, he gave me a slight but unmistakable wink. It was a tricky gesture to interpret. It seemed unlikely that you'd wink at someone just moments before you destroyed them, but then again if you wanted to lull them into a false sense of security to make the destruction that much more painful, you might do precisely that.

My attention was understandably scattered, and the silver and grey woman had been speaking for some time before I cottoned on to what she was talking about.

'That's why, on balance, we're very pleased with what you've accomplished here,' she said. She was addressing Kincaid, but I could feel the tide of approval rolling in to include Alicia and me. 'I'm sure your techniques won't be without their critics. Whose are? Yet it seems to us those techniques are clearly working.'

Kincaid nodded, but he wasn't simply agreeing with her, wasn't accepting a compliment. He was just acknowledging her acceptance of what had been obvious to him all along: that he was right, that his methods worked, that he was a genius.

'We very much want you to carry on the good work,' Dr Driscoll said. 'We want to be facilitators for you. And we want you to be able to make the so far rather limited evidence even more compelling.'

I stole a glance at Bentley. He was placid. No wink this time, nothing. I wondered what he was up to. If 'we' were indeed to carry on the good work then logic suggested he couldn't be about to expose me. He certainly couldn't have told the other two about me yet, and he was surely leaving it late. It was all very well to humiliate me at the last possible moment, but if he didn't say something soon, he was in danger of making himself and his colleagues look pretty damn silly as well.

Dr Driscoll continued, 'Your current patients have obviously benefited enormously from Kincaidian Therapy, so much so that we feel they're ready to move on, to go back into the outside world, or at the very least to move on to a less regimented form of care.'

'Mmm,' said Kincaid.

This sounded very alarming to me. Sane or not, malingerers or not, whether Kincaidian Therapy worked or not, whether we'd erected a bulkhead or not, I still couldn't imagine how the patients would fare if suddenly returned to the outside world.

'And then,' Dr Driscoll continued, 'we'd like to bring an entirely new group of patients to the clinic and have you apply your methods to them.'

'Yes,' said Kincaid. 'I see. I see.'

This alarmed me even more. I wasn't sure I could face starting again, getting to know a whole new group of lunatics, learning their quirks, making peace with them, getting them to write, et cetera, et cetera. And yet even as I had these worries I realised they were of the sort that only arose if I was going to remain at the clinic, an assumption I couldn't possibly sustain. What the hell was Bentley up to?

There was suddenly a terrible crash and the door of Kincaid's office flew open, as Carla fell into the room and on to the floor. As in the cheapest, weariest kind of farce, she had been listening at the door, and it had come open. I wondered if she'd done it deliberately. She scrambled to her feet, playing the hapless but endearing comic heroine. Nobody was endeared, least of all Kincaid.

'Get out, you idiotic girl,' he said, and Carla slunk away like a whipped, knock-kneed spaniel.

Kincaid offered his apologies for the interruption and they were accepted easily enough. A single bit of buffoonery from one stupid eavesdropper was hardly going to be enough to invalidate what had gone before. Kincaid consulted his diary, discussed dates and institutions and budgets with the two doctors, and then suddenly the meeting seemed to be drawing to a close. There was talk of keeping in touch and scheduling a second meeting when practical details could be finalised, and then the two trustees were shuffling away papers, closing up their briefcases, about to shake hands and depart.

I still couldn't quite believe it. Was I really going to get away with it? Had Bentley come all this way simply to sit and say nothing? No, of course he hadn't. Very quietly he said, 'There is one small matter I think I'm duty bound to bring up. Though I'm sure it's nothing.'

Did he really consider my fate such a small matter? Did he really think I was nothing? And how was he going to do this? How excruciating was he going to make it? I watched in fascinated terror as he took a pristine white envelope out of his jacket pocket and from it unfolded a couple of photocopied sheets.

'I have here a copy of a review of *Disorders*. It's about to be published in a respectable, if small circulation, Cambridge journal. I think it just possibly merits some of our attention.'

I was baffled. A simple denunciation, a simple statement of the facts, of my lies and general deceit, was surely all that was required. Why was Bentley getting so fancy about it?

'I only have the one copy so perhaps it would be best if I read it out,' he said.

The others weren't any more comprehending than I was, but nobody was going to stop him. Bentley began to read in his best, most persuasive and patrician lecturing voice.

'"Certain readers professed to having problems with Gregory Collins' first book, *The Wax Man*. It was clear that here was a book with moments of irony, moments of high seriousness, moments of low comedy; the difficulty was determining which were intended to be which. To put it another way, although readers frequently found the book hilarious, they were generally unsure whether they were laughing with the book or at it and, perhaps more problematically, whether the book was laughing at them. A few readers found this indeterminacy delicious, but most did not. They had a simpler desire to understand the author's intentions, to know, as it were, what was going on.

'"With *Disorders*, the latest book to appear with Mr Collins' name on its cover (the need for this formulation will become clear), such uncertainties are most definitely not banished, but the book is such a highly wrought, relentlessly, ferociously sustained piece of irony and literary mayhem, that these uncertainties not only remain delicious, they also become the book's *raison d'être*.

'"Mr Collins sets up a meticulously preposterous fictional framework. The text purports to be the results of work done with a set of inmates at an experimental and dubious-sounding mental hospital called the Kincaid Clinic. We are given an introduction by the eponymous Dr Eric Kincaid, the supposed head of the clinic, which is a wonderfully savage and deadpan parody of psychiatric banality. Collins then invents a persona for himself as writer-in-residence at this establishment. In a gloriously ill-written preface he tells us it has been his job to encourage the patients' creativity; a job he has performed not wisely but too well. We are to understand that the rest of the book is a mere sampling, the tip of a vast, lumbering iceberg of the patients' manic literary efforts. These samples are splendidly, brilliantly awful.

'"The book contains all that is good and bad, compelling and objectionable, satisfying and infuriating, intriguing and laughable, about modern experimental writing; sometimes it is obscene, sometimes it is trite and empty. Passages evoke echoes of almost everyone in the modern canon, from Burroughs to Artaud, from Bataille to Robbe-Grillet, from Huysmans to Freud, by way of Kafka, de Sade, Beckett et al.

'"Sometimes these pieces appear to be offering genuine, or at least convincing, insights into the disturbed human mind, as though they were acts of psychotic ventriloquism; but just as often Mr Collins simply aims for the comedic jugular and provides good, militant, satirical, dirty-minded, intellectual fun. Parts of this book are screamingly funny, all of it is wildly, decadently inventive.

'"One's first impression might be that these insane voices form a discourse claiming to be independent of dominant 'sane' ideological practices, and if that were the case one might indeed carp at this overweening ambition. Yet Mr Collins is more ambitious and more slippery still. It dawns on the reader that for all Mr Collins' inventiveness and virtuosity, he can't successfully impersonate so many different voices. We feel he has bitten off more than he can chew. But then, slowly, and what a thrill it is when the realisation comes, we see this is, so to speak, the whole point. One realises that these voices are not intended to be so very different after all. They are in fact all one. They are acts not of ventriloquism but of soliloquy. Mr Collins is, if you will, speaking all the lines, and speaking them to himself. The patients do not exist, the 'real' Gregory Collins does not exist either, and the fictional author is locked in the asylum of his own head, a sort of literary madhouse. The author is the only patient, the book's only begetter. All we are reading is words, words, words. The book is the diary of a literary madman, and it is magnificent."'

Bentley folded the pages and placed them on Kincaid's desk. Nobody else moved. I cannot imagine blanker faces than the ones that stared at Bentley and then at each other.

'I don't know what this means,' said Dr Gutteridge.

He spoke for all of us I think, and yet Bentley's revelation was so different from the one I'd been expecting, that I found myself garrulously on the offensive.

'Well, it's obviously just nonsense, isn't it?' I said. 'Are you really trying to say I made it all up, wrote the whole of *Disorders*? That it's a *novel*?'

'*I*'m not saying that,' said Bentley. 'But somebody is.'

'Who wrote this review, anyway?' Alicia asked.

'Somebody called Michael Smith,' said Bentley. 'A name I'm not familiar with.'

And then he winked at me again. I started to sweat. Where had this review come from? Why was my name on it? Who'd written it? Why was Bentley doing this? What was he going to get out of it?

'But it's transparently not true,' I insisted. 'I didn't make up this clinic. I didn't make up Dr Kincaid. I didn't make up the patients.'

'No, the reviewer is clearly mistaken there. The charge is more simply, and more seriously, that *Disorders* is not a work of collective pathology, but a work of fiction created by a single hand.'

'Well, that's obviously not true either, is it?' I said with some passion. 'Why would I do that? Why would anyone? What would be the point?'

Bentley shrugged extravagantly.

'Well,' said Dr Driscoll, very slowly and judiciously, 'one point might be in order to validate an experimental form of therapy, mightn't it? An unscrupulous doctor might, I suppose, employ a professional writer to create an accomplished piece of writing and attribute it to his patients in an attempt to prove that his therapy worked, and that his patients were, so to speak, cured.'

This sounded like Alice in Wonderland stuff to me.

'I can show you the manuscripts,' I protested, and then I realised that I couldn't. Gregory or the publisher now had them, and if I'd thought about it any further it was obvious that thousands of sheets of typed manuscript actually proved nothing at all.

'It just didn't happen,' I said. 'I'll take a lie detector test. Anything.'

The moment I said that I wished I hadn't. God knows how I'd have done on a lie detector. Would it have picked up the fact that I wasn't even who I said I was? Fortunately nobody took me very seriously.

Dr Gutteridge turned to Bentley and said, 'Are you asking us to believe that the assertions in this review are true?'

'I'm asking nothing,' Bentley replied.

'But you're saying that *Disorders* may be, what, a literary hoax?'

Bentley said. 'I'm merely presenting you with a text. It is no part of my intention to influence your interpretation of that text.'

Kincaid looked paralysed, as though he might be about to give in to some explosive, calamitous impulse, and could only hold himself in check by adopting a sort of catatonia. Alicia tried to come to his aid.

'Please,' she said. 'A moment ago we were all perfectly content. We were moving forward. I don't see how one over-ingenious book review can make such a big difference. It's only one person's opinion and we know it's wrong.'

'I don't know any such thing,' said Dr Driscoll.

'This really does make a difference,' Dr Gutteridge agreed, and he picked up the photocopy of the review, scouring it for undiscovered clues.

'We understand that,' said Alicia. 'We understand your position completely, but still ...'

She was trying to sound optimistic, as though the mere fact of understanding their position somehow meant we were all on the same side, but we clearly were not, and the visiting doctors were quite unconvinced.

Dr Gutteridge turned to Bentley and said, 'Let me ask it more simply. Do *you* think the text of *Disorders* is the work of a single hand?'

Bentley sucked air in between his clenched teeth. He wanted us to know this was difficult stuff. He was not a man for rash decisions, for easy conclusions. He was prudent, thoughtful, authoritative. But at last he had to say, 'If you really press me, if you really demand an opinion from me, then I think it probably is, yes.'

'So you think that Mr Collins here wrote every single word of *Disorders*?'

Bentley spread his palms wide and said, 'He is a very clever, skilful and persuasive young man. And if not him, then who else?'

Doctors Driscoll and Gutteridge nodded gravely. Here was a man they could trust, one of their own, someone whose opinions they had to take seriously, someone they could believe in. I felt almost deranged with anger. What was wrong with these people? How could they think I was the author of this book, I who could barely string two paragraphs together? And regardless of whether I was capable of doing it or not, the simple fact was, I hadn't. And I knew there was no way I could possibly convince them.

My God, Bentley was good. I stared around the blank walls, looking for inspiration, and my eyes fell on the window. I got the fright of my life. As did the trustees.

'Oh my God, what's that?' said Dr Driscoll.

There was a face at the window, actually a whole body. Charles Manning had found his way up a drainpipe and was now perched on the window ledge, peering in, spying on us. As a covert operation it lacked finesse. The ledge was narrow and he had to press himself against the glass in order not to fall off. Then we saw another detail. His fly was open, his penis was out, and it took on a squashed, doughy appearance as it was flattened against the pane.

'Oh Jesus,' said Alicia.

Then the office door flew open again and a naked Charity pranced in looking zonked, and did a circle of the room, arms and legs flailing, while singing some song of undifferentiated mysticism.

'Perhaps we should—' Alicia said, but she was too late. The trustees had already gathered up their belongings and were heading for the door, although Bentley seemed less inclined to run away. He was enjoying this. Nevertheless, we all followed the two doctors as they left the office, Alicia mouthing what she took to be words of reassurance. Kincaid and I were both speechless but we too felt the need to keep up.

Charity danced and twirled ahead of us, like a naked sprite leading us who knew where. When we had passed through the clinic and stepped outside into the open air she left us and ran full tilt towards the dried-up fountain. We didn't go after her since the trustees were rapidly moving in the opposite direction, towards the gate and an immediate exit, but we couldn't help following Charity with our eyes, and the events taking place in and around the fountain were undeniably compelling.

I expect the word orgy is often applied rather casually and inexactly. Let's just say that Charity leapt into the fountain and joined the other nine inmates of the Kincaid Clinic who were already arranged around the statue of the mermaid. They were stripped down and participating in an ornate and spectacular bout of group sex. One small consolation was that at least Gregory Collins wasn't part of the show.

I expect once you've seen one orgy of lunatics you've seen them all. There are only so many things hands and mouths and genitals are capable of, and certainly the patients weren't doing anything beyond the bounds of possibility. They were just doing everything they could. Only three things really stood out for me. One, that an otherwise naked Carla was wearing a Che Guevara T-shirt that looked identical to the one I'd once owned. Two, that Byron, who was only intermittently involving himself in the activities, was taking photographs with what looked very much like my missing camera. And three, that Charles Manning, having come down from the window ledge and removed the rest of his clothes, was masturbating while looking at what was undoubtedly a naked picture of Nicola that had been in my missing collection of photographs.

Need I tell you, nothing about this spectacle was remotely erotic? The patients were whooping it up, making inarticulate noises that in other contexts might have seemed joyous or abandoned, but to me it sounded like the soundtrack of a bad porn film – forced and very badly acted. There was nothing spontaneous or authentic or even very sexual about it. Obviously they weren't faking as such, since they were really having sex, and yet I felt they were doing it for effect, not for pleasure. And when they started wordlessly signalling to the doctors Bentley, Driscoll and Gutteridge, inviting them to come and join in, the effect was complete.

Our visitors were out of there in seconds flat, and perhaps the orgy would have ended then regardless, but to make absolutely certain, the porters arrived dragging garden hoses behind them and started spraying down the patients with icy water, bringing things to a drenched and inevitable conclusion. Then the porters began to manhandle the patients, brutally strapping them into straitjackets and, in a move I hadn't seen before, putting thick black nylon bags over their heads, and dragging them away to their rooms. You might have thought the patients had numbers on their side and could have put up quite a struggle if they'd wanted to, but they didn't resist much, not even Anders. It was as though they thought this punishment was their due.

Alicia watched sadly but did nothing to intervene and it was left to me to make a feeble, futile protest, to say to Kincaid, 'And is this part of your precious Kincaidian Therapy too?'

He was not in the mood to be doubted. He gestured to the porters and I was instantly silenced. They grabbed me and did to me what they'd already done to the patients: the straitjacket and the bag over the head. I was outraged. Nothing is more maddening than being treated like a madman. I struggled and shouted, but only in the most ineffectual way. I could hear Alicia asking the porters to be gentle with me, but that had predictably inverse results. They kicked and punched me a little, and then dragged me back to my writer's hut, where they abandoned me and where I remained for some considerable time.

29

A man can entertain some strange thoughts while he's lying on the floor of his hut, bound in a straitjacket with a black nylon bag tied over his head, and the particularly strange thought I came to entertain was that I finally knew what was going on. Something clicked and I was certain I knew what Kincaid and the patients were up to. Consequently I felt myself seething with indignation and righteous anger, desperate to communicate this precious truth that I'd worked out.

My opportunities for communication were strictly limited, however. At first there had been bangs and crashes outside the hut, shouting, some laughter, some barked orders from Kincaid, the sound of glass breaking, a noise that could have been someone being pummelled with a truncheon. And then it had all gone perfectly quiet, though that in itself was no source of comfort. I wondered what kind of coshes, chemical or otherwise, what kind of shock treatments, what 'experimental techniques', Kincaid and the porters might be performing out there. And where was Alicia in all this?

Time passed painfully. I tried to breathe slowly and regularly, tried not to fret too much about the cramps developing in my arms and shoulders. Finally, hours later, I heard footsteps coming into the hut, just one person, not the two porters as I feared, and it sounded like a woman's tread. Then a pair of hands was on me, pulling the bag from over my head. It was Alicia, and I was exquisitely relieved. I thought everything was going to be all right now.

I was expecting a great flood of light when the bag came off but it was night, the hut was in darkness and Alicia was working by the glow of a small pencil torch. It seemed a little melodramatic but perhaps it was necessary.

'I'm really sorry about this,' Alicia said. 'It's all my fault. I should probably never have brought you here.'

It was tempting to agree with her, but I said, 'I wouldn't have missed it for the world.'

'You're an interesting case,' she said.

'More than you might imagine.' And then with the flawless confidence that the hero always displays, I said, 'Listen, I can explain everything.'

'You can?' said Alicia, and I thought she sounded impressed. 'What do you mean by everything?'

She was right to make me define my terms. There was a certain amount I was still going to leave unexplained, like who I was for instance, but I said, 'For a start I know why the patients suddenly went crazy like that.'

'Crazy?'

'Yes. I think having group sex in front of the visiting trustees is crazy in anybody's book.'

'Perhaps,' she said grudgingly.

'Could you take this straitjacket off me?'

'First tell me your theory.'

I was disappointed not to be instantly freed, but I was so eager to tell my story I was prepared to tolerate it.

'The patients went crazy simply because they wanted to,' I said. 'They wanted the trustees to see they were mad. Carla was listening at the door, remember? She heard them say that Kincaidian Therapy had worked and it was time for the patients to move on. They don't want to move on, so they have to prove they aren't sane. She reported back to the other patients and they knew they had to do something pretty spectacular.'

'Possibly,' said Alicia.

'But they were obviously in a double bind, the one I now see they've been in all along. If they appear completely sane then Kincaidian Therapy is declared a success and they're sent on their way. But if they appear completely mad then Kincaidian Therapy is declared a failure and they're sent somewhere else anyway. So the trick all along has been for them to show just enough progress to make Kincaid continue the treatment, but also to make sure they're never completely "cured", whatever that means.'

'They were playing us along all the time, you mean?' she asked.

266

'Yes. Malingering if you like. But the so-called literary evening threw everything out of kilter. The trustees were right. The patients *did* behave like more or less sane people on that night, and that was their undoing. They looked too good. So obviously they had to behave like totally insane people today. Personally, I think they went about a million miles too far, but obviously it's a tricky thing to get right.'

'Poor Dr Kincaid,' Alicia said.

'Kincaid I'm coming to, but wait. Now, obviously Carla didn't hear Bentley read out the review of *Disorders*. She'd gone by then, so she couldn't have known that I was being accused of having written it all. She didn't know that part of the game was up, although I'm absolutely sure she knew I wasn't the author. And, for reasons I'll explain, she obviously knows who is – Kincaid.'

'Dr Kincaid?' said Alicia in slightly extravagant wonderment.

'Yes. Bentley may have been out to get me, but he knows what he's talking about. If he says there's textual evidence that *Disorders* was all written by one person, then I'm prepared to believe him. But it's not me. It's Kincaid. He's the single author who wrote the whole book. I don't know exactly how he made it work, but if I had to guess I'd say he probably did it in his therapy sessions, in his office when the blinds were drawn.'

'How?' said Alicia.

'I think he probably just dictated things to the patients. Maybe he was doing preparation when I saw him pacing in his office at night, and then when the patients came in to see him he let it all pour out, giving vent to his literary ambitions. The patients wrote it all down in their notebooks, then they went to the Communication Room and typed it up and gave it to me as their own.'

'But would they do that?'

'They would if Kincaid told them to. If they'd refused he'd have kicked them out of the clinic.'

'But why would Dr Kincaid do it?'

'For all the reasons that Dr Driscoll said. To make himself look good, to prove to the world that Kincaidian Therapy actually worked. And he might have got away with it if it hadn't been for Dr Bentley. And of course it was very handy for Kincaid that Bentley accused *me* of doing the dirty work. It let him off the hook. It made him look like the innocent party. And it's even more convenient that he can now use me as a scapegoat.'

'Well,' said Alicia. 'It's very ingenious. You're very clever, aren't you?'

'It's not just clever. It's true.'

Alicia looked at me a little less tenderly and admiringly than I'd have liked. I wanted her to acclaim me as the all-knowing hero, instead she looked troubled. But, then again, why wouldn't she? Even if she accepted what I said was true, it didn't solve anything. What was the next step? A break out? An insurrection? The lunatics taking over the asylum?

'It's got a little bit crazy out there in the clinic,' Alicia said.

'You don't say.'

'All the patients are in their rooms, straitjackets on, bags over their heads.'

'Very therapeutic,' I sneered.

'That's what Dr Kincaid says. And there's been a power cut. Or perhaps he's turned off the electricity. He says darkness is good for the patients. It's keeping them fairly quiet, anyway. And Dr Kincaid, well, I wouldn't want to put a label on it, but he does seem to have gone a little mad. And he wants to see you. That's why I came here. To get you.'

'OK then,' I said, still the cliché-ridden leading man. 'If he's ready for me, I'm more than ready for him. Let me out of this straitjacket, will you?'

'I'd like to, I really would, but Dr Kincaid has said I shouldn't, and this would be a really bad time to disobey him.'

There was something in that, but it left me feeling extremely vulnerable.

'He's waiting for you in the library,' said Alicia. 'I'll take you there.'

She led me by the feeble light of the pencil torch. I couldn't picture what would happen once I got to the library. I wondered what constituted 'a little mad' in the case of Kincaid. I couldn't imagine what roles he and I were going to play, and perhaps that was just as well.

He was seated at the library table, an arc of stubby candles in front of him casting a streaky, restless light on to his smooth, glossy cheeks. He looked both glum and threatening. His body leaned forward, his head like the end of a battering ram. He looked at me fearfully, as though I might do something crazy, as though I was the mad, dangerous one, although how dangerous could I possibly be in a straitjacket?

'How are you, Gregory?' he asked in his best condescending, medical, bedside voice.

'Top notch,' I said. 'Nothing I like better than a little straitjacket time.'

'I had hoped you might see its value.'

'Wrong once again, doctor.'

He gazed at me dolefully, as though I was an enigma to him, one of his rare but devastating failures.

'Why did you do it?' he asked.

He was speaking more in sorrow than in anger, though I sensed the anger might not be very far away.

'Do what?' I demanded.

There were so many things he might have been accusing me of, and I thought it best to be clear.

'Why did you write *Disorders*? Did you think it was a joke?'

I was furious. 'I'm not playing this game, you bastard,' I said.

He looked genuinely surprised by my reaction, as though he might have been expecting regret or defiance, but this simple denial confused him.

'You're not pinning this on me,' I said. 'Oh yes, I realise that review's very convenient for you—'

'Convenient?' he exploded. 'Could you please try to explain to me, for the love of God, what is in any conceivable way convenient about all this?'

His anger was formidable but I could handle it.

'It's convenient because it makes me the fall guy,' I said. 'You're still the great doctor, and I'm the one who deceived and betrayed you. But I'm not having it.'

He blinked at me with perplexed dignity. 'You're not really still trying to claim you didn't write the book, are you?' he said.

'Fuck this. We don't have to go through this charade,' I said. 'Credit me with some intelligence. I know *you* wrote it.'

We glared at each other in fierce mutual accusation, and as we stared and glowered we both caught something in the other's eye; something that was very rare indeed around the Kincaid Clinic. We both saw that the other was not pretending. It was clear that we both really believed what we were saying, believed that the other was the culprit. And suddenly we both knew we were wrong. Kincaid realised I wasn't the author of *Disorders*, and I realised he wasn't either. We continued to stare at each other. We didn't know what to say.

Alicia broke the silence and said, 'It looks like another one of those linguistic-philosophical conundrums, doesn't it? The two of you have convinced each other that you're both telling the truth. That doesn't necessarily mean you both are, but you both *believe* you both are. And if neither of you wrote *Disorders*, then you have to ask who did.'

It was a good question, but not one I felt remotely able to answer.

'How about the patients?' Alicia suggested. 'Maybe Dr Bentley was wrong after all. Maybe they really did write it.'

Kincaid and I shook our heads. No, that didn't seem like an option. We'd stopped believing in that possibility.

'Then how about Byron?' she asked eagerly. 'He looks like a writer. Or how about Anders? He looks completely *unlike* a writer – maybe it's a disguise. Or Sita? Who knows what she gets up to behind that quiet exterior?'

Kincaid and I remained silent and unconvinced. I was actually finding Alicia's behaviour a little embarrassing. I couldn't see why she was so desperate to come up with a quick, easy answer.

'Oh, all right,' she said suddenly, resignedly, 'I admit it. It was me.'

Kincaid and I said 'What?' simultaneously.

'I wrote it all, well, dictated it to the patients in my office, in our therapy sessions, then had them type it up, just like you said. After all, "psychiatrist" is an anagram of "typist's chair".'

'Did you really do this?' I asked, not fully persuaded.

'Why would you?' said Kincaid.

'For all the reasons everyone said. I wanted Kincaidian Therapy to look good, to be declared a success.'

'I wanted it to succeed too,' said Kincaid, 'but why this way?'

'Because you're a great man and a genius, and Kincaidian Therapy is a great thing, and because this man here,' she meant me, 'wasn't capable of inspiring the patients. And because I love you,' she said.

Kincaid was as taken aback by this declaration of love as I was. I'd never thought Alicia was in love with me, but neither had it crossed my mind that she was in love with him. Fortunately, I didn't have to ask the obvious question: why had she been sleeping with me, if that was the case? Alicia was already explaining away that apparent contradiction.

'I only slept with Michael to make you jealous, Dr Kincaid. That's why I made so much noise, why I was so verbal. So you'd hear me. So you'd pay attention. So you'd love me.'

This sounded plain crazy to me. Was it true? Or was she just manipulating Kincaid, trying to get control over him? She said he'd gone a little mad, yet he seemed more or less rational to me, if you discounted turning off the power and treating the patients like political prisoners; whereas the things Alicia was saying seemed far more insane.

'Who's Michael?' Kincaid asked.

In the confusion I hadn't even been aware that Alicia had used my real name.

'Michael. Gregory. What's in a name?' said Alicia.

Kincaid looked distressed and bewildered, and I couldn't blame him. Straitjacketed though I was, I felt the urge to help him out.

'Gregory Collins isn't my real name,' I said quickly. 'It's a pseudonym. My real name's Mike Smith. Not much of a name for an author. You can see why I changed it.'

Kincaid was satisfied, at least for a moment. As for Alicia, if she knew I wasn't really Gregory Collins, then she'd been playing a much longer and more bizarre game than I'd realised.

'But just a second,' Kincaid said, shuffling his wits. 'Michael Smith was the name of the man who wrote that blasted review. Did you write it? Did you do all this deliberately?'

'No, no,' I said. 'This is not what I wanted at all.'

You could say that again. Kincaid seemed to be on the brink of defeat, and yet there was an undeniable strength about him as he said, 'It's time somebody told me what's going on.'

Alicia and I glanced at each other like the conspirators we apparently were, and then I told Kincaid everything. He sat in stately suspended animation as I ran through all the ramifications that had resulted from not being who I said I was. It took some doing. It was hard enough to keep the story clear in my own head, and even harder to make it clear to someone else. Kincaid listened intently, and the more it sank in, the more he looked as though he wanted to kill me or Alicia or both of us.

When I'd eventually finished he turned to Alicia and said, 'And you've known about this all along?'

'Well, it depends what you mean by "all along", but essentially yes,' she said.

His head swayed, looking robotic, and his mouth moved slowly as though not quite in sync with his words. 'Between you, you've destroyed me,' he said.

'No,' said Alicia passionately. 'No. I love you. I need you. I dream of us together, driving away from here together, at speed, into the night, a black man in a black car, the headlights pointing the way through the impenetrable night, and then suddenly you turn off the lights and you put your foot to the floor, the engine roars and the car accelerates and we continue careering into the unknown dark. The blackness enfolds us. It's all right. I trust you. You know the road by heart, every twist and turn, you don't need visual data, you touch the wheel deftly, confidently, and you carry us away into the night, into this darkness and oblivion, into—'

Kincaid slapped her, the way people slap hysterical women in films. The problem here was that Alicia wasn't actually hysterical at all, but the moment Kincaid hit her she began to scream, loudly and deliriously. Kincaid didn't know what to do, and neither did I. I think we were both relieved when the porters arrived. They just happened to have another straitjacket and black nylon bag with them, and they strapped Alicia in, despite her fighting and screaming, and then carried her away into the night.

Kincaid and I were left alone in the library. I feared for what he might do to me, but he was a better man than I had any right to expect. He did nothing, said nothing, just stared at me long and hard, and then he left me there, walked out of the library, locking the door behind him.

I thought of trying to kick open the door, but I didn't see how that was going to do me any good. Not having the bag over my head was a real improvement but the straitjacket was causing stabbing pains all over my torso. I'd once seen an escape artist get out of one of these things in about half a minute and I'd been unimpressed at the time. Now I wished I'd watched more closely.

I don't know how long it was before Gregory arrived, and I wasn't sure how he'd got there. Apparently he'd found a way of escaping from his padded cell, and a way of arming himself with a flaming torch – a length of tree branch with a paraffin-soaked rag tied round its end. Then, avoiding the porters and Kincaid, he had shinned up the front of the clinic to the window of the library, and now he was forcing his way in.

'It's like a bloody madhouse out there,' he said as he climbed into the room. A wayward, flapping light and the reek of paraffin filled the library. 'This is a right place you've brought me to.'

There was no point arguing that he had come entirely of his own free will and that I'd much rather not have had him there at all. I said, 'Unstrap this thing, will you, Gregory?' I hardly thought I was asking too much. Why had he come to the library if not to free me? But he was no keener to undo the straitjacket than Alicia had been. He was now strolling round the room, looking at the books on the shelves, inspecting them by the light of his flaming torch. I had the urge to explain everything to him, but there was so much information I would have needed to impart that I was relieved at his distracted condition, although that in itself created other problems.

'You know, this is a very dodgy collection of books,' he said. 'I noticed that when I was here before but I had other things on my mind then.'

'Yes, well, beggars can't be choosers,' I said.

'Can't they?'

'No, Gregory, they can't. Now let me out of this thing, will you?'

He said, 'I see *Disorders* got an interesting review. By someone with your name. Now there's a turn up for the books.'

'You wrote it, didn't you?' I said. That was another thing I'd worked out.

Gregory tilted his head modestly. 'Oh yes. I most certainly did.'

'It was a very perceptive review as it turns out. You were right. There was only one author.'

'Of course,' he said. 'It was me. *I* wrote *Disorders*.'

'Oh please, Gregory.'

I was reminded of that scene at the end of *Spartacus* where the Romans say they'll let everybody go if Spartacus stands up and lets himself be crucified and, one after another, hundreds of people get up and every one of them says, 'Take me. I'm Spartacus.' 'No, I'm Spartacus.' 'No, I am.' So they crucify the whole lot of them.

'Gregory,' I said, 'could you be a real pal and unstrap me and then we can have a good long talk about this?'

'I know it sounds a bit barmy,' he said, making no move to help me, 'but it's not all that complicated really. It's like inspiration. I sit up there in Yorkshire and I transmit these brain waves, these inspirational vibrations, and they go through the ether and they arrive in the minds of the patients here at the Kincaid Clinic and they write it all down, and it's like a group project, like divine dictation, and it comes out a bit garbled in the transmission, a bit scrambled, and that's why I needed to come along and edit it and make it my own again. And obviously that's why my name's on the front of the book—'

Gregory had lost it. Either the trauma of the abandoned wedding or the shock of being in the padded cell had pushed him over some vertiginous edge. This was not what I needed. I didn't know what the consequences were either for him or for me. On the other hand, how sane did he have to be to do a simple thing like get me out of the straitjacket?

'Can we talk about this later?' I asked.

'Later may be too late,' he said, and he perused the bookshelves again.

'When Ernest Hemingway was young he worked for Ford Madox Ford at *transatlantic review*, and Ford told him that a bloke should always write a letter thinking what posterity will make of it. This pissed Hemingway off so much that he went home and burned every letter in his flat, especially the ones from Ford Madox Ford.'

'But, Gregory—'

'And when Goebbels lit a bonfire in Berlin in nineteen thirty-three to commemorate the new spirit of the German Reich, he used up twenty thousand books. Not bad, eh?'

He fixed his attention on some scruffy old volumes on a bottom shelf of the library.

'It's not exactly the Alexandrian Library in here, is it?' he said. 'And you know what happened to that. Well, actually, nobody's all that sure. Caesar definitely burned down some library or other during the Alexandrian wars, but it probably wasn't *the* Alexandrian Library. Because if Caesar had really done so much damage there wouldn't have been much left to destroy come the really big burning of AD 642 when the Caliph Omar ordered the destruction of the library on the grounds that if the manuscripts in it agreed with the

Koran they were superfluous, and if they disagreed with it they should be destroyed anyway.

'And frankly that's how I feel about my own books, Michael. The works of Gregory Collins are pretty much the only ones anybody should ever need. The rest can go to blazes.'

'Gregory, all I'm asking is that you undo this straitjacket.'

'I couldn't possibly do that,' he said. 'That would be against doctors' orders. In fact, I think you're in need of a little more therapy.'

He reached into his pocket and produced another of the black nylon bags, which he rather deftly, with one hand, slipped over my head, and then he torched the library, the Kincaid Clinic and me.

Now

30

Welcome to the present. I'm writing this in the here and now, and inevitably you're reading it in the here and now. Of course. There's no other way. That's the strange and unique bargain that a book makes with us. When you pick up *Bleak House* you're there with Dickens, when you pick up *Mein Kampf* you're with Adolf Hitler – in the same shared here and now. I think this is totally different from what happens with a painting or a piece of music or a play or a movie; and if books have any capacity to endure, to face up to what I suppose we might as well call the 'electronic media', then I suspect it's largely because of this, that they allow a profound connection across huge swathes of time and space between two individuals. You'll find some French lads who'll give you an argument, who'll say it's really all about presence and absence; but hell, you can't spend your life worrying about what the French think.

It has felt very strange to be writing about the person I was all those years ago. Needless to say, I'm no longer precisely him. Thank God, I've changed, matured, wised up a bit; and yet as I describe the things I thought and did back then I don't feel I'm describing an entirely different person, don't feel that I've had to actually invent or reconstruct a character. A part of me is still that gauche twenty-three-year-old, just as a part of me is still the child on his first day at school, the ten-year-old discovering the joy of books, the hopeless adolescent trying to work out what love and sex were all about.

The twenty-five years or so since those days at the Kincaid Clinic have been, on balance, good to me. There are some lines in the *Four Quartets* about how as you get older the pattern becomes stranger, but I'm not so sure. In lots of ways the years seem all too simple, like a ride down a ski slope: continuous, sometimes exhilarating, occasion-ally scary, but in the end not so very convoluted, not ultimately unpredictable. I realise I've been quite lucky in this.

I've been married and divorced. There were no children, nothing really worth fighting about, and yet the split was bitter and damaging. But who would have expected anything else? Both my parents have died, I've put on weight, lost some hair, had a couple of bad bouts with a stomach ulcer; but today I'm living with a good woman and we say we love each other, and we believe it, which seems to be as much as anybody can ask. I think you would have to say that, all things considered, I'm happy, that I've had my full ration of happiness. There are plenty of stories that could be mined out of those years, but I don't want to tell them here and now. They seem simultaneously too personal and too commonplace.

If by some sorcery I was now able to go back, knowing nothing of the intervening years, and meet the person I was then, I think I'd look at him and say, my God, what the hell is ever going to become of him? He has no prospects. He has no ambitions. He has no way of making a living. He completely screwed up his future when he took that job at the Kincaid Clinic. What's he going to do with his life? And yet I suppose I'd be reasonably confident that somehow or other he'd survive. He mightn't win any glittering prizes, but he surely wouldn't end up entirely destitute and lost. Perhaps I could have looked at him as if at a character in a soap opera and thought, 'Oh yes, it'll be interesting to see how this plot develops.' But I wouldn't have held any hopes that it was going to be one of the great dramatic storylines.

The truth is I became a writer of sorts; not exactly the stuff of soap opera. When the Kincaid days were over, and after I'd eventually put myself back together, I returned to London and started to do some freelance journalism, nothing very exciting, nothing very cutting-edge, but eventually, by a minor fluke, I got a job working for an in-flight magazine. I did everything: interviews, travel writing, book reviewing. I wouldn't say these were areas where my looks didn't matter – I suspect no such world exists. But let's say this was a job where I didn't have to show my face to the public. I wrote articles, I had a byline, that was all. I was just a name.

This went on steadily and unspectacularly until, when I was in my mid-thirties, one of those odd little arbitrary, life-changing things happened. I got the chance to interview a rather grand old English travel writer, one of those who rarely gave interviews, and he was only prepared to see me because I'd given his book such a ridiculously fulsome review in the magazine. I was granted an audience. According to his publisher it was quite an honour for me.

I'd always used a crappy little pocket tape recorder when I'd done interviews, but this time a friend at a local radio station offered to lend me a professional machine. It would provide a broadcast-quality tape they might be able to use on air. It was OK by me, but I wasn't sure the grand old man would want to be recorded, yet oddly enough he agreed to it. It must have been my charm. Or something. It seemed like the most insignificant event at the time. I was still thinking of myself as a print journalist, not as a radio interviewer, and perhaps because I didn't care about it too much I was very relaxed and the interview went well. It was friendly and funny and revealing, and when it was broadcast it was regarded as quite a coup; and that was the start of my career in radio.

I'd never given any thought to my voice. It was just a voice as far as I was concerned. But now people were telling me it had an engaging warmth to it, that it established an easy intimacy with the listener. It made individual members of the audience feel I was talking to them directly. This apparently is what good radio voices do. It's not entirely unlike reading a book, I suppose.

My life got surprisingly easy from then on. I turned out to be a natural. I did a few more interviews as part of other people's radio programmes but then very quickly I got my own show on local radio. Most of it was pretty banal, reading traffic reports and birthday requests; but once in a while I got to interview a novelist or biographer or playwright. I was damn good at it, and I got a bit of a reputation for being smart without being stuck up, a guy who seemed to have read everything but who wore his learning lightly, and who could fight his intellectual corner if he needed to.

I moved on to a late-night show on a small London station, and now I have an evening show on a much bigger London station. We do some round-table discussions, some film and exhibition reviews, even a few phone-ins, but books and author interviews are what I do best and what I'm known for. When big-time authors have a book they want to plug on radio, they plug it with me. People tell me I'm a cult. People tell me it's a crying shame I can't do TV. I say that's OK, I do voice-overs instead; they help to top up the really pretty humble wage I get from the radio.

The title of my programme is *I'm Afraid I Haven't Read Your Book* – a double bluff. It mocks all those crappy radio interviewers who say those words to their authors; and the real joke is that I always *have* read the book. I've read everything. I'm famous for it. If you get the joke you get the show.

I come across as this benign, well-informed, intelligent, warm-voiced host who makes the authors feel relaxed enough to let their guard down; and if they're smart, modest, reasonable, then all well and good. But if they start being precious or pretentious or glib, then I fillet them, gut them and hang them out to dry. There are worse jobs.

Some of my critics, and yes I'm a big enough name to have critics, say I hate books, which is clearly nonsense. Others say I hate authors, but that's not exactly true either. The people I hate and the people I enjoy eviscerating on the show are those who adopt the *pose* of authors, who behave the way they think great authors behave.

'Tonight we have with us David Bergstrom, author of *A Light Rain in the Appalachians*. Hello, David.'

'A pleasure to be here, Mike.'

The author is American, smooth, deliberate in his speech. He considers himself an old hand at this interviewing lark. He doesn't look at all like his author photograph.

'I've read your book, of course,' I say.

A nervous laugh from the guest. He doesn't get the joke. He's far too full of himself to imagine there's anyone in the world who hasn't read his book. Why wouldn't they have when it's obviously such a masterpiece?

'Good,' he says.

He tells us the plot, not that it's exactly one of those plot-rich novels, you understand. The book limns (his word) the elements of a difficult father-son relationship. It's largely autobiographical, based on the problems he went through with his own offspring. 'It's very hard,' he says, 'to love someone so much who hates you so much in return.' But it's better now. They've achieved a balance, a synthesis, a sort of redemption; just like in books.

'What does your son think about the novel?' I ask.

'He's proud,' says the author. 'He's proud. And that makes me feel very humble.'

This goes on for quite a long time. I don't challenge him, don't mock him. I trust that my listeners are clever enough, cynical enough to find this man as preposterous as I do. We move on to more general matters.

'And who are your influences?'

'Faulkner, Walker Percy, Pynchon, Melville perhaps.'

'Proust?'

'Proust inevitably.'

'And tell me, how exactly do you write?' I ask. 'What are the nuts and bolts of how you work?'

'I get up every morning at six a.m., leave the house, go to the little writing cabin I have up on my land. There's no phone, no heat, no electricity. I smoke one small cigar and then I start. I write by hand in unlined, hand-crafted notebooks that I have specially made by a local papermaker and bookbinder. I find it's the only way.'

'And what if you couldn't get those books?'

'Then I couldn't write. And then I guess my life would be over.'

'Your writing life?'

'My life.'

'Is he in good health, this bookbinder?'

'Excuse me?'

'I mean, what if he dies before you do?'

'It doesn't bear contemplating.'

'Oh, I think it probably does. Well thank you, David Bergstrom, you've told us all we need to know. *A Light Rain in the Appalachians* is available now in all good bookshops, and probably in quite a few crappy ones as well.'

That was it. I brought the music in, trailered the next programme, and it was over; not a great show, not a bad one. David Bergstrom's publicity girl whisked him off to his next appointment. I unstrapped my headphones, came out of the studio, out of the padded silence and the flat lighting, exchanged a couple of long-suffering looks with my teenage-prodigy producer, picked up some faxes and e-mails, and went out into the lobby. It's comfortable in that airport lounge, cheap-but-durable-modular-upholstery kind of way and there's a photograph of me up on the wall, taken from my good side, my name along the bottom edge, the station's logo in the corner in a bigger typeface than my name.

There are always one or two people hanging around in the lobby waiting for who knows what. Even with the photograph, or perhaps because of the photograph, they don't recognise me. That's the beauty of radio. However, I was aware of a woman staring at me with more than just the usual curiosity. She stood up and moved towards me. The receptionist indicated that this woman was waiting to see me and suddenly I realised who it was, someone from a distant past: Nicola.

I hadn't seen her for a very, very long time. There was no reason why I should have. That's what I mean about the pattern getting less strange. Your life gets set, you see the same few people over and over again. One day you realise you haven't seen some of your 'good friends' for the best part of ten years, and somehow it doesn't matter. You carry on and they carry on, and what difference does a decade make? And let's face it, Nicola and I were never even 'good friends', and yet I felt pleased to see her again. The years had been very good to her. They had given her elegance, an attractive patina. She was a good-looking woman of a certain age: middle-age, my age. She looked sleek, efficient, and she carried a briefcase. Her clothes were expensive, the effect was worked on and knowing. I thought she looked great, better than she ever had.

'Nicola. Amazing.'

'Hello, Mike. Busy?'

'No more than usual.'

'Can we talk? It's important.'

'No time for the niceties, eh?'

'Sorry, yes, there's time for niceties. I'm a little over-eager. I was afraid you might not want to talk to me.'

'Why not?'

'Oh you know, everything.'

'I'd like to talk to you,' I said.

'I'm staying in a hotel round the corner. They have a bar. We could talk there.'

The hotel was small, exclusive, costly. I knew I must have walked past it any number of times without noticing it. You had to pay a premium for that kind of discretion. Nicola had done well for herself, but who would have expected anything else? Gregory Collins had obviously just been a blip, a youthful indiscretion, as had I, for that matter.

We sat in the bar, in plum-coloured leather chairs, and a waiter took our order. Nicola quickly brought me up to date: living in

Oxfordshire, married to a man who did amazing things that involved the Internet and Hong Kong. Two more or less grown-up children at university. She said she was comfortable, not unhappy, not unfulfilled, though sometimes a little bored. She did freelance editorial consultancy work, which required her to be in London occasionally, hence the stay at the hotel.

'Your face is looking—' and then she stopped. She didn't know what to say about my face. It's not exactly a new problem for me.

When I said that Gregory torched the library, the Kincaid Clinic and me, I was exaggerating a little. He made a game attempt to set fire to the books in the library, but he didn't get very far. The library didn't really burn, and the clinic escaped more or less unscathed, but for me it was a different story. Gregory managed to press his flaming torch right into my face so that the nylon bag over my head caught fire. My arms were strapped into the straitjacket. I could do nothing to help myself and, believe me, nylon sticks. You could argue about whether or not Gregory was of sound mind, about how responsible he was for his actions, but that's not an argument I'm inclined to indulge in. The bag only burned comparatively briefly, but the nylon adhered to my left cheek and reduced that part of my face to the consistency of ruined pork.

I'm a bit vague about the exact sequence of events after that. Kincaid knew something was going on. He came running back to the library, saw the state I was in, dealt with Gregory in some fashion, and did what he could for me on the spot. Then, reluctantly I'm sure, he called for an ambulance. I was taken, in agony and shock, to the burns unit in Brighton, where they did rather more for me, though actually at the time it struck me as surprisingly little. They said it could have been much, much worse, but I suppose they say that to all their patients, and I suppose it must always be true.

My memories of the treatment are mercifully vague. I know there was endless washing and dressing of my face, which didn't seem like sufficient intervention, but eventually there was an operation, excision they call it, then sheet grafting – taking stretches of my own skin from my buttocks to my cheek. That could certainly have been far worse. In some cases I understand they have to use skin from pigs or cadavers.

Sometimes I felt they weren't taking my burns quite as seriously as I was. They were third degree, which is serious enough by anyone's standard, but they were over such a small area, just part of the face, that they weren't life-threatening, and it's been my experience that once doctors know you're not going to die on them they have a tendency to lose interest in you. I thought they'd want to know how it happened. I thought the police might get involved, but no, nobody showed anything other than professional concern. I was a routine and not very engrossing case.

The treatment took a long time but it was declared to have worked. There was scarring and contraction, all absolutely standard, I was told, and the left side of my face became, and remains, taut and fixed, setting into a pattern of livid, marbled pink and purple, like a minor work of Abstract Expressionism, though I couldn't tell you in whose style; not Rothko, certainly not Pollock. The distortion of the skin has given a sad droop to my left eye, and pulled the corner of my mouth up into a twisted, asymmetrical little smile. There seems to be something very appropriate about that.

I neither want to exaggerate nor underplay the extent of the scarring. I'm not the Phantom of the Opera. People don't stop in their tracks and cover their children's eyes; but they do sometimes stare in morbid fascination, and sometimes they can't bear to look at me at all. If you're the sort of person who's alarmed by these things then I suppose I look alarming, though only from one side. Once in a while well-meaning morons ask me whether I couldn't have plastic surgery to improve my face. I want to scream, 'I've *had* plastic surgery, you fuck! What do you think I'd look like if I hadn't?' But I don't say that. Nobody likes an angry, bitter burns victim.

My parents came to see me in hospital, but I only got one 'real' visitor, and it wasn't Alicia. It was Nicola. She came down from London for the day, visited me in the hospital, visited Gregory, her recent fiancé, who was still in the Kincaid Clinic at that moment, though not for very much longer, and then very understandably she ran away from it all. At my bedside she told me another version of the wedding story. Hers was that neither she nor Gregory had turned up at the church, that they'd both independently made the same decision and both chickened out, but by then I wasn't much interested in playing detective to work out which story sounded more plausible.

I eventually went home and stayed in my parents' house. I had nowhere else to go. We called it convalescence, but really I was just hiding. I was afraid to show my face. I was offered some group therapy, some counselling to help me deal with the psychological trauma, but I turned it down. I'd had enough of psychology. I sat in my old room and watched television: old black and white films, horse racing, cricket, children's nature programmes. It seemed to help. It stopped me thinking or feeling, and I needed that.

It was months later before I got up the courage to go out in the world, but as soon as I was able, I took a trip to Brighton, to the Kincaid Clinic. I had no idea what I'd find there. I'd heard nothing from anybody. As I got off the train at Brighton station it was raining and I could imagine it might be just like my previous arrival, standing outside the clinic, getting wet, trying to make somebody inside aware of my presence. I got into a taxi and told the driver where I wanted to go. He was one of those who preferred to keep his eyes averted from my face.

'You don't want to go there,' he said. 'They closed it down.'

'When?'

'A while ago.'

'Who closed it down?'

'I don't know. The authorities, I suppose.'

'What happened to all the patients?'

'I don't know. I'm only the bloody taxi driver.'

I had him take me there, nevertheless. I wanted to see for myself, although inevitably there was nothing much to see: a high wall, a locked gate, the main building visible inside, its doors tightly closed, its windows dark. I didn't even bother to get out of the car.

'Did you know somebody in there?' the taxi driver asked.

'I knew a lot of people in there.'

'Sorry to hear that,' he said.

He drove me back into Brighton where I walked round the town, feeling displaced and exposed, feeling people were staring at my mutilated face, as some undoubtedly were. But by chance, or at least it felt like chance, I found myself walking past Ruth Harris's bookshop. I was about to hurry away but Ruth saw me through the window and came bustling out to drag me inside.

'Oh my. What happened to you?' she said, with a refreshing lack of inhibition. She was surprised by the state of my face, but she didn't seem repelled. She was as warm as ever, and I had stopped expecting anyone to be warm to me.

'Book-burning accident,' I said.

She was happy enough with that as an explanation. If that was all I wanted to tell her she wasn't going to press me.

'Sometimes I think that might be the answer to all my problems,' she said. 'Set fire to this place. Burn it down for the insurance.'

'Good luck,' I said.

'Is there anything you need?' she asked.

I had no answer. I knew I had all manner of needs but I could barely articulate them, and I didn't for a moment think Ruth Harris was likely to be able to satisfy them. As it happened, I was wrong. I said I'd like a drink and she opened a bottle of cheap red wine and we got a bit drunk.

'If it's of any interest,' she said, 'just as many women will find you attractive now as did before. They'll have different reasons but they'll be there.'

I started to cry. I hadn't dared articulate my fears about the future, of how I feared that my facial transformation might prevent me ever again being loved or touched. Ruth Harris's words of reassurance opened the flood gates.

Ruth Harris and I had sex in the back of her bookshop, in the dusty, rickety, lean-to room where I'd done the reading all that time ago. The sex was friendly and consoling and strangely passionless, yet it did me the world of good. Ruth Harris was big, soft and generous, and I had a lot to thank her for.

And later I discovered she was right. A little facial disfigurement doesn't stop you getting laid. Some women would see the scarring on my face and feel the need to mother me or protect me. Some thought I looked ruined and degenerate. Some, I'm sure, went to bed with me out of sympathy, because they imagined nobody else ever would, and some perhaps because they thought it was cool and exotic to be going to bed with a burns victim. The best of them would eventually see past the scarring and it would become irrelevant, but they always had to fix their gaze firmly on the scars before they could see the man beneath. And a surprising number did.

In the end, there was no great mystery about what had happened to the Kincaid Clinic. The trustees had simply pulled the plug. What choice did they have? The doubts about Kincaidian Therapy, the doubts about the authorship of *Disorders*, the public display of group sex, these would have been enough, even without Gregory's attempt to burn both books and people. But the medical profession being what it is, the closure was done very quietly and discreetly. There was no scandal, and everyone had to save face. Except, obviously, me. The patients, Gregory included, were redistributed among other institutions. Kincaid was given early retirement. Alicia was given a job at a hospital somewhere in Scotland.

I learned these facts from a number of sources. Ruth Harris was a mine of information, putting out feelers among her many contacts in Brighton. The rest I gleaned from a letter Alicia eventually sent me. It was short and very unsatisfactory. It told me all too little. She said she was sorry, though she wasn't sure what 'sorry' meant, and I certainly didn't know which of the many possible things she was actually sorry about. There was no return address on the letter and I'm sure I wouldn't have written even if there had been.

For a long time I used to imagine I might see Alicia again, run into her by chance when I was least expecting it, but the years passed and it never happened. And I did very occasionally think of tracking her down. If she was still a doctor it wouldn't have been all that hard, but in the end I never did anything.

Naturally there were a lot of questions I had, and sometimes still have, about Alicia. For instance, do I think she really wrote *Disorders*? Well yes, on balance, most days of the year, I do. It's convenient for me to think that, but I also happen to believe it's true. I think she did dictate it to the patients. I think she invented stories for them, provided them with the words they couldn't provide for themselves, had them write the sort of things they'd have written had they been writers. I know it wasn't a very sensible thing to do, maybe even an insane thing to do, and the sheer number of words might be regarded as indicative of logorrhea or tachlogia, which are themselves, I now know, characteristic of the manic phase of what we these days call bipolar disorder. But I like to believe she acted out of the best intentions: to make Kincaidian Therapy look good.

I have more difficulty deciding when she realised I wasn't Gregory Collins. Was it when she saw I wasn't writing anything? Or was it when the real Gregory turned up as Bob Burns? Or did she know all along? Maybe she'd looked at me at the reading in Ruth Harris's bookshop, used her psychological training and said to herself, 'This man isn't Gregory Collins. He isn't an author at all? But so what?

He'll do for what I have in mind.' I was good enough to make Kincaid jealous.

And do I think she 'loved' Kincaid? Do I really think she slept with me to get to him? Well yes, I suppose I do. I suppose I have to admit that I was used by a crazy woman; but on the whole, on balance, most days of the year, I'd be hard pressed to say I didn't enjoy being used.

I have no idea what Kincaid did next. Perhaps he enjoyed a long and happy retirement, finally able to give vent to his literary ambitions. God knows what he was up to in his office on all those evenings. I suppose he was working on his intractable *magnum opus*, just another unpublishable, not to say unwritable, book by someone who thinks he's a genius. I suppose there's a reasonable chance that he's dead by now. Strange as it may seem, I tend to think he emerged from events better than any of us. Yes, he'd lost his job, his clinic, his therapy, but at least he'd retained his integrity. He may have been deluded, he may have been insufferable, but he wasn't a fake like the rest of us. He was a true believer. He really was trying to do some good.

And what do I think about Kincaidian Therapy these days? Well, what can I say other than that I think Kincaid may have had a point? You don't need to be a raving Luddite to wonder if the tidal wave of images that washes over us is in any sense 'good' for us. God knows I'm not being holier than thou about this. I may make my living in radio, but I watch as much TV as anyone else. I have my video library, I paddle the Internet, I take photographs on a pretty good digital camera, and I've even been known to play the odd video game. It's not a reaction against my days in the Kincaid Clinic, and neither does it feel like embracing Satan or going mad. It just feels like being part of what's going on. I can understand why someone might want to lock himself away from it all, in a white room, in a block of wax. That doesn't seem insane to me, but neither does it seem very smart. It certainly doesn't seem very useful. It feels like rejecting the wheel.

These days, from what little I know about the treatment of mental illness, nobody believes in fancy new therapies or grand theories any more. People believe in drugs, in making adjustments to brain chemistry. If it works, then why not? On the other hand, I tend to think Freud had it just about right: love and work are the only true therapy, but no doubt drugs are considerably easier to come by.

As for the patients from the Kincaid Clinic, I've never seen any of them again. I think about them sometimes, wonder whether they're alive or dead, free or locked up, mad or sane. And sometimes I still wonder what they were up to at the Kincaid Clinic, what game they were really playing and why. These days I'm prepared to live with any amount of uncertainty, prepared to accept that I'll never altogether know. I suspect there isn't one answer that fits all the cases, but if I'm pressed, I tend towards the opinion that they were mad north northwest. I don't think they were all sane people pretending to be mad, or all mad people pretending to be sane; but I do think by and large they could tell a hawk from a handsaw, whatever that means.

I heard from Ruth Harris that some local vandals eventually got into the clinic and smashed what they could, but they must have been a pretty inefficient bunch. They managed to demolish the writer's hut, but the fabric of the building wasn't much damaged, and after a while it was renovated and turned into an upmarket, not to say fashionable, addiction clinic, with a swimming pool, hot tubs, and a TV in every room. How could it fail?

Nicola and I sat in the hotel bar and she looked at my face with a steadier gaze than most people can manage.

'Does it hurt?' she asked.

'It's just skin,' I said. 'You can touch it if you want to.'

She was hesitant. The etiquette of what to do when a man with a mutilated face asks you to touch his cheek is not well established, and you wouldn't want to do the wrong thing. Nicola took a sip of her drink, then leaned across, pressed her lips to my scarred cheek, and kissed me. I was impressed.

'Gregory's dead,' she said.

I laughed in that way people do when they're given a piece of news they can't quite believe, and yet know must be true. In fact, I'd heard from Gregory a few times in the intervening twenty years. He'd written me inappropriate, chatty, newsy letters without a hint of regret or remorse, without any sense of the horror of what he'd done to me. He had got on with his life. His brush with madness had been brief. From the Kincaid Clinic he'd gone to an institution in his native Yorkshire and made a remarkable 'recovery'.

He'd quickly returned to teaching, in a minor public school, where, to his own professed amazement, he'd found himself coaching football and swimming, and enjoying it. There had never been any reference in the letters to a girlfriend or wife, and there had been no mention of his doing any writing. He had certainly said nothing about Nicola, the Kincaid Clinic or *Disorders*. I had not replied to these letters.

I'd be lying if I said there hadn't been times when I thought of hunting down Gregory Collins and revenging myself on him, and various people had suggested that I could have him arrested or sue him or sue Kincaid or the trustees of the clinic, or someone. But ultimately I hadn't wanted to do any of those things. They would only have prolonged the agony. I liked to think I no longer had any unresolved feelings about Gregory Collins. Somehow or other, in my unscientific layman's way, I'd explored and worked through my anger, my resentment, my murderous rage, and I'd come out the other side, not unscathed, but at least in working order. There were times when I still liked to imagine performing satisfyingly gruesome acts of vengeance on Gregory Collins, but the fact that I imagined them meant I would never do them. I liked to think of them as therapy. News of Gregory's death shocked me.

'Not all that recently, actually,' Nicola said. 'About six months ago. Died in hospital after a short illness. Liver.'

'He drank?'

'Apparently.'

'Poor bugger.'

Gregory's death was revelation enough and yet I knew Nicola hadn't sought me out solely to deliver that particular bit of information. Both Nicola and I had complex and ambivalent feelings about Gregory, but his death alone would not have been enough to bring us together.

'He left me something in his will,' said Nicola. 'Something for both of us.'

'Oh shit.' I knew what it was going to be. 'The manuscript of an unpublished novel, right?'

'Very good,' said Nicola.

'You've got it with you.'

'Naturally.'

She tapped her briefcase.

'And you want me to read it,' I said.

'It's not that simple.'

'No, I didn't think it would be.'

'We're in a bit of a Max Brod situation here,' she said.

Max Brod, friend, biographer, champion and literary executor of Franz Kafka. When Kafka died he left Brod all his books and manuscripts with instructions that he should burn them. It was obviously an absurd and duplicitous legacy. If you want your books burned you do it yourself, like Gogol did. It's not a thing you get somebody else to do for you. Furthermore, Kafka entrusted the job to the one person he could be sure wouldn't do it. Brod didn't burn the books. He published and publicised them, spent the rest of his life spreading the good word about his dead friend. I wondered precisely how our situation resembled that of Max Brod.

Nicola said, 'Gregory left me the manuscript in his will. The instructions are that I read it, pass it on to you so that you can read it. Then we burn it.'

'Can't we burn it before we read it?'

'In some ways you haven't changed at all, have you, Mike? In any case, I've already read it.'

'And?'

'I like it. A lot.'

I thought I could see where this was going and I wanted no part of it.

'I'll bet you think it's publishable,' I said.

'Publishable? What does that mean? When you see the crap that gets published these days.'

'But you think it's worth publishing.'

'Yes.'

'So send it to a publisher.'

'I want to do the right thing by Gregory. If he wanted us to burn the manuscript then I think we probably should. After you've read it. He obviously wanted that.'

Was I irredeemably cynical or was Nicola unspeakably naive? I stood by my original analysis of the situation. If Gregory had really wanted his manuscript destroyed he'd have done it himself. The twist here was that Nicola and I were only to perform that destruction after we'd read it. Did that mean the manuscript contained something so private or scandalous that it was really for our eyes only?

I said, 'You've made a photocopy, obviously.'

'Actually not. I thought that would complicate everything.'

I was going to say something about Walter Benjamin or even, God help me, about Baudrillard, but I decided against it.

'It looks like you trust me,' I said.

'Yes, I suppose I do.'

'That's nice.'

She took the manuscript out of her briefcase. It was slim, neat, bound between black plastic covers. I was relieved to see it was so short. Twenty years was time enough for Gregory to have come up with something truly monstrous.

'Does it have a title?'

'*Untitled 176.*'

'Ah well, what's in a name?' I said.

'Are you a quick reader?'

'I'm famous for it.'

'Take it home with you. Read it overnight. Meet me here tomorrow. We'll have breakfast.'

'That'll be nice,' I said.

I went home and told my girlfriend I had some important reading to do – nothing very unusual about that – and I spent the rest of the night with Gregory Collins' *Untitled 176.* It was an extremely hard book for me to read, not because it was especially dense or impenetrable or because it had a difficult prose style, but because it was a little too close to home. It told the story of a good-looking but essentially empty scoundrel who impersonates our noble but absent hero, a northern schoolteacher who's published a fine but misunderstood first novel. This scoundrel goes to work as a writer-in-residence at a lunatic asylum somewhere outside Brighton, where he gets all the love, sex, respect, glory and attention that's not his due. Ultimately it all turns very sour and he dies in a horrible and very convenient fire.

For obvious reasons it wasn't precisely 'my story', since Gregory didn't know all that much about life in the Kincaid Clinic, and his inventions were both more predictable and more lurid than what had actually gone on there. For instance, one of his female characters had religious visions, and regularly spoke in tongues, tongues that Gregory had lovingly invented. Another inmate had developed an infinitely complicated secret language, which again Gregory had been at pains to set down in print. I knew this had something to do with

Wittgenstein, although I wasn't sure what. There was also sex and violence, though not the kind I'd ever encountered in the Kincaid Clinic, and some of the 'experimental techniques' that Gregory invented and described were not only illegal and immoral, but by and large physically impossible. Mercifully the manuscript contained nothing that resembled my relationship with Alicia, and the head of the clinic wasn't even remotely like Kincaid.

Nevertheless, something about it was surprisingly accurate. Gregory had managed to create a convincing atmosphere of enervation and perplexity that rang absolutely true. His ruminations about what madness is and what madness does were very much the ones I'd had myself. I had to conclude that the book was pretty good. It certainly seemed much better than *The Wax Man*, although naturally enough I hadn't read that book in a very long time. Unlike Nicola, I'd have hesitated to say whether or not it was publishable. What I was absolutely certain of, was that I didn't want it to be published.

I didn't get a lot of sleep that night, but by the morning I knew what I was going to do. I didn't turn up for breakfast at Nicola's hotel. By the time she'd have realised I wasn't coming I was already on the train to Cambridge, seeking out Dr John Bentley, a man I thought could help me.

I called him on my mobile from the train. He was surprised to hear from me, even more surprised than I'd been when I saw Nicola, but given our history he wasn't going to say no to me, now was he? We talked only briefly on the phone but I thought I'd conveyed that something significant was afoot.

I arrived at the college. I'd been there occasionally over the years, and my feelings were always much the same; a simultaneous familiarity yet strangeness, a nostalgia, a sense of loss, a dislocation. The college had been there since the sixteenth century. I'd been there for three years. I was nothing to the college, yet for those three years it had been more than enough for me.

I walked through the main courtyard to Bentley's rooms. He'd lived in the same place all these twenty-odd years, the place where we'd gone for our book-burning party, and when he opened the door to me, he looked remarkably unchanged; certainly he appeared no older than when he'd taught me. I felt as though I had aged and deteriorated while he'd remained in a state of delicately shabby preservation.

He invited me in. His rooms were smaller than I remembered them. Perhaps they'd filled up over the years with the accumulation of books and papers, the clotting together of knowledge and scholarship. I noticed he owned a very sleek laptop. Bentley was quite chummy, as though I was one of his favourite, roguish students dropping in for one of my regular visits. In fact, we'd spoken just once over the years, shortly after I got out of the hospital. I'd called him on the phone and asked him who the author of that 'Michael Smith' review was: him or Gregory Collins or somebody quite else? Gregory, of course, had claimed authorship, but at a time when his grasp on truth and reality had been decidedly patchy.

Bentley had categorically denied that he was the author, although he admitted he wished he had been. The review had provided him with an elegant solution, a way of ending my tenure as Gregory Collins, of exposing me to all concerned, without making himself look petty or vindictive. He thought the review was a very good joke. He had repeated that he liked jokes. I trusted him enough to believe he wasn't the author. I could see no reason for him to lie. So I accepted that Gregory had written the review. I could live with that.

As I walked into his rooms, Bentley's eyes lingered just a little too long on my scarred cheek, but I didn't blame him for that. It made him seem human. He brewed tea and we sat in wing chairs on either side of the cold fireplace. There was an arrangement of pine cones and teasel heads in the grate that suggested there hadn't been a fire there in a long time.

I began by asking him if he'd really burned the copy of *The Wax Man* Gregory had sent him, as he'd promised in his letter, and he said no. He hadn't thought the book quite good enough for that. He also insisted that his book-burning days were far behind him. The parties had only seemed worthwhile so long as there were undergraduates who understood the perverse principle of the thing. For all that the world now claimed to be thoroughly post-modern and ironic, people just didn't 'get' the idea of book-burning parties any more. He thought it probably had something to do with Salman Rushdie.

I told Bentley about my current dilemma, what to do with Gregory's legacy, *Untitled 176*. I opened my bag, pulled out the bound manuscript and set it down on a low table between us. Bentley looked at it without interest. He was finding this a good deal less intriguing than I'd expected. We talked briefly about Kafka and Brod, and about one or two other famous literary incendiarists (Bentley's term): Isabel Burton, Thomas Hardy, Thomas Moore – the burner of Lord Byron's journals. We agreed that these precedents didn't necessarily have a great deal to teach us.

'You could read it if you'd like,' I said.

'I think not,' said Bentley, as though I'd suggested a bracing dip in the North Sea on Christmas Day.

That was fine by me. The manuscript sat between us looking flat and dead.

'And I suspect you've already decided what you want to do,' he said.

'I know what I *want* to do, but I'm not sure I should do it.'

'What stops you? Fear of being condemned by posterity?'

'In a way.'

'And you need some sort of dispensation from me, from the world of academe? I didn't think our opinions meant so much to anybody any more.'

'You'd be surprised,' I said.

'Or did you just want me to strike the first match?'

'Possibly,' I said. 'But I think the real reason I'm here is because I want all this stuff to have some shape, some outcome.'

'You want things to come full circle? Isn't that a little humdrum?'

'I need a sense of an ending.'

'Closure? Isn't that what people call it these days?'

'Yes,' I said.

'Ultimately, I'm not quite sure what you want from me, Michael. Do you want me to help you burn the manuscript or beg you not to?'

'Either would probably be all right,' I said.

Bentley did his pondering act and finally said, 'I think you're entirely on your own here, Michael, but for what it's worth, if you really want my opinion, I think that burning Gregory's manuscript might be a little bit glib, a tad too neat. Don't you think so?'

'I'm sure you're right,' I said.

He invited me to have lunch in the college, but I declined. We said polite goodbyes and I left his rooms and walked out through the college into the streets of Cambridge. They were full of clean, harmless-looking students who made me feel very old. Had I ever been so innocent, so pristine?

I wandered down to the river and stood on King's Bridge. It was busy with people coming and going and I feared there might be something a bit melodramatic about standing there and throwing Gregory's manuscript into the water, but nobody paid the slightest attention to what I was doing. Then I wondered if the manuscript might float, sit on the top of the water and some punting undergraduate might salvage it and return it to me, but no, I was worrying unnecessarily. I let go of the manuscript and it fell softly from my hand, hit the surface of the water and disappeared unspectacularly into the thick shallows of the river. It didn't have the drama or the finality, and I certainly didn't experience the sadistic thrill, that combustion would have provided, but perhaps that was no bad thing. It was good enough. The deed was done.

I walked back to the railway station, a long and not especially interesting route, but it gave me time enough to think, to make some resolutions and decisions. I knew what I was going to do when I got home, something I'd been resisting and yet moving towards for a very long time. I would start writing. I already had my title.